TIM WAGGONER

Nekropolis

ANGRY
ROBOT

ANGRY ROBOT

A division of HarperCollins*Publishers*
77-85 Fulham Palace Road
London W6 8JB UK

www.angryrobotbooks.com
Dead brilliant

Expanded from a short novel first published by Five Star
Books in 2004
This revised and expanded edition published 2009
1

A catalogue record for this book is available
from the British Library

ISBN-13: 978 0 00 732386 9

Set in Meridien by Argh! Nottingham

Printed and bound in Great Britain by
Clays Ltd, St Ives plc

NEKROPOLIS

ONE

I was sitting in Skully's, nursing a beer that I couldn't taste, and which I'd have to throw up later, and trying real hard to look like I was minding my own business, when the lyke walked in.

He (I knew it was male only because I'd been told) stood well over seven feet tall. But he didn't have to stoop to enter the bar. Since Skully's is located close to the Wyldwood, a lot of his customers are lykes, who often wear their wildforms, and he'd designed the nine foot-high doorway to accommodate the specialized – and mutable – physiognomy of his clientele.

The lyke, Honani by name, stone-cold killer by rep, was one of the newer shapeshifter breeds, a mixblood: lyke biology tweaked by the hand of genetic engineering. But as far as I was concerned, he was an ugly mess. I could pick out badger, puma, crow and what I thought was a bit of snake around the eyes. He looked almost as ugly as one of Lady Varvara's demon kin. Almost.

Skully's doesn't offer much in the way of décor, but that has more to do with the owner's practicality than any lack of aesthetic sense on his part. The nine-foot high door is solid iron, and there are no windows so customers aren't tempted to throw anything – or anyone – through them. The walls are unpainted brick and the floor smooth concrete so Skully can hose the place down every night and remove the bloodstains. The tables are solid oak and bolted to the floor to make it more difficult to use them as weapons, and the chairs are easily replaceable cheap wood because they have an extremely short life-expectancy. There's no mirror behind the long oak bar – not only because it would be just another damned thing to break, Skully once told me, but because it would annoy the vampires.

Honani stomped across the floor, the concrete shuddering beneath his considerable weight. Even for a lyke, he was massive.

The jukebox in the corner had been singing a fairly decent rendition of "I Ain't Got Nobody," but the three heads bolted to the top of the machine had gone silent when the huge lyke entered, and now they watched him pass by with nervous gazes. The multitude of scars, bruises, welts, and fresh cuts on their flesh testified to how hazardous their job could be, and they knew trouble when they saw it.

Skully stood on the other side of the bar close to me, sizing up the mixblood. "He looks bigger than I expected," he said softly. "Meaner, too."

"You're supposed to be my friend," I replied, just as softly. "Try to be a little more encouraging."

"That *was* encouraging. What I really wanted to say is he looks like he could tear your head off with just his little finger."

I grimaced. "Thanks." Unfortunately, I couldn't disagree with him.

Skully's is always open, and the man himself is always behind the bar – or at least he is whenever I go there. I'm not sure what he is exactly. He looks like a stocky, broad-shouldered human, at least from the bottoms of his feet up to the top of his fleshy neck. But resting on that neck is a skull. Just a skull: no hair, no skin, no organs. Hence his name, obviously. Skully always wears a white shirt with the cuffs rolled up, a black apron, black pants, and black shoes. To the right of the bar is a second iron door which leads upstairs. I assumed Skully had quarters up there, but he'd never said anything about them, even when I'd pried a bit. There are no other servers in Skully's, and he doesn't bring drinks to your table. He'll mix your drinks when he gets around to it, you have to come to the bar to fetch them, and if you don't like it, you can get the hell out.

As Honani continued heading toward the bar, Skully's other patrons looked up to assess the nightmarish hodge-podge's threat potential. An insectine demon with tangleglow delivery tubes surgically grafted to its chitinous head sat next to me at the bar. The demon glanced at Honani once, and then quickly found an

empty corner of the room to turn its attention to. A pair
of black-clad vampires – one male, one female – sitting
at a nearby table were playing a game of bloodshards,
the game pieces appearing in the air between them,
projected from the holographic implants where their
eyes had once been. Though neither looked in Honani's
direction, I could tell by the way the crimson shards
momentarily faded that their attention was on the lyke
instead of their game. The table next to the holo-vampires was occupied by two men and a woman who
were working on finishing off a pitcher of beer. Their
clothes were simple – flannel shirts, jeans, boots – and
at first glance, they seemed human enough, but each
of their eyebrows met in the middle, a sure sign that
they were shapeshifters. As Honani passed, the trio
growled softly and wrinkled their noses in disgust.
From their reactions, I knew the three were un-en-
hanced lykes who had just made their low opinion of
their genetically altered cousin clear. I half-expected
Honani to stop and snarl a challenge at the trio, but he
just kept on walking. The other lykes continued to glare
at his back, but from the way the tension in their bodies
eased, I could tell they were relieved he'd kept going.

"He cowed those three lykes without doing a thing.
Impressive."

"Not helping, Skully," I muttered.

Honani continued toward the bar, passing a table
where a lean heavily pierced man with a shaven head
and a black T-shirt with an anarchy symbol on the front
was sitting. A soft shimmer of argent energy passed

over the man's piercings as Honani went by, and I knew the punk was one of the Arcane, a magic user, and that he'd just activated a battery of defensive spells. There was something naggingly familiar about the warlock, but I didn't know what. I figured I'd probably seen him around the Sprawl somewhere before. Sitting at the table next to the warlock was a fluid shadowy mass that sometimes resembled the silhouette of a person, sometimes a formless blob. I had no idea what the thing was, but as Honani walked by, the shadowy thing flowed down to the floor, became a black puddle, and then quickly oozed toward the exit and slipped beneath the closed iron door.

The last customer in the bar was a reed-thin blonde dressed in tight black leather sipping a glass of aqua sanguis alone at a corner table. The woman's gaze was focused intently on Honani, her brow furrowed in concentration. She looked alert, but not especially worried. She was extremely attractive, and if I'd still been alive – but I wasn't, so I turned my attention back to Honani.

The big lyke reached the bar and slapped a paw on the shoulder of the insectine demon sitting next to me and threw him/her/it backwards. The demon squealed in fright as it sailed across the room and smashed into the table where the holo-vampires were sitting. Despite how sturdy the table was, it collapsed, and the blood-shards winked out of existence. The demon, tangleglow leaking from cracked tubes, squealed in terror and scuttled off into a corner where it rolled into a quivering ball and attempted to make itself look as non-threatening as possible. The vampires, who looked so much alike they could've been brother and sister, turned toward Honani and hissed in cold anger, displaying their incisors. But as much as the vampires might have liked to, they didn't make a move toward the lyke. He was just too damned big.

"Whisky," he growled, the words barely recognizable coming out of his inhuman mouth.

Skully trained his empty sockets on Honani for a long moment before finally nodding and setting a bottle on the counter in front of the lyke. Skully unscrewed the cap with his fully fleshed fingers, set it down, and then reached for a glass.

"Forget the glass," Honani said, then grabbed the bottle and drank the entire contents down in three gulps. He tossed the empty over his shoulder and it shattered against the concrete floor.

Skully normally doesn't put up with much crap. He keeps a silver broadaxe behind the counter, but he hardly ever has to use it. Rumor is that he has ties to the Dominari, Nekropolis's version of the Mafia, and while he's never admitted it to me, he hasn't denied it, either. A rumor like that, true or not, can head off a lot of trouble before it starts. If the Descension celebration hadn't been in full swing, and Honani already likely drunk before he even came in here, he would've had more sense than to act like such a jackass. Probably. But Skully didn't reach for his axe. Instead he looked over at me – at least I think he looked at me; it's kind of hard to tell when the person you're talking about doesn't have any eyes. I nodded. Show time. If I still had a pulse, it would have been racing.

I stood up.

"My friend," I said just a bit too loudly, "you are the butt-ugliest sonofabitch in the city." And considering the citizenry of Nekropolis, that was saying something.

The thick muscles in Honani's shoulders rippled and tensed beneath his fur. The other people (and I use the term extremely loosely) in the bar drew in surprised gasps of air. Those that breathed, anyway.

Honani turned around. His lips curled back from his sizable teeth in a snarl, and his eyes burned feral yellow.

"I ain't your friend."

The lyke was damned intimidating, but I stood my ground. There's only one cardinal rule when it comes to surviving in Nekropolis: *Show No Fear.*

"That's true. If you were my friend, I'd suggest you have a street-surgeon remove your ass and graft it onto your face. It'd be a vast improvement."

The big lyke just stood there a moment, blinking in confusion while his alcohol-sodden brain struggled to process what I'd said. Either he figured it out or decided to give up and just assume I'd insulted him. Either way, he let out an ear-splitting roar and came at me.

You know the old cliché about how time seems to slow down when you're in danger? It's true. Unfortunately, being dead, my reflexes aren't what they once were, so the shift in time perception didn't do me any good. But twenty years' experience as a cop can make up for a whole hell of a lot, and thus I was able to side-step just as Honani's claws – which had lengthened to twice their previous size and were still growing – raked the air where my chest had been a moment earlier.

I was a bit slow, however, and the lyke's razor-sharp talons sliced through my Marvin the Martian tie, de-capitating the cartoon spaceman. I watched Marvin's headless body flutter to the floor.

"Damn it! Do you know how hard it is to come by ties like that around here?"

Honani didn't sympathize with my sartorial loss. In-stead, he lunged forward, mouth wide open, jaw distended farther than should have been anatomically possible, and fastened his twisted yellow teeth on my shoulder. I didn't feel a thing – except regret that along with my tie, I'd also lost a perfectly good suit jacket and shirt.

But before he could take a hunk out of me, he pulled back, his face scrunched up in disgust, and spat great gobs of foam and saliva to the floor. "You're a deader!" he accused.

"Guilty as charged. You'd have known that if you'd bothered to smell me." Mixbloods' patchwork physiol-ogy doesn't always function properly. It was quite possible his sense of smell was no better than an ordi-nary human's.

Though the idiot should've been able to tell just by looking. It'd been a while since my last application of preservative spells, and I wasn't too fresh – skin gray, dry, and beginning to flake. I probably didn't taste too good either.

As if emphasizing this last point, Honani spat once more then looked at me with disdain. "Go back to the Boneyard, zombie. Your kind isn't wanted around here." And then he turned and walked toward the bar.

Honani's reaction was understandable. Most zombies are little more than undead automatons under the control of whoever raised them, and hardly a threat to a lyke as strong as Honani. But I'm not most zombies.

I removed a glass vial full of gray dust from the inner pocket of my suit jacket and pried off the cork. And then I made a leap for Honani.

My reflexes may be slower, and I'm no stronger than I was when alive, but I can get the job done when I have to. I threw my left arm around Honani's chest and with my right jammed the vial into the lyke's massive mouth and emptied the contents. There wasn't much in the vial, but a little was all that I needed.

Honani choked and sputtered and then I felt a distant tearing sensation. I stepped back from the lyke, still clutching the mostly empty vial. Something was… and then I realized what had happened: my left arm was gone. The preservative spells were breaking down fast.

Honani whirled around and brandished my detached limb like a club. Behind him, I saw Skully lifting his silver axe, ready to strike, but I shook my head and he lowered his weapon.

"You… damn… corpse!" Honani advanced on me, no doubt intending to pound me into grave mold with my own arm. But he only managed a few steps before he doubled over in pain. He dropped my arm and it hit the floor with a meaty plap! His breathing became harsh, labored, and he started whining like a wounded animal, which, I suppose, he was.

"You shouldn't have killed her, Honani," I said. "Lyra was a simple working girl; it wasn't her fault you couldn't get it up." Like I said, mixblood physiology doesn't always work right.

He fell to his knees, breathing rapidly now. His entire body shook, as if a great struggle were occurring within him.

"That dust I dumped into your mouth was part of Lyra's ashes. Not much, but enough. You took her life; now you're going to give it back."

He rolled onto his side, quivering uncontrollably in the throes of a violent seizure. His eyes had lost all of their anger and wildness and were now rolled up in their sockets.

This was it.

With my remaining hand, I reached into one of my jacket's outer pockets and removed a small clay jar. I shook off the lid, which was attached by a short length of twine, then knelt down next to Honani's head and held the open jar in front of his mouth.

His exertions lessened bit by bit and finally his body grew still. And then, as I watched, thin whitish wisps curled forth from between his teeth, lazily at first, but then the jar's magic began to draw them in, and they flowed out of his mouth faster and faster, until at last they were done. I sat the jar on the floor, put the lid back on tight, and then slipped Honani's soul into my pocket.

Honani – or rather his body – began to stir. I put my right hand beneath one of the lyke's sweaty armpits and lifted. I don't know how much help I was, but a few moments later, the body was on its feet again.

Lyra swayed dizzily and for a moment I thought she might fall, but then she steadied herself and gave me a toothy smile.

"It worked!" The voice was Honani's, but yet it wasn't.

I nodded. "Of course. Didn't Papa Chatha say it would?" I decided not to tell her that sometime Papa's spells failed, often in quite spectacular – and deadly – fashion. Why spoil the moment?

She ran her hands across her new body. Luckily, Honani's claws had retracted during the struggle for possession of his form, or else she would have sliced herself to ribbons.

"It feels so strange… and I'm male now, aren't I?" She reached down to check and I politely looked away.

"Yes," I said. "But it's better than being dead, isn't it?"

"Oh, yes, much!" And then she looked at me. "I'm sorry, I didn't mean–"

I held up my remaining hand. "That's okay. I know what you meant." Would I have traded in my undead carcass for Honani's body? Maybe. Probably. I don't know.

She pointed at my empty, ragged left sleeve. "Your arm!"

"Don't worry about it. Occupational hazard. Papa'll fix it up for me." I hoped.

She regarded me for a moment, and I could see the confusion in her eyes.

"Something wrong?" I asked.

"I… I don't know what to do now." She shrugged her massive shoulders.

"You're alive – do whatever you want."

She grinned, and even though I knew it was Lyra inside the body, the sight of all those teeth being bared still unnerved me. "You're right." She came forward and gave me a hug that, if I hadn't been dead, most likely would have killed me on the spot.

"Thank you, Matthew."

I wanted to respond, but I couldn't pull any air into my dead lungs to do it. She released me, and then with a wave she left the bar for whatever her new life held in store for her. I couldn't help but envy her.

Everyone watched her go, and then Skully said, "All right, show's over," and his customers returned to drinking, talking, laughing, the incident well on its way to being forgotten. Just another day in Nekropolis.

I walked up to the bar and sat on one of the stools.

"Looked pretty hairy there for a minute," Skully said. "Pun intended." He grinned at that, but then he always looks like he's grinning.

"You know, I can never figure out how you talk without lips or a tongue."

"Just talented, I guess."

"Right." I got off the stool. "Thanks for letting me conduct my business here."

"No sweat. What're friends for?"

"Gotta go. Papa's waiting." I started to leave.

"Matt? Don't forget your arm."

"Oh, yeah. Right." I bent down to retrieve it, more than a little embarrassed, and then continued toward the door. I was half aware of some of the bar-goers watching me as I left, especially the blonde in leather.

However, it wasn't until later I learned that as soon as I left, she got up and followed.

TWO

Papa Chatha's shop was on the other side of the Sprawl from Skully's, and while navigating the maze of cramped streets was never easy, this time of year it was a nightmare, both figuratively and literally. It was the anniversary of the Descension, and the Sprawl, always party central for Nekropolis, had become a mix of Las Vegas and Disneyland (assuming the Haunted Mansion had exploded and taken over the entire park) during both Mardi Gras and New Year's Eve. Beings of every description – and quite a few who defied description – choked the streets, drinking, shouting, singing, groping, slapping, hitting, dancing, screwing... You name the verb, they were doing it. It was Halloween as scripted by Franz Kafka, with costumes and set design by Salvador Dali.

Umbriel, the shadowsun, hung motionless in the starless sky, fixed in the same position it holds day in, day out, its strange diffuse light maintaining the city's perpetual dusk. And directly below Umbriel, rising forth from the ground like a gigantic obsidian talon, visible from anywhere in Nekropolis, rested the Nightspire, home to Father Dis, founder of Nekropolis and its absolute ruler. And in many ways, its God.

Over three hundred years ago, the Darkfolk, rather than deal with an increasingly populous, aggressive, and technologically advanced mankind, decided to leave Earth. Led by Father Dis and the five lesser Lords, they traveled to a distant dark dimension where Nekropolis was born. This leavetaking, which the Darkfolk call the Descension, is Nekropolis's most sacred holiday.

As far as I'm concerned, it's a gigantic pain in the ass.

The Sprawl was crowded at the best of times, but this was madness. Normally, the streets were filled with traffic, vehicles of every type and description – and many that defied description – racing this way and that, drivers searching impatiently for whatever pleasures they'd come to the Sprawl to find. But because of the Descension celebration, the Sprawl was presently closed to vehicular traffic, and masses of partiers thronged the streets, as if determined to take advantage of the one day during the year when Nekropolitans could stand in the middle of the street and not risk getting run down by cars… or devoured by things only *pretending* to be cars.

The sidewalks weren't much better, but I shoved my way through the crowds as best I could, past bars, clubs, restaurants, and establishments offering more esoteric – and often stomach-turning – entertainments. I'd have kept one hand on the few darkgems I carried to prevent pickpockets from taking them, but I needed my good arm to carry my detached one.

I was passing by Sawney B's, a fast-food franchise established by descendents of the infamous Scottish cannibal, when a trio standing outside the restaurant's cave-entrance façade turned to look at me. A bald man with large spider legs growing out of his head held a container of lady fingers, while his friends – a being who looked like a lobster in a leisure suit and a well-built woman with pythons instead of arms – sipped a marrow shake and nibbled homunculus nuggets, respectively.

The bald man was about to pop a lady finger with cherry-red nail polish into his mouth when he stopped and pointed the finger at me. "Hey, check it out! The guy's been disarmed!"

The three gourmands laughed. I stopped walking and turned to scowl at them.

"I only need one arm to yank those legs off your head and shove them where Umbriel doesn't shine."

The laughter died in their throats and I continued on my way to Papa Chatha's.

The architecture in the Sprawl is a mad conglomeration of styles – Art Deco, Tudor, Baroque, Victorian, Post-Modern, Frank Lloyd Wright, and buildings which look like structures made from regurgitated insect resin. The whole place is like an M. C. Escher fever dream. But the Sprawl is Lady Varvara's Dominion, and zoning isn't exactly high on the Demon Queen's list of priorities.

After struggling through the drunken, drugged-up throngs for what could only have been an hour or so but which felt more like a handful of eternities, I saw the greenish tint against the sky which told me I was nearing the flaming river Phlegethon and the Bridge of Nine Sorrows. Papa Chatha's was close by – finally.

And then I felt a hand on my shoulder; or rather, I felt the pressure of a hand on my shoulder, as that was all the sensation my dead nerves were capable of conveying.

"Excuse me."

The voice was soft, feminine, and nervous. But while I'd been in Nekropolis only a couple years, that was long enough to know that in this place appearances mean jack. So I stepped forward, and whirled about, body tensed, ready to fight, holding my detached arm out before me like a weapon.

The woman – the leather-clad blonde I'd seen at Skully's – took a step back, startled by my action. But then she regained her composure, or at least a good portion of it, and said, "I watched you handle that lyke in the bar. A most impressive performance, Mister Richter."

She was barely five feet tall, slim to the point of being model-thin, with pale porcelain skin. Her short hair was bright blonde, almost white. Her eyes were large and red, as if from crying. Or perhaps too much celebrating. "Yeah, well the next show isn't till midnight. Now if you'll pardon me, I have to go see a voodoo priest." I turned to go.

"Wait, please!"

The urgency in her voice, almost panic, made me hesitate. "Look, whatever it is, can't it wait? I'm no expert, but as I understand these things, if I don't get my arm reattached soon, I'll lose it for good."

"I… it's just…" She looked around, as if afraid someone might be listening, though how anyone could overhear us talking in the din of celebration, I didn't know. Hell, I could barely hear us. She leaned forward and mumbled something.

"I'm sorry, you'll have to speak up."

She looked around once more and then said, with exaggerated lip movements so I'd be sure not to miss it this time, "I need you."

I was flattered, and like I said earlier, she was very attractive. Still, I couldn't take advantage of her offer even if I wanted to. "Sorry, I don't go in for that kind of thing anymore. I'm dead. And I don't get off on fulfilling other people's necrophiliac fantasies. Enjoy the festival." This time I did go, forging a path through the partiers in the general direction of Papa Chatha's.

"You don't understand." Her words sounded in my ear, and although I couldn't feel her breath, I was sure it was cold, like a draft from an open grave.

"Vampire, right?" I said without turning around. "That's why I didn't hear you come up behind me just now."

"Please, we prefer the term Bloodborn."

"And I'd rather be referred to as Previously Living, but at the end of the day I'm still just a damned walking corpse." I would've loved to shake her off my trail, but even if the street hadn't been so crowded, I probably couldn't. I'm not as fast as I used to be, and at my fastest, I'm still standing still compared to a vampire… excuse me, one of the Bloodborn.

So I just kept on slogging through the crowd toward Papa Chatha's, and hoped she'd get bored soon and go find another dead man to put the moves on. I'd used my handvox – Nekropolis's version of a cell phone – to call Papa earlier. He'd been out celebrating at his favorite hangout, the Bar Sinister, but when I told him I needed some serious repair work, he promised he'd be home when I got there. Papa's the best houngan a dead man could have.

"They say you're a detective."

That's when I realized the vampire wasn't warm for my undead form. I felt stupid, but I wasn't about to show it. "They say wrong. When I was alive, I was a cop, yes. But I'm not alive anymore." I wiggled my detached arm to emphasize my point.

"But you helped that woman, the one the lyke killed."

"Sometimes I do favors for people – for a fee. Preservative spells don't come cheap, you know."

"I am in desperate need of a favor. And I can pay. Please!"

She sounded as if she might burst into tears at any moment. But that wasn't what made me stop. I knew Papa Chatha would only give me so much for Honani's soul. And now thanks to that miserable lyke ripping off my arm, I needed more work done than when I'd decided to help Lyra. More work than Honani's rotten spirit would pay for.

It wasn't her beauty, and it wasn't the threat of her tears. It was the money. Really.

I turned around. "All right, Miss…?"

"Devona," she supplied. "Devona Kanti."

"You can come along, Devona. We can talk after I see Papa. But I'm not promising anything," I cautioned.

"Of course." But she smiled in relief just the same.

I rotated my left arm and then flexed it a couple times.

"How's it feel?" Papa Chatha asked.

"A bit loose," I admitted.

Papa ran long, slender black fingers through his short gray hair, and then sighed. "That's what I was afraid of."

"I don't like the sound of that."

Papa Chatha was a dignified, handsome black man in his sixties, with a tattoo of a blue butterfly spread across his smooth-shaven face. The edges of the butterfly's wings seemed to ripple, but it was probably just my imagination.

I scanned the shelves in Papa's workroom, taking in the multitude of materials that a professional voodoo practitioner needs to perform his art: wax-sealed vials filled with ground herbs and dried chemicals, jars containing desiccated bits of animals – rooster claws, lizard tails, raven wings – candles of all sizes and colors, varying lengths of rope tied in complicated patterns of knots, small dolls made of corn shucks and horsehair, books and scrolls piled on tabletops next to rattles and tambourines of various sizes, along with pouches of tobacco, chocolate bars, and bottles of rum. Papa said he used the latter three substances to make offerings to the Loa, the voodoo spirits, and while I had no reason to doubt him, I've noticed that he tends to run out of rum before anything else.

Papa sat on the only chair in his workroom, a simple wooden stool, and smoothed his loose white pants which matched his pullover shirt. He then tapped his bare toes on the wooden floor.

I had the impression he was stalling.

"You're a self-willed zombie, Matt. Do you have any idea how rare that is?" He had a deep, resonant voice that was usually full of good humor. But he was somber today.

"From what you've told me, pretty damned rare."

He nodded. "Most zombies are merely reanimated corpses, bereft of souls, linked to the life-force of the sorcerer who raised them from the dead. It's this link, this sharing of a living being's life-force, which prevents their dead flesh from withering away. But you have no master." He frowned. "How did you become a zombie, anyway, Matt? You've never told me."

"Just too stubborn to die, I suppose."

Papa looked at me a long moment before going on. "Since you have no master–"

"I know," I interrupted. "I need you and your magic to keep my body in tip-top condition."

Papa gestured at the collection of odds and ends that cluttered the shelves and benches of his workroom. "My meager arts can only do so much, Matt. And I fear they've done all they can for you."

I don't feel emotions the same way I did when I was alive, but I felt an echo of fear at Papa Chatha's words. "What do you mean?"

"That this last application of preservative spells almost didn't take. And they may not last more than two, three days."

"You mean–"

"We've staved off the inevitable as long as we could, my friend. I'm sorry."

I felt like a man who'd just been told by his doctor that he only had a short time to live. And I suppose in a way, I was.

"Nothing personal, Papa, but is there anyone else who might be able to help me? After all, Nekropolis is lousy with all sorts of witches and magicians. Maybe one of them–"

Papa shook his head. "I'm afraid not. While it's true there are others more powerful than I, there is only so much power can do."

I thought for a moment. "Could my spirit be caught, like Honani's, and implanted into a second body?"

"Perhaps," Papa allowed. "If you are willing to steal another's form."

So much for that. After what he'd done to Lyra, Honani deserved to be evicted from his body. But I couldn't do that to someone else just to save my own life. If I did, in effect I'd be a killer, no better than Ho-nani.

I stood there, trying to come to terms with what Papa had told me. I wasn't going to die. I couldn't; I was already dead. But my body was going to… what? Collapse into a puddle of putrefaction? Or just flake away to dust? And when it was gone, what would happen to me? Would I end up wandering Nekropolis, a disembodied spirit like Lyra? Or would my soul depart for some manner of afterlife? Assuming, of course, that there was any beyond Nekropolis. Or would I just cease to be, my spirit rotting away to nothing along with my body?

As much as I hated my mockery of a life, it was the only mockery I had, and I didn't particularly want to lose it. There had to be a way for me to continue existing, a way that wouldn't result in my having to steal another's body. I'd just have to find it within the next couple days.

I shook Papa's hand. "I appreciate everything you've done for me." I reached into my pocket, intending to hand over the soul jar containing Honani's spirit to pay for Papa's services.

"Keep it, Matt." He smiled sadly. "This one's on the house, okay?"

I didn't know what I'd do with Honani's soul, but Papa refused to take it, so in the end I walked out with the jar still in my pocket. I had two souls now, when what I needed was another body. Life – and death – is full of little ironies, isn't it?

* * *

Devona was waiting for me outside, leaning up against
the wooden wall of Papa's shack, arms crossed, survey-
ing the Descension Day celebrants in the street with a
wary, nervous gaze. The crowd was thinner this far
from the center of the Sprawl, but there were still a lot
of loud, drunken monsters about, and they bore watching.

Devona's leather outfit clung to her like a second
skin, and even though I no longer had any libido to
speak of, I couldn't help appreciating how good she
looked in it.

I had my own problem now, and no time for hers.
But I thought I could at least hear her out. Maybe her
problem would turn out to be something simple. And I
could use the darkgems; I would need them if I was
going to find someone else – someone more powerful
than Papa – to extend my unlife.

"All done. I'm ready to talk." I didn't feel a need to
mention the bad news I'd received. After all, Devona
and I had just met.

"Not here. We need someplace private."

Like I'd told her, I wasn't a detective, no matter what
she'd heard from them, whoever the hell they were,
and I didn't have an office. But my apartment wasn't
far from Papa Chatha's.

"How about my place?"

She nodded.

A few more blocks of negotiating our way through
the chaotic riot of partiers – which for Devona meant
slapping more than a few males of various species and

states of life and death who decided to grab her shapely leather-clad posterior – and we were there.

My neighborhood is actually one of the more mundane sections of the Sprawl, a street of urban townhouses, which, except for the fact that the bricks appear to be made of gristle, looks perfectly ordinary.

We went up the front steps, inside, and up more steps to my apartment. I had unlocked the door and was just about to grip the knob when a voice behind us said, "Hey, Matt!"

"Hell," I muttered, and turned around to greet my neighbor. "Hi, Carl," I said without enthusiasm. "What's up?"

Carl was a grizzled old fart in a rumpled seersucker suit which had probably once been white but was now mostly yellow.

He grabbed a sheet of paper from the stack under his arm and thrust it into my hand.

"Just finished printing out the latest edition of the *Night Stalker News*. I'm breaking a major story this week."

I glanced at the headline: WATCHERS FROM OUT-SIDE PLOT CITY'S DESTRUCTION.

"Sounds ominous, Carl. I'll be sure to read it."

I quickly opened the door and gestured for Devona to go in; she did and I hurried after her.

Carl scowled. "Don't you humor me now, Matt. It's true! None of the other media will have anything to do with the story. It's too hot for the *Tome*, and even that rag the *Daily Atrocity* won't touch it. If we don't do something about it soon, we'll all be–"

I closed the door in Carl's rapidly reddening face, cutting him off.

"Just you wait!" came his muffled voice from the other side of the door. "You'll be singing a different tune when the Watchers come!"

He shouted a bit more before finally moving off, grumbling to himself about idiot zombie cops.

"Who was that?" Devona asked.

"Just some nut who lives upstairs. Used to be some sort of tabloid reporter back on Earth, but he can't find work on any of the papers in the city. The stories he comes up with are too crazy even for Nekropolis. Don't worry; he won't bother us anymore. He'll no doubt head out into the street to harangue the festival-goers with his latest paranoid expose." I crumpled Carl's so-called "paper" into a wad and tossed it into an empty corner while Devona surveyed the room.

"It's better than a tomb, even if it does have about as much personality," I said, feeling only a little self-conscious. A threadbare couch, a single wooden chair – with one leg shorter than the others – and a Mind's Eye set sitting atop a wooden stand comprised the sole contents of the living room. No pictures, no rugs, not even curtains. No toilet facilities, either, but then I don't need them. One of the perks of being dead.

Nekropolis doesn't have television. Instead we have Mind's Eye Theatre. Mind's Eye is exactly what it sounds like: psychic transmissions are received by your set and then relayed straight into your brain. The process is kind of hit and miss for me, probably because my zombie brain doesn't get good reception, so I tend not to watch too often. I read instead, hence the reason for the piles of books stacked in the corners of the room. Right now the set was off, the large eye closed, its lashes crusted with yellowish crud, probably because it had been so long since I'd turned it on. I wondered if the set had some kind of infection, and I told myself to remember to call a repairman.

"Do you have a bed?" Devona asked.

"I told you: I don't do those kinds of favors."

She gave me a look which said I was being less than amusing. "I'm just curious. Do zombies sleep? I've never thought about it before. But then, I've never been to a zombie's apartment, either."

"I have a bed." Though it was just a lumpy mattress sitting on the floor, no sheets, no covers. "I don't sleep, exactly, but sometimes I feel a need to… rest. To relax."

"And so you just lie there and stare at the ceiling?"

"Sometimes. Sometimes I close my eyes. So tell me, what's it like to sleep in a coffin? Ever feel like a sardine?"

"Bloodborn don't sleep in coffins," she said disdainfully.

"Even when they're half human?"

Her eyes widened in surprise. "How did you know?"

I shrugged, the gesture a bit lopsided thanks to the bite Honani had taken out of my shoulder, which Papa hadn't been able to repair completely. "Little things. You don't move as gracefully as other vampires. Your pallor isn't as white. And whatever your problem is, it's got you tied up in knots inside. I've never seen a full-blooded vampire afraid. It doesn't seem to be an emotion they're capable of."

I went into the bedroom, and she followed. Aside from my mattress, the only other items in the room were my laptop computer, the desk it sat on, and the chair I sat on when I used it. In Nekropolis, the computers are organic, fashioned from bone, cartilage, muscle, sinew, and specialized organs. The machines breathe, gurgle, and moan – especially when doing difficult tasks – and have even been known to burst blood vessels if asked to perform too many functions at the same time. The damned things literally get sick when they catch a virus and become all mopey and lazy, refusing to do any work until they get better. The spoiled things are worse than pampered cats.

My computer made a soft humming sound to catch my attention, and I grudgingly went over and scratched the top of its casing. In response, it let out a moist, phlegmy purr.

"You use your bedroom as your office too?" Devona asked.

"I don't have an *office* because I don't have a *business*," I said. "I mostly use the computer to play DVDs – it works better for me than the Mind's Eye – and to hop on the Aethernet from time to time." The Aethernet is Nekropolis's answer to the Internet back on Earth. Information is swiftly transported through the system by data-ghosts: the spirits of executed criminals sentenced to spend their afterlives ferrying bytes back and forth for the rest of us.

"So you can check out zombie porn?" Devona asked with a wry grin.

"You ever see one of those sites? No? Well, if you get curious, take my advice and don't eat for a week or two before logging on."

I removed the soul jar from my pocket, and placed it on the desk next to my computer. I then walked over to the closet and removed my torn jacket, tie, and shirt. I opened the closet door, dropped my ruined garments on the floor next to my footlocker, and scanned my pitifully small collection of clothes for replacements. If Devona felt any disgust upon seeing so much of my bare zombie skin with its slight grayish cast revealed, she showed no sign.

"You said you don't think vampires experience fear," Devona said, picking up the thread of our earlier conversation. "But they do. They just don't like to show it. But you were right about me; I'm only half Bloodborn. My mother was human."

From my closet's meager offerings, I chose a brown shirt, yellow paisley tie, and a brown jacket. I could wear whatever I want, I suppose. I'm not a cop anymore, and besides, I'm dead. Who cares how I dress? But old habits – and old cops like me – die hard, I guess. And besides, wearing the sort of clothes I wore in life makes me feel more… well, human.

I dressed and stood before the cracked mirror hanging on the wall and adjusted my tie. Thanks to Papa Chatha's latest round of spells, I didn't look too much different than I had in life, grayish skin aside. Black

hair, brown eyes, features on the ordinary side of handsome (or so I'd been told by my ex-wife; I'm no judge
of such things). Face a bit thinner than when I'd been
alive. Death is a great diet plan.

I put the soul jar in the pocket of my new jacket. I'm
not really sure why; it just didn't seem like the sort of
thing a person should leave lying around, and then I
turned to face my guest. "And who's your father?"

She hesitated a moment before answering. "Lord
Galm."

If my heart had been functional, it would've skipped
a beat or two right then.

"I think you'd better leave now," I said.

Confusion spread across her face. "Why?"

"It's nothing personal; I just make it a policy never
to get involved with Darklords if I can avoid it. And that
includes getting involved with their relatives."

Lord Galm is an ancient, powerful vampire, ruler of
the Bloodborn, and of Gothtown, the Dominion where
the vampires live, or rather, exist. And like any Darklord, he's dangerous as hell. I'd rather run up to a
Mafia don in his favorite restaurant, dump his
spaghetti marinara in his lap, and accuse him of did-
dling his grandchildren than I would mess with a
Darklord.

"Please, at least let me—"

I held up a hand to cut her off. "I'm sorry. Really, I
am. But getting involved with a Darklord is what got
me killed and resurrected as a zombie. I hate to think
what might happen to me the next time. Being dead

isn't all that much fun, but I've lived in Nekropolis long enough to know it could be worse. A lot worse."

She cocked her head to one side and looked at me as if seeing me for the first time. "Which Darklord was it?"

"I'd rather not talk about it, if you don't mind. And I don't want to talk about your problem either, not if it involves Lord Galm."

She crossed her arms and gave me a calculating look. It didn't appear as if she were in a hurry to leave.

"I don't know a lot about zombies, but I know they need to have preservative spells regularly applied to keep them from rotting." She smiled. "And as I've seen, they occasionally need limbs reattached. Spells like that cost money."

"I can get darkgems somewhere else," I said, trying to sound more confident than I felt. And besides, I wasn't worried about mere preservative spells now. I needed to find a way to keep my body from rotting away to nothing. I imagined I could already feel the slight itch of decay – one of the few sensations I can feel.

"One hundred? Two? Three hundred?" she countered. "Three hundred darkgems would pay for quite a lot of spells."

"They would at that," I was forced to admit. That would be roughly the equivalent of several thousand dollars back home in Cleveland. But would even three hundred darkgems be enough to buy the kind of magic I would need to keep my body intact?

And then it hit me. I needed the kind of power few beings in Nekropolis possessed: the power of a

Darklord. If I helped Devona, perhaps she would intercede with her father on my behalf – and Lord Galm could use his magic to "cure" me.

I cautioned myself not too get excited, that it was a long shot, that even if Devona asked, Lord Galm might not help me. But right then it looked like the best – and only – shot I had. Besides, if I did have only a few days left in my existence, I'd rather spend them working than sitting around my place staring at the walls.

"All right, Devona, tell me about your problem."

"I'm seventy-three years old," she said. "Surprised?"

"Not really," I said. "Seventy-three is young for a vampire."

We were sitting in the living room. Devona was on the couch, and I'd taken the chair. The sounds of the Descension celebration out in the street – blaring music, laughter, shouting, and the occasional scream – served as a muted background to our conversation.

"Although," I added, "you're the best looking seventy-three year-old I've ever seen."

She blushed slightly. Another sign that she was half human. A full-blooded vampire can't blush.

"Lord Galm didn't exactly love my mother. But he came as close to it as a being like him can, and when I was born, he brought me from Earth to Nekropolis."

"And your mother?"

"Died delivering me," she said softly. "Human women usually do when giving birth to a half-Bloodborn child." She looked down at her lap, where the thin, fine fingers of her delicate hands played nervously with each other. "We have our teeth early, you see, and we're born hungry…"

The resultant images in my mind might've nauseated me if I still had a working digestive system. "I understand. Go on."

"I was raised in the Cathedral. I didn't see my father very often – he was usually busy ruling Gothtown or engaging in power struggles with the other Lords. I was cared for and taught by Father's staff, and I grew and learned."

"I thought vampires didn't age."

"Those that were originally human and transformed into Bloodborn do not. But those like me, who are half human, do age, only very, very slowly."

"So you'll die one day?"

She nodded. "And afterward, I may rise as one completely Bloodborn. Or I may not. No one can say."

"Could your father transform you, make you a full vampire?"

"He could try. But there's no guarantee I would survive the process and be reborn. At this point, I'd rather wait and take my chances."

"I don't blame you."

"When I reached my forty-fifth birthday, Father called me in to his study and told me that he wished me to join the staff of the Cathedral and serve him. It was a great honor, and I accepted thankfully."

"What did he want you to do?"

"I was given charge of his Collection, and I have taken care of it for the last twenty-eight years."

I noticed a black spot on the far wall – a spot which hadn't been there when we'd started talking. It was a roach-like insect. Gregor, or rather one of his little informants. I nearly waved hello, but I didn't want Devona to think I wasn't listening to her. Besides, the bug didn't care if I acknowledged its presence or not. All it wanted to do was observe.

"His… Collection?" I said, returning to the conversation.

"Father is incredibly ancient; how old, even he isn't certain. Thousands and thousands of years, at least. And in all that time, he has acquired quite a number of items. Some are merely mementos of lives lived, countries and cities long dead; others are trophies: of triumphs, conquests, battles won, enemies defeated. Still others are tokens of magic, mystical objects of great power – any of which the other Darklords would dearly love to get their hands on in order to increase their own strength.

"As I said, I have watched over, cared for, and guarded the Collection for nearly three decades. And I have never had any problems," she said proudly. But then she lowered her head. "Until yesterday."

"Let me guess. You went to check on the Collection and found something missing."

"How did – of course, you're a detective."

I almost protested that I wasn't, that I was just an ex-cop – and ex-human – who did favors for people, but I decided to let it lie.

"Yes, something was missing. And I want you to help me get it back."

I thought for a moment. "Why come to me? Why not go to Lord Galm? He's a Darklord. With the powers at his command, I should think he'd be able to locate the object easily."

"Perhaps. But I cannot go to my father. Lord Galm is not especially... understanding of failure. Or forgiving. My only hope is to recover the object on my own, or at least discover what has happened to it. If I am unable to do either..." she trailed off, shuddering.

"But you're his daughter."

"Yes, but the Bloodborn have a different set of values when it comes to determining family relationships. Those who are chosen for transformation are considered true children, and are closest to their sires' hearts. Half-human get like me... well, I suppose the closest human equivalent would be children born out of wedlock. Our sires still care for us, just not as deeply.

"Most of Lord Galm's staff are children of his, whether fully Bloodborn or partially. And there is a great deal of competition among us for our father's favor."

"And so you can't turn to any of them, either."

She nodded. "That's why I need your help. You have a reputation for not only getting the job done, but for keeping quiet about it as well."

"I didn't know I had a reputation. I don't suppose you heard anything about my sparkling personality or my dazzling wit?"

She smiled. "Unfortunately not."

She had a beautiful smile, the effect spoiled only slightly by her revealed canine teeth.

"Tell me about the object."

"It's a crystal a little larger than my fist called the Dawnstone. What it does precisely, I'm not certain. While I tend his Collection, Father doesn't entrust me with complete knowledge of it. The Dawnstone is one of those items whose secrets he wishes to keep to himself."

I thought it ironic a vampire would own an artifact called a "Dawnstone."

"But you know it's powerful," I said.

"Of course. Why else would Father be so secretive about it? And the wardspells which protect it are among the most potent in the Cathedral."

"Yet someone got past those spells."

"Yes."

"How do you know Lord Galm didn't just take the Dawnstone himself and forgot to tell you?"

"Father is a stickler for procedure. In twenty-eight years he has never failed to inform me when he removed an item from the Collection."

"Still, there's always a first time," I pointed out.

"I suppose. But I can hardly go up and ask him, can I? If he hasn't removed the Dawnstone, my asking after it would alert him to its disappearance."

"And buy you a world of trouble."

"Yes."

She definitely needed help – and I needed the aid of

a Darklord if I was to survive. I stood. "I have more questions, but I can ask them on the way."

"The way to where?"

"The Cathedral, of course. One of the first steps in any investigation is to examine the scene of the crime."

I looked over at the spot on the wall where the bug had been, but it was gone now. Gregor's tiny minion had probably heard enough and moved on to find something more interesting to observe.

Devona stood. She smiled, took my hand, and gave it a squeeze. "Thank you, Mr. Richter."

I could only feel the pressure of her hand, but I could imagine how smooth and soft her skin was. "Call me Matthew."

Detective or not, I was on the job once more – and this time, I was working not only to help my "client," but to save my own life.

Talk about incentive.

THREE

Before leaving, I strapped on my shoulder holster and then made a few selections from the foot locker on the floor of my closet. My 9mm handgun – a souvenir from my days on the force back in Cleveland – along with a few other goodies that I'd picked up since. I slid the 9mm into the holster and hid the rest in various places about my person, mostly in the extra pockets sewn into in the inner lining of my suit jacket, and then I was ready. Or at least as ready as I was going to get.

As we walked down the front steps of my building, Devona eyed the street full of drunken revelers. "It's going to take some time to get through this mess."

"You could go on ahead, and I could meet you."

"Go on? Oh, you mean shapeshift. I don't possess the capability of assuming a travel form. Not many half-human Bloodborn do. Although I do have other… talents."

Before I could think of a witty reply, a shriek went up from the festivalgoers at the far end of the street, and the crowd began to part like water before a large yellow object careening toward us.

"Oh, no," I moaned. "It's Lazlo."

Sure enough, with a rattling and knocking of the engine and a roar of purplish exhaust, Lazlo's cab carved a path through the suddenly terrified partiers, only running down one or two in the process. Lazlo pulled up to the curb in front of my building with a pitiful squeal of brakes begging to be replaced and sent on to car-part heaven.

"Heya, Matt! How's it hanging?"

"I'm dead, Lazlo, remember? Hanging is all it does anymore."

Lazlo guffawed violently, his laughter a combination of genuine amusement and someone in desperate need of the Heimlich maneuver. Lazlo's a demon whose face looks something like a cross between a mandrill and a ferret, with a little carp thrown in for good measure. And although I can't testify to this personally, I've heard he smells like a toxic waste dump.

Evidently the rumors were true, for Devona recoiled as if she'd just taken a sledge hammer blow to the side of the head.

Before Lazlo could say anything else, one of the festival-goers came lumbering toward us. I'd seen it around the Sprawl before, but I didn't know its name and I'd taken to mentally referring to it as Tri-bod. The creature had one extremely large head which looked something like a half-rotted flesh-colored pumpkin with humanoid eyes, noise, and mouth. Supporting that immense dome were three bodies – the outer two male, the one in the middle female. The two male bodies wore tuxedos, while the female was garbed in a sequin-covered evening gown. The female body could've graced the cover of any high-profile beauty magazine back on Earth… as long as the photographer made sure to shoot her from the neck down.

Tri-bod's mushy facial features were contorted into an angry scowl, and when it spoke, its voice was a combination of male tenor, female alto, and male bass.

"What the hell do you think you're doing, dumbass? You can't drive on the streets today! They're closed!"

Tri-bod came up onto the sidewalk and one of its male components shoved me aside so it could lean down and look at Lazlo while it yelled at him. To help keep its balance, all six of Tri-bod's hands grabbed hold of the cab at various points.

"You really don't want to do that," I warned.

Devona shot me a questioning look, but before I could answer, the hood of Lazlo's cab sprung open, revealing a maw filled with razor-sharp teeth. A serpentine tongue whipped through the air toward Tri-bod's middle neck and wrapped tight around the soft feminine flesh.

"I only got one rule," Lazlo said calmly. "Hands off the cab."

Though Tri-bod had two other sets of lungs to breathe with, its face nevertheless began to turn purple. I guess a head that big needed all the oxygen it could get.

I leaned close to one of Tri-bod's misshapen ears. "Ever see a kid pop the head off a dandelion? If I you were you, I'd apologize."

Tri-bod's eyes bulged from a combination of terror and air loss. Its flabby lips moved silently several times before it finally managed to gasp out, "Sorry" in its two male voices. The female voice was silent.

Nothing happened right away, and for a moment I thought the cab wasn't going to accept Tri-bod's apology. But then the tongue released the woman-neck, receded into the toothsome mouth, and the hood slammed shut.

Lazlo smiled at Tri-bod, the expression truly grotesque on the cabbie's inhuman face.

"Now, what were you saying about my not being allowed to drive here?"

"N-nevermind," Tri-bod wheezed. The creature leaned back, took its hands off Lazlo's cab, and beat three pairs of feet out of there. It quickly merged with the crowd and did its best to disappear into the throng. If there was anyone else around who was displeased with Lazlo's driving, they decided to keep their feelings to themselves.

Lazlo looked up at me, his hideous smile widening into a truly appalling grin. "Need a ride, pal?"

"You know I do. When else do you show up?"

He guffawed again, sounding this time like he was about to cough up a kidney. "You slay me, Matt." He put the engine in park, hopped out, opened the rear door, and gestured for us to climb in, bowing as he did so.

"Your chariot awaits."

Lazlo, despite my attempts to convince him that it would be in the best interests of the entire citizenry of Nekropolis, refuses to wear clothing. His body resembles a spider that's been turned inside out and then stomped on. I've gotten somewhat accustomed to his rather unique anatomy over the years, but Devona's eyes goggled.

"No offense," she said, "but I'd prefer to walk."

I'm sure Tri-bod's reception by Lazlo's cab was as much behind her reticence to get into the vehicle as was the sight – and smell – of the demon's unclothed body.

"Don't worry," I told her. "The cab won't do anything as long as Lazlo vouches for us. Besides, every moment we waste is another moment for your father to find out what's happened." I added this last bit softly, so Lazlo wouldn't overhear.

She hesitated, but finally agreed. "I may have to hold my nose the whole trip, though."

"Go right ahead." I didn't tell her it wouldn't help. She'd find out soon enough.

We got into the cab; Lazlo closed the door, hopped behind the driver's seat, and put the car in gear.

"Surprise me, Lazlo," I said, "and try not to drive like a maniac for a ch–" That's as far as I got before Lazlo slammed on the gas and I was thrown back against the seat.

He hung half out of his open window, shouting, "Out of the way, morons!".

Most of the celebrants scattered, but despite what had happened to Tri-bod a few moments ago, a massive bull-headed man wearing an I'M HORNY T-shirt wasn't – pardon the expression – cowed so easily. He planted his feet firmly on the ground and braced himself for impact.

"Look at the size of him!" Devona cried. "Swerve!"

But there was no point shouting at Lazlo. He never listened to passengers' suggestions. "After all," he once told me, "*I'm* the professional."

"Hold on!" I warned Devona, and then there was a loud crash and the cab shuddered and jerked; but it kept moving. Behind us, falling quickly away in the distance, came the wounded bellow of one very unhappy – but lucky to be alive – minotaur.

"Hah!" Lazlo barked in triumph. "That'll teach that udder-sucker to play chicken with me!" He turned around to look at us, and grinned. "So where we headed, folks?"

"Put your eyes back on the road, and I'll tell you," I said nervously. The last time Lazlo turned around to talk to me, we almost ended up taking a flame bath in Phlegethon.

Lazlo laughed, but did as I asked, so I said, "The Cathedral. And we'd like to get there in as close to one piece as possible."

"Gotcha. You two just sit back and enjoy the ride." He pointed his cab in the general direction of the Bridge of Nine Sorrows – the crossing point between the Sprawl and Gothtown – and pressed down on the accelerator.

"Enjoy the ride?" Devona said, her nails digging into the greasy fabric of the seat. "Not until it's over!"

I had to agree.

A few blocks from my townhouse, Lazlo was forced to stop when a fight erupted between a group of lykes and several vampires. Even Lazlo wouldn't try to drive through that mess. Things got pretty bloody for a bit, until a Sentinel came charging through the crowd, knocking aside those who didn't get out of its way fast enough, and broke the conflict up, basically by breaking the combatants up. The Sentinels are Father Dis's police force: eight feet tall, massive, gray-fleshed, featureless golems that are strong as hell and, as far as I know, completely invulnerable. The lykes and vamps tried to fight back, but they never had a chance. When it was over, the Sentinel tossed their bloody, broken bodies into an alley and stomped off. The fighters would heal, eventually, but in the meantime, they wouldn't be bothering anyone.

As Lazlo pulled away from the scene, I said, "Every time I see a Sentinel in action, I can't help thinking we could've used a few during my days on the force in Cleveland. Sure would've made life a lot easier."

"For the cops, maybe," Lazlo said. "But the morticians would've been a hell of a lot busier."

"I've never seen a Sentinel before," Devona said quietly.

I looked at her, surprised. "You're kidding."

She gave a small shrug. "I don't get out of Gothtown, much."

From her tone, I knew she wanted that to be the end of it, so I leaned forward and said to Lazlo, "Hear anything interesting on the street lately?"

We'd reached the Obsidian Way, the only road that passes through all five of the Darklords' Dominions. There was a Hemlocks next to the on-ramp, and a skeletal being in a sombrero who looked like a picture on a Mexican Day of the Dead postcard came out of the coffee shop, carrying a grande-sized drink of one sort or another. The bone-man made the mistake of stepping into the street just as Lazlo came barrel-assing along, and the demon barely yanked the steering wheel to the right in time to avoid turning El Hombre Muerte into a pile of bleached-white pick-up sticks.

Lalzo flipped off the bone-man as the cab roared onto the Obsidian Way. The road's glossy black surface is hard as diamond, though it's not slick, and there's never a crack or chip in it. Despite how crowded the streets of the Sprawl were, the Way was empty of anything save other vehicles. The road was constructed by Father Dis two hundred years ago, at the end of the Blood Wars, when the Darklords fought each other for control over Nekropolis. One of the Accords that resulted from the war states that travel throughout the city on the Obsidian Way, including across the Five Bridges, is not to be impeded for any reason, not even by the Darklords themselves. Once travelers leave the Way, however, all bets are off and they go at their own not inconsiderable risk.

Of course, just because that was the law didn't mean that everyone always followed it – Darklords included. So it paid to keep an eye out for trouble when traveling on the Obsidian Way. Traffic was lighter than usual because of Descension Day, but there were still a fair number of vehicles sharing the road with us. Some were ordinary-seeming vehicles imported from Earth – sensible fuel-efficient cars, sports cars built for speed and status, family-sized vans and gas-guzzling SUV's. But this was Nekropolis, which meant most of the vehicles rolling along the Obsidian Way were of a rather more exotic nature.

I saw an Agony DeLite, a car made out of a dozen masochistic humans – their hands and feet providing the motive force instead of wheels. Such vehicles are powered by their components' suffering. They moan at idle, yell when moving, and scream when the vehicle is traveling at high speed. The humans that form the car love the pain, and they're enchanted so that all of their wounds heal instantly. But from what I understand, the drivers have to work damned hard to hurt the vehicles in just the right ways to coax maximum performance out of them, and in addition the upkeep is a real bitch. You can spend a small fortune buying new and ever more deviant S&M equipment.

There were several Carapacers on the road as well, hollowed-out giant insect husks animated to serve as vehicles, scuttling along at high speeds, and something I'd never seen before: a gigantic chrome-covered flatworm which undulated past us so swiftly I barely got a good look at it. Lazlo's cab growled as the thing flew by, but the demon shushed it softly and patted the dashboard to keep the vehicle calm.

Once the cab had settled into a groove, Lazlo responded to my question. "I hear lots of things, Matt. Rumor has it that the Conglomeration tried to absorb one too many bodies and ended up in the Fever House, where it's being treated for separation anxiety. I also heard there was a riot at Sinsation last night when they ran out of aqua sanguis and tried to replace it by draining water out of the toilet tanks and adding red food coloring."

"Fascinating," I said, "but I was thinking more along the lines of crime-related activity. For example, hear about any big thefts recently?"

Devona frowned, but she didn't object to my asking.

"Big thefts? How big?"

"Big. We're talking about an object of power, Lazlo. A lot of power."

"Can't say as I have, Matt. But I'll keep my ear to the ground."

"Just so long as you keep your wheels on the ground, Lazlo."

The demon guffawed as turned on the cab's radio and turned it to Bedlam 66.6, the most popular station in the city.

A song ended and the DJ's fake-enthusiastic voice came through the cab's tinny speakers. "That was the latest from Midnight Syndicate's new album, *The Dead Matter*. Happy Descension Day, Nekropolis! Eat, drink, and be scary! And now, by request, let's give a listen to the music of Erich Zann."

Unearthly sounds that bore only the faintest resemblance to music filtered forth from the speakers, and Lazlo hummed along in voice that sounded like a rabid weasel slitting its own throat. The demon kept the gas pedal jammed to the floor as he continued the insane kamikaze death-race he called driving, and Devona and I held on for dear life, or at least a reasonable facsimile thereof.

Once we crossed the Bridge of Nine Sorrows and entered Gothtown, Lalzo pulled off the Obsidian Way, and we drove through the Dominion's narrow streets. I really could've done without the cobblestones, though, especially at the speed at which Lazlo drove over them. Before long, even my dead kidneys were starting to ache from the abuse.

The Sprawl is to Nekropolis what the French Quarter is to New Orleans – which is exactly the way Lady Varvara likes it – and thus the majority of the Descension celebration was taking place there. But that didn't mean Gothtown was deserted. Lazlo passed a number of horse-drawn carriages clip-clopping along, as well as midnight-black stretch limos silently cruising the streets, all likely bearing their occupants to various private parties. The older vampires tend to keep to themselves and their Dominion; it's the younger ones who seek out the more decadent lifestyle offered by the Sprawl.

Gothtown itself lives up to its name: every street looks like a set-piece for an old Universal horror flick, buildings of gray stone sporting arches, spikes, towers, turrets, and gargoyles. Gothtown is the cultural, historical, and artistic center of the city, which only makes sense given how long the Bloodborn live. They prefer anything of a classical nature, meaning anything as old as they are. The best art and historical museums, the grandest concert halls, and the most-respected theatre district in the city are all located here. And while the elder Bloodborn tend to look down their undead noses at other species in general, they admire non-vampires who display high intelligence or exceptional artistic skill, so it's not uncommon to find a demon painter with a Bloodborn patron living in Gothtown, or a mixed-species orchestra performing in one of the concert halls. Nekropolis's hospital, the Fever House, where the poor Conglomeration was evidently at that very moment missing out on all the Descension fun, is also located in Gothtown. The Bloodborn aren't particularly known for their mercy, but they do have an ancient tradition of keeping blood – both theirs and that of their food supply – pure, hence their highly developed knowledge of medicine.

We kept driving for a time and finally the Cathedral hove into view. I asked Lazlo to let us off a couple blocks away.

"Will do, Matt."

Lazlo slowed and actually came to a stop without slamming on the brakes and fishtailing for a half dozen yards as he usually does. Maybe his driving skills were beginning to improve. Or maybe he figured we'd suffered enough for one ride and decided to take pity on us. Whichever, he stopped and we got out. Being dead, I guess my sense of balance was less affected by the tumultuous ride than Devona's. As soon as her feet touched the cobblestones, her knees buckled under her. She would've fallen if I hadn't managed to catch her in time.

I helped her stand, and she nodded to indicate she was okay. I wasn't so certain, but I took my hands away. She stood a trifle unsteadily, but she stood.

She turned to Lazlo. "How much do we owe you?"

The demon's fur turned crimson, and his cab began to growl beneath the hood. "Owe me?" he said, as if grievously insulted. "Lady, Matthew Richter and his friends never have to pay to ride in my cab – not after what he did for me!" And then with a wave and a wink of one bulbous bloodshot eye, he roared off to endanger lives elsewhere in the city.

"What did he mean by that?" Devona asked.

"I've done favors for other people besides you. But I don't think Lazlo would appreciate me discussing the particulars."

She scowled. "You didn't seem too reluctant to discuss my problem when you were asking him questions. 'Hear about any big thefts recently?' I told you I don't want anyone to find out what's happened – especially Lord Galm."

"One of the things I hated the most when I was alive was people trying to tell me how to do my job. And that hasn't changed now that I'm dead. You want me to find the Dawnstone? Then I'm going to have to ask questions. And you'll just have to trust me to do so as discretely as possible. You don't have to worry about Lazlo. He won't say anything; he's good people, even if he is a demon."

She looked like she was going to say something, but then thought better about it. "All right. I'm sorry I questioned you. Now let's go."

We started walking toward the Cathedral.

"By the way," Devona asked, "how did Lazlo know to come get us?"

"I have no idea. Sometimes he just shows up when I need him."

"That's odd," she said.

I laughed. "You're a half-human vampire who's asked a zombie ex-cop to help you track down a stolen magic crystal – and you think Lazlo's odd?"

She smiled. "You've got a point."

We walked to the end of the street, turned the corner, and before us lay the Cathedral, the seat of Lord Galm's power. I've never been to Europe, but I've seen pictures of the great Gothic cathedrals. But this place made them all look like tarpaper shacks. It rose four, maybe five hundred feet into the sky (Umbriel's strange shadowlight sometimes makes it hard to judge distances correctly). I'd never been this close before, and if I still breathed, the sheer insane scope of the structure would have taken my breath away. If I hadn't known this was Galm's home, I wouldn't have been surprised to discover the name "Jehovah" stenciled on the mailbox.

A number of carriages, and one or two limos, were lined up outside the Cathedral. Handsome men and beautiful women with chalk-white skin were disembarking and entering through the vast entranceway between twin black oak doors at least fifty feet tall. The Bloodborn's clothing represented numerous eras in Earth's history: ancient Rome and Greece, Elizabethan England, medieval France, colonial America, the Aztec and Mayan Empires, feudal Japan, and many more time periods, cultures, and countries that I didn't recognize. I was impressed despite myself.

"Lord Galm always hosts a reception for the elite of the Bloodborn before the Renewal Ceremony," Devona said. "A number of dignitaries even return from Earth to attend."

"There are still vampires on Earth? I thought all the Darkfolk, vampires included, had migrated to Nekropolis."

"Most did. But some remained behind, hidden, to look after the Lords' interests on Earth – and to keep trade routes open."

That explained how so much modern technology had found its way to Nekropolis. Even across dimensions, the law of supply and demand still held sway.

I felt a pang at the thought of the dimensional portal housed within the Cathedral. Each Darklord had one; I had entered Nekropolis through Lady Varvara's. But any one of them would return me to Earth, if not to my hometown of Cleveland. But they wouldn't do me any good now that I was dead.

I had heard of the Renewal Ceremony before, of course, but I didn't know much about it. But I had more immediate concerns right then. "Maybe this isn't the best time to examine the Collection. Things look awfully busy right now."

"No, it's the perfect time. Everyone is so caught up in the reception that no one will notice us."

"I don't think too many zombies received engraved invitations to Lord Galm's party."

"There'll be quite a few humans there as well. Ones who are… drawn to the Bloodborn."

"I know what you mean. Shadows." Vampire groupies who get their rocks off by having their blood drained, or who hope to form a relationship with a vampire and become one of the Bloodborn. Or both. They're called Shadows because they stick close to whichever vampire claims them – and because over time the cumulative blood loss makes them thin, pale shadows of their former selves.

"If anyone takes note of your pallor, and the way you walk, they'll just think you're another Shadow." She smiled, almost shyly. "My Shadow."

I frowned. "What's wrong with the way I walk?"

"Never mind." She took my elbow, the strength of her grip surprising me even though it shouldn't have, and led me across the cobblestone street toward the Cathedral. I tried very hard not to feel self-conscious about my slightly stiff-legged zombie gait.

A crimson carpet, appropriately enough, had been laid out for the occasion, and we walked across it, up the steps, and toward the open doorway. Above the entrance perched a clutch of snarling stone gargoyles, and as we came closer, I could have sworn that one of them moved the slightest bit. I tried to tell myself that it was my imagination, but I wasn't very convincing.

Whether they were just statues or something else, the gargoyles remained motionless after that, and then we were in.

Before us stretched a long stone corridor with torches burning in wall sconces. The flames were green-tinted – the same fire as that which burned in Phlegethon? I didn't know. But whatever the nature of the flame, it produced no smoke. No heat, either, as near as my dead nerves could tell. Still, I didn't want to get too close. No sense taking a chance on becoming zombie barbecue.

"We'll just take the corridor to the ballroom, and then keep on going," Devona whispered.

I nodded slightly. We were on her turf; all I could do was follow her lead.

As we continued, the mingled sounds of merriment – tinkling glasses, the buzz of conversation punctuated by an occasional burst of laughter, the soft lyrical sound of a string quartet – grew louder. The couple before us, who were garbed in Roman togas as white as their alabaster skin, were greeted enthusiastically at the ballroom entrance by a large burly vampire dressed like a Scottish highlander.

The highlander said something I didn't catch, and the three of them broke into peals of laughter. But their merriment had a dark edge to it, and I was glad I hadn't overheard what had sparked it.

We reached the ballroom and kept going, passing the Romans and the highlander, who were still chuckling over whatever black joke had amused them. And although I shouldn't have done it, was risking drawing attention to ourselves – or specifically to my non-vampiric, non-human, not-invited-to-the-party self – I couldn't resist taking a quick look into the ballroom. What can I say? A curious nature was one of the things which led me to become a cop in the first place.

The ballroom was gigantic, four stories high at least. The floor and walls were completely covered by a smooth, mirrored surface that reflected the greenish light from the wall sconces, a scattering of people whom I took to be human, and nothing else – despite the fact that the room was packed with men and woman garbed in all manner of historical dress. Among those whose reflections were visible, however, were strolling human musicians who wandered through the room, along with equally mortal singers, comedians, jugglers, acrobats, and stage magicians. When the humans' performances met with the Bloodborn's approval, they received polite applause, and if the vampires were particularly amused, they might slip a performer a few darkgems as well. But when the performers didn't quite measure up... well, the humans had more to offer than their meager talents, and the

Bloodborn weren't shy about taking their entertainment in liquid form.

I tried to catch a glimpse of myself in the wall mirror, but there was so many people milling about I couldn't. I did, however, see a hazy ghost image of a petite blonde for just a moment. Devona was half human. It only made sense she would cast half a reflection.

But as impressive as the gathering of Bloodborn royalty was in and of itself, one thing was more impressive still. In the center of the room stood a great marble fountain, and bubbling forth from it a thick shower of reddish-black liquid. I told myself the viscous fluid couldn't really be what it seemed; that it was either aqua sanguis, the synthetic blood substitute produced in the Sprawl, or a decorative effect of some sort achieved through Lord Galm's dark arts. I almost believed it, too.

And then Devona and I were past the ballroom and continuing down the corridor.

"I don't think anyone noticed us," Devona said, relieved.

"I hope you're right."

After a few dozen more feet we came to a winding stone staircase. Devona removed a torch from a sconce on the wall and started up the stairs. I held back a little. Maybe the torch wasn't lit with real fire, but zombie-flesh is dry, bloodless, and very flammable. I wasn't about to take any chances.

Devona led the way up: two, four, seven floors. I don't tire as I did when alive, but just to break the silence, I said, "I wonder if Lord Galm has ever considered installing an elevator."

"Most Bloodborn don't need to rely on stairs," she answered. "They have their travel forms. Besides, Father won't have anything to do with technology. He thinks it a decadence which promotes laziness of the mind and spirit."

I wondered what Galm thought of those Bloodborn who'd arrived in limousines that night. I thought of asking Devona, but I decided to stick to business instead. "I didn't notice Lord Galm in the ballroom."

"He's probably still meditating, marshaling his power for the Renewal Ceremony."

I thought I might take the opportunity to find out more about the ceremony – it struck me as awfully coincidental that one of Lord Galm's most powerful mystic objects should just happen to vanish so close to the Renewal Ceremony. But then we reached the ninth floor and Devona gestured that we should stop.

Devona stuck her head into the corridor, looked both ways, and then motioned for me to follow. I did, but to the right I saw a window, and I couldn't resist stepping over to it and taking a quick peek outside.

The window was covered with thick iron bars, but that wasn't the only protection. I could hear, or rather almost hear, a hum in the air, like the ultrasonic whine of an alarm system.

"Don't stand too close," Devona said. "The wardspell on the window is a particularly deadly one."

"Thanks for the tip."

The borders of Nekropolis form a perfect pentagram, and the points of the pentagram – connected by the flaming barrier of Phlegethon – are the strongholds of the five Darklords. This window faced outward from Nekropolis and toward the Null Plains: a flat black featureless expanse which stretched to the horizon. A whole hell of a lot of Nothing.

I'd only seen the Null Plains a couple times before, but viewing them always gave me the creeps. There was something about the blackness that the human (or zombie) eye couldn't quite deal with, a subtle movement, nearly undetectable, like glacially slow tides of solid darkness sliding and swirling against one another.

I thought of crazy Carl and the headline of his idiotic "newspaper" – WATCHERS FROM OUTSIDE PLOT CITY'S DESTRUCTION – and I couldn't help shuddering. Looking out at the endless darkness, I could almost believe something was out there, watching, waiting…

"Not much to see," Devona said.

"Not much," I agreed, turning away from the window. There was nothing out there, certainly not any Watchers. Carl was a loon, and that was the end of it.

We continued down the corridor past a series of solid-looking wooden doors, each of which appeared to be exactly like the one before it, until we came to a door which didn't seem particularly special, but evidently was, for Devona stopped.

"This is it. The entrance to the Collection." She unzipped her leather jacket halfway to her waist to reveal an iron key hanging on a chain between her partially exposed breasts.

As she detached the key from the chain, I asked, "Is this the only key to the chamber?"

She nodded. "Not even Lord Galm has one. But then, he doesn't need a key. The door is spelled to open at his touch." She moved to insert the key in the lock – not having bothered to zip up her jacket (like I said, I pay attention to details) – but I grabbed her wrist before she could.

"Let me have a look first." I let go of her wrist and knelt down to examine the lock.

There aren't too many good things about being a zombie, but one of them is that, while my thought processes sometime take a little longer than they used to, I'm able to focus my attention and concentrate like crazy. The dead aren't easily distracted.

The lock appeared to be made of the same iron as the key. The door handle rested directly above it. I looked closely for scratches, nicks, or dents – anything which might indicate the lock had been picked or forced. There were none.

I straightened. "Let's go in." I stepped aside, and Devona inserted the key. The lock turned with a metallic *clack*, she pushed open the door, and Lord Galm's great Collection was laid bare before us.

FOUR

And most impressive it was.

The stone walls were covered with weapons, from simple wooden spears and bows to highly polished swords and ornate jewel-encrusted daggers. There were broadaxes far too large for anyone possessed of merely human strength to wield, and a series of maces and morningstars, each covered with larger and crueler spikes than the last.

The floor was taken up by stone tables, daises, and columns upon which rested a variety of non-military objects: a tiny golden skull which glowed with a soft, gentle yellow light; an Egyptian scarab carved from jade, but which nevertheless moved, scratching away at the inner surface of the glass globe which imprisoned it; a stereopticon constructed entirely of what appeared to be spider silk, a stack of picture cards next to it, displaying what looked like Tarot images; and on and on. There were no placards, no labels to name the objects, but after nearly thirty years of tending the Collection, I doubted Devona needed any.

The Collection communicated an almost tangible sensation of antiquity, and for the first time I had an inkling of what it truly meant to be immortal.

"I'm surprised everything's out in the open like this," I said.

"They're protected by wardspells placed by Lord Galm himself."

"I don't much know about magic, but as I understand, certain spells have to be renewed from time to time." Like the preservative spells which, up until that point anyway, had kept me from crumbling into a pile of rotten hamburger. "Maybe some of these, specifically the one protecting the Dawnstone, are due for a recharge."

She shook her head. "My job is to oversee the Collection, which means that I primarily monitor the wardspells. Lord Galm saw to it that I was taught just enough spellcraft to check the wards, but not enough to actually tamper with them. The wardspells Lord Galm employs are powerful and intricate. It takes me over six hours to check them all. And the first thing I did when I realized the Dawnstone was missing was examine the ward which protected it. The spell was intact and not due to be recharged by Lord Galm for some time."

"Is it possible for someone with enough magical know-how to circumvent the wardspell?"

Devona thought about that for a minute.

"I suppose, but it's highly unlikely. Another Darklord might be able to do it, but then a Darklord could never enter the Cathedral without Lord Galm knowing."

It was my turn to think. "How about any of the visitors from Earth? Do any of them possess enough power and skill?"

"There are some who are almost as ancient as my father, and certainly as cunning," she admitted. "But Father keeps a very close eye on them when they're in Nekropolis."

"Might he have brought one of them up here to show off his Collection and—"

"No," she interrupted. "Father is a private man, and not given to bragging."

"I see. It strikes me as odd that someone—" I couldn't bring myself to call Lord Galm a man – "who is so secretive and possessive about his Collection should entrust its care to another, no matter how worthy of that trust she might be."

"Father is very, very old, and his mind..." She paused. "After millennia of existence, time doesn't mean the same thing to him as it does to you and me. Not only would the constant examination of the wardspells waste hours which he could be spending on more important matters, quite frankly, months, perhaps years, might go by before he remembered to check the wards."

"So you got your job because your dad has a lousy memory."

She smiled ruefully. "Something like that."

I nodded. It was looking more and more like Lord Galm – despite Devona's assurance that he would never do so – had removed the Dawnstone for reasons of his own, reasons he had elected not to share with the guardian of his Collection. But I decided to continue my examination of the room anyway. After all, that's what she was paying me for.

"Show me where the Dawnstone was."

Devona led me through the maze of clutter that was Lord Galm's Collection until we came to a narrow stone column with nothing on it.

"It was here. Don't get closer than a foot or so," she warned. "The wardspell's still active."

"And we don't want to alert Lord Galm that we're here. Right." I stood as close as I could and took a look at the spot where the Dawnstone had rested. I didn't know what I thought I might see, but then I never do; that's why you look.

At first glance there appeared to be nothing special about the flat surface of the column. Just smooth gray stone, no cracks, no sign of age. The column might have been chiseled yesterday for all I could tell. Part of the wardspell's protective qualities?

Another thing about being dead: my patience has increased. When I was alive, I would've given the column a quick look or two, and then moved on. But now I scanned each inch thoroughly, and then I did it again. It was on my second pass over the column that I saw, in what from my vantage was the far righthand corner, a couple tiny specks of white powder.

I smiled. Score one for the dead man.

I pointed the specks out to Devona. "Know any vampires with dandruff?"

She ignored the joke and instead leaned forward and looked closely at the white grains.

After a bit, she straightened and said, "I have no idea what that is. Do you?"

"Maybe," I said, declining to elaborate. "There's no way we can reach it, is there? Not without setting off the wardspell's alarm."

She nodded.

"Figures. Well, if there are two specks, maybe there's more." I asked Devona to stand back, and then got down on my hands and knees – my zombie joints creaking in protest – and did my best impersonation of a bloodhound, crawling slowly across the floor, face only inches above the stone and searched. I had the patience, the ability to hyper-focus my attention, and I didn't breathe, so I didn't have to worry about accidentally blowing any specks away before I could find them.

It took some time, but I located five more grains, all of which I collected with a pair of tweezers and slipped into a small white envelope. I never was a Boy Scout, but I know enough to be prepared all the same. And the gods of evidence collection were in a beneficent mood that day, for I also stumbled across a hair.

I gripped it in my tweezers, stood, and showed it to Devona. It wasn't especially long, but longer than mine (which doesn't grow anymore; another of the few fringe benefits being a zombie: no trips to the barber).

It was difficult to tell the color in the greenish light of the torch, but it appeared to be–

"Red," Devona pronounced.

"I think you're right. Lord Galm's?"

"He has brown hair; and his is much longer than this."

"Well, it's not yours. That is, unless you're not a natural blonde."

She smiled. "As half Bloodborn, I suppose I qualify as an unnatural blonde. But no, I don't color my hair."

I took another envelope out of my jacket and carefully placed the hair within. I didn't bother to seal it – no saliva, you see – and tucked the envelope and tweezers away in a pocket.

"Know anyone with red hair who might somehow gain access?"

"Well… There's Varma, I suppose. But I don't see how he could possibly get in here."

"Who's Varma?"

"One of Lord Galm's bloodchildren – a human that's been fully transformed. He's one of Father's favorites, though why, I don't know. He's an irresponsible hedonist."

"That's a fine way to talk about your own brother." As soon as the words were out of my mouth, I knew they were the wrong thing to say: Devona's jaw tensed and her eyes flashed. Literally.

"He's not my brother!" she snapped. It might have been my imagination, but her canines seemed longer, sharper. "In Bloodborn terms, we're considered the equivalent of cousins. Distant cousins at that."

I held up my hands in what I hoped was a placating gesture. "Okay. I'm not here to untangle the roots of your family tree. I'm here to help you find out what happened to the Dawnstone."

She glared at me for a moment longer, and then, with a sigh, relaxed. "I'm sorry. It's just that half-humans like me are looked down upon by the fully Bloodborn. To put it mildly. I'm not sure Father would ever have given me my position if I hadn't displayed a talent for magic. It's one of the few advantages of being half human: we tend to possess more aptitude for magic and psychic feats than the fully Bloodborn."

I understood then why her position and its attendant duties meant so much to her. It was a way for her to feel important, to be something more than just a mere half-breed in the eyes of the fully Bloodborn – and most significantly, in the eyes of her father.

I understood how she felt, at least a little. I was a zombie – not human anymore, not even alive. I'd seen the looks of disgust, heard the jokes and taunts, especially when my latest batch of preservative spells started to wear off and I didn't look my best. I knew what it was like to feel less than everyone around you.

If she couldn't get the Dawnstone back, she'd consider herself a failure to the Bloodborn, to her father, and especially to herself.

I was determined to do my best to see that didn't happen, whether I kept my body from crumbling to dust or not.

"I didn't mean to snap at you like that," Devona said.

"Forget it. We've all got something that pushes our hot button."

"What about you?"

"With me, it's flies who mistake me for a nursery. Now let's go see if we can find Varma. I've got a few questions to ask him."

FIVE

Devona wasn't too thrilled with what I had in mind. Truth to tell, neither was I. But we needed to talk to Varma, and in order to do that, we had to find him. And the most likely place to look was Lord Galm's party.

"You said yourself that Galm won't be there, that he'll be meditating to prepare himself for the Renewal Ceremony. And I can stay out in the corridor while you hunt for Varma in the ballroom. Then the three of us can go somewhere private and we'll see what your cousin has to say for himself."

She agreed, but she didn't look happy about it.

We went back downstairs, and I took up a position in the corridor about fifty feet from the ballroom entrance.

"Good luck, Devona. Oh, and you, uh, might want to zip yourself up."

She looked down at her jacket, which was still open halfway to her waist. She smiled. "I suppose I should if I don't want to attract any more attention than necessary." She pulled the zipper tab upward, and then headed for the ballroom. Considering how tight her leather outfit was, I thought she would attract attention no matter what she did.

I crossed my arms and leaned against the wall and waited. I'd waited quite a bit during my two decades as a cop, and I was real good at it – and being dead made it even easier. I listened to the sounds of celebration wafting from the ballroom, stared at the opposite wall, and let one part of my mind wander, while another kept watch for Devona's return.

I don't know how much time passed, but eventually I became aware of someone approaching. I turned, expecting to see Devona, hopefully with Varma in tow, but instead a middle-aged woman in an elaborate pre-French Revolution gown and a towering white wig staggered down the corridor toward me. Her skin was ivory white, and I doubted it was because she powdered it. She wore a fake beauty mark in the shape of a tiny bat on her left cheek. Cute.

"Pardon, Monsieur, could you direct me to the–" That was as far as she got before doubling over and vomiting a gout of red-black liquid all over the corridor floor.

I was sympathetic vomiter when alive; all I had to do was hear someone retch and my own gorge would start to rise. My zombiefication had cured me of that, but I was still uncomfortably aware of the booze I had drank at Skully's while waiting for Honani to show up, still sitting undigested in my stomach. I knew I had to get rid of it soon, before it pickled my dead innards.

When she was finished, she straightened and wiped her mouth with a dainty hand. Her wig had gone slightly askew, but she didn't bother to right it. She smiled shyly at me.

"Forgive me, but I have such trouble resisting the temptation to overindulge at these affairs."

I was hoping that would be the end of it, and she would return to the party. But she stood looking at me expectantly, so I said, "No apologies necessary."

She looked into my eyes and I noticed a thin red line dimpling the flesh of her neck. From an encounter with Monsieur Guillotine? "Well, aren't you a gallant one?" She reached out and drew a long, blood red fingernail lightly down my cheek. "And you're rather handsome, in a consumptive sort of way."

Some compliment. But I didn't say anything.

She smiled lopsidedly. "Did you know that the Bloodborn do not cast shadows? It's true. And I miss mine something awful. Perhaps you would be a gentleman and take its place for a while?"

Before I could answer, she linked her arm in mine, and started pulling me forward. Despite appearing middle-aged and being inebriated, she was still a vampire and strong as hell. I couldn't resist, not unless I wanted an arm torn off for the second time that day.

"I'd be honored," I said as she dragged me toward the ballroom. At least she'd mistaken me for a Shadow. I could only hope Lord Galm's other guests would do the same.

* * *

"Matthew, allow me to present the honored Amadeo Karolek. Amadeo, this is my new Shadow, Matthew."

The male vampire, who was dressed in a coat of gold brocade, didn't bother to hide his disgust. "Charmed," he said in a voice which let me know he was anything but.

I almost offered my hand to shake, just to irritate him, but the way he glared at me, he'd most likely have crushed it, and then torn it off.

"Excuse me, Calandre, but I see someone I really must say hello to." And then Amadeo collapsed into a pool of black water and flowed away across the floor.

Calandre – which meant lark, she'd told me – still had a death grip on my arm. But after introducing me to more than a dozen vampires, all of whom acted like I was some new species of giant maggot, I was considering sacrificing the limb, like an animal caught in a leg-hold trap, desperate to escape. But I'd already had an arm reattached once that day, so I resisted the urge.

I knew next to nothing about Bloodborn etiquette, but from what I was able to observe as Calandre hauled me about the ballroom, Shadows were supposed to walk or stand at least three feet behind the vampires they belonged to, keep their heads down, and remain quiet. But Calandre, still drunk – or whatever the vampiric equivalent was of gorging on too much blood – was parading me around like I was her new lover. And the other vampires definitely did not like it. I had the impression her behavior was akin to that of a human woman going to a party and introducing everyone to her favorite vibrator.

So much for my keeping a low profile. I could only hope that Devona would eventually find me and come to my rescue, or that Calandre would tire of me and let me go.

Calandre licked her lips. "I'm dreadfully thirsty, Matthew." She smiled, displaying her incisors. "Dreadfully."

This was bad. If she bit into my flesh, she'd realize I wasn't alive. My blood had long ago turned to dust in my veins. It'd be like someone expecting a nice, refreshing drink of water suddenly getting a mouthful of chalk instead.

I returned to contemplating spending the rest of my unlife as a one-armed zombie, when a statuesque woman in an Edwardian frockcoat walked up, her features scrunched into an expression of supreme distaste.

"Really, Calandre, this is too much, even for you!"

Calandre drew herself up haughtily, which wasn't easy since her wig looked as if it would topple off her head any moment. "I have no idea what you're talking about, Naraka, nor do I care. Now why don't you take your little penis-envy pageant elsewhere?"

Naraka made a sound deep in her throat, and I realized she was growling. This did not look good, especially since Calandre still had hold of me; I didn't relish the prospect of being caught in the middle of a catfight between two vampires.

"Ladies, please, there's no need for–"

"Silence, Shadow!" Naraka's hand flashed out and her nails, which had suddenly become claws, raked my left cheek.

"Really, Naraka, you didn't..." Calandre's voice trailed off, and I had a pretty good idea why. She had noticed that the deep scratches Naraka had inflicted on my face weren't bleeding.

"Father Dis!" Naraka swore in disgust. "It's one thing to drag a human around as if he were one of us. But a zombie!"

"But I... He... I didn't..." In her surprise and confusion, Calandre released my arm, and I decided that, zombie-slow or not, I was going to make a run for it.

And then the torches along the ballroom walls dimmed, and the noise and music ceased as if a switch had been thrown. Everyone looked upward, even Calandre and Naraka, who seemed to have forgotten all about me. I didn't know what was happening, and I didn't care. I was just grateful for the distraction.

I started to edge away from the two vampire women, but then I stopped. The atmosphere of the ballroom felt charged with energy, like before a violent storm breaks loose. It had to be a psychic and not physical sensation, or else I probably couldn't have perceived it, but whichever, it stopped me in my tracks and made me look up along with everyone else.

Darkness gathered along the mirrored surface of the ballroom walls, thickening and growing. And then the darkness exploded into a thousand shards which darted and whirled through the air, a cyclone of shadow. One of the black fragments dipped near my head, and I could see that what had been formless pieces of darkness had assumed the shape of large bats. Not actual three-dimensional animals, but instead shadowy silhouettes circling madly about the room.

And then the flock of shadow-bats drew close together directly above the gushing fountain of red, and coalesced into the form of a huge, well muscled man, who wore only a loincloth, boots, and a cape made out of black fur. His skin was white as bone, and his body looked hard as marble. He had long brown hair, and an equally brown beard which spilled onto his chest. His eyes were frost-white and cold as glaciers.

I didn't need a formal introduction to tell me this was Lord Galm, progenitor of the Bloodborn and ruler of Gothtown – and, if I was lucky and Devona managed to persuade him to help me, my eventual savior.

"My children." Though Galm spoke softly, his low rumbling voice echoed through the ballroom in tones as cold as an arctic plain at midnight.

As one, the assembled vampires fell to their knees and bowed their heads. "Our Lord," they chanted in unison.

I was about to kneel myself to keep from drawing the Darklord's attention, when I felt someone grab my arm and start dragging me backward. It was Devona – and she looked scared.

I didn't know what to do: stay and risk being exposed as a zombie and a party-crasher – thus earning Galm's wrath – or go with Devona and risk drawing the vampire lord's ire for not displaying the proper obeisance. In the end, simple fear won out and I turned and we both ran like hell for the exit.

I felt a freezing-cold sensation on the back of my neck, as if it were suddenly coated in ice. I didn't have to turn and look to know the Darklord was watching us. But for whatever reason, he did nothing, and we reached the corridor, turned left, and kept going.

As we ran, I thought it was a good thing I was dead. If I'd been alive, I would surely have needed a change of underwear at that point.

We didn't stop running until we were a couple blocks from the Cathedral. Devona put her hands on her knees and gulped air – another sign that she was half human; a full-fledged vampire wouldn't have needed to breathe, let alone catch her breath. I just stood and waited for her to recover, not fatigued in the slightest myself, although I thought my left arm was a trifle looser than it had been.

"Will Galm send someone after us?" I asked Devona when her breathing had returned to normal.

She shook her head. "He's going to be too busy receiving guests for the next few hours. But I'm sure he'll tend to us later." She slumped back against the wall of a building and rubbed her forehead, clearly upset.

I laid a hand on her shoulder. "Maybe Galm will be more forgiving of our disrupting his entrance if we can recover the Dawnstone, or at least discover what happened to it."

She gave me a weak smile. "Perhaps. It's something to hope for anyway." She stood straight, took a deep breath, and did her best to regain her composure. And then she noticed the cuts on my face. "Oh, you're hurt!"

She reached a hand toward my wounds, but I took a step back. I didn't want her smooth, half-living hands touching my dead flesh, didn't want to see her possibly pull away in disgust.

"I'm a zombie; I can't be hurt. Don't worry, Papa Chatha will just take care of it the next time I see him." Or in a couple days I'd be gone, and a few scratches wouldn't matter anymore. I changed the subject. "Did you locate Varma?"

"No one had seen him. He's probably off celebrating in the Sprawl somewhere."

"Do you have any idea where he might be? Any favorite hangouts?"

"I know a couple places that he frequents. So we're off to the Sprawl, then?"

"Not just yet. First, we need to find out as much about the Dawnstone as we can."

"How are we supposed to do that? We can hardly ask Father, can we?"

"Maybe not. But I know someone else we can ask."

"Who?"

I smiled. "Do you have your library card on you?"

SIX

"You can't be serious," Devona said.

We were on the Avenue of Dread Wonders, where museums housing the rarest and strangest artifacts in all Nekropolis were located. The neighborhood here was deserted and blessedly free of Descension Day chaos. I guess a museum district isn't exactly high on anyone's list of party destinations. Before us, nestled between the Pavilion of Nightmares Incarnate and the Hemesphere, stood the Great Library. I'd never visited the Pavilion, and from the way its shadowy architecture continually shifts and reforms itself into ever more sinister configurations, I'm not sure I ever will, but I had poked my head into the Hemesphere once. Inside the large round building is a museum that exhibits blood samples from famous people – both Darkfolk and human – acquired throughout history. The place doesn't do much for me, but then I don't have a sense of smell, let alone the enhanced sensory apparatus necessary to tell the difference between one blood sample and another. From what I've been told, you need to be a vampire or shapeshifter to fully appreciate the experience.

The Great Library didn't look like much from outside, especially not compared to the two grander structures flanking it. It was just a simple wooden building, more appropriate for a cobbler's or a baker's. Devona's doubts had nothing to do with the Library's appearance, though. Everyone in Nekropolis knew what it looked like; no, what she didn't believe was what I'd just told her.

"You really expect to just walk up to the door," she said, "knock, and be let into the repository of not just the sum total of Bloodborn history but the accumulated knowledge of the entire Darkfolk?"

"No," I deadpanned (I'm good at that). "I've never had to knock before."

"Matthew," she said in the tone of an adult speaking to a mistaken child, "no one just goes into the Great Library whenever he wants. That's not how it works."

So it was *Matthew* now. I wondered when in the last couple hours we'd gotten on a first-name basis.

"Call me Matt. And yes, that's precisely how it works for me."

"Waldemar is very selective about who he allows inside the Library and when. And no one knows how he chooses who may enter. I've never been inside. Even Lord Galm cannot just drop by whenever he feels…"

She broke off when she saw me reach out and open the door. Her jaw dropped. "That's… impossible!"

"Are you sure Waldemar's reputation isn't just exaggerated? Like I said, the door's always been open every time I've come here." Even Nekropolis, a place where so many myths and legends are real, still has its share of tall tales.

"I don't..." Whatever she was going to say, she decided against it and finally just shook her head.

"C'mon, let's go." I held the door open for her and gestured for her to enter. She walked past me and stopped on the other side of the threshold and swayed dizzily.

I shut the door quickly and put a hand on her arm to steady her. "I'm sorry, I really should have warned you. The shift in perspective hits you pretty hard the first time."

We stood inside a vast room, far larger than such a small building as the Library appeared to be from outside could possibly contain. And the room was filled with case after case, shelf upon shelf, of books, papers, parchments, and scrolls. And what the shelves couldn't hold were stacked on the floor, piled on top of cases, shoved into corners, jam-packed into every nook, cranny, and crevice available.

I didn't have a sense of smell anymore, but I could imagine the wonderful musty odor of ancient knowledge and thought that permeated the place. Breathing this air would be like breathing Time itself.

"So what do we do?" Devona asked in the hushed, respectful voice people only use in churches and libraries.

"We start wandering around. Eventually Waldemar will show up."

She looked skeptical, but she didn't say anything. After all, the front door had opened as I said it would. We started walking.

As big as the Great Library looks when you first enter, you don't really get a sense of how truly enormous it is until you start exploring. Room after room: some large, high-ceilinged, footsteps echoing against tile floors; some small, cramped, barely bigger than a closet, with hardly enough room to squeeze through the moldering books and papers jammed against the walls. There was no obvious source of light: no torches – naturally enough in a place filled with paper – no electric or fluorescent lights, and no magical equivalents to any of the above. Nevertheless, every corner of the Great Library was clearly illuminated, and we had no trouble making our way.

After a time, Devona asked, "Do you know where we are?"

"Of course," I answered, even though I had no idea. It didn't really matter, not here.

I don't know how long we wended through the maze of books and papers, but eventually we came to a circular room with a high domed ceiling fifty feet about the floor. The walls were lined with bookcases which rose nearly all the way to the ceiling, leaning against them at irregular intervals stood a half dozen long, rickety-looking ladders to provide access to the upper reaches of the shelves. In a regular library, the ladders might have had wheels. Here, they had tiny clawed lizard feet. They might have been for purely decorative purposes, but I doubted it.

"We're wasting time, Matthew," Devona said, exasperated. "Waldemar obviously doesn't wish to talk to us. Instead of wandering aimlessly through here, we should be trying to locate Varma."

"I understand how you feel, but the more we can learn about the Dawnstone, the more–" I broke off, frowning. "Do you hear something?"

Devona's brow furrowed as she listened. It was faint, but there was a definite *skritch-skritch-skritch* coming from an overburdened shelf of books against the far wall.

"What is it?" she asked.

Despite the fact that my nervous system was as dead as the rest of me, a chill rippled down the length of my spine. "So you do hear it. Damn! I was hoping it was just my imagination."

The skritching became louder.

"Matthew, just tell me what the hell it is!"

Before I could answer, the bookshelf exploded, sending fragments of torn paper, parchment, and vellum flying toward us. Devona hissed in pain as the sharp edges of the paper-storm sliced through the flesh on her face and hands. I suffered similar injuries, of course, but I didn't feel them. Even if I had, I wouldn't have cared right then. I was too busy watching the thing that was responsible for the explosion step forward from the hole in the wall where the bookshelf had been. A seven foot tall insect with a silvery carapace stood upright on its four rear legs, sheafs of paper clutched in its upper two limbs. Antennae quivering nervously, the giant bug stepped forward into the room, jammed the paper it held into its mouthparts, and chewed noisily.

"Just what I was afraid of," I said. "It's a goddamned silverfish."

Devona goggled at the monstrous insect. "*That's* a silverfish? It should be the size of the end of my little finger, if that!"

I shrugged. "This is the greatest library that's ever existed, so it only makes sense that it would attract the largest pests in existence."

The silverfish finished its snack and regarded us dispassionately with cold black eyes. The creature's antennae continued to quiver, as if drinking in every bit of sensory data it could find, but otherwise, its body remained unnaturally still. But a certain tension radiated from the giant insect nevertheless, as if the thing might dash toward us in an instant if we made the wrong move.

Devona, as if sensing the silverfish's mood, spoke in a hushed tone. "What does it want?"

"Mostly, just to be left alone to gorge itself on paper," I said. "It's trying to decide whether or not we're a threat to it."

"You mean it's afraid we might be the exterminators?" she asked in disbelief.

"Something like that."

"And if it should decide we mean it harm?"

"While the giant silverfish that dine at the Great Library might prefer a diet of paper products, they've been known to eat other things from time to time," I said. "This *is* Nekropolis, after all."

"When you say 'other things', I don't suppose you mean popcorn and potato chips."

"Afraid not."

The silverfish shifted its weight from side to side then, as if working up the courage to attack.

"So what do we do?" Devona asked. "Slowly back away, keeping our gazes trained on it the whole time?"

"You've watched one too many nature documentaries," I said. "That's a sure way to get us both eaten. There's only one way to deal with a monster silverfish." I'd known we'd probably end up at the Great Library sooner or later, and so I'd come prepared. Slowly – very, very slowly – I reached into my jacket pocket and removed a small white plastic container.

The silverfish's entire body began to quiver then. I unscrewed the container's lid, careful not to make any sudden moves. Devona watched me, a puzzled frown on her face.

"Is that... glue?"

"Not just any glue," I answered. "It's really thick... and it has sparkles in it."

The silverfish's antennae blurred with anticipation, and it legs began tap-tap-tapping on the floor, like an excited little dog getting so worked up it was going to start peeing any minute.

I slowly held the container of sparkle-glue out before me. "Back on Earth, silverfish eat more than just paper. They also eat the glue in book bindings. And this is really *good* glue. Expensive, top-of-the-line stuff, imported from an art supply store near the Louvre."

The silverfish's body began to undulate rapidly, almost as if it were swimming underwater, the strange motion a major reason for its species' name. The giant insect took a single hesitant step forward, then a second...

"Whatever you do," I said to Devona, "don't move."

Before she could ask why, the silverfish darted forward. I spun around and hurled the open container of glue through the nearest doorway. The silverfish became an argent blur as it scuttled past – missing us by only a few inches – and raced out of the room in mad pursuit of the treat I had brought it. A moment later loud, enthusiastic slurping noises came from the outer chamber, quickly followed by a heavy thud.

"Poison?" Devona asked.

I started to answer, but before I could say anything, a new sound disturbed the Library's quiet. A soft papery rustling. A sheaf of torn book pages blew into the room on what I imagine was a musty, antiquity-laden breeze, tumbling and scratching against each other like dry autumn leaves caught in a windstorm. The pages stopped in front of us, whirled about in a column, faster and faster, closer and closer, until they merged together and resolved into the form of a friendly-faced, middle-aged man wearing granny glasses. He looked like Ben Franklin by way of Shakespeare's tailor.

"There's no need for poison," Waldemar said. "A rich meal of French glue just makes the poor things logy." He sighed. "I try my best to keep them out, but somehow they always manage to find their way in again."

"Maybe if you wouldn't keep leaving scraps of paper in the back alley for them to eat," I said.

Waldemar grinned, displaying a small set of fangs. "And where would be the fun in that, I ask you?" He took my hand in both of his pale, pudgy ones and pumped vigorously. "Delighted to see you again, Matthew, my boy!"

"Good to see you too, Waldemar." I was about to introduce Devona when he released my hands and took hers, shaking them just as energetically.

"Devona Kanti – it's a privilege and a joy to finally meet you! And how is your esteemed father?"

Devona looked at Waldemar for a moment, his effusive greeting catching her off guard. I guess she hadn't expected Nekropolis's most respected historian to act like someone's effusive uncle.

"He's, uh, rather busy right now, actually," she said.

Waldermar nodded. "Of course, of course. It is the anniversary of the Descension, after all. The three hundred and seventy-third, to be precise." He paused and touched a finger to his lips. "Or is it three hundred and thirty-seven? Oh, well, it's one or the other. I think." Then he looked at me and brightened, as if he'd forgotten all about us and had just remembered.

"Now, how may I be of service to you and your lovely companion, Matthew?"

Waldemar's befuddled scholar pose didn't fool me. I'd known him too long. He was a vampire as old as Lord Galm, perhaps older. And when I looked closely into his gray eyes, I sometimes got a sense of the ancient, vast intelligence at work between them. I had no doubt he'd be able to tell us what we needed to know.

"We'd like to learn about a mystic artifact called the Dawnstone."

Waldemar's finger returned to his lips, only this time to tap them thoughtfully. "Dawnstone, Dawnstone…" His eyes got a far away look in them, and not for the first time after asking him a question, I had the impression that I had set a complicated process into motion, as if I'd asked a computer to divine the meaning of life and then balance my checkbook.

Waldemar began meandering about the room, muttering softly to himself, the words unintelligible, except for the occasional repetition of "*Dawnstone.*"

Devona looked at me as if to ask what we should do now. I shrugged and started after Waldemar.

"Dawnstone, Dawnstone, Dawnstone…" He pulled books off the shelves, seemingly at random, flipped them open, and barely glanced at their pages before putting them back. Once, I swore he checked a book, replaced it, and then immediately removed and looked at it once more before moving on.

Curious, I pulled the book in question off the shelf myself and opened it. I wasn't particularly surprised to find that the page I had chosen – like all the pages, in fact – was blank.

I reshelved the volume and wondered if all the books, scrolls, and parchments in this room – maybe in the entire Library – were also blank.

As I watched Waldemar continue randomly searching his collection, I had the impression that he wasn't consulting books so much as sifting through the immense reaches of his unfathomably ancient mind, and that perhaps the Great Library itself was nothing more than a physical manifestation of his memories. And if that was true, what about the giant silverfish? Were they really pests or were they simply Waldemar's way of forgetting?

Another thought occurred to me then. If Devona and I truly were standing somehow within Waldemar's memories made real, what might happen if his absent-mindedness wasn't an act after all, and he really did forget we were here? Would we vanish, just two more minor memories, no longer needed? I didn't want to think about it. I had all the existential dilemma I could handle just being a possibly soon-to-be-rotted-away-to-dust zombie, thank you very much.

"I have a number of interesting references regarding dawn," Waldemar said as he continued looking. "Some lovely bits of poetry, and quite a few more references dealing with stone, stone cutting, stone working... Especially fascinating is a song cycle from an ancient aboriginal people dealing with a man who wanted to mate with a boulder shaped like a woman. His chief difficulty lay in his inanimate paramour's lack of the requisite, ah, anatomy. He solved the problem by constructing a crude hammer and chisel and—"

"We just want to hear about the Dawnstone, Waldemar," I cut in. "Not to be rude, but we're in something of a hurry."

He looked a bit hurt, but thankfully didn't resume his story. Instead he took a volume which appeared to be bound in green scale from the shelf, flipped it open, and ran a finger along the righthand page. "Ah, yes, here it is! No wonder it took me so long to find it. The object in question is only mentioned in several obscure pre-Atlantean myths, and only once as the Dawnstone. Other names include the Eye of the Sun and–"

I must have been frowning because Waldemar looked at me, cleared his throat, and said, "So on and so forth. While the details of the myths vary somewhat, the basic story is the same. A loathsome demon carries off a beautiful young woman to a shadowy underworld with the intention of making her his bride. The maiden's paramour, a strong and clever hero, ascends into the heavens and steals one of the Sun's eyes. He takes it down into the underworld, and – after overcoming sundry obstacles – confronts the demon and unleashes the eye's light. The creature of darkness cannot withstand the Sun's all-powerful illumination and perishes. The hero escorts his love back to the surface world, and then returns the eye to its rightful owner, the Sun."

Waldemar snapped the book shut. "Quite an amusing little fable. It rather puts one in mind of Orpheus and Eurydice, doesn't it?"

"Is that all?" Devona asked, sounding like a kid who's opened all her Christmas presents and discovered that Santa not only brought her underwear this year, it's full of holes.

"I'm afraid so, my dear," Waldemar said. "But I have quite a selection of other myths dealing with similar themes. For instance, there's a story among the Native American Indians regarding–"

"Thanks, anyway, Waldemar," I said hurriedly before he could get too far into this latest digression. "But we really must be going."

"So soon? Ah well, if you must, you must, I suppose. You'll have to promise to stop back and see me again, though, Matthew."

"I will," I said, knowing it was a promise I might not be able to keep. "Same price as usual today?"

"Of course." And then Waldemar reached into my chest – or seemed to; I was never clear on that – and pulled forth a scrap of paper, leaving my flesh and the shirt that covered it unmarked.

I felt a wrench deep in my soul, and then a sense of loss which quickly began to fade.

"Father Dis!" Devona swore in surprise. "What…?"

"Waldemar's standard price for information," I explained. "A page out of your life."

Waldemar held the page up to his face, adjusted his glasses, and quickly perused its contents. "Most interesting, most interesting indeed." He sniffed the paper like a bloodhound trying to catch a scent, and then in a single, swift motion crumpled the page and stuffed it into his mouth. He chewed greedily, noisily, a thin line of saliva rolling down his chin. Then he swallowed and grinned.

"Most delicious, Matthew. Thank you."

Devona had gone as pale as a full vampire. I took her by the arm, said goodbye to Waldemar, and led her out of the room with the domed ceiling, the master of the Great Library licking his fingers behind us as we left.

I knew it didn't matter which route we took as we departed. However we went, we'd eventually discover the way out or it would discover us. And sure enough, before long we found ourselves back at the entrance, and then outside on the Avenue of Dread Wonders once more. The sidewalk was still deserted, and everything was still quiet. For some reason, the stillness made me uncomfortable, and I wondered if I'd gotten too used to living in the chaos of the Sprawl.

I started walking, but Devona took hold of my arm to stop me. I turned to look at her, glad to see that the vicious paper-cuts she'd received thanks to the silverfish were almost fully healed. Before long, not even scars would remain to mar her flesh. I wished I could've said the same.

"What happened in there?" Devona asked. "Waldemar didn't actually–"

"Devour a snatch of my life? He sure did. Most vampires live on blood. He subsists on memories."

"You mean you gave up one of your memories just for some information… to help me?"

I didn't want to tell her that it hardly mattered, seeing as how I'd be zombie guacamole in a couple days. So I just nodded.

"Which… which memory did you lose?"

"I don't know. I never do. Once they're gone, they're gone completely. It could have been something as boring as failing an algebra test in high school."

"Or something as important as the first time you fell in love."

"I suppose. But it doesn't matter now."

She thought for a moment. "How many times have you done this, Matthew? Given Waldemar one of your memories?"

Too damned many, I almost said, but then I realized it would cheapen what I had done in her eyes – cheapen me, too, for what kind of a man, living or dead, thinks so little of his own memories that he's willing to spend them like money?

"Only a couple," I lied.

"You shouldn't have," Devona said. "It's my case you're working on; I should've been the one to pay."

But you're not the one who may die soon, I thought. "The important thing is we've gained some vital information about the Dawnstone."

"Assuming what he told us was more than just an old, forgotten myth. And even if it was, I'm not sure we learned anything useful, certainly not anything worth the price you paid."

"We learned that the Dawnstone is probably the most potent weapon Nekropolis has ever seen. For what could be more devastating in a world of shadows and darkness than a piece of the sun itself?"

SEVEN

We started walking through Gothtown, away from the
Great Library, heading toward the Bridge of Nine Sorrows. Devona kept looking around nervously, as if she
were expecting trouble.

"Worried that Lazlo's going to show up and run us
over?" I asked, only half-jokingly. "Don't be. His fre-
quency of appearances, like everything else about him,
tends to be erratic. A month might go by before I see
him again." Not that I might be here – or anywhere for
that matter – in a month, but I decided not to mention
that particular tidbit of information.

"It's not that," she said, shooting a quick glance over
her shoulder. "I think we're being followed."

On TV and in the movies, cops always sense when
they're being tailed, as if they have a sixth sense or
something. It's true that you do develop certain instincts after a while, but when you live in Nekropolis,
where quite a few of the residents possess the physical
capabilities to sneak up on a fly, instincts don't do you

a lot of good. Besides, Devona's half-vampire senses were much sharper than my dulled zombie ones; I decided to trust her.

I reached into one of the homemade inner pockets of my jacket and removed another of the little surprises I'd picked up before we left my apartment. I held it down at my side, and gestured with my other hand for Devona to stop. I quickly scanned the street, looking for cover, but there was nothing. We'd just have to fight in the open.

"Hey, deader! What you doing here in Bloodsville?" The voice, a male's, came from out in the street, but no one was in sight.

"Maybe he's come to see how his betters live," came a second voice, this one female.

"Or maybe he's looking to upgrade." Another male. "Trade in his rotten zombie teeth for a nice new pair of shiny fangs."

Disembodied laughter echoed up and down the street.

"Who–" Devona started to ask, but I cut her off and pointed to the end of the street.

"Just watch," I said.

Moments later a roiling wall of crimson mist came wafting around the corner. It rolled forward, gathering momentum, completely filling the street. The mist stopped when it reached us, and quickly dissipated, as if scattered by wind. But the air was still.

Standing in front us were now three young (or at least young-seeming) vampires, two male, one female. Instead of wearing clothing, their fish-belly white bodies were wrapped in tangles of multicolored wire, cables, and circuitry. The bodysuits might've been high-tech, but I knew they were powered by the vampires' own dark lifeforces, making their outfits a fusion of science and magic. All three had clean-shaven skulls, and in their foreheads were embedded tiny silver crosses, the flesh around the holy objects swollen, cracked, and festering. They smiled, displaying their canines, the left incisors painted bright ruby red – the calling card of the Red Tide, one of the most vicious street gangs in Nekropolis.

"How are you two doing this fine Descension Day?" asked the girl, whose body appeared to be that of a fourteen year-old girl, fifteen tops. A pair of glowing tesseracts dangled from her lobes like earrings. The latter were a nice touch, I thought.

"Us, we're bored bloodless," said one of the males, who was tall, lean, and looked to be in his mid-twenties.

"Then you three ought to head to the Sprawl and live it up with the rest of the city," I said.

The other male, short, stocky, and looking like he was in his early thirties, spat a gob of blood-colored saliva onto the cobblestones. "Fuck *that* noise. Bunch of lame-asses running around drunk in the streets. Not our kind of fun, is it, Narda?"

The girl gave a wicked, lopsided smile. "Not at all, Enan."

The lean male giggled, a high-pitched, crazy sound.

"What *is* your kind of fun?" I asked, though I had a damned good idea.

Narda answered. "Thought maybe we'd take ourselves apart a zombie."

"See what it looks like inside," added Enan.

The still nameless male just kept giggling.

Narda looked at Devona and frowned. "What are you doing with this corpse, honey? Can't find yourself a real man?"

"Maybe she likes 'em dead," Enan said.

"Dead and limp," added the giggler.

"Why don't you just go on ahead and find a party somewhere, honey?" Narda said. "And leave the deader to us."

I'd had enough of this, and was about to step into the street and confront them when Devona spoke, her voice shaky with barely contained fear.

"Do you have any idea who I am?"

Nada wasn't impressed. "Yeah, you're a dumb half-breed blood-slut who ought to have better taste than to hang around with a pile of walking hamburger like him." She nodded in my direction.

I signaled for Devona to be quiet, but she ignored me and went on.

"I am Devona Kanti, daughter of Lord Galm and guardian of his Collection," she said haughtily, or at least as haughtily as she could while trembling.

I groaned inwardly. That was exactly the wrong thing to say.

"You're lying, bitch," Narda said. "And if you aren't, you're just plain stupid. The Red Tide doesn't give a damn about the high-and-mighty Lord Galm."

"Galm hates tech," Enan put in.

The giggler raised his forearm and made a fist. The wires around his arm quivered like hungry worms. "And Red Tide is wired, man."

As if in agreement, the holo-cubes dangling from Narda's ears flashed red. "Wired *solid*," she finished.

Screw this, I thought, and raised my surprise and leveled it at the three undead gang bangers.

"You'll get the hell out of here if you know what's good for you," I said in my best I'm-a-cop-and-I'm-through-taking-shit voice.

They saw what I was holding and burst out laughing.

"A squirt gun?" Narda said, incredulous. "Deadboy, your brains must have rotted away to goo!" She turned to her two companions. "C'mon, let's each grab a limb and make a wish."

They started forward and I aimed my plastic green squirt gun at their heads and pumped the trigger three times in rapid succession. Three streams of liquid flew out of the nozzle, one for each vamp.

When the fluid struck them, their undead flesh sizzled and popped and steam rose into the air. I imagine it didn't smell too good, either. They screamed and fell to their knees, clutching their wounded faces in their hands.

"That's a mixture of holy water and garlic juice," I said. "And unless you want some more, you'll–" Before

I could finish, Narda – her burns already beginning to heal – pointed at me and a thick tentacle of braided wire and circuitry shot forth from her arm. The tentacle wrapped around my gun arm and squeezed. Sparks crackled where the wire connected with my arm, and I could hear my own flesh begin to fry. I knew I had to do something quick, before my dry zombie skin caught fire.

I dropped my gun, intending to catch it with my left hand and continue squirting, but my zombie reflexes were too slow. I missed and the plastic gun clattered to the street.

I tried to bend down to retrieve my weapon, but Enan stabbed his hand forward and a thick black cable lashed out toward me like a whip. It coiled around my neck and Enan grunted as he yanked me forward. I slammed face-first onto the cobblestones and got to listen to a few of my ribs break for good measure.

This wasn't exactly going as well as I'd hoped.

The Giggler decided to get into the act then. Thin tendrils of wire uncoiled from around his arms and came snaking through the air toward me. Like Narda's, electricity coruscated up and down the length of the Giggler's wires, but unlike hers, his streaked toward my mouth. I realized then that the bastard intended to cook me from the inside out.

I clamped my mouth shut tight and struggled to roll over onto my side. I would've pinched my nostrils shut to prevent the Giggler's wires from entering me that way, but I only had one hand free, and I had a more important use for it. I reached into my jacket and groped for something else that might fend off the vampires, but before I could get hold of anything they started shrieking anew. I looked up and saw that Devona had retrieved my squirt gun and was dousing the Red Tide members with my holy water and garlic combo.

"For godsakes, be careful!" I warned. "You don't want to get any of that stuff on you!"

The three tech-vampires retracted their cables and wires, releasing me. She and the other two vamps didn't look so hot. Their faces were a mass of burns, and their combination hi tech and magic body suits were starting to short circuit, throwing off showers of miniature fireworks.

The vampires staggered to their feet and stumbled off, howling in pain. At the end of the street, Narda turned, and fixed us with a hate-filled stare from her single remaining eye.

"The Red Tide's going to store this in permanent memory, fuckers! Bet on it!" Then she turned and continued running after the other two, leaving us alone on the streets of Gothtown. They were vampires; their injuries would heal eventually. But it was going to take some time.

I pushed myself to my feet with my left arm, and stepped over to Devona. She still pointed the squirt gun in the direction the Red Tide vamps had gone, holding it in an iron grip. Her entire body shook, and her breath came in ragged gasps. I'd only fired my weapon twice in the line of duty when I was cop – before coming to Nekropolis, that is – but I understood what Devona was feeling.

"Why don't you give that back to me before you break it and that crap leaks all over your hands?"

She looked at the gun as if realizing for the first time what she was holding, and she handed it over to me gingerly, like it was a live grenade. I suppose for a vampire – even a half-vampire – it was.

I checked the water level, saw that the squirt gun was almost empty, and then replaced it in my jacket pocket.

"Thanks for taking care of those three, Devona. You probably saved my unlife." *At least for another day or two*, I added mentally.

"I didn't think about it; I just grabbed the gun off the ground and started shooting." She sounded amazed, as if surprised by her own actions. "Where in Nekropolis did you get holy water, anyway? It's extremely illegal. If Father Dis found out–" She stopped and looked at me in horror. "The Hidden Light! You're a member of the Hidden Light!"

She started backing away and I held up a hand – my right one – to calm her. It was a little hard to control, thanks to Narda sizzling my arm, but it still worked. "Take it easy. I'm not one of the Hidden Light, but from time to time they supply me with certain items I can't get any other way."

That didn't do much to reassure her. "They're a terrorist version of the Inquisition, Matthew: radical Christians completely dedicated to the destruction of

Nekropolis and the Darkfolk by any means necessary!"

"I don't condone their actions, but if it wasn't for them, I wouldn't have been able to get me hands on the holy water that just helped save your butt."

"I don't care what your reasons are. It's because of people like them that my kind had to leave Earth in the first place. People like them – and like you." She looked at me like I was the lowest form of life imaginable.

I knew the intensity of Devona's reaction was an emotional aftereffect of the battle we'd just survived – most likely the first she'd ever fought – but despite that I couldn't control my rising anger.

"If you don't want my help anymore, just say so. Maybe you'll get lucky and the Dawnstone will just show up on its own. And if it doesn't, maybe Lord Galm will have mercy and kill you quickly." It was a rotten thing to say, and I immediately wanted take it back, but I didn't know how. I've never been good at apologies.

Devona was silent for a few moments, and I could tell that she was considering walking away and being done with me. But in the end her dedication to her job – and fear of her father – won out.

She let out a long sigh and then in a tired voice said, ""All right. Where to now?"

I was glad she stayed. I needed her to intercede with her father on my behalf, get him to use his powers, or his influence with the other Lords or even Father Dis himself, to save my undead excuse for an existence. Not because it mattered to me what happened to her… and definitely not because I was starting to care for her.

Honest.

"We head back to the Sprawl," I said. "To find Varma and – with any luck – the Dawnstone."

EIGHT

I wouldn't have been all that unhappy if Lazlo had shown up then, truth to tell. I wasn't looking forward to battling the crowds in the Sprawl again. But of course he didn't, and so we had no choice but to walk. There were no coaches or cars for hire in Gothtown that night; they'd all been previously engaged by Bloodborn for transportation to the Cathedral.

To pass the time, and more importantly because it might have something to do with why the Dawnstone was stolen, I asked Devona to tell me everything she knew about the Renewal Ceremony. I was familiar with the basics – every Nekropolitan was – but I hoped that as the daughter of a Darklord, she might be able to provide more insight into the specifics.

"The river Phlegethon, the air we breathe, and in some ways the city itself are all maintained by the power of Umbriel. When the Darkfolk first came to this dimension, Father Dis and the five Lords created the shadowsun and set it above the Nightspire to sustain their people in their new home. But Umbriel isn't eternal; it needs to be recharged once a year."

"And thus the Renewal Ceremony," I said.

She nodded. "The five Darklords conserve their powers for months and then, on the anniversary of the Descension they gather in the Nightspire along with Father Dis to perform the rite which will revitalize Umbriel. Nekropolis's most illustrious citizens are invited to witness the ceremony. I never have, though. My rank among the Bloodborn isn't high enough to merit an invitation." She said this quietly, without self pity. "Do you think there's a connection between the theft of the Dawnstone and the Renewal Ceremony?"

"Maybe," I answered. "The Darklords don't particularly like being equal; they're always trying to gain an advantage over each other."

That's what caused the Bloodwars two hundred years ago, and though a lasting peace was finally negotiated – or, as I've heard it, violently enforced by an extremely fed-up Father Dis – to this day the Darklords continue to spy on and plot against one another. I suppose all the intrigue and power-struggles prevent them from getting bored as they while away Eternity.

I went on. "From what Waldemar told us, it sounds like the Dawnstone would be a powerful weapon – especially against a vampire. Because of the Renewal Ceremony, this day is the one time of the year when the Darklords' minds are on matters other than their endless bickering… a good time to take an opponent by surprise."

Devona stopped walking, grabbed me by the arms, and turned me toward her. She might have only been a half vampire, but she was still strong as hell. "You think someone – perhaps Varma – is plotting to destroy my father?"

"Possibly."

"Then we must return to the Cathedral and warn him!"

She let go of me and started to run in the direction of Lord Galm's stronghold, but it was my turn to grab her, and I took hold of her arm to stop her. She struggled, and she was more than strong enough to break free of my grip if she wanted to, so I knew I had to talk fast.

"You told me you didn't want your father to know about the Dawnstone being missing before we had a chance to at least find out what happened to it."

"That was before you said he might be in danger. Now let me go!" She tried to pull away from me, but I tightened my grip, praying her exertions wouldn't snap off my fingers.

"Listen to me for a minute: if someone does intend to kill Lord Galm, whoever it is won't try now. Think. You told me the Darklords conserve their power for months before the Renewal Ceremony – right?"

"Right."

"So who would be foolish enough to attack Galm at the height of his strength? No, the best time to kill him would be during the Ceremony, when he's distracted and expending his power to help recharge Umbriel. He's safe until then."

Devona didn't look completely convinced, but she stopped trying to tear away from me, which was good, because as strong as she was, she probably would've taken my arm with her when she left.

I pressed on. "Even if you did try to warn him, as busy as he is right now, would he even talk to you?"

"Perhaps not."

"And don't forget that there's a good chance your father is angry with you right now for bringing a zombie to his pre-Ceremony celebration. Besides, what do you really have to tell him, other than vague suspicions? The more we can learn, the greater the chance we can make him listen to us. Make him believe us. Look, how long do we have before the ceremony starts?"

She shrugged. "Hours, at least. We'll know it's near when the Deathknell of the Nightspire sounds."

"So we have time to try to find Varma."

She sighed. "I suppose."

"All right, then let's quit talking and start walking."

She nodded, but she didn't look happy about it.

We started in the direction of the bridge again, but immediately stopped. There before us was a midnight black coach hitched to two large ebony horses. And perched in the seat on top sat a man in a top hat and cloak which looked as if they'd been fashioned out of solid darkness, a horsewhip cradled in his lap. He turned his face toward us, but I couldn't make out his shadowy, indistinct features. He inclined his head and touched the brim of his hat in greeting, but said nothing.

The coach had made no noise whatsoever pulling up, but either Devona hadn't noticed or it didn't bother her.

"Look, Matthew, perhaps we won't have to fight our way through the crowds after all." She stepped toward the coach, but I grabbed her elbow and pulled her back.

"That's the Black Rig, Silent Jack's coach," I said harshly. "You *don't* want to ride with him."

She frowned at me. "Why not?"

"That's right; you said you didn't get out of Gothtown much. Let's just say that Jack has a thing for the ladies. And his fares are quite steep."

Jack's shadow-shrouded face remained pointed at us a moment more, then he turned forward, raised his whip, and cracked it soundlessly over his horses, Malice and Misery. The animals whinnied silently, displaying teeth as black as their hides, and then the rig vanished, winking out of existence as if it had never been.

"You know," Devona said in a shaky voice, "Suddenly walking doesn't seem so bad after all."

Bars, nightclubs, strip joints, and bad theatre are as common in the Sprawl as scales on a Gill-man. But the hottest, trendiest, most debauched entertainments can be found in only one place: Sybarite Street. It's jam-packed with pleasure-seekers at the best of times, but during the Descension celebration, you couldn't cut your way through the throngs with a high-precision laser. Still, if Varma were anywhere in Nekropolis, he was probably here, so Devona and I made our way the best we could.

According to Devona, Varma frequented quite a few establishments on Sybarite Street, so we decided to start with the first one we came to: the Krimson Kiss. I'd never been inside before, but I'd heard a few things about it. I wasn't looking forward to finding out if they were true.

Outside, the Krimson Kiss wasn't much to look at. A large blocky stone building with two large neon K's on the roof, blazing – what else? – crimson light into the darkness. Like everywhere else on the street tonight, there was a long line of less-than-patient would-be patrons standing outside. But I figured there was a good chance I would rot away to a pile of zombie dust before the line budged a foot, so I took hold of Devona's hand and pulled her along with me to the front. A tall, broad-shouldered satyr was working the Krimson Kiss's door that night, and he stood behind a velvet rope barrier, well-muscled arms crossed over his body-builder chest, grinning at the crowd through his curly reddish-brown beard. He was naked, as was customary for his kind, but since he was covered with thick fur from beneath his washboard abs down to his cloven-hoofed feet, he didn't really need any clothing.

I started to say something to the satyr, but before I could get a word out, I felt pressure as a hand gripped my shoulder. I turned around to see a petite woman dressed in a 1920's flapper outfit glaring at me. Her skin was covered with pulsating lesions, and when she opened her mouth to yell at me, I saw that her tongue was covered with blood-fattened ticks.

"What the hell do you think you're doing?" she said, her words made mushy by all those ticks. "I've waited *hours* in this line, and now that I'm next, I'm not about to let some chewed-up deader and his leather-clad slut cut in front of me!" She bobbled her head as she spoke, making the locks of her page-boy hair cut swish back and forth and causing the ostrich feather tucked into her headband to jerk about spasmodically. Her lesions began to throb violently, presumably as a result of her anger.

"Surely those aren't those real ticks." I leaned close to the flapper and squinted my eyes, while at the same time reaching into one of my pockets and palming one of the objects I found there.

"Of course they're real!" she said indignantly. "They're the very latest thing. Take a look if you don't believe me."

The flapper stuck out her parasite-infested tongue for my inspection, and that's when I flicked my lighter and touched the flame to the insects. The blood-gorged bugs popped and sizzled and leaped off the flapper's tongue like... well, like dying ticks leaping off a burning tongue. The woman shrieked and batted her blazing tongue with both hands, while tears streamed down her face. "My babies!" she shouted. "What have you done to my babies?!"

At least, I think that's what she said. It was kind of hard to tell with that flash-fried tongue of hers.

I then turned to glare at the rest of the people at the head of the line, and in my best gruff cop voice said, "Anybody else got something to say?"

A tall man dressed like a mortician with an inside-out face stepped forward, but before I could do anything, Devona bared her fangs at him and hissed like a cougar on crack. The tall man swallowed – a very disturbing sight considering the state of his face – and quickly stepped back in line.

I looked to Devona. She kept her fangs bared, but I could see the satisfied twinkle in her eyes.

A hearty laughed boomed out, and Devona and I turned to face the satyr.

His teeth were perfectly white, perfectly straight. "Thanks for that – it was the most fun I've had all night! But even though I'm a great fan of street theatre, I'm afraid the two of you will just have to wait in line like everyone else."

There was some half-hearted applause from the people behind us, but it cut off when Devona whirled around and hissed again.

I sighed. It had been a long day, and I'd never had much tolerance for people who thought they were God's gift – on in this case, Dis's gift – to the world. "We're going into the club to look for someone, and you're going to let us in. Now."

The satyr's left eyebrow climbed toward one of his horns. "Really?" he said, his voice dripping sarcasm. "And just how is this miraculous event going to take place?"

The asshole was really getting up my nose, but even though I was no longer a cop, I had a cop's training, and I knew that it's best to negotiate whenever possible.

And I did have a few darkgems on me to offer as a poor excuse for a bribe.

"It depends," I said. "What would it take for you to help *make* it happen?"

The satyr ran his fingers thoughtfully through his shaggy beard. "Oh, I don't know." Then he looked at Devona. A smoldering lust came into his gaze and a sly smile spread across his face. "She's not bad-looking, and even better, she's feisty. Fifteen minutes alone with her in the back alley, and I'll let you both in. What do you say?"

Devona's pretense of fierceness dropped away, replaced by shock. She looked to me, unsure how to respond. But that was all right – I knew exactly how to respond.

I still had hold of my lighter, and now I slipped it back into my pocket and exchanged it for a small burlap-wrapped ball tied with a thin white ribbon. I tossed it toward the satyr and said, "Catch."

He caught the ball in one hand and then turned his palm up to examine it.

"What's this?" he said, frowning in suspicion.

"Inside is some hair shed by a hellhound with a serious case of mange. As for what it does, it functions as a highly effective depilatory spell."

The satyr's frowned deepened into a scowl. "Depilatory? What's that mean?"

A second later, he found out precisely what it meant when all of his hair – atop his head, on his face, and most especially from his waist down – slid off his body and fell to the ground in large clumps.

The people in line took one look at what the satyr's groin fur had been hiding and started to laugh – and despite her injuries the burnt-tongue flapper laughed loudest of all.

"You wanted fifteen minutes with me?" Devona said, giving a certain portion of the satyr's anatomy a pointed look. "That thing's so small, it would've taken me half an hour to find it."

More laughter, and the satyr – who was now absolutely and undeniably naked in the most profound sense of the word – wailed with embarrassment and took off running. The crowd on the sidewalk obligingly parted for him as he clip-clopped away on his goat hooves, bawling like a baby, which I decided was only appropriate considering he had an infant-sized wee-wee.

The satyr had dropped the hellhound fur ball when he ran, and I bent down, retrieved it, and tucked it back into my pocket. As I straightened, Devona said, "Is there anything you don't have in those pockets of yours?"

"Yeah. A wallet. Who needs one in Nekropolis?"

I offered her my arm, she took it, and together we walked into the Krimson Kiss.

The atmosphere of the Krimson Kiss was even seedier than Skully's. Bare dirt floor, crude wooden tables and chairs, guttering candles shoved into beer bottles... Vermen servers scuttled from table to table, the humanoid rodents taking and fulfilling orders with

obsequious speed. The creatures stand between four
and five feet tall and usually walk with a hunched-
over shuffle, though they can move damned fast
when they want to. They only wear clothes when
working for humans (or humanlike beings), and the
servers in the Krimson Kiss wore white waistcoats lib-
erally splattered with bloodstains, equally stained
white shirts, black pants, and black bow ties. No
shoes, though. No amount of darkgems could get Vermen to cram their long clawed toes into such
tortuously uncomfortable things. One passed close by
me, carrying a tray loaded with pewter tankards. It
was a female, I think, though I have a hard time
telling one gender from another when it comes to
vermen. She twitched her whiskers as she went by,
and I couldn't help feeling a wave of disgust. I've
made a lot of adjustments since coming to Nekropolis,
but for reason I've never have been able to get used
to vermen. Maybe my mother was frightened by a
Mousketeer when she was pregnant.

The Krimson Kiss's clientele was a mix of vampires,
lykes, and ghouls, with a scattering of demon kin and
a few less identifiable beings. Some were watching a
horror movie playing on big screen TV – I didn't recognize it, but it was one of those English ones, in color,
with lots of blood – and laughing uproariously. But
most were busy gorging themselves on the establishment's specialty – plates heaping with slabs of raw, wet
meat and tankards brimming with blood, all provided
by the Krimson Kiss's claim to fame: the Sweetmeat.

The ghastly thing filled a recessed pit in the center of the club, a grotesquely fat blob of pink, boneless flesh from which a dozen stunted, withered arms and legs jutted forth. Vermen waiters ringed the creature, cutting off hunks of its flesh and slapping them on serving trays, filling mugs from brass spigots surgically implanted in its sides, all as fast as the ravenous crowd could order them.

Once a verman sliced off some meat, he took a step to the right and cut another. By the time he had taken three more steps, the first cut he had made was already healed.

The Sweetmeat possessed a horrendous, toothless maw on its back, and a line of vermen passed down metal buckets full of a grayish glop which they dumped into the obscenely gaping mouth. Bucket after bucket after bucket. No slowing, no end in sight.

"Lovely, isn't it?" I said sarcastically.

Devona didn't answer; she looked like she was too busy trying to keep from vomiting.

"Do you see Varma?"

She took her eyes off the Sweetmeat – and was more than likely quite grateful for a reason to do so – and scanned the room.

"No."

"Then let's start asking around."

It would've been more effective if Devona and I had split up, but I was mindful of the fact that she didn't have much experience outside Gothtown – maybe even outside the Cathedral, I suspected – so I thought it best if we stuck together. I didn't see any friends or better yet, anyone who owed me a favor. But I did recognize a few of the beings stuffing their faces, so we began with them.

Glassine, also know as the Transparent Woman, was eating alone. Supposedly she was the descendent of some English scientist who'd invented an invisibility potion a century or so ago. Unfortunately, her attempts to recreate her relative's formula had only met with partial success, rendering her skin invisible but not the muscles, veins, organs, and bone underneath. She didn't mind answering a few questions, but she'd never heard of Varma and had never seen a Bloodborn of his description at the Krimson Kiss. She actually turned out to be rather chatty and even invited us to join her, but we declined as politely as we could.

Glassine sighed. "I get that a lot, especially when I dine out. I tend to spoil people's appetites."

I said something about not having an appetite anymore myself, but I couldn't help sympathizing with Glassine. In my current condition, I doubted too many people would want to have a meal in my presence, either.

Next we spoke to Legion – or at least, whoever was inhabiting his body at the moment. Legion appears to be an ordinary-looking human in his late twenties, usually dressed in T-shirt, jeans, and running shoes, but he makes his living by renting out his body to spirits who are eager to experience physical pleasures once more. Whoever – or whatever – was possessing Legion at the moment was so busy cramming food and drink into its host's mouth that he barely paused to answer my questions.

"Yeah, I've seen Varma around a few times. He comes in here now and again for a tankard of blood, but far as I know, he hasn't been in for a couple weeks." Legion burped loudly and wiped a smear of blood off his mouth with the back of his hand.

"I don't suppose we could talk to any of the other entities inside you for a moment, just to see what they might know?" I asked.

"Hell, no!" Legion – or rather his current occupant – said. "I paid good money for my time in this body, and I'm not about to give up so much as a second of it!"

"Speaking of money, tell me something," I said, genuinely curious. "Where do spirits get darkgems anyway?"

A sly look game into Legion's eyes. "You'd be surprised at the sorts of things you can find out when you're both invisible and intangible. There are all kinds of valuables out there, ripe for the taking – if you know where to look. Now fuck off and let me eat."

Legion returned to gorging himself, and Devona and I walked away from his table.

"Do you think he makes good money renting himself out like that?" Devona asked, mouth pursed in distaste.

"I don't know, but I bet buying antacids and paying for detox treatments must cut a damned big chunk out of his profits."

We moved on to the Mariner's table. The old man looked miserable as ever, and while he wasn't partaking of any food or drink himself, the dead albatross hanging around his neck was tearing at a raw chunk of Sweet-meat with sickening gusto.

When we asked him about Varma, he shook his head. "But you know who you should be asking?" The Mariner turned and pointed to an obese ghoul sitting at a large table in the rear of the place. "Arval. He owns the place."

I'd heard of Arval, but I'd never met him before. I thanked the Mariner, and we started to go.

"Wait!" he said desperately. "I have a tale to tell thee!"

"Sorry, but we're rather busy at the moment," I said and started to pull Devona away from the old man's table. Once he got going with his story, there was no stopping him.

Devona resisted and stood her ground. "We really are too busy to stay, but why don't you go on over and tell her?" she said, pointing to Glassine. "I'm sure she'd be glad for the company."

The Mariner glanced over at the Transparent Woman, and for the first time since I'd known him, he broke into a smile.

"Thanks. I think I'll do that."

"Not until I'm done with my meal, you old fart!" the albatross squawked.

The Mariner gave the undead bird a solid thump on the head to quiet it. "That's old salt, featherbrain." He gave us another smile and a nod, picked up the plate with his bird's meal, and started toward Glassine's table, walking with a rolling seaman's gait.

I looked at Devona and she shrugged.

"So I'm sentimental," she said. "Sue me."

"I can't. No lawyers in Nekropolis. They're too scary even for this city."

Devona and I made our way over to the Arvel's table. Given the way they eat, ghouls tend to run to fat, but this specimen was the largest I'd ever seen. His face was practically all jowl, his thick-fingered hands so swollen they resembled flippers. He was bald, as all ghouls are, male and female alike, and he had the same eyes – completely black, no white of any kind. His fleshy lips were ridged like a reptile's, and his mouth was lined with double rows of tiny piranha teeth, top and bottom.

Ghouls normally go naked, and Arvel was no exception. We were saved, however, from having to gaze upon the entirety of his body by a large drop cloth that was spread across his chest and belly, a cloth covered with bloodstains and gobbets of partially chewed meat.

Arvel was so huge that he had to sit in a specially constructed chair made of steel and bolted to the floor in front of a cherrywood table which had been cut in a half moon in order to accommodate the vast spill of the ghoul's stomach.

Vermen waiters tended him constantly, bringing him a steady stream of meat and blood which they shoved and poured into his mouth. Arvel chewed and swallowed, his flipper-hands resting on the tabletop, unneeded. I wondered how long it had been since he'd last lifted them. Quite some time, I suspected.

His moist black eyes were fixed on the big screen TV and the image of a buxom young English actress who was succumbing to the satanic charms of Christopher Lee's Dracula. He didn't take his gaze off the movie as we approached his table.

"Excuse me," I began.

"Shhh!" he admonished, a bit of bloody meat falling out of his mouth and sticking to one of his upper chins. "Forgive me, but this is the best part!"

Christopher Lee made his move and the girl swooned as Dracula put the bite on her.

Arval let out a wet, bubbling chuckle. "They always react so melodramatically when he bites them. A ghoul wouldn't waste precious eating time on such carnal preliminaries." He looked up and saw us for the first time. "Pardon me for speaking so crudely, Miss. I didn't realize a lady was present."

Devona didn't respond. Vampires and ghouls, despite their dietary similarities, don't get along too well. Vampires consider ghouls disgusting mistakes of Unnature, while ghouls view vampires as little more than walking leeches with an unholier-than-thou attitude. I tend to agree with both sides.

"What can I do for you two fine people this glorious Descension Day?" Despite his appearance and physical mannerisms, Arval's voice was smooth and cultured, as if he'd OD'd on *Masterpiece Theatre*. Even so, he didn't stop his gluttony to talk to us, but rather continued speaking his refined words through mouthfuls of meat and blood, spilling liberal amounts onto the drop cloth as he conversed.

I introduced us, and his lamprey mouth twisted into a delighted grin. "Your reputation proceeds you, Mr. Richter! I've heard quite a bit about your exploits, but I never thought I'd be fortunate enough to actually meet you!"

He clacked his teeth together twice, and a verman scurried up.

"Bring chairs for my friends," he ordered, his tone cold, completely devoid of feeling. When the rat-man had scampered off, Arvel was once again the gracious host. "Carbuncle will be back momentarily. While we wait, would either of you care for a beverage?" He smiled sheepishly, suddenly embarrassed. "Forgive me, Mr. Richter, I forgot that you have no need of nourishment. But surely you won't pass up a tankard, Ms. Kanti? We serve the best blood in Nekropolis. It's the real thing, too. None of that horrid aqua sanguis for us here at Krimson Kiss." His smile widened, and I could see bits of flesh caught between his tiny sharp teeth.

Devona didn't say anything at first. I don't know if it was because she was too disgusted to answer, or whether she was actually thinking it over. After all, she was a half vampire.

"No, thank you. I fed earlier."

I hadn't seen her drink any blood during the time we'd been together, and I wondered if she was lying, or if perhaps she'd managed to sneak a quick snack while we were separated at the Cathedral.

"Pity," the ghoul said. "You don't know what you're missing." A verman hurried up with a full tankard. Arvel opened his mouth and the rodent poured the gore straight down his gullet. The ghoul didn't even have to swallow.

Carbuncle returned then, carrying a pair of the simple wooden chairs that everyone else in the place but Arvel was using. The rat-man set them down at the table, took a few steps back, and waited for more orders, his whiskers twitching nervously.

Devona looked at me and I nodded. I wasn't feeling especially sociable, but my years as a cop taught me that sometimes it's better to go along with the program if you want to loosen someone's tongue. We sat.

Arvel was brought another mouthful of meat followed by a mug of blood. As he devoured them, I said, "This is certainly an... interesting place you have here."

He belched loudly. "Pardon me. Yes, it's quite nice, isn't it? Though I dare say that has everything to do with my delectable Sweetmeat. Dr. Moreau over at the House of Pain created the dear thing for us, using a combination of vampire and shapeshifter DNA, mixed with a few special ingredients of his own, of course. The Sweetmeat's wounds heal almost instantly, and it quickly replaces the flesh and blood it's lost – as long as we keep it well fed with the special nutrient solution the good Doctor developed. For all intents and purposes, the Sweetmeat is immortal. It will live – and taste delectable – forever." Arvel shook his head, or rather, wobbled it from side to side a fraction. "Whenever I take another delicious bite of the Sweetmeat, I wonder why some of the Darklords are so against importing human technology from Earth."

I thought of the misbegotten thing trapped in Arvel's pit, constantly being bled and cut for the ghoul's patrons. And if what Arvel said was true, the creature was immortal and could conceivably suffer this treatment for eternity.

"I can think of a few reasons," I said.

Arvel ignored the dig. "Tell me, Mr. Richter, is it true what they say? That you're responsible for Lady Talaith's recent ill fortune?"

"I'd really rather not discuss it, if it's all the same to you."

More meat, more drink. "Ah, but there is something else you wish to discuss, no?" He licked a smear of red from his lower worm-lip. "Quid quo pro, Mr. Richter. We ghouls have an ancient aphorism: You feed me, and I'll feed you." He smiled smugly. I wanted to punch him in the mouth, but I'd probably just have shredded my hand on those teeth of his.

"Yes, it's true. But it was a couple years ago, when I first came to Nekropolis."

"Please, go on."

I sighed. "My partner and I were investigating a series of killings on Earth. There was no connection between the victims' age, race, gender, economic status, or location. The only similarity was in the way they were killed. Each victim showed no signs of having been in a struggle. It was as if they'd all just dropped dead, despite the fact that all of them were healthy with no history of serious medical conditions. Autopsies revealed something else strange: a tiny segment of their frontal lobe was missing – despite the fact that their skulls had all been intact before their autopsy."

"Sounds like quite a mystery," Arvel said as he chewed another in his endless mouthfuls of meat.

"It was. To make a long story short, through dogged detective work and more than a little luck, my partner and I tracked the killer down to a park near the lake. But just as we were about to catch him, the killer disappeared through a strange shimmer in the air."

"A portal," Arvel said.

I nodded. "Varvara's. My partner Dale and I followed, and found ourselves in the basement of the Demon Queen's lair. The killer was gone. It took a bit for us to acclimate to Nekropolis—"

Arvel laughed. "I imagine it did!"

"But once we had our bearings, we continued to search for the killer. At first, we thought the warlock had ties to Varvara, but we learned Talaith had been using the Demon Queen's portal because hers had been damaged in a previous struggle with Lord Edrigu. When we learned the truth, we headed to Glamere, determined to bring the killer back to Earth to face justice."

"And what happened?" Arvel's black eyes were shining; he was hanging on to my every word as if were a child being told a favorite bedtime story.

So I continued.

NINE

I stood with my back flattened against a smooth wooden wall, 9mm held easily at my side in my right hand, a small device gripped tightly in my left. The corridor was lit by a series of gently glowing blobs of yellowish light hovering near the ceiling, and the shadows they cast seemed to slither across the floor as if possessing a life of their own. From what I'd seen of this insane city so far, I knew it was quite possible that the shadows really were alive, and I reminded myself to keep an eye on them. A bead of sweat rolled down the back of my neck and across one of the many small wounds covering my body. It stung, and I started to take in a hissing breath of air out of reflex, but I forced myself to take a deep, calming breath instead.

You swore an oath to serve and protect, Matt. And even if you are a bit out of your jurisdiction, that's exactly what you're going to do.

My partner stood next to me, gun held ready as he peered around the corner.

"How many?" I whispered.

Dale pulled his head back and turned to face me. "Two," he said, speaking softly. "Both male, big and tough-looking. The corridor stretches a long way – a couple hundred feet, easy – and they're standing guard in front of a large wooden at the end of it. No obvious weapons that I could see."

"They don't need to carry physical weapons," I reminded him. "Not in this place."

"Don't I know it."

Dale Ramsey was a lean African-American man in his early fifties. His short black hair was starting to grey at the temples, and the lower half of his face was covered with thick stubble. People thought he did that to look stylish, but I knew it was because he often forgot to shave, sometimes for days. He wore a sharp-looking blue suit and, despite his slightly scruffy physical appearance, his outfit was dry-cleaned and neatly pressed as always. Dale had been my partner in the homicide division for the last five years, though I'd known him even longer, all the way back to when I'd started on the Cleveland force as a patrol cop and he was working Vice.

Thin lines of blood trickled from tiny wounds peppering Dale's forehead, and he bent his head forward and used his tie to wipe away the blood so it wouldn't run into his eyes. He'd used his tie instead of the back of his hand because his hands – like mine – were covered with similar wounds and were bleeding too. Not a lot, certainly not enough to be life-threatening, but definitely inconvenient.

Dale looked at the new smear of blood on his tie and grimaced. He hated getting his clothes dirty. "Who uses a barrier of animated thorn bushes as security? I mean, really."

"Just be glad we got through without being sliced to bits."

"I think that little lizard you picked up the Sprawl helped some," he said.

"Salamander. They're amphibians." At least, I thought the creature I'd used to clear a path through Talaith's thorn barrier was an amphibian. The dealer who'd sold it to me had said the small bright-red animal was a salamander in the mythological sense, meaning that it blazed with intense magical fire when threatened. I didn't care what species it was, just as long as it worked as advertised. When Dale and I approached the thorn barrier surrounding Woodhome, and I'd had to do was removed the little guy from my pocket, and toss him into the thorns. The instant one pricked him, he opened his tiny mouth and let loose a blast of flame that would've done Godzilla proud. The salamander's fireblast cut a swatch through the thorns, and Dale and I had to run like hell to reach the entrance to Woodhome before the barrier closed up again. We'd made it, but not without getting pricked, scratched, and slashed in the process. I didn't know what had happened to the salamander, but I wasn't worried. As the little guy had so amply demonstrated, he could take care of himself.

I was only sorry that the creature's magical fire hadn't been strong enough to set Woodhome itself ablaze. But from what I understood, Talaith wasn't only a witch, she was a Dark Lord – one of the most powerful beings in Nekropolis. And that meant her stronghold was protected by some serious magic, and since it was basically a gigantic tree – really a living mass formed from dozens of huge ancient trees intertwined – she'd been smart enough to fireproof it. But not, it seemed, smart enough to do the same to her thorn barrier. Or maybe she simply hadn't wanted to waste the magic on her thorns. I didn't know from magic, and I had no intention of learning. Dale and I had come to Woodhome for one reason: to track down the warlock who'd been killing people in Cleveland and bring him to justice. After that, Dale and I would head home and this place would be nothing more than a nightmare that both of us would work damned hard to forget.

Inside, the corridors and chambers of Woodhome looked as if they'd been grown instead of built. The ceiling, walls, and floors were smooth but somewhat uneven, and instead of running straight, the corridors had a tendency to curve right or left, up or down. There were no signs to help us tell which way to go, but I'd picked up a few other items in the Sprawl besides the salamander, and one of them was the object I held in my left hand.

"You sure this is it?" he asked.

In response I held up the compass. Beneath the glass was the tiny figure of a skeleton lying flat, right arm stretched over its head, index finger pointing toward the wall – or rather, toward the chamber on the other side of the wall.

"How are we supposed to know if that thing's working right? Or if it is working, it's functioning as advertised?"

I shrugged and tucked the compass into one of my jacket pockets. "It's supposed to locate sources of powerful magic. And if what the seer in the Sprawl told us is true, what we're looking for should be the most powerful device in this place. Besides, I can't think of any other way to find this Overmind thing. Can you?"

Dale made a face as if he'd just taken a bite of what he thought was prime rib only to discover someone had snuck a turd onto his plate when he wasn't looking. "I hate this place. I like to keep things simple: good guys, bad guys, witnesses, and evidence. I could do without all this hocus pocus."

"You and me both, partner," I said. "But when in Rome…"

"I've never been to Rome, but I'm confident it's nothing like this shithole." He sighed. We'd worked together for so long that I knew Dale's quirks and mannerisms as well as my own. Better, in fact. That sigh was Dale expelling the last bits of tension from his body as he geared up for action. He raised his gun and fixed me with his soft brown eyes. "You ready?"

I reached into one of my pockets with my left hand and took out a small mirror.

"Let's do it."

Without another word, we turned the corner and started running down the corridor.

The guards were exactly as Dale had described – big and mean-looking, but then they were guards: that was how they were *supposed* to look. They were two of a kind, Literally, they were twins. Both wore their black hair pulled back in pony-tails, both sported Vandyke beards, and both wore black tunics, black pants, and high black boots. I'd only been in Nekropolis a couple days, but I'd already learned that in this city, black was the new black. The warlocks looked surprised at first to see us, but they only hesitated a few seconds before raising their hands and gesturing wildly as they prepared to throw some very nasty magic our way.

The twins' hands began to glow with silver-tinted energy, and Dale and I poured on the speed.

"That damned mirror better work!" Dale shouted.

"Look on the bright side," I yelled. "If it doesn't, we'll be dead before we find out!"

Before Dale could come back with a witty rejoinder, the twins thrust their hands forward, sending a pair of lightning bolts crackling down the corridor toward us. Still running, I held out the mirror in front of me, and it drew the lightning toward its glossy surface and swallowed it whole. The glass vibrated and grew hot in my hand as it struggled to absorb the mystical power of the twins' strike.

"How many spells is that thing good for?" Dale shouted.

"Three," I said, "so we have two–" My words cut off as the mirror exploded in my hand, glass shards piercing the soft flesh of my palm.

"Fuck!" I shouted. My hand was bleeding like crazy and hurt like a sonofabitch. I lost momentarily lost my concentration and started to stumble, but Dale caught hold of my elbow and steadied me. "Make that one," I said through gritted teeth. Whether on Earth or in Nekropolis, it seemed you couldn't trust a goddamned street vendor.

Dale and I had covered half the distance to the chamber at the end of the corridor, but the twins started gesturing and chanting once more, both of them grinning with dark anticipation. They had us and they knew it.

Still running, Dale and I raised our guns and started firing. One thing about spellcasters: it's hard for them to shift gears when they're in the middle of working an enchantment. Our aim wasn't perfect, but it was good enough, and several 9mm slugs slammed into the warlocks, and while their black tunics might've been the latest in magical guard chic, the cloth didn't do a damned thing to stop bullets. By the time Dale and I reached the wooden door, the twins had slumped to the floor, bleeding from their wounds. Dale had gotten his twin twice – once in the shoulder, once in the gut – and I'd hit mine in the chest. Both were still alive, but they were in too much pain to concentrate on working any hoodoo on us.

If we'd been on Earth, Dale and I would've cuffed the two warlocks and called for an ambulance. But this was Nekropolis, and even if it wasn't we didn't have time to do things by the book. Dale and I slammed our gun butts into the twins' heads, and they fell onto their sides, unconscious. I knew there was a chance one or both of them might die from their injuries, but they *were* warlocks. There was an equally good chance they'd find a way to heal themselves soon. At least, that's what I told myself to assuage my conscience.

Dale took a second to check his weapon. "I'm out of ammo."

"Me too." And neither of us had reloads. We'd used up all our bullets over the last couple days just surviving long enough to get this far. I holstered my gun, and Dale did the same. "Guess we'll just have to improvise," I said.

"Fair enough." Dale grabbed the door handle, but before he opened it, he said, "How much you want to bet there's no lock on it?"

"Who needs locks when you have a pair of beefcake warlocks to guard your secret chamber of evil?" I said.

Dale laughed as he opened the door, and we rushed inside. I'd been expecting the chamber to be like the rest of Woodhome – smooth, barkless wood – but instead it was spherical and covered with glimmering metal panels. The chamber reeked of ozone and overheated circuitry, and a low thrumming filled the air, the sound of a powerful machine in the process of warming up. In the middle of the room was a huge pinkish mass the size of a bull elephant. Its wrinkled surface was slick with blood, and dozens of black cables extended from its pulpy substance out to different points on the walls and ceiling.

This was the Overmind.

Dale and I stopped to look at the obscene thing.

"I thought brains were gray," he said.

I shook my head. "That's only after they've been preserved. Inside our skulls, they look like that: all pink."

Dale and I weren't alone in the chamber, though. There were two others standing before the Overmind. A male warlock with long flowing blond hair and a neatly trimmed beard standing next to a handsome middle-aged woman with short black hair. The warlock wore a dark red robe – not quite black, but close enough, I supposed – while the woman was garbed in an old-fashioned Puritan dress of severe black-and-white. I didn't recognize the warlock, but I had a pretty good idea who the woman was: the Dark Lady Talaith, ruler of Glamere and mistress of the Arcane.

Dale immediately fixed his attention on the warlock. "Let me guess. You're the sonofabitch who's been killing people in my town back on Earth." We'd tracked the killer down in Cleveland, even watched as he'd disappeared back through Varvara's mirror portal, but neither of us had gotten that good a look at him. But now, standing here gazing at the bastard, both Dale and I knew this was our man.

If the warlock was surprised to see us, he didn't show it. He stepped toward us with a casual confidence that said he was used to having his evil rituals interrupted by a pair of out-of-town cops. *Very* out-of-town.

"I'm afraid I'm unacquainted with you two gentlemen, but I'm impressed that you made it this far." He looked us over. "Though I must say that you both appear somewhat the worse for wear."

Despite the fact his weapon was out of ammunition, Dale drew it and leveled it at the warlock's head. "You can cut the 'It's a pleasure to meet you, Mr. Bond' crap. Just tell me if you're the person responsible for the death of seven men and women in Cleveland."

Amusement flickered in the warlock's eyes, and I wondered if he could somehow sense that Dale's gun was empty. "I am. Though as you can see, they've been reborn." He gestured toward the Overmind. "So technically, I suppose I'm not a killer. I'm more of a…" a slow smile spread across his face. "A recycler, I suppose you could say."

Despite ourselves, Dale and I turned to regard the Overmind once more.

"The coroner's report said the people you killed died without outward signs of violence," I said. "We've already figured out that you used some kind of spell to stop their hearts. But the coroner also said that portions of their brains were missing, even though each of their skulls was intact."

The warlock bowed his head in mock-humility. "I must confess to possessing a certain modicum of skill at psychic surgery."

I ignored the arrogant bastard and went on. "So you're telling us that you used the brain matter you stole from those people to build the Overmind?"

The warlock stepped closer to the giant brain and laid his hand on it as if stroking a beloved pet. "Precisely.

Those seven people were all extremely gifted psychically, but none of them knew it. Moreover, they'd never even used their preternatural abilities, which meant their brain matter was completely unspoiled. Pristine minds – virgin minds, if you will – are almost impossible to find in Nekropolis. They need to be… imported."

Up to this point, Talaith hadn't said anything, but now she stepped toward the warlock, grabbed his shoulder none-too-gently, and spun him around to face her. "We don't have time for this foolishness, Yberio. We need to finish powering up the Overmind and use it strike against Edrigu before he becomes aware of what we're trying to do! The fool may be Lord of the Dead, but doesn't mean he's as slow-witted as his mindless subjects. We only have moments before he senses what we're up to."

She glanced past Yberio at Dale and me, and I could feel the hatred blazing in her eyes as if it were a physical force. "Kill them while I continue the ritual."

Yberio's jaw muscles tensed, telling me that he didn't appreciate being spoken to as one of the help. "Yes, my love," he answered through gritted teeth.

"Forget the 'my love' shit and just do it!" she snapped. She turned to face the Overmind, raising her hands over her head and chanting harsh, guttural words in a language I didn't recognize, but which hurt to hear. It felt like someone was jamming rusty metal spikes into my ears.

Dale and I exchanged a quick look. Understanding the emotional stressors on your opponents is just as important as knowing what weapons they have – sometimes more so. It was obvious that Yberio was Talaith's lover and that he thought that relationship made them equals. It was just as obvious to Dale and me that Talaith thought differently.

Yberio glared at Talaith for a moment, but she ignored him as she continued working whatever magic was necessary to get the Overmind to do its thing. Yberio turned back to face us, and from the dark expression on his face, it was clear he intended to take out his anger toward Talaith on us.

Dale kept his empty gun trained on the warlock, and with his free hand he gestured to me behind his back. *Get ready.*

My left hand still had fragments of glass in it – and still hurt like hell – but my gun-hand was free and uninjured, and I took a half-step behind Dale to cover my motion from Yberio as I reached into my jacket pocket and removed the last device we'd managed to acquire in the Sprawl. It looked like a simple pocket watch, old and badly in need of polishing, but otherwise unremarkable. Lady Varvara – who was very displeased that Talaith had made use of her dimension portal in her latest scheme to attack Lord Edrigu – had given the device to us before we left the Sprawl. She'd said it was called the Death Watch and that all we would have to do was push the switch to activate it when the right time came. After that, we'd know what to do.

I hoped like hell she was right – and that she was telling the truth. She was a demon, after all, and her kind had a reputation for being somewhat lacking in the truth-telling department.

If Yberio had seen me take hold of the Death Watch, he gave no sign. Perhaps he simply thought he was too powerful to worry about whatever meager magics Dale and I might have acquired during our brief stay in Nekropolis.

"You gentlemen were quite correct in your earlier surmise," the warlock said. "I did use magic to kill those people. The spell is a quite simple one, really." He smiled coldly. "Allow me to demonstrate it to you."

That sure as hell sounded like a cue to me. I thumbed the switch atop the Death Watch, and the black hands on the clock face began spinning wildly. Dark energy spread outward from the watch, so cold that it felt as if I'd plunged my hand into ice water. I wanted to drop the damned thing, but I forced myself to hold on to it.

Talaith continued chanting, but she shot me a quick look, and her eyes widened in shock when she saw what I held. Yberio stared at the Death Watch and the spreading ebon energy that surrounded it, his jaw hanging open in a way that might've been comical in other circumstances.

"You can't possibly have that!" Yberio shouted. "There's no way you could've gained possession of a token of such power!

Talaith broke off her chanting to yell at him. "Don't be an idiot! That bitch Varvara must've have given it to them! But it doesn't matter how those poor excuses for mortals came by it, just kill the morons before they can use it!"

Yberio's head jerked as if she'd just physically slapped him, and he blinked several times before raising his hand and pointing his index finger at me. I understood then what was going to happen to me: Yberio was going to use his magic to stop my heart, just as he had done with the seven men and women he'd killed on Earth. By this time the dark energy emanating from the Death Watch had formed a black sphere around my hand about the size of a soccer ball. My hand felt frozen, and I could sense tremendous power building up within the sphere, but I still had no idea what to do with it.

C'mon, Varvara… you said I'd know what to do when the time came…

Yberio spoke a word and a thin beam of white light shot forth from his finger and headed straight toward me. But Dale threw himself between me and the warlock, and the light speared him straight through the heart instead. He made no sound, but his entire body stiffened as if a massive electric current passed through him, and then he simply collapsed to the floor. No final words, no last look passing between us. It was like Yberio had reached inside my partner, found his life switch, and flipped it off.

Yberio grinned as he looked down at Dale's corpse, then he raised his head to look at me.

"That's eight," he said. "And you'll make nine." He lifted his hand and aimed his index finger at me.

And then, just as Varvara had promised, I understood what I had to do.

"Fuck you –" I looked to Talaith – "both." And then I turned to the Overmind and thrust the hand holding the Death Watch into the pulpy mass of the gigantic brain. I heard Talaith shout "No!" followed by the sharp sensation of Yberio's magic beam cutting through me. And then I heard the Overmind's voice in my mind – a chorus of six voices combined, actually, and it whispered two words:

Thank you.

And then a darkness blacker, deeper, and colder than anything I had ever imagined rushed in to fill me, and I knew nothing more.

"When I woke up, the Overmind was nothing but a pool of necrotized tissue on the floor on the metal chamber, the cables that had attached it to the walls dangling useless in the air. I crawled over to Dale – my limbs were stiff and uncooperative, and at the time I thought it was just due to the aftershock of the Overmind's destruction – and I checked his pulse. I wasn't surprised to find he no longer had one. Yberio and Talaith were both lying on the floor as well. I assumed they'd been hit by some kind of psychic or magical backlash when the Overmind exploded, but I had no idea if it would cause them any permanent damage. After all, I was still alive. Or so I thought.

"I checked their pulses. Yberio didn't have one. Talaith did, but hers was weak. I was a cop – supposedly one of the good guys – but I confess at that moment, I seriously considering wrapping my hands around Talaith's throat and finishing what the destruction of the Overmind had started. Instead, I turned away and did a quick search for the Death Watch. I'd lost my grip on the device when I blacked out, I couldn't find it in the mess of what remained of the Overmind. For all I know the Death Watch was destroyed, but if not, I suppose Talaith has it. I really don't know, and to tell you the truth, I don't care. I gave up looking for the watch, picked up Dale's body, and carried him out of the chamber."

Devona, who'd been listening to my story as raptly as Arvel, if not more so, put a hand on my shoulder and squeezed hard enough so I'd be sure to feel it. "I'm sorry for your loss, Matt."

I nodded my thanks for her sympathy. Dale was a good man, a good partner, and a good friend. I don't know how I would've made it through my divorce if he hadn't been there for me. He saved my life more than once on the streets of Cleveland, and in the end he'd given his own life so that I could live a few moments longer to finish the last case we'd ever work together.

"He was a hell of a cop, and he died in the line of duty." It was all the epitaph I could bring myself to say aloud, but maybe it was enough.

"Yberio was a Demilord," Arvel said, "one of the high-ranking Darkfolk who, while extremely strong, weren't quite powerful enough to be chosen by Dis to help him create Nekropolis. There's been no mention of him on the streets for the last couple years." The ghoul smiled with his blood-stained lamprey mouth. "Now I know why."

"What happened to Talaith?" Devona asked.

"She's a Darklord," I said. "I assume her powers enabled her to withstand the blast, but considerably weakened. She's recovered some since then, but she's still not up to her full strength. Needless to say, I haven't been to Glamere many times since. And I make sure to watch my back when any Arcane are around."

Arvel smacked his lips. "A most… delicious story, Mr. Richter. But you left out one salient detail: how you became a zombie."

"Remember how I said the murder victims showed no sign of external injuries? It's because Yberio threw a deathspell at them and stopped their hearts instantly. That's how Dale died, and Yberio did the same to me – just as I released the power of the Death Watch into the Overmind. Somehow, Yberio's spell, the Death Watch's magic, and the release of psychic energy when the Overmind died all combined and when I awoke, I was dead, but in a way still alive, too." I shrugged. "That's Papa Chatha's theory, anyway."

"Fascinating!" Arvel gushed. "I knew some of the details, of course, but I've never heard the full story. Tell me, what arrangements did you make for the disposal of Mr. Ramsey's remains?"

I felt a wave of anger and disgust. Ghouls had an unhealthy preoccupation with dead bodies, and I wasn't about to tell Arvel where and how I'd laid Dale to rest, just in case the gluttonous monster decided to go in search of my dear, departed partner.

"Not to be rude," I said, not caring if I was or not, "but my associate and I are in something of a hurry."

"Ah, another case full of danger and intrigue! You must let me know how it turns out!"

"I will," I said. It was an easy promise to make, since I knew there was a chance I might not be around to keep it. "Now if you could *quid quo pro* us right back?"

"I'll be happy to answer your questions; once I've finished attending to nature's call, that is."

I was about to ask if he needed any help getting up, but then I noticed the large metal washtub beneath his chair. Arvel clicked his teeth and Carbuncle scuttled over and pulled a lever on the side of the ghoul's chair, releasing a trap door in the seat.

As the next few moments passed – along with a number of other things – I was more grateful than ever that I had no sense of smell.

TEN

As we left the Krimson Kiss, Devona looked like she was suffering from shellshock.

"My father is anything but a saint, and during my time at the Cathedral I've seen some terrible things. But I have never experienced anything as sickening as that ghoul!"

"He's disgusting, no doubt about it. But he did give us some useful information."

Devona snorted, but whether because she didn't agree with me or because she was trying to get the stink out of her nostrils, I don't know.

"All he told us was that while Varma used to frequent the Krimson Kiss, he hasn't been around in the last few weeks."

"You're forgetting what he said about Varma being a heavy drug user."

"That's no surprise; I told you he was a hedonist. Besides, drugs don't affect Bloodborn physiology the same way they do the human body. Varma would need to take large doses to get even mild effects."

Nekropolis has all the drugs you'd find on the streets of any city on Earth – marijuana, coke, crack, heroin, crystal meth – as well as quite a few locally produced specialties, such as tangleglow and mind dust.

"But that gives Varma a motive for stealing the Dawnstone beyond mere lust for power" I said. "He wouldn't be the first junkie to steal to support his habit. And don't forget the traces of powder we found in the Collection room. They could very well be drug residue of some sort."

Devona shook her head. "I told you, Bloodborn handle drugs differently than humans. We don't get addicted. I suppose it's because the need for blood supersedes all other needs."

"Maybe," I allowed. "We'll just have to ask Varma when we find him, won't we?"

We continued walking down Sybarite Street and checked a couple more places, including the Freakatorium and, as Father Dis is my witness, a country vampire bar named Westerna's. I'll never forget the sight of vampires in cowboy hats, jeans, and boots line dancing – though I intend to spend the rest of my existence trying like hell.

Finally, we'd penetrated to the heart of the Sprawl, and one of the hottest of its hot spots: the Broken Cross. From the outside, it looks like any trendy Earth night club: all chrome, glass, and glitter. The only difference is the day-glow neon sign above the entrance; it looks like the sixties' peace symbol, only without the circle. An upside down and broken cross.

The street outside the club was completely jammed
with people who wanted in. Half a block away was the
closest we could get. I steered us toward a fluorescent
street light, and we took up a position alongside it.

"Now what?" Devona asked. "Are you planning to
introduce the Broken Cross's doorman to the wonders
of instant hairloss or do you have yet another surprise
in those pockets of yours?"

"As a matter of fact, I do." I reached into one of my
jacket pockets and brought forth two of the most dangerous weapons in my entire arsenal – a string of
firecrackers and my trusty lighter.

"Would you like to do the honors?" I offered.

She frowned, unsure of what I was up to, but she
took the lighter and lit the firecrackers.

"Throw them as close to the entrance as you can," I
instructed.

She heaved the firecrackers over the heads of the
crowd and, thanks to her half-vampire strength, they
fell within five feet of the entrance.

I cupped my hands to my mouth and shouted, "The
Hidden Light! They're attacking!"

And the *pop-pop-pop* of firecrackers exploding began.
The sound wasn't very impressive, but then it didn't
have to be, given what I'd just yelled. People screamed,
shrieked, bellowed, and howled in fear, probably believing incendiary grenades were going off in their
midst, or perhaps a hail of silver bullets rained down
upon them. Whatever they thought, they had a single
common desire: *escape*.

"Grab hold of the pole and don't let go!" I told Devona. We held tight as a panicking mass of Darkfolk and humans rushed past, nearly sweeping us away. We got battered pretty good, but we managed to hold on, if only barely.

Several minutes later, the street was clear.

Devona looked at me. "That wasn't very nice."

"Tell you what, you find me a blackboard, and I'll write, 'I'll never fake a terrorist attack again' a thousand times – after we find the Dawnstone." I started across the empty street and Devona followed, looking like she was trying hard not to laugh.

Inside, the party was going strong. Either word of the faux Hidden Light assault hadn't filtered into the club, or everyone was too high or drunk to care. I suspected the latter.

Techno-rave music throbbed and pulsed, the jams cranked out by Nekropolis's most sought-after DJ, the Phantom of the Paradise, and laser lights flashed in time with the beat. Beings of all sorts gyrated wildly on the dance floor, looking more like they were engaging in foreplay or ritualistic warfare – perhaps both – rather than dancing. Above their heads played out a holoshow depicting various scenes of torture. It looked as if MTV had produced a special on the Inquisition.

Though all of Nekropolis's many and varied types of Darkfolk were represented in the Broken Cross, the club was a favorite with Bloodborn, and they predominated tonight. One of the things about vampires, especially the younger ones, is that because of their supernatural healing abilities, they go in for the most extreme forms of entertainment. Not so much because they enjoy pain more than anyone else, but because of how much physical punishment they can take. For example, in one corner of the Broken Cross, a vampire who called himself Anklebiter – appropriately enough, since he appeared to be no more than three years old – was taking on all comers in a one-on-one, no-holds-barred mixed martial arts battle. Whoever was dumb enough to accept Anklebiter's challenge got to make the first move. Anklebiter then got the second, which was also usually the last. In another corner, a vampire wearing only a pair of black shorts stood with his back against the wall, while a group of enthusiastic knife throwers used him for target practice (no silver blades allowed, though).

Perhaps most disturbing of all was Mimi the Conflagration Artist. She danced naked in an iron cage that hung down from the ceiling above the middle of the dance floor, just below the holographic torture scenes. She thrashed and writhed along to the music while flames licked at her pale undead flesh. Before performing, she slathered her body with a chemical that kept the fire from burning too fast or too hot, so it wouldn't devour the flesh before her Bloodborn physiology could repair the damage. I'd had occasion to speak with her a time or two, and I'd once asked her if she enjoyed her work. She'd shrugged and replied, "At the risk of making a terrible pun, it's a living."

Devona leaned close to my ear and shouted in order to be heard over the racket. "How are we supposed to find Varma in this chaos?"

"The same way we've been doing: we start asking around."

I caught sight of Patchwork the Living Voodoo Doll on the dance floor, and I took Devona by the hand and led her over to him. Patchwork was gyrating bonelessly to the throbbing dance-club beat, arms and legs flopping about wildly. As his name implies, Patchwork is made up of cast-off scraps of cloth, all different sizes, patterns, and colors, and he has two large black buttons for eyes. I have no idea how he sees with those things, but then I also can't figure out how he can stand upright with no skeletal system.

Patchwork is a hair under six feet tall, and while he normally had dozens of hat pins sticking out of his body, he'd thoughtfully removed them before starting to dance. That, or he'd lost them all doing his whirling dervish act and they were scattered across the floor, or had become embedded in his fellow dancers.

The music was so loud that I had to lean close to Patchwork's ear – or at least where an ear would've been if he'd had one sewn on – and shout.

"Hey, Patch! I'm looking for a vampire named Varma!"

Patchwork shook his head. "Never heard of him, but you want me to put a hurt on him for you?" Patch's voice sounded like rustling cloth and came from a small flap of a mouth sewn into the bottom of his face. "Free of charge for you, Matt!"

Despite his somewhat whimsical appearance, Patchwork was one of the deadliest beings in Nekropolis. All he needed was a personal token of a target – a photo, a piece of clothing, or better yet a lock of hair or a nail clipping – and wherever he stabbed himself with his pins, his target felt the pain. Depending on his clients' wishes, Patchwork could simply annoy a target, make life miserable for him or her, temporarily or permanently disable them or – if he jabbed a long enough, sharp enough needle into the right place on his artificial body – kill them.

"I appreciate the offer, but I'm trying to locate Varma, not perforate him!" I shouted.

"Suit yourself! Let me know if you change your mind! You might ask Fade, though. I saw her over at the bar not too long ago!"

Then Patchwork spun away like a cloth top and lost himself in the pounding beat once more.

I turned to Devona. She was watching Patch's performance and bobbing her head from side to side in time with the music. Earlier, she told me she didn't get out of the Gothtown much. I wondered if what she'd really been saying was she didn't get out of the Cathedral often. It was quite possible she'd never been to a nightclub before. I felt the urge to start dancing with her, but I checked it. I knew we didn't have time to waste on such foolishness... plus I'd never been the greatest dancer when I was alive, and my damaged and swiftly rotting zombie body wasn't going to help that situation any.

I led Devona off the dance floor and we wended our way through the crowd and headed toward the bar. We found Fade deep in half-drunken conversation with a vampire named Ichorus. Outwardly Fade looked like a normal club-crawler – early twenties, petite, purple lipstick, dark green eyeshadow, long brunette hair past her waist, black combat boots, little black dress that fit her in all the right places, and a pair of barbed-wire hoop earrings that were almost as large as her head. Fade has a problem, however. She's reality-challenged. For reasons she keeps to herself, her existence is so tenuous that if she isn't careful to constantly reinforce her own reality, she's in danger of vanishing into nothingness, hence her nickname. So in order to ensure her survival she had to make sure to see and be seen, which was why she spent almost all her time club-hopping. The more time she spent alone, without anyone around to validate her existence, the more she risked fading away completely. That's also the reason she took a job as gossip columnist for the *Daily Atrocity*. Knowing everyone, whether they liked it or not, made her perfect for the job, and the more people that read her byline, the more anchored she was in reality.

She looked pretty solid right then. Descension Day was always a good time of year for her. Tons of people for her to interact with – and right now she was interacting with Ichorus.

One of the Accords that came out of the Blood Wars set limits on air travel in Nekropolis in order to make it more difficult for the Dark Lords to attempt sneak attacks across Dominion borders. No one is permitted to travel by air over Phlegethon, for example, and everyone – whether possessing the power of flight or not – has to use one of the Five Bridges to travel from one Dominion to another. Ichorus doesn't just hate the restriction imposed on air travel; he utterly loathes it and does everything he can to fight it.

He's a stereotypical vampire type: tall, lean, dark-haired, handsome. But what makes him stand out is the pair of huge ebon wings growing out of his back. The feathers are made of lightweight super-strong metal, and their edges are razor-sharp. Whether they're magical or some kind of technological augmentation, I don't know. Ichorus goes shirtless because he refuses to constrain his wings, so he wears only a pair of black pants. No shoes either, but I don't know if that's because it helps him fly or he just doesn't like shoes. His chest is covered with dozens of criss-crossing scars, the result of numerous less-than-welcome receptions he gets from flying throughout the Dominions in defiance of the Accords. Since he's a vampire and can heal any injury, his scars are a testament to how seriously the Darklords take anyone transgressing on their airspace – and how strongly they and their servants will fight to stop him. But Ichorus still flies on, undeterred in his endless quest to defy authority.

We approached the pair and asked them about Varma. Ichorus didn't know him, but of course Fade did; she knew everyone, as a matter of self-preservation, if nothing else. But she hadn't seen him tonight.

"Go check with Shrike," she said. "I was talking to him earlier over by the VR booths." She gestured vaguely toward the other side of the club. I thanked her and reached out and briefly patted her arm. She smiled gratefully. Talking with people helps her maintain reality, but I knew that being touched helped her more.

Before Devona and I could walk away, Ichorus said, "I've got a big flight planned next week, Matt! I've heard rumors of an invisible moon that orbits around Umbriel, and I'm going off in search of it! Should be quite an adventure!"

Fade grinned at him. "Should make quite an article for the *Atrocity*."

Devona looked at me and raised a questioning eyebrow.

"Don't look at me. I've never heard anything about a moon in Nekropolis, invisible or otherwise." I turned back to Ichorus, shook his hand, wished him luck, and then Devona and I went off in search of Shrike. True to Fade's word, we found him by the Mind's Eye virtual reality booths.

Despite Shrike's chronological age, which I had no way of knowing, he resembled a skinny boy in his teens. His hair was a wild tangle of black the same shade as his deliberately ragged t-shirt and pre-torn jeans. He was talking on his handvox, ever-present cigarette in his mouth. As he exhaled, he became transparent, solidifying again only when he took his next puff. Handvoxes have the same basic design as Earth cellphones, except they're made – or maybe grown – from flesh. There's an ear for you to speak into, and a mouth that relays the words of whoever is on the other end, and which speaks in their voice, too. I find the damned things more than a little disconcerting, especially when the person on the other end tries to make the vox's mouth kiss, lick, or even bite you. That's why I hardly ever use mine.

Shrike saw us approaching, shut his handvox, and tucked it into his pants pocket. He grinned, displaying his elongated canines.

"Matt!" He had to shout to be heard over the din. "What the hell are you doing here? This isn't exactly your kind of scene." Then he looked at Devona, ran his gaze along her body from foot to head, and back again. "Wow. Your taste in friends is *definitely* improving, my man."

"Shrike, this is Devona Kanti. Devona, this is Shrike."

"Lord Galm's kid? Cool." He took a battered pack of cigarettes out of his back pocket and held it out to Devona. "Want one?"

Devona shook her head. "No thanks."

I noticed the brand: *Coffin Nails*.

I nodded toward the pack. "The name's a cute touch."

He grinned again. "I like to think so," and put the pack back in his pocket.

I don't know why he carries the pack around. In all the time I've known him, I've never seen his cigarette burn down, no matter how many drags he takes on it.

"What's up, Matt? You've got to be working a case. I can't imagine any other reason why you'd be here." He leaned toward Devona as if about to confide a secret. "The man's sense of fun is as dead as the rest of him." Then he looked at me and frowned. "Say, you all right, Matt? You're not looking too fresh, if you know what I mean." He pointed to the wounds on my face.

If I was alive, I could've run my fingers over my cuts to check their condition. As it was, I'd just have to wait until I came across a mirror. But from Shrike's comment, I doubted they looked very good. Injuries don't hurt zombies, but they do tend to start rotting before the rest of the body.

"You're not looking all that hot yourself, kid," I said. "Maybe you should think about trying the nicotine patch."

Shrike grinned. He always gets a huge kick out of my calling him kid. Probably because he's a hell of a lot older than he looks.

He put an arm around my shoulder and addressed Devona. "If it wasn't for this guy, I wouldn't be here today. Hell, I wouldn't be anywhere today! I love this guy!" and then he planted a loud, wet kiss on my cheek, despite its less-than-attractive condition.

"Get off of me, you lunatic!" I said good-naturedly as I shoved him away.

Devona laughed. "Another favor?" she asked me.

I nodded. "Shrike got himself into trouble over at the House of Dark Delights a while back."

"One of their girls accused me of making her Bloodborn without her permission. I was innocent, but it took Matthew to prove it. Good thing, too. Madam

Benedetta was so mad, she'd sicced a Soulsucker on me." He frowned. "Or was it Master Benedict who did it? Whichever. I still get nervous when I think about it." He took a long drag on his cigarette, his hand shaking slightly.

Me too. Defeating a Soulsucker isn't easy. I still have a few psychic scars left over from that battle.

"So what can I do you for, Matt?" Shrike said, cheerful again. "You name it, you got it."

I removed one of the evidence envelopes from my jacket and handed it to him. "Know what this stuff is?"

He opened the envelope, stuck his finger inside, and brought out a couple of the white grains I'd gathered in Lord Galm's Collection chamber. He smelled them, then took his omnipresent cigarette out of his mouth and gingerly touched his finger to his tongue.

His reaction was immediate. "Jesus Christ!" As soon as the holy name passed his lips, his mouth burst into flame.

I grabbed a beer out of the claw of a demon at a nearby table and splashed Shrike in the face, hoping to douse the fire. It worked: the flames died, leaving Shrike's lips charred and his tongue blackened.

"I've told you before, kid, you've got to be careful what you say when you're upset!"

The demon had risen from his chair, and was coming toward me, his leathery gray lizard hide turning battle-angry red. I tossed a couple darkgems at him – her? it? who could tell? – to pay for another beer and that ended the matter.

"Do oo know what dis stuff is?" Shrike said as best he could with his ravaged mouth.

"No, that's why I asked."

He looked around to see if anyone was listening, then leaned forward. "It's veinburn." He leaned back. "Ashully, it's prolly a good thin' I swore. Maybe burned ou' the shit 'efore it got inna my shystem."

"C'mon, Shrike, it was only a couple grains."

He took a puff on his cigarette, and while his mouth didn't heal all the way, it improved noticeably. I bet the Surgeon General would've been surprised to see that.

"It doesn't take much to get you hooked." His speech was a little clearer, too. "Where'd you get it?"

"Never mind. Is it new? I've never heard of it before."

"New and nasty. It's really strong and highly addictive – even for Bloodborn."

Bingo. Sometimes I love being a detec – doing favors for people. "Who produces it?"

"I don't know. But I wouldn't be surprised if the Dominari have a piece of that particular action."

"Makes sense." I said. "I've got another question for you."

"Shoot." Shrike's mouth was almost completely healed now, just singed a little around the edges.

"You seen a vampire named Varma tonight?"

"Varma? You mean the one who's Lord Galm's bloodchild, right? Yeah, sure. He was out on the dance floor last I saw him. That was probably, oh, an hour ago, maybe less."

"Think you could make a quick circuit of the club for me, see if he's still here?"

"Sure. Be back in a minute." He took a deep drag on his cigarette, became solid, and blew out a long stream of gray-white smoke, his body turning transparent as the smoke left his lungs and then fading altogether until he was gone. The smoke Shrike had blown out wafted purposefully toward the dance floor.

"That's his travel form?" Devona asked. "Interesting."

"Yeah, Shrike's got his own style, that's for sure."

She leaned close to me so I could hear her better over the music. "I've been thinking. I have an idea of how Varma might have been able to get into the Collection chamber and past the wardspell on the Dawnstone."

"Go on."

"Even though Varma isn't biologically Lord Galm's child, the transference of blood necessary to turn a human into a vampire makes him Galm's son in a metaphysical sense. It's possible that since the door to the chamber and the wardspell both are keyed to recognize and permit access only to Lord Galm, they could be made to recognize someone who shares the same blood – provided this someone had the right magical help."

"Are you sure?"

"Remember, I'm no mage; I was taught only enough magic to monitor the spells on the Collection chamber. But from what I understand, it might be possible."

The way things were going, the Dawnstone would be back in Lord Galm's Collection before he returned from the Renewal Ceremony. Devona would hang on to her position and her dignity, and maybe, just maybe, she could convince her father to help me stave off my dissolution.

I should've known better. Life – and death – is never so easy.

"Matthew Richter?"

I turned around. "Yes?"

Before me stood a tall raven-haired woman in a red mini dress. She might have been pretty if her features hadn't been so sharp, her expression severe. Her eyebrows met in the middle. A sure sign she was a lyke.

"My name is Thokk. Honani and I were littermates."

Her dress ripped away as she began to change.

ELEVEN

Thokk was a mixblood, like Honani, but where he'd turned out a hodgepodge mess, whoever engineered her had done the job right. She was primarily lupine, the most common wildform for lykes. After all, as Waldemar once told me, the word *lycanthrope* comes from the Greek: *lykoi* for wolf and *anthropos* for man. But the term, and its abbreviated version, *lyke*, has become common parlance for any of the shapeshifters under Lord Amon's rule. Still, Thokk displayed signs of other animals in her mixblood lineage too – her stomach was hairless and scaled, resembling a snake's, and her gray fur held a greenish tint. Her eyes were reptilian as well, cold and staring, and when she opened her canine jaws, long, curved fangs sprang forward, glistening with venom.

"You killed Honani, zombie." Her barely intelligible voice was a deep growl with a slight hiss to it.

I was aware of the club-goers around us abandoning their tables, having decided that being in my proximity at the moment wasn't conducive to their continued good health. I didn't blame them.

"Technically speaking, he's not dead," I pointed out. "His body's still alive." I was uncomfortably aware that I still was carrying the soul jar containing Honani's spirit in one of my jacket pockets.

Thokk pulled her head back and in a single liquid motion, jerked forward and spit a stream of venom into my eyes. If I'd been alive, the venom probably would've started me shrieking, perhaps cause me to fall to the floor in agony and Thokk would've moved in to finish me off. But I felt nothing and calmly wiped the venom away with my tie. My vision was a trifle blurry, but it was nothing I couldn't deal with.

"What good is the body if the soul is gone?" She swayed back and forth, her torso undulating bonelessly.

"According to some folks, zombies don't have souls, and I feel just fine," I countered. "Besides, Honani's body does have a soul. It just happens to be a new one."

For a second I considered offering to give Thokk the soul jar which contained her brother's spirit, thinking it might placate her. But then I realized she'd probably attempt to return it to its original body, evicting Kyra from her new home. I couldn't allow that.

"Your littermate was a killer, Thokk, and he got what he deserved," I said. "End of story. Now why don't you leave, unless you'd like some of the same?"

She hissed and came at me.

I reached under my jacket and drew the 9mm from my shoulder holster. The gun was loaded with silver bullets, but one would be all I needed to take care of Thokk. I aimed and started to squeeze the trigger.

But I was too slow. Thokk's arm lashed out and she smacked the gun out of my hand, sending it tumbling through the air toward the suddenly deserted dance floor. The Phantom of the Paradise remained at his station, though, to keep the throbbing dance beat going, either because he was too caught up in his work to flee or because he wanted to provide some appropriate background music for my battle with Thokk. Thoughtful of the bastard, wasn't it?

I reached into my jacket, but Thokk was on me before I could pull forth anything from my dwindling supply of surprises, slamming into me and coiling her python-supple arms around my midsection, pinning my arms to my sides. She lifted me off the floor and began squeezing.

I felt pressure, but no pain. I couldn't breathe, but all that meant to me was that I couldn't pull in any air to make my voice work. Still, I was concerned. If she snapped my spine, I'd survive, but I'd be unable to walk. And after I was immobilized, it would be a simple matter for her to take my head in her hands and crush my skull. Once my brain was destroyed, no amount of preservative spells, no matter how powerful, could restore me.

I was wracking my dead excuse for a brain, trying to get it to come up with a brilliant plan that would, if not defeat Thokk, at least get me out of her clutches, when a gurgling sound came from deep inside me, and I remembered the beer that had been sitting in my dead stomach since I'd dealt with Honani at Skully's.

You picked the wrong zombie to squeeze tonight, Thokk, I thought, and then a gout of sour-smelling fluid jetted out of my mouth and struck Thokk in the face.

The lyke roared with fury, but she didn't drop me as I'd hoped. Instead she gripped me tighter and opened her mouth wide. I doubted she was going to try to eat me; most lykes can't stand the taste of dead meat, unless they have scavenger wildforms. More likely she intended to get a solid grip on my head with her teeth and then rip it off my shoulders.

I watched helplessly as her mouth descended, and then she stopped, stiffened, and shrieked. Her arms uncoiled, dumping me to the floor, and I saw what was happening. Devona had leaped onto the lyke's back and was tearing into the beast's neck with her own teeth. Thokk's arms curled over her shoulder, grabbed Devona, yanked her off, and threw her forward – into me, just as I was starting to rise.

We went down in a tangle of undead and half-undead limbs. Thokk advanced on us, the ragged neck wound Devona had inflicted already healing.

With vampiric grace and speed, Devona disengaged herself from me and stood before Thokk, fingers touching her temples.

"Stop," she said in an even, measured voice.

Thokk hesitated.

"Leave this place now," Devona continued. "Go."

Devona had told me she had a certain amount of magical training, and now it seemed she was attempting to use her abilities to influence Thokk's mind. At first, it looked like Devona's plan was going to work. Thokk stopped coming toward us. She lowered her hands to her sides and seemed about to turn away, but then she chuckled – the sound like a snake's rattle – reared back, and spat venom into Devona's face. Devona screamed and frantically began wiping at the poison, trying to get it out of her eyes.

Thokk knocked Devona aside easily and came stomping toward me once more. But I'd had enough time to fish a small metal box out of my jacket. I flipped open the lid, stood, and flung the contents at Thokk's muzzle. Her eyes teared up instantly and she began wheezing.

"Powdered wolfsbane," I said. "Never leave the grave without it."

Her eyes began swelling shut and her wheezing took on a more desperate, labored tone. Her throat was closing. I allowed myself to feel smug. All lykes are allergic to wolfsbane to some degree, some more so than others. But it appeared Thokk –

I stopped my self-congratulating in mid-thought. Thokk's breathing became easier and the swelling around her eyes lessened. Her mixblood physiology was counteracting the effects of the wolfsbane. Like I said, whoever designed her had done it right.

I had nothing left in my bag – or rather jacket – of tricks that would stop her. I glanced toward the dance floor. I doubted I could reach to my gun before Thokk recovered. But I had to try.

I started toward the dance floor, running as best I could in the slow, stiff-legged way we zombies have and hoped that it would take just a few more seconds for Thokk to fully throw off the effects of the wolfsbane.

My hope was in vain. Claws raked the right side of my head, knocking me to the floor.

"I'm going to shred you to gobbets for that," Thokk said, her voice hoarse and thick with mucus. "Very, very slowly."

I rolled over to face her. After all, dead or not, a man should look his fate straight in the eye.

She lifted her clawed hands to strike, disturbing a cloud of smoke hovering over her head. And then the smoke darted toward her mouth and curled down her throat.

Thokk howled in agony, and thrashed about as if her every nerve was on fire. She coughed up a gout of blood and crashed to the floor, rolling back and forth, her limbs flailing spastically. But finally her exertions slowed and then ceased altogether.

A moment later tendrils of smoke wafted from her mouth and coalesced into the form of Shrike, his ever-present cigarette the last thing to solidify.

He took a drag and exhaled. "Did you know you can do a lot of damage by partially solidifying inside some-one?"

"Do tell." I hauled my undead carcass to its feet. "Is she dead?"

"Nah, not even the kind of damage I did to her can kill a lyke. But I bet she's not going to be moving too fast for a few weeks. Unless, of course, someone does something about her first." He nodded toward my gun.

It was tempting. Thokk had tried to kill me, and would no doubt try again when she recovered. And it wasn't like anyone would try to stop me. But that wasn't the way I operated.

I shook my head. "Why don't you retrieve the gun while I see to Devona?" Without waiting for Shrike to reply, I turned and headed back toward my client – I mean, the person who I was doing a favor for.

Devona knelt on the floor, her face cradled in her hands.

"Are you okay?"

"Not exactly. I'm blind."

I helped her stand and kept a hand on her elbow to steady her. She took her hands away from her face, but she kept her eyes shut tight.

She took in a hiss of breath. "Dis, but it hurts!"

I didn't know what to say. I'd been human for most of my existence, and in that time I'd known my share of pain. You'd think I'd remember what it was like to hurt. And I do, sort of, but the memory's hazy, indistinct, like a memory of a memory. I suppose a lot of people would've been grateful for that. But it made me feel cut off from Devona, distant, as if we were at the moment inhabiting two vastly different worlds, and there was no bridging the gap between them.

Shrike came up, holding my gun gingerly by the butt with two fingers – like shapeshifters, vampires aren't especially fond of silver. He was carrying a glass in the

other hand: a glass filled with thick red liquid – and I
doubted it was aqua sanguis. He handed me the gun,
then offered the glass to Devona, saying, "Drink; it'll
help."

Her nostrils flared as she picked up the scent of blood,
the real thing. She reached out and Shrike placed the
glass in her hand. She brought it to her lips, but then
hesitated.

At first I couldn't figure out why she wouldn't drink.
And then it hit me. Though being half human was a
negative to most Bloodborn, it was important to Devona, maybe even a secret source of pride for her. And
humans didn't drink blood.

"Go on," I said. "Shrike's right, it'll help."

She hesitated a second more, but then drank, slowly
at first, but then with increasing enthusiasm, gulping
down the last few swallows.

Devona shuddered as if she'd just downed a glassful
of hard liquor and couldn't stand the taste. A few moments went by, during which a couple lykes came
forward. From the way they glared at me and snarled,
I thought they were going to cause trouble, and I wasn't
sure I was up to it just then. But the lykes merely took
hold of Thokk by the arms and hauled her out of the
club, probably to take her back to the Wyldwood so she
could convalesce. Soon the noise level in the club returned to normal and people were back on the floor,
dancing. No one bothered to wipe up the blood Thokk
had vomited. Perhaps they thought it added to the
club's ambience.

Devona gingerly opened her eyes. She blinked a few times, and then smiled. "Much better."

Like lykes, vampires heal fast, but only if they've fed recently. Otherwise their wounds don't heal any faster than a human's.

I holstered my gun and then turned to Shrike. "Thanks for taking care of the lyke. I owe you one, kid."

"Hardly. I've got a few hundred more favors to do for you before we're close to being even." Shrike grinned. "Besides, it was fun."

"That kind of fun I can do without, thank you." I turned back to Devona. "And thank you for jumping into the fray too."

"What for? All I did was manage to get myself blinded."

"If you hadn't attacked when you did, Thokk probably would've squeezed me in two. And what was that other thing you tried? It looked like you were casting a spell on her or something."

"Remember when I told you I can't assume a travel form but had other talents? Besides my minor skill with magic, I also possess some rudimentary psychic abilities, as half Bloodborn often do. Not that they did anyone much good today. All I did was make Thokk hesitate."

"When you're fighting for you life, sometimes that's enough," I said.

"That's nice of you to say, but I still–" She broke off and frowned. "Matt, are you missing an ear?"

Shrike snapped his fingers. "Almost forgot!" He reached into the pocket of his jeans and brought out a grayish-colored ear. "Found this on the floor, not too far from your gun. Thokk must've torn it off you some-time during the fight."

I brushed my hair back and felt the open dry wound where my right ear had been. "Probably happened when she knocked me down the last time." I took my ear from Shrike and, without any place better to put it, stuck it in one of my jacket's handy pockets.

"Won't you lose it if you don't get it reattached right away?" Devona asked, concerned.

"Maybe not. An ear isn't all that complicated, not like an arm. It'll keep longer." I had no idea if that was true or not, but I didn't have time to bother with one ear, not when I had the survival of the rest of my body to worry about.

That reminded me of why we'd come to the Broken Cross in the first place.

"Shrike, did you spot Varma?"

"In all the excitement, I forgot you were looking for him. Yeah, I found him. He was sitting alone at a table in the back, looking like he was higher than Umbriel." He turned and pointed. "Right over–" Pointed to an empty table. "He was there just a minute ago, I swear to Christ! OW!"

I sighed as Shrike's mouth sizzled. He'd never learn.

Varma had probably cut out when Thokk attacked. I doubt he recognized me, but he surely recognized De-vona. He didn't have much of a head start on us, though.

"How are you feeling?" I asked Devona.

"Well enough; let's go."

I thanked Shrike again, but he was too busy frantically slapping his tongue in an attempt to extinguish the flames. Devona and I headed for the table Varma had until only recently occupied – the one next to the door marked EXIT.

The door opened onto a trash-strewn alley.

"Which way?" Devona asked.

I pointed left. "But there's no need to hurry. Not anymore."

Lying face down on the ground not twenty feet away, surrounded by a massive pool of blood, was the body of a redheaded male.

Varma.

TWELVE

I was pretty sure Varma was dead, but I looked to Devona – and her heightened senses – for confirmation. She nodded, her eyes moist with tears. I was surprised; I'd thought there was no love lost between Devona and her "cousin."

Nekropolis has more than its fair share of scavengers. Stray dogs and cats brought from Earth as pets and then abandoned and left to fend for themselves. The poor animals often end up mutating into bizarre and dangerous forms upon repeated exposure to the strange magics coursing through the city. And there are rats, of courses, far larger and meaner than back home, if nowhere near the size and ferocity of vermen. But there are a number of home-grown varieties as well. Carrion imps are tiny, primitive versions of ghouls that scuttle about in their endless quest to fill their bellies with dead flesh. I can't tell you how many times I've been meditating in my bedroom and opened my eyes to find one or more of the little bastards gnawing on

me. Leech vine is a vampiric plant that grows on buildings, especially in the Sprawl where no one bothers to
kill it. There was some growing on the walls of the alley,
but I wasn't worried about it. Leech vine doesn't move;
it's only dangerous if you're foolish enough to brush up
against it – and once it has you, if you can't escape fast
enough, it'll drain you dry just as fast as a flesh vampire.

But one scavenger always gave me pause. It was one
of the deadiest of the city's bottom feeders, and a prime
specimen was standing at the edge of the blood pool on
four tiny legs, lapping daintily at the gore.

"What *is* that horrid thing?" Devona cried, and
started toward the small creature, intending to scare it
away from Varma's body. I grabbed hold of her arm to
keep her back.

"Don't. That's a chiranha. It's alone, but if it calls for
its pack, we're done for."

She looked at me with disbelief. "You can't be serious! It's so tiny!"

The creature under discussion raised its head, glared
at us with beady black eyes, and let out a soft, high-
pitched growl. It resembled a small dog with short tan
fur blended with fish scales, and its mouth was filled
with rows of razor-sharp triangular teeth.

"Chiranha are either someone's idea of a sick joke or
the result of some very unnatural evolution, but either
way, the damned things are dangerous as hell. Believe
it or not, they're a hybrid of chihuahua and piranha
fish. They may look harmless at first glance, even

adorable in their way, but get them in a pack, and they can strip the flesh from your bones within seconds. I once saw a pack take down a sasquatch – the poor sonofabitch didn't even have time to scream."

"Use your gun," she said. "Fire a bullet in the air to scare it away."

"The little fuckers are fearless," I said. "Besides, I doubt he'd even hear the gunshot with all the noise coming from Sybarite Street. I could shoot him, but the one thing guaranteed to bring a pack of chiranha faster than a bark from one of their own is the smell of chiranha blood. They tend not to eat vampire flesh – not unless they're *really* hungry, that is. Let's just wait a minute. With any luck, this one will decide to go seek his dinner elsewhere."

The chiranha growled at us a few seconds longer, before leaning down to sniff Varma's blood once more. Then after giving us a parting glare to let us know it wasn't afraid of us, the chiranha turned and padded off down the alley in the other direction.

"All right. It should be safe to approach now."

I moved forward to examine Varma's body, trying not to step in blood, unable to avoid it. He was thin, and shorter than I'd imagined. I realized that somehow I'd expected him to resemble Galm, even though he wasn't the Darklord's biological child. He was dressed in the white silken weave of spidermesh, a fashion popular in Nekropolis at the time, and one with partially techno-logical origins – a rebellion against his bloodsire? Or just the latest in a series of trends he'd followed over the

centuries? Or maybe he'd just liked the way it felt; Devona had said he was a hedonist.

From the back, there appeared to be no marks on the
body to account for so much blood. I put my hands
under Varma, intending to roll him over, but my damaged right arm refused to cooperate. I had no choice but
to ask Devona to help me.

She did so, fighting tears, but when Varma's blood-
smeared face was revealed, she lost the battle and
sobbed.

His skin was bone-white, dry, and brittle like the cast-
off husk of a cicada. He stared lifelessly, eyes wide,
whites completely red, pupils dilated so much they
were practically nonexistent. His skin was white as polished bone. Dry, cracked lips had pulled away from his
teeth to reveal sickly gray gum. The inside of his desiccated mouth was caked with blood-soaked clumps of
whitish powder. Veinburn.

No sign of a wound on his front, either. I looked more
closely.

"He overdosed on veinburn, didn't he?" Devona
asked as she wiped tears from her eyes. "When one of
the Bloodborn's blood supply is contaminated beyond
the power of his system to cleanse it, his body casts it
out – all of it – and unless he can replenish it within
moments, he dies."

"I didn't know vampires could die of bloodloss. Interesting."

She looked at me as if I had just slapped her. When
she spoke, I thought she might yell at me, though I had

no idea why she would want to. But all she said was, "It's very rare."

"Shrike said veinburn was an extremely powerful drug, but I'm not sure Varma did this to himself."

"What do you mean?"

"The veinburn in his mouth. You said a vampire's blood is poisoned, he has to get rid of it. I assume it would be vomited out."

Devona's expression became steely, and she wiped away the last of her tears. "Primarily."

"Then why is there veinburn left in his mouth? Wouldn't the blood have washed it away?"

Devona glared at me. She was obviously upset with me, but I still didn't know why. "Perhaps it had been in his stomach and became lodged there, perhaps after he fell forward onto his face."

"Maybe, but then why is it still partially white? With the all the blood Varma brought up, the veinburn should be completely soaked. And there are these." I turned Varma's forearm so Devona could see the five tiny puckered marks arranged in a half circle.

"They look like needle marks," she said.

"They sure do, don't they?"

"So perhaps Varma injected the veinburn."

"Then why is there some caked in his mouth? And where's the needle? There isn't one lying around, and spidermesh is skin tight; no room for pockets. Not that Varma needed them. I assume that as the bloodchild of a Darklord, he could charge whatever he wanted to Galm's account – when he just didn't get things handed to him free, that is. "In my experience, addicts don't usually vary how they ingest drugs. There's more than one reason they're called drug habits." I ran a finger over one of the marks. Why, I don't know; it wasn't like I could feel it. "And these marks are fresh. All of them."

"That merely means that Varma died before they could begin to heal."

"Which means he died fast. And that he injected quite a bit of veinburn into himself at one time. Literally one time, for if he'd given himself five shots with one needle, the first mark would've started to heal before the last was made."

Devona's eyes widened in comprehension. "Unless it had been some time since Varma had fed, the first mark would've fully healed before he made the fifth."

I glanced at the pool of blood surrounding us. "I think it's safe to say it hasn't been that long since his last meal."

Devona's lips tightened, but she didn't respond.

"So if the first mark is as fresh as the last, that means Varma was injected by five different needles at the same time. And I doubt even the bloodchild of a Darklord is talented enough to do that – and then make the needles disappear the instant before he dies. No, Varma was killed. Probably to keep him from revealing what happened to the Dawnstone." I looked up and down the alley. "No tracks. Whoever injected Varma took off before he started puking." Too bad; I could have used an easy-to-follow set of bloody footprints just then.

I stood. "Damn it!" I swore in frustration. With Varma dead, and no clues as to who killed him, I didn't know what to do next.

And then I saw a tiny black shape I hadn't noticed before scuttle quickly away along the surface of the alley wall. A roach. Or something so close to a roach as to make no difference.

I knew then what we could do – if I was willing to risk it, that is. But given Papa Chatha's prognosis for my survival, what choice did I have?

Time to pay Gregor a visit.

"C'mon, Devona. We need to talk to someone."

"Talk – Matthew, Varma's dead. We have to take care of him."

"Take care… what are you talking about? He's dead; for real this time. There's nothing we can do for him now."

"We can not leave him lying in an alley like discarded refuse," she said tightly.

"Well, we can't very well take him with us. Even in Nekropolis, carrying a bloody corpse around attracts attention. Besides, you didn't seem to care very much for him when I made the mistake of calling him your brother. In fact, you seemed quite offended."

"Varma was not especially kind to me, it's true. But he was related to me, after a fashion. He was family. And besides, you just don't leave a person to rot in an alley when he dies – it just isn't right!"

"Now I *know* you don't get out of the Cathedral much. Most of the people in this city would do just that and not think twice about it. Hell, I doubt they'd even think once about it."

"I'm not most people. But I guess you are, eh?"

"What are you insinuating?"

"I can't believe how cold you're being, Matt. The way you didn't blink an eye when we found Varma... examined him as if he were just a piece a meat. He was alive and now he's dead. Doesn't that mean anything to you? Doesn't it do anything to you?"

"I'm a zombie, Devona. And zombies don't feel emotions, at least not the same way–"

"Normal zombies don't think, either; they only do what their masters tell them too. But you think just fine. If you don't feel anything, perhaps it doesn't have anything to do with your being a zombie. Perhaps that's who Matthew Richter really is – a man who was dead inside long before he died on the outside."

She pushed past me and ran out of the alley. I just stood and watched her go, her words having hurt me in a way I didn't think I could be hurt anymore. I told myself I'd only been doing my job, had been focused on trying to help Devona and prevent my final end.

Maybe she was right, maybe I should have, could have, felt more. But Christ, I was a cop for twenty years, and in that time I saw more cruelty, despair, and death than I can remember. You had to become numb eventually to survive, to get through the day without losing it, climbing up a water tower, and taking potshots at pedestrians. All cops knew it; it was part of the price you paid when you signed on to serve and protect.

But human beings aren't machines: they can't turn off their emotions at work and then turn them on once they get home. So they get into the habit of leaving them off all the time. That's why so many cops are divorced, like me. Or end up substance abusers or suicides.

Maybe Devona was right; maybe I had been a zombie long before I came to Nekropolis.

I looked down at Varma, and tried to feel something – sadness, pity, disgust. But I didn't feel anything. I hadn't known Varma. But I did know Devona.

I bent down and, as best I could with my bum right arm, I lifted him over my shoulder and carried him out of the alley.

Devona didn't say anything when I caught up with her. We walked in silence, making our way through the crowds in the street as best we could. I had been wrong about one thing: no one paid any attention to us. Since it was the Descension celebration, I guess everyone assumed that we were escorting a friend who'd ingested a little too much fun. That, or they had ingested a little too much of their own and didn't give a damn about anything except remaining upright.

I didn't know what Devona expected us to do with the body. If we took Varma back to the Cathedral – to Lord Galm – that would be the end of our investigation. Galm would learn of the Dawnstone's theft, punish Devona (and perhaps blame her for not informing him about the Dawnstone earlier so that he could have taken steps to prevent his son's death), and in a day or two I'd be a pile of Kellogg's Zombie Flakes. Unless Lord Galm in his anger decided to destroy Devona and me on the spot.

Preoccupied with these cheery thoughts, I almost didn't notice when Devona held up a hand for me to stop. She pointed to a hulking gray figure stomping unimpeded down the street as if the crowd didn't exist.

"Sentinel!" she called out.

The faceless – and for that matter earless – golem stopped, and then turned in our direction. It regarded us for several seconds before heading toward us with its stiff-legged gait, parting the crowd before it like the Moses of ambulatory clay.

It stopped and regarded us with whatever sensory apparatus it possessed. It looked like every other Sentinel I'd ever seen, save that this one had faint line about nine inches long down the middle of its chest. Probably a souvenir left by one of Nekropolis's more powerful – and foolish – denizens resisting arrest.

"My friend and I found this man," she indicated Varma, "in the alley behind the Broken Cross. We believe he died of a drug overdose."

The Sentinel stood impassively for a moment and then pointed with a thick finger at the ground. The message was clear; I set Varma down. The Sentinel bent forward from the waist as if hinged, and examined the body. At least, I assumed it examined the body. I had no real way of telling for certain.

When it was satisfied, the Sentinel straightened and pointed down the street. Again, the message was unmistakable. We were free to go.

If I'd been alive, I'd have probably had to release a relieved breath. There had been a good chance that the Sentinel might've wanted to take us to the Nightspire for questioning by an Adjudicator. Maybe there was too much going on during the Descension festival for the Sentinel to bother. Even in Nekropolis, where the police force had been mystically manufactured, there weren't enough cops to go around.

I nodded, one cop to another, and we got the hell out of there before the Sentinel could change its mind. When we were halfway down the street, I looked back to see that the Sentinel had slung Varma's body over its shoulder and was moving off in the opposite direction – toward the Nightspire.

"The Adjudictors will eventually identify Varma, and then inform Lord Galm," Devona said. "And Father will claim the body and see that it's laid to rest." She sounded relieved.

"Then you intend to continue searching for the Dawnstone?"

"Of course. Whatever gave you the idea I wanted to stop?"

Human, vampire, or a combination of the two – sometimes women just didn't make any sense to me.

"Oh, and Matt? Thanks." She smiled gratefully.

It was one of the best smiles I'd ever been favored with. "Sure. And now we need to find a way to–"

I was interrupted by the loud *blat-blat-blat* of some idiot leaning on a car horn.

Across the street, parked halfway on the sidewalk, was a cab.

"Hey!" Lazlo shouted. "You two need a ride?"

THIRTEEN

"Are you out of your worm-eaten mind?" Lazlo shouted as he swerved to avoid a being that resembled a pair of giant Siamese frogs.

"I've gone through Glamere a couple times since my run-in with Talaith," I said. "And you've taken me on nearly every occasion. We got through okay then."

"That's because of my finely honed driving skills and a hell of a lot of luck." Lazlo roared across the Bridge of Nine Sorrows, taking us from the Sprawl and back into Gothtown. "But luck doesn't hold forever, Matt – and you've used more than your fair share over the last couple years."

"Life's a gamble, Lazlo." Especially when you might only have a day or two of it left. "The case I'm working on is stalled, and I need Gregor to give it a jump start. Besides, if you think about it, this is the safest time for me to cross Glamere. Talaith is undoubtedly conserving her strength for the Renewal Ceremony. She won't have the time – or the energy – to worry about me."

"Maybe," the demon allowed, "but if your bones end up hanging on a wall in Woodhome, don't say I didn't warn you."

"Duly noted." I sat back against the seat and turned to Devona. "Maybe you should think about letting us drop you off before we get to Glamere. If Talaith detects my presence, things will get very ugly, very fast."

"I understand the risk involved, but I still want to go. It's my problem we're trying to solve, after all. And I've never been to Glamere or the Boneyard. Besides," – she paused – "I think we make a good team."

I smiled. "I think you're right."

We didn't say much more after that, just sat, gripped the armrests, and prayed that Lazlo wouldn't swerve off the Obsidian Way and slam us into a building. After a time, we drew near the Bridge of Shattered Dreams, the entrance to Glamere. As we drove across, I hoped the bridge's name wouldn't turn out to an omen of things to come.

Glamere – the Dominion of the Arcane, the magic workers of Nekropolis – is a series of medieval villages nestled in a bucolic countryside. The buildings range from simple huts and shacks to wood-and-stone houses with thatched roofs. Nearly every house has a garden full of herbs, flowers, and plants, some recognizable, most not... and some which sway and undulate as if more than just exotic-looking vegetables. Emblazoned on the outside of each building, sometimes in crude soot-drawn lines, sometimes in elaborately painted colors, are an infinite array of hex signs. I couldn't decipher any of them, so I asked Devona.

"I only recognize those that serve as wardspells," she said. "As to the rest, your guess is as good as mine."

The roads in Glamere are little more than unpaved wagon routes for the most part, but since we were traveling on the Obsidian Way, our ride was smooth and we made good time. We often saw fires in the distance, probably surrounded by chanting witches and warlocks celebrating the Descension in their own pagan way. Besides producing most of the city's spells, potions, and magic devices, Glamere was also the primary farming center, and on a normal day we might have run into (literally, with Lazlo driving) ox-drawn carts full of produce or herds of animals being brought in from pasture. But this was Descension Day. No one was working and aside from Lazlo's cab, the Obsidian Way was thankfully deserted.

If I'd been alive I would have been holding my breath ever since we'd crossed over into Talaith's Dominion. But we were halfway across Glamere – or at least I thought we were; it's hard to judge distance since there are no road markers or prominent landmarks – and nothing had happened yet. I actually allowed myself to start thinking this was going to be the easiest part of the case yet.

Stupid of me.

Lightning flashed across the sky, startling me. Not because I'm afraid of storms, but because Nekropolis normally doesn't have weather. No sun, only Umbriel's eternal shadowlight, no heat, no rain, no snow – nothing except wind, and never very strong at that. No, this lightning wasn't natural. And that could only mean one thing.

"Talaith's aware of us," I said. Thunder rumbled from somewhere off in the distance, probably originating from Woodhome.

"How?" Devona asked. "She should be husbanding her power for the ceremony!"

"Maybe she doesn't care," Lazlo said. "And by the way, Matt, I told you so."

"Get exorcised," I snapped. "How much farther do we have to go until we reach the Boneyard?" Darklords don't directly use their powers in another Lord's Dominion – not unless they want serious trouble from Dis. I knew if we could make it to the Boneyard before Talaith attacked, we would be safe. Hopefully.

"Too far," Lazlo answered. He stomped on the pedal, and the cab, which had already been doing what seemed to me close to the speed of sound, accelerated.

Go as fast as you like, Richter, said a smug, slimy voice in my head. *It won't do you any good.*

More lightning. And the thunder which followed was closer this time.

You're mad, Talaith, I thought back. You can't afford to waste your energy like this. The Renewal Ceremony is approaching. And Dis won't be pleased if you're too weak to fulfill your part in it.

I'm touched by your concern, she thought mockingly. *You'll be relieved to know that I'm not using a single iota of*

*my own power. My loyal subjects are thoughtfully allowing
me to borrow theirs.*

I realized the significance of all the fires we'd seen.
The Arcane weren't celebrating; they were conducting
a rite to transfer mystic power to their Lady.

A series of lightning flashes this time, much closer,
and the crack of thunder sounded almost immediately.

How'd you know we were coming? I thought. I doubt
you've been wasting power constantly scrying for me –
you don't have it to spare. Not in your present condition.

I sensed her anger at my taunt. *I always conduct an augury using a mourning dove before every Descension Day to
determine how things will go. This year, the bird's entrails told
me that you would be passing through tonight. And so I prepared. Glee and anticipation suffused her thoughts. With the
help of my people, I'm going to destroy you once and for all,
Matthew Richter, and your friends along with you. What do
you think of that?*

Lightning crashed outside the cab, thunder cracked,
rattling the windows. A driving rain began to fall. Lazlo
hit the wipers.

What if I told you that I'm due to decompose in another day or so anyway? Why bother wasting magic
power, even if it isn't your own, to destroy me if I'll be
gone in a handful of hours?

Talaith didn't respond right away, and the rain slack-
ened, but didn't let up entirely.

*I sense you're telling the truth. And in that case letting you
go would be the sensible thing. But I don't want to be sensible;
I want revenge.*

The rain picked up, coming down so hard now that visibility was near zero, but Lazlo didn't let up on the gas. The lightning and thunder were constant now. I wondered how close we were to the Bridge of Lost Souls. Not close enough, I feared.

Instead of destroying you, perhaps I'll try to merely incapacitate you. That way you'll get to see your friends perish, and afterward I can bring you to Woodhome and have the pleasure of watching you rot away to nothing. Yes, that sounds quite lovely.

I had one last card up my sleeve. It wasn't an ace... hell, it wasn't even a deuce, but it was all I had, so I played it.

What would you say if I reminded you about the Accord that states travelers on the Obsidian Way aren't to be interfered with?

I'd say, "What Accord?"

And then I felt Talaith's foul presence depart my mind. If I could have, I would've taken my brain out and given it a good scrubbing to get rid of the mental aftertaste of the Witch Queen's thoughts.

"Uh, guys, we have a problem."

"No shit we have a problem!" Lazlo shouted over the riotous thunder. "I can barely see two feet in front of us, and these so-called roads are rapidly turning into mud!"

I filled them in on my mental tête-à-tête with the mistress of the Arcane.

"An augury!" Lazlo said in surprise. "Those went out with evil eyes and love potions!"

"This is no time to discuss fashion trends in magic," I said. "We have to figure a way out of this!"

"We better figure fast, then." Lazlo pointed at the sky beyond the windshield. There, highlighted against black clouds, was the figure of an angel with wings of lightning. But this was a dark angel with wild raven hair, hate-filled eyes, and lips twisted in cruel laughter that boomed louder than thunder. Talaith, or at least a reasonable facsimile, getting ready to swoop down for the kill.

I looked out the windshield. Talaith's avatar had left her position in the sky and was swooping down toward us, dark glee and anticipation blazing on her face.

Talaith's avatar closed on our cab. She plucked a bolt of lightning from her wings and it shaped itself into a sword crackling with electricity. As she neared, she shrieked like a banshee experiencing labor pains, lifted the glowing yellow-white sword, and, as she reached the cab, swung.

But Lazlo was ready for her. Just as she brought the sword around, he jerked the steering wheel to the left and hit the gas. A sizzling sound filled the interior of the cab and then we were spinning out of control. I grabbed Devona because I hoped my zombie body might absorb some of the impact – neither of us were wearing seatbelts because Lazlo's cab doesn't have them. He tore them out because, as he once explained to me, they "show a real lack of confidence in the driver" – and together we bounced around the back seat as Lazlo swore mightily and struggled to regain control over his machine.

But it was no good; the car tipped, bounced, and rolled five times before finally crunching to a stop. The cab – what was left of it – was resting on its hood in the middle of a rain-soaked field. I still had hold of Devona.

"You okay?" I shouted above the still rollicking storm.

"I think so. Plenty of aches, but I don't think anything's broken."

"Lazlo?"

He moaned and I thought he'd been hurt. But then he said, "My cab! What did that bitch do to my beautiful cab?"

If any of us had been human, or in Devona's case all the way human, we most likely would've been killed. As it was, it looked like we were going to survive long enough for Talaith to kill us in person.

I kicked out the safety glass of the shattered rear window, which wasn't easy since my left leg didn't work quite right anymore, and pushed Devona through the opening. I yelled for Lazlo to get out of the car, and then crawled after Devona.

Getting up wasn't easy with my latest injury, but once I was up, I could stand okay. Devona pointed to the cab's passenger-side tires: they were nothing but melted globs on the rims.

So Talaith's avatar had gotten in a shot after all. I suppose the air was filled with the greasy-oily stink of burning rubber, though my dead zombie nose couldn't detect it. The rest of the cab didn't look much better than the tires.

The driver's door burst off and flew into the field as Lazlo forced his way out. The demon's a lot stronger than he appears. As soon as he got a good look at what Talaith had done to his beloved cab, he began sobbing. The vehicle's hood had been torn off, exposing its inner mouth. Numerous teeth had been broken off, the cab's long tongue lolled onto the ground, and a pool of dark liquid that might or might not have been oil was spreading beneath the vehicle. Devona hurried over to console Lazlo, and I looked to the sky, expecting to see Talaith's avatar gazing down at us and laughing with dark delight. But there was no sign of the Witch Queen, and a moment later the rain ceased and the clouds began to clear.

"What's happening?" Devona said as I walked over to join her and Lazlo next to the demon's dearly departed death-machine.

"I don't know," I said. "Maybe Talaith used up the magic power she borrowed from her people and couldn't maintain her avatar any longer."

Bright white light flared into existence around us, revealing a dozen men and women carrying wooden staffs with glowing lux crystals attached to the ends. Most of them wore tunics, but three – two men and a woman – wore loose-fitting hooded robes. I didn't have to guess who was in charge.

One of the robed men, a portly fellow with a gray mustache and goatee stepped forward.

"Or maybe," he said with a sinister smile, "instead of wasting more power, our Lady sent us to retrieve you."

"That's another possibility," I said.

"You sure know how to show a girl a good time, Matt."

"How long have you been waiting to use that line?" I said.

"A few hours," Devona admitted.

"You two are a riot," Lazlo said. "Are you guys always this funny or only when you're tied to stakes and surrounded by pissed-off witches and warlocks?"

Our Glamere welcoming committee had brought us – by force, naturally – to the village of Merrowvale. They'd hustled us into the village square and then tied us to three large wooden stakes atop a stone dais. The three robed Arcane, who I took to be the village Elders, then ordered children to begin piling firewood around Devona and Lazlo's feet. But not, I noticed, around mine.

The entire square was filled with villagers, young and old, all decked out in medieval dress. It looked like a renaissance fair, only without the funnel cakes and ATM machines labeled *Queen's Treasury*. Only about half of them carried magic staffs with lit lux crystals, but that didn't mean the other half were harmless. Even the smallest child here was capable of casting at least some rudimentary spells. Both Devona and Lazlo were strong enough to break free from the ropes binding them if they wished, but they knew they couldn't hope to escape from this many Arcane, and so they simply remained where they were while the children stacked the fuel for a good old-fashioned stake-burning at their feet.

The Elders stood at the base of the dais, and I caught the portly one's eye.

"Why don't I get any wood? You people have something against the smell of burning zombies?"

"Don't answer him, Zorian," said the Elder standing to the portly man's right, a tall middle-aged woman with her graying brunette hair tied up in a bun. "He's not worth the breath it would take to speak to him."

I almost fired off a witty comeback, but I noticed something odd about the woman's face. I looked at her more closely, and it didn't take me long to figure out what was bothering me about her. I examined her fellow Elders, and then I turned my head as far as I could – given that I was tied to a stake – and gazed upon as many of the good folk of Merrowvale as I could. And when I was finished, I smiled to myself. These people had a secret, and they weren't hiding it very well. But I decided to keep that to myself for the moment.

"Hush, Gizane," said the third Elder, a tall beefy man with a neatly trimmed brown beard who looked as if he would have made a hell of a quarterback on Earth. "Let Zorian have some fun. After all, it is Descension Day." He grinned at me, a savage gleam in his eyes. He reminded me of a mean little boy who'd caught a trio of insects and couldn't wait to start tearing their legs off.

Zorian nodded to the other man. "Thank you, Ortzi." Then the warlock turned to me. "We have no intention of burning you, Mr. Richter. Our Lady wants you all for herself, and we'd be poor subjects indeed if we kept the pleasure of destroying you for ourselves."

A scattering of laughter passed through the crowd, but it was more dutiful than enthusiastic.

"She's en route now," Ortizi said. "She's coming here personally to claim you, though to be honest we're not sure whether she'll destroy you on the spot or take you back to Woodhome and save you for after the Renewal Ceremony. Me, I'm hoping for on the spot. I'd love to see the Lady in action."

"That would be a treat," Gizane admitted.

"Once her avatar forced the three of you off the road, she mentally contacted the three of us," Zorian said, "and we – along with a few of the more powerful members of our village – went out to find you and escort you back to Merrowvale. Our orders are to hold you here until Talaith arrives, Mr. Richter."

Ortzi grinned. "But she told as that as a reward for our service, we can do anything we like to your two friends. So we're going to burn them alive at the stake – while you watch, helpless to save them. Won't that be just *awful*?"

The children finished piling up the wood, and they stepped off the dais and returned to their parents. Ortzi's lux crystal began to glow orange and flames flickered to life around it. The warlock made no move to step forward and touch the flaming tip of his staff to the wood yet. He wanted to make this last as long as he could.

"Uh, Matt?" Lazlo said, his bulbous demon eyes transfixed by the fire atop Ortzi's staff. "If you have any brilliant ideas, now would be an excellent time to implement them."

"Don't worry," Devona said. "He'll think of something."

The simple confidence in her voice was both heartwarming and heart-breaking. I did have an idea, but if it was going to have any chance of working, I had to stall just a bit longer, to give Talaith time to get closer to Merrowvale.

"Out of curiosity," I said, "how's Talaith traveling here? Broom? Magic carpet? A pair of ruby slippers?"

The three Elders only glared at me, and someone in the crowd shouted out, "Quit talking and light the goddamned fires!"

I decided I'd better move on to something else, and quickly. "All right, forget that. But tell me this: just how close to the Bridge of Lost Souls were we when Talaith's avatar knocked us off the Obsidian Way?" When none of the Elders responded right away, I added, "Come on… you'll just make us more miserable by telling us." When they continued to hesitate, I said, "You know, if Talaith were here she'd tell me… Now there's a woman who *really* knows how to torment a man – and not in the good way."

"Very well," Zorian said. "You were less than a mile and a half from the Bridge."

"You might have made it, too," Gizane said, nodding toward Lazlo. "If that idiot demon was a better driver."

"Too bad ugly – or body odor – doesn't equate with driving skill," Ortzi said. "Otherwise, he'd be qualified for the Grand Prix back on Earth."

Lazlo ground his teeth, sending small sparks shooting out of the corners of his mouth. He glared at Ortzi, and from the way his muscles were bunched up, I knew my demonic friend was getting ready to burst his bonds and show the Elders what happens when someone insults his driving.

I couldn't afford to stall any longer.

"Tell me something, Gizane. Where do you get your make-up?"

Gizane drew up the hood of her robe as if to hide her face and gave her fellow Elders a sideways glance.

"I don't know what you're talking about, zombie."

"I'm not criticizing," I said. "It's nicely understated the eye shadow, the eyeliner, the rouge, the lipstick… all very natural-looking. And you, Ortzi. Your beard is a deep, rich brown, but the color is a slightly different shade than your hair, and you've got a significant amount of gray at your temples. A man's beard usually goes gray before his hair. I suppose you imported the stuff you use to color it from Earth."

Ortiz started to cover his beard with his hand, but then he must have realized he was only drawing attention to it and lowered his hand once more – though it looked like it took an effort for him to do so.

I turned to Zorian then. "And unless my dead eyes deceive me, I see a small flesh-colored hearing aid nestled in your right ear, Zorian. Another import, I take it?

Zorian glanced at his fellow Elders, and all three of them looked nervous as hell.

"I don't understand, Matt," Devona said. "Now that you've pointed out those things about them, I can see them all, but why would Arcane bother using mundane items like that? Wouldn't they just use their magic to improve their appearance or repair their hearing?"

"I'm sure that's what Talaith would prefer. But these three aren't the only ones who prefer non-magical ways of solving problems – or just enjoying life. Take a good look at the crowd. You'll see people wearing wrist-watches, talking on cell phones – the real thing, not handvoxes – texting on BlackBerrys, taking digital pictures and video of us... More than a few folks are listening to music on their iPods, and a number of the children are playing handheld videogames. And if you'll look really close at that alley over there, you'll see someone sitting on the ground typing furiously on a laptop. Probably blogging about our imminent demises. All of them are trying to hide their toys, but they're doing a crappy job of it."

Now the assembled villagers were starting to look nervous too.

"I still don't get it, Matt," Devona said. "Lots of people in Nekropolis use imported Earth technology, whether in its pure form or adapted somehow by dark magic. What's the big deal?"

"The big deal is that these people are subjects of Talaith," I explained. "And she's not particularly fond of technology – especially not after how things turned out with the Overmind. By Talaith's edict, technology of any sort is illegal for the Arcane to possess or use as long as they are within her Dominion. If she catches any Arcane with technology, she punishes them." I smiled at the three Elders. "Most severely."

The Elders paled.

I went on. "Talaith has a huge problem trying to enforce her edict, because pure technology is fascinating to the Arcane, almost to the point of addiction. Chemicals, medicines, and machines that can perform wonders without requiring a spellcaster to use her or her own energy to power them? What could be more wondrous? Merrowvale is one of the outlying villages in Glamere, so close to the Boneyard that it's a simple matter to smuggle technology in and far enough away from Woodhome that they don't worry too much about getting caught. If you went into their homes right now, you'd probably find flat-screen TVs, DVD players, videogame systems, personal computers, refrigerators, microwave ovens, washers and dryers... you name it, they've got it, and portable generators to power it all. And now they've captured us and their mistress is coming here to get me." I smiled at the Elders. "What makes you think you're going to be able to hide all your toys from Talaith when you couldn't hide them from me – and I'm not even a Darklord."

Gizane grabbed the collar of Zorian's robe and turned him to face her. "He's right! Talaith will find out! She may even already know!"

"And if she doesn't," I said, "I'll make sure to tell her the moment she arrives."

People in the crowd began wailing and crying. They had a good idea what sort of reaction they could expect from their mistress once she discovered their village's tech-fetish.

"Don't panic!" Ortzi said. He gave me a sly look. "If we destroy the zombie along with his friends, there will be no one left alive to tell Talaith anything."

Gizane and Zorian looked at him hopefully.

"But Talaith gave you specific orders not to destroy me," I pointed out. "If you burn me up along with my friends, how will you explain it to Talaith? And even if you could come up with an excuse that she'd buy, she'd punish you all for stealing her chance to get revenge on me."

Gizane and Zorian no longer looked so hopeful. In fact, they both looked as if they might vomit at any moment.

"Then we're lost!" someone in the crowed wailed. "There's nothing we can do!"

"There is one thing," I said. "You could let us go."

"Are you mad?" Ortzi shouted at me. "Talaith would be sure to punish us in ways beyond imagining if we did that!"

"That's true," I admitted. "But not if the citizens of Merrowvale release us, then tell Talaith we got away because the three of you screwed up and allowed us to escape."

"Is your brain as dead as the rest of you?" Ortzi snapped. "Zorian, Gizane, and I would never permit the villagers to do that – and even if somehow they succeeded, we'd simply tell the Dark Lady what really happened."

"True again. But the villagers could tell Talaith that after you let us escape, they killed you in her name for your incompetence. Then there would be no one left to tell Talaith about what really happened, the villagers could keep all their toys, and the Dark Lady would be none the wiser."

Zorian tried to look calm, but the lines of sweat trickling down his face told a different story. He kept shooting sidelong glances at the crowd in the square. "I think you've underestimated the good folk of Merrowvale, Mr. Richter. They would never do anything so heinous simply to keep their..." He broke off as he noticed the villagers staring quietly at him and his two fellow Elders. The lux crystals of the villagers who carried staffs began to glow a baleful red, while others started making intricate hand gestures and chanting mystic phrases.

I turned my head so I could see Devona and Lazlo.

"You might want to close your eyes. I have a feeling this is going to get real ugly, real fast."

The villagers let out a roar as they surged en masse toward the dais.

Devona, Lazlo and I were hoofing it on the Obsidian Way. I'd been tempted to ask the villagers if we could borrow some horses, though the beasts tend to shy away from me, probably because of my smell. And if they turned up their noses at me, I couldn't imagine how they'd react to Lazlo's stink. But after seeing what the villagers had done to their Elder – and the zeal with which they'd gone at it – I decided not to push our luck. A mile and a half isn't that far to walk, even on stiff, partially damaged zombie legs. But time, as they say, was of the essence. Talaith had already been on her way to Merrowvale when the villagers released us, and it wouldn't take her long to arrive. Once she saw that we'd escaped, she'd come looking for us, and as long as we were in her Dominion, we weren't safe. We needed to get to the Boneyard, and we needed to get there fast, and I doubted we were going to make it on foot. If worse came to worst, I would give myself to Talaith and urge her to let Devona and Lazlo go, but I knew the Witch Queen wouldn't go for it. She'd kill the both of them just to hurt me further. So either we all made it or none of us did. Once more, I attempted to cudgel my zombified brain into providing a way out.

I knew the Darklords constantly strove against one another – within the boundaries set by Dis, that is. They spied on and schemed against one another, tried to outdo the others' accomplishments and win favor in the eyes of Dis. They ruled their individual Dominions and the inhabitants thereof absolutely, though some of the Lords were more involved in their subjects' lives than others. Still, it was considered an act of great transgression for a Darklord to interfere with another's Dominion and its subjects.

I also knew the four remaining Darklords had to be aware of what Talaith had been up to tonight. Even if

it was borrowed, the sheer power she was expending
would stand out to them like an atomic bomb detonat-
ing at a July Fourth celebration. In fact, the other Lords
were likely keeping close watch on the situation right
now, if for no other reason than to make certain Talaith
wasn't somehow gearing up for an attack on them.

And then I had an idea.

I lived in the Sprawl. That made me a subject of Varvara, didn't it? If I called upon the Demon Queen,
might she intervene to save one of her subjects? No, I
decided. Varvara liked me well enough, but we weren't
friends. What she liked about me was the amusement
value I offered as a zombie ex-cop trying to survive in
Nekropolis. But I doubted she'd find a confrontation
with Talaith amusing, especially when the Witch Queen
was filled with the combined mystic power of her subjects. Varvara might miss me when I was gone, or she
might get a laugh out of my demise, but she wouldn't
help me.

I looked up, trying to see if Talaith was on her way. I
saw no sign of the Witch Queen.

As if reading my mind, Devona said, "I feel psychic
pressure at the base of my skull, Matt. She's coming."

I quickly explained my idea about the Darklords
watching.

"If they are, then that means Father is watching too,"
she said thoughtfully. "And he knows I'm here and in
danger. But if that's the case, why hasn't he done anything?" She looked up into the sky. "Father!" she cried.
"Father, help us!" But nothing happened.

Maybe I'd been wrong about the Darklords watching. Or maybe they were, but Galm was constrained by one of the Accords, or maybe he just couldn't afford to expend any of his power so close to the Renewal Ceremony, even to save the life of his own daughter. Or maybe his reasons were political. From what I understood, Galm and Talaith, while not the best of friends by any means, had about as cordial a relationship as any two Darklords can.

But I knew a Lord who Talaith wasn't on such good terms with – a Lord she'd planned to attack with the Overmind before Dale and I destroyed it.

A voice whispered in my mind then, thick with barely restrained fury. *Another valiant attempt to escape me, Matthew, but you're too late. Look up.*

I did and saw a figure swiftly approaching from the western sky. Talaith sat upon an airborne throne of black marble held aloft by a pair of giant flapping raven's wings growing from the throne's back. Despite myself, I was impressed. Much classier than a broom or carpet. I knew we had only moments before she reached us. Once again, it was time to do something desperate.

I raised my hands to the heavens. "Lord Edrigu! Hear me! You are Master of the Dead; I am a zombie! Will you allow Talaith to insult you by attacking one of your own subjects? I ask you to help us, if for no other reason than to spite her!"

I waited, but nothing happened.

Nice try, zombie. Talaith's thought-voice was smug. *But Edrigu would never da–*

And then, as if Talaith's comment was a cue, the air near us shimmered and a shadowy coach appeared.

It was Silent Jack's Black Rig.

We didn't have time to think about it.

"C'mon!" I shouted, grabbing both Devona's and Lazlo's arms and pulling them toward Jack's coach.

"I'm not going to ride in a ghost hack!" Lazlo protested. "I'm a real cabby! Besides, I'm not going to leave my cab. We have to go back and—"

Talaith was close enough now for us to hear her voice, and she shrieked, furious at Jack's sudden appearance. She gestured and a bolt of lightning crashed to the ground less than three yards from where we stood.

"I'm going to shut my mouth and get inside," Lazlo finished.

The door of the coach sprung open of its own accord, and we climbed in: Devona first, Lazlo second, me last. I pulled the door closed after us, and it shut with a muffled click. The interior of the coach was dark and the wood looked... insubstantial, somehow, as if you could put your finger through it if you pressed hard enough. But what else could you expect from a ghost coach? At least it was solid enough to keep the rain out.

I thumped on the roof to get the driver's attention. "Let's go, Jack!"

Silent Jack, true to his name, didn't reply. His whip cracked soundlessly, Malice and Misery let out a pair of inaudible whinnies, and we began to move. But the horses didn't pull us, at least not in the usual way. The entire coach, horses, slid forward as if on a conveyer belt, slowly at first, but with increasing speed. There was no bouncing or juddering; the ride was eerily smooth.

I pushed aside the curtain over the rear window and saw Talaith pursuing us, eyes flashing with mystic energy and blazing bright with anger and frustration. The Witch Queen poured on the speed, but inch by inch, we began to outdistance her.

Damn you, Richter! a furious voice thundered in my head. *This isn't over!*

It is for now, I responded, and settled back in my seat. I'd survived another encounter with the mistress of Glamere.

I looked up at the ceiling and thought of Jack sitting atop the coach, driving the horses onward in silence. We'd gotten away, but, I wondered, at what price?

FOURTEEN

The coach neared the border between Glamere and the Boneyard, but instead of heading for the Bridge of Lost Souls, it aimed straight for Phlegethon. Before we could protest, the coach had passed through the wrought iron fence at the side of the road – somehow allowing us to pass through as well – and continued through the air as if the road had never ended, bearing us easily across the river of green fire. I wonder if any Lesk, the giant serpents that plied the flaming waters of the river, were looking up, disappointed we hadn't fallen in. But I didn't look out the window to check. Some things are better left a mystery.

Now that we had crossed over into Edrigu's Dominion, Talaith no longer pursued us. But that didn't necessarily mean we were safe. Nekropolis doesn't do safe.

As soon as we reached the other side, the Black Rig glided to a stop on the Obsidian Way.

"It wasn't as much fun as a car," Lazlo said, "but I have to admit it was a pretty decent ride." He tried to open the door, but it wouldn't budge. "Hey, it's locked!" Lazlo gripped the handle tighter and shook it for all he was worth, but despite his demonic strength, the door remained closed. "What gives?"

"I believe it's time to settle the matter of our fare," Devona said.

I remembered the rumors about Silent Jack, about how much he liked the ladies. And from the look on Devona's face, she was thinking the same thing.

"I'll get this one, Jack," I said loudly.

The door sprung open.

"Matt, no!" Devona protested. "You shouldn't pay for all three of us!"

"She's right," Lazlo agreed. "We all three rode; we all should pay."

I shook my head. "I'm the one who requested Lord Edrigu's assistance, so I'll be the one to settle the tab. Now go ahead and get out, both of you."

Devona refused, so I looked to Lazlo. The demon sighed. "All right, Matt; if that's the way you want it. Let's go, Devona." He took her hand and pulled her struggling from the coach. As strong as Devona was, Lazlo was stronger. As soon as they were both out, the door *snicked* shut once more, and Silent Jack appeared on the seat opposite me. This was the closest I'd ever been to him, but I couldn't make out any facial features. It was as if he were formed entirely out of shadow, just like his cab and the horses that drew it.

The ghostly coachman held out a gloved hand, but I was fairly certain he wasn't asking for darkgems.

"Name your price, Jack."

He put his hand in his lap, held it out again, and then pointed to me. The message was clear – he wanted me to hold out my hand. I extended my left hand palm up. Jack reached out and with the sharp ebon nail of his index finger traced four lines on my palm. When he removed his finger, my flesh puckered and scar tissue formed in the shape of a letter E. *E for Edrigu*. What did it mean?

I started to pull back my hand, but Jack gripped my wrist, and with his other hand got hold of my pinkie and yanked. There was a snapping, tearing sound, and my finger came loose in his hand. He inserted the finger in his vest pocket, tipped his hat to me, and then vanished.

The door opened.

I climbed out and stood next to Devona and Lazlo. We watched as Silent Jack – who sat once more atop the coach – and his Black Rig faded from sight.

"What was his price?" Devona asked.

I showed them the mark on my palm.

"What do you think it means?" I asked.

"I'm not certain," Devona said. "Perhaps merely that you are in Lord Edrigu's debt. Or perhaps that you now have a new master."

A master. I couldn't deal with all the implications of what that might mean. I'd always been my own man, even when I was on the force in Cleveland. And now I had a master?

Edrigu was Lord of the Dead – had he perhaps repaired the damage to my body? I took a quick inventory. No, my face was still scratched, my ear still missing, my right arm and left leg still damaged. Edrigu hadn't bothered to fix me, which meant that I was still in the process of decomposing for the final time. It didn't make any sense. Why would Edigru have Jack put his mark on me if he wasn't going to bother preserving me?

And then I felt an echo of a chill run along my dead spine. What if Edrigu wasn't interested in my undead body? What if he wanted my soul?

Well, if that was the price I had to pay to save my friends, it was worth it. But I wasn't about to give up on Devona's case or on trying to find a way to keep my body intact. Lord Edrigu might have a lien on my soul, but that didn't mean I had to make it easy for him to collect.

Devona noticed my pinkie was missing. I told her what had happened to it.

"I don't understand," she said, puzzled. "Why would Jack take your finger if you'd already paid Lord Edrigu's price?"

"For his tip," Lazlo said, "what else?"

Bereft of transportation, we had no choice but to hoof it. We left the Obsidian Way and began walking along the Boneyard's cramped, narrow streets. But foot travel wasn't a problem in this Dominion, even during the Descension celebration. With the exception of the occasional shade drifting across our path, the streets were deserted. Everything was in a state of arrested decay:

the roadways buckled and bulged, bricks cracked and crumbling; the buildings covered with dead, dry ivy, shutters hanging by one hinge, roofs full of holes or collapsed entirely; the trees and bushes lining the streets twisted, gray, and barren. And, according to Devona and Lazlo, the air was still, stagnant, and stale.

We caught glimpses of movement out of the corner of our eyes, flashes of darting wraith-like shapes that disappeared when you tried to look at them directly. I seemed to be more aware of them than either Devona or Lazlo, maybe because I was dead myself. Not for the first time I wondered just how many spirits inhabited the Boneyard. If we could see them clearly, would we find the streets full of people, perhaps celebrating the Descension along with the rest of the city? Were we even now walking among – walking through – throngs of laughing, shouting merrymakers, oblivious to their presence?

The Boneyard isn't strictly the Dominion of the dead, though. Many living beings – warm ones, as the dead refer to them – also live there. Those who for whatever reasons feel more comfortable living in the presence of death. Some simply like the quiet and solitude, while others go there only for the sake of morbid fashion. And then there are those disturbed individuals who are drawn to death like moths to a cold dark flame, such as the Suicide King and Overkill, who can only truly feel alive when they come as close to death as possible.

Me, I feel more alive around the living. Weird, huh?

Ghosts aren't the only supernatural inhabitants of the Boneyard. Anything dead falls under the rule of Lord Edrigu: poltergeists, skeletons, liches, mummies, wights, wraiths, and others dwelled within his Dominion. Most of these creatures preferred keeping to the shadows or haunting their lairs, waiting for those curious or foolish enough to seek them out or stumble blindly across them. As the three of us walked, we caught the occasional glimpse of a shambling thing lurking in an alley or dark eyes peering through broken shutters in an abandoned building, but we made sure not to disturb them and they in turn didn't seek to devour our souls. A good arrangement all the way around, as far as I was concerned.

Unfortunately, there was one type of dead creature more aggressive than all the others, and as we turned a corner, we saw a group of them coming down the street toward us, walking with stiff, spastic movements and groaning softly.

"Are those… zombies?" Devona asked.

There were eight of them – nine if you counted the partially decayed dog carrying a severed hand in its mouth. Three women, five men, aged anywhere from twenty to sixty at the time of their demise. Their clothes were torn and stained with patches of blood, some of it relatively fresh. Their flesh was a mottled grayish-green color, and their bodies displayed various types of damage: cuts, gouges, tears, and bite marks. A couple were missing arms – I couldn't help feeling a pang of sympathy toward them – and one was missing a good portion of his scalp. It took the zombie horde, such as it was, a moment to realize we were there, but as soon as they did, they began moaning, "*Braaaaiiiinssss...*" and started heading toward us as fast as their dead bodies would permit.

"Idiots," Lazlo said. "Why are they always obsessed with brains? Don't they know how hard it is to bite through a skull?"

"I do *not* want to know how you came by that knowledge," I said.

As the zombies – dead doggie included – shuffled closer, Devona stepped closer and grabbed hold of my arm, as if seeking my protection. I wanted to put my arm around her and hold her closer, but I didn't. I told myself this wasn't the right time, and anyway, it wouldn't be professional. But in truth, I was afraid if I tried, she might pull away from me in disgust. After all, right then I didn't look, or smell, any better than the walking corpses slowly coming toward us.

"What's wrong with them?" Devona asked. "I've seen zombies before – normal ones, not self-aware ones like you, Matt – and they don't act like that. For the most part, they just stand around and wait for someone to give them an order."

"You're thinking of voodoo zombies," I said. "Those are corpses resurrected by a voodoo priest or priestess for the purpose of being a servant. Those zombies–" I nodded toward the moaners – "are a more recent breed."

"Not to mention more annoying," Lazlo out in. "They're always wandering out of the Boneyard and into the other Dominions, staggering around and trying to feast on the flesh of the living. The only good thing about them is that you have to shoot them in the head to kill them. Makes them good target practice."

"Where did they come from?" Devona asked. "And more to the point, why are we just standing here if they want to crack open our skulls and slurp up our brains?"

The zombies had crossed half the distance to us in the time we'd been talking, and they were becoming more excited the closer they got, moving with more urgency, and all of them were loudly moaning, "*Braaaaiiiinssss…*"

I decided to ignore Devona's second question and answer her first. "No one's sure where they originated from. Some say they're the result of voodoo zombies mutating after exposure to some kind of supernatural or science-based power source. Others think that one mad scientist or another got hold of an old Earth flesh-eating zombie movie on DVD, saw it, and decided to see if he could actually make them."

The zombies were almost upon us by then.

"Wherever they came from" Lazlo said, "I'd wish they'd go back and stay there." He glanced at me. "No offense, Matt. You're in a way different league than these moaners."

"No offense taken," I reassured him.

The first of the zombies was just about within arm's reach now, and she stretched a trembling hand toward us that was more bone than flesh. Her milk-white eyes stared hungrily at us, her leathery lips moving as if she were anticipating the meal to come.

"*Brains…*" she whispered softly in an eerie, hollow voice.

Devona was pressed against me so tight now that I feared she might break a few more of my ribs.

"Guys…" She sounded on the verge of panic, but before she could do or say anything else, the zombie woman paused.

Her dead nostrils flared as they took in our scents, and I was jealous. I couldn't smell, but then I didn't need to hunt down brains to devour, either. The zombie's features twisted into a mask of pained disgust, and she stuck out a slimy black tongue.

"*Yuck,*" she spat, then turned to face her fellow zombies.

She said or did nothing obvious to communicate with the others, but they stopped and gazed at her with their dead eyes. And then as one the entire group, zombie-dog included, slowly turned and began shuffling away.

Devona relaxed a bit, but she made no move to step away from me. Not that I was complaining.

"What just happened?" she asked.

"That breed of zombie only feasts on living human flesh," I explained. "Not demon, not half-vampire, and certainly not another zombie."

Lazlo shook his head as he watched the zombies slowly depart. "That's the other thing I hate about them: they're picky eaters."

Devona ignored the demon and gave me an irritated look. "You could've told me that sooner."

I smiled. "What, and spoil the surprise?"

She hauled off and punched me in the arm using her full strength. It might have been my imagination, but I thought it actually hurt a little.

We resumed walking and eventually came to an open field containing the bent, broken, and rusted hulks of hundreds of cars, with a faded, weather-beaten sign proclaiming the place to be Riffraff's Revenants. A junkyard. It made sense, I suppose. After all, this Dominion was reserved for the dead, right? And what was a junkyard other than a cemetery for machines?

Lazlo stopped and stared, a beatific expression on his hideous face. He looked like a demon who had died and, much to his surprise, gone to heaven.

"Look." He pointed to a crumpled hunk of yellow metal that had once been a taxicab and grinned. "I thought I'd never see it again."

"Surely you don't think that's yours," Devona said.

"Look at the tires on the passenger side," I said. "They've been melted."

She shook her head. "It's not possible."

"Maybe this is where cars go when they die," Lazlo said in wonder.

"Or maybe it's part of the deal I made with Lord Edrigu. Whichever, it sure looks like your cab."

"I'm going to check it out, see if anything's salvageable. Maybe, with enough work, I can even get the poor thing running again. You guys go on ahead." He started forward.

"We can't just leave you here," I said.

Lazlo stopped. "Why not? What can happen to me in the Boneyard? Everything's dead here."

I thought of the E emblazoned on my palm. "This is Nekropolis, Lazlo. Just because something's dead does-n't mean it isn't dangerous."

He chuckled. "You worry too much."

"We almost died in Glamere," Devona pointed out.

"We didn't, though, did we?" Lazlo countered. "But my cab did. Maybe now I have chance to get it back. You two take care, and good luck." And with that he shufled toward the remains of his pride and joy.

"Let's go, Devona."

"But–"

"Lazlo's cab is his whole life. And you've seen him drive. Once he starts, he doesn't slow down, and he doesn't listen to anyone telling him to stop. He's like that about everything. He'll probably mess around with the cab for a few hours, realize it's no use, mourn his loss, and then head on back to the Sprawl. Eventually, he'll either find another cab, or he'll be forced to go into a new line of work and the pedestrians of Nekropolis will be able to breathe a little easier."

Devona looked at Lazlo – who was walking around the wreckage of his cab, shaking his head and mutter-ing – one last time, and then together we continued down the street toward Gregor's.

* * *

The streets in the Boneyard had no names, and there were no particular landmarks, just block after block of decay and dissolution, so finding Gregor's place wasn't easy. Eventually we passed a large factory that looked something like a medieval castle with three towering smoke stacks pumping black clouds into the already ebon sky. An intricate lattice of metal beams and wires stretched upward from the roof of the building, and electricity sizzled as it swept through the lattice, bolts cracking like thunder as they leaped from one connection point to another. A high wrought-iron fence surrounded the facility, tipped with sharp spear points to prevent any curiosity-seekers from being tempted to climb over.

Devona gazed upon the factory with wonder. "Is that–"

I nodded. "The Foundry. Home, laboratory, and production facility of Victor Baron, otherwise known as Frankenstein's Monster."

"It's bigger than I imagined," she said.

"Baron lives to create things, and that includes his facility. He's been expanding it for over two hundred years, and he shows no signs of stopping anytime soon."

"Do you know him?" she asked.

"Only by reputation. From what I understand, he doesn't leave the Foundry much."

For the last two centuries, Victor Baron had been Nekropolis's prime supplier of what he terms *reanimation technology* but which most people call meatwork.

Baron is responsible for the city's Mind's Eye technology, handvoxes, flesh computers, and anything other tech based on resurrecting the dead. Just look for the label, often tattooed into the flesh of your device: *Another Victor Baron Creation*. From time to time I'd toyed with the idea of making an appointment with Baron to see if he could anything to stabilize my zombie state or, better yet, return me to the living, but Papa Chatha counseled caution.

Magic and science don't always get along as well as they could, Papa once warned me. *Baron's technology would be as likely to destroy you as help you.*

I sometimes wonder if Papa feels more than a little professional jealousy toward Baron, but since my houngan has kept me going for years, I've decided to trust his advice.

Devona and I kept walking. Gregor's place wasn't far from the Foundry, and I soon recognized a broken beam here and a shattered wall there, and before much longer we stood before the ruins of a stone building: roof collapsed, walls fallen, columns broken and time-worn.

"This is it," I pronounced. "Good thing Gregor has the columns, or I'd never be able to find this place."

"Who is Gregor, precisely?"

"Gregor is probably Nekropolis's best kept secret. He's an information broker on a par with Waldemar. But where Waldemar specializes in the past, Gregor deals in the present." I smiled. "If he doesn't know something, it's because it hasn't happened yet."

"Then why didn't we come here in the first place?"

"Because to do so we had to go through either Glamere or the Wyldwood. It's suicide for anyone but a lyke to travel the Wyldwood – and you experienced Talaith's hospitality. Gregor may be the best source of information in the city, but he's not exactly the most accessible."

"I understand." She surveyed the ruins. "How do we get in?"

I led the way up the cracked and broken steps and we walked carefully through the rubble of Gregor's building until we came to a shiny black rectangle set into the ground.

"It's me, Gregor. And I brought a friend."

Nothing happened for a moment, and then the rectangle parted as the tiny black shapes which comprised it scurried off.

Devona took in a hiss of air. "Insects!"

"Gregor's little friends – and his informants."

As the roach-like bugs retreated, they revealed stone stairs leading down into the earth.

"Try not to make any sudden moves," I told Devona. "Gregor and his friends tend to be on the skittish side."

I took out a pocket flashlight, thumbed the switch to low, and shined its beam down the steps, sending more insects fleeing, thousands of hair-thin segmented legs whispering across stone. Gregor didn't keep his underground lair lit, so the flashlight was a necessity for me – one which he tolerated. And even though I had no reason to fear Gregor, none that I could name, anyway, I always felt better visiting him with flashlight in hand.

We started down into the darkness, roaches scuttling away from the steps and walls as we descended. I'd been here only a handful of times since coming to Nekropolis, but I'd never gotten used to seeing so many of Gregor's friends in one place. My dead nerve endings didn't work anymore, but I still felt itchy when I visited.

When we reached the bottom of the steps, Devona turned around.

"The insects have closed up behind us." Her voice was steady, but I detected a hint of nervousness beneath her words.

"They always do that; don't worry about it."

We were in a large, empty basement which seemed cloaked in tangible darkness, except for the small circle of gray stone around us illuminated by my flashlight.

"Is this place… filled with them too?" Devona asked me in a whisper.

"Try not to think about it," I whispered back, and then in a normal voice I said, "Thank you for seeing us, Gregor."

A faint clicking sound emerged from the darkness where the opposite wall should be.

"Always a pleasure, Matthew." The voice was soft and the words rustled like insect carapaces sliding against one another. "Ms. Kanti, it's quite an honor to meet you."

"The honor is, uh, all mine." As a half-vampire, Devona's eyesight was far better than mine, and I was sure she could see through the basement's gloom to Gregor.

"Please, both of you, come closer. But keep your flashlight pointed downward, if you don't mind, Matthew."

"Not at all," I replied, and we walked forward, the carpet of insects which blanketed the floor flowing out of our path like living oil. We stopped about nine feet from the gigantic insect huddled against the basement wall. He leaned back like a humanoid, though his body wasn't really built for it: he looked as if he might topple over any second. I wondered, as I had before, whether this was a natural position for him, or if he assumed it to seem more humanlike. If the latter, the attempt was a dismal failure.

Gregor was a gigantic version of the far smaller insects which served as his spies throughout the city. Somewhat like a roach, but his head was too large, his legs too many, and his eyes... they didn't resemble a human's, but then they didn't look all that much like an insect's, either. They looked more like obsidian gems set into the hard shell of his carapace.

A constant stream of the smaller Gregors ran up his body, over his head, and touched their antennae to the tips of his far larger feelers. They then scuttled back down as another took their place, and then another, and another. The flow of information from his spies never stopped, even when he was involved in a conversation.

"You'll have to excuse me if I seem a bit distracted today," Gregor said. "But the Descension celebration is the busiest time of the year for us – so much happens around the city – and the sheer tidal wave of information my children bring me can be a bit overwhelming at times. Please bear with me."

"No problem," I said. "So I don't waste your time or ours, Gregor, why don't you tell us how much you know about why we've come? I assume you at least know a little. After all, I did see one of your children in my apartment when I first spoke with Ms. Kanti, and I saw another in the alley where we found Varma's body."

Gregor made a high-pitched chittering sound which I took for laughter. "Very observant, Matthew. Suffice it say I have a fair grasp of your basic situation."

I knew that was all we would get out of him on the subject. Gregor never gave away more information than he had to.

"I'd like to ask you a few questions."

"Of course you do. Why else would you be here?" More chittering. Then he folded his legs across his abdomen – a sign he was preparing to listen closely.

"First off, do you know who stole the Dawnstone?"

"Regrettably, no. My children have a very difficult time penetrating the Darklords' strongholds. Their protections are too strong, too intricate."

"Are you aware of anyone trying to fence the Dawnstone?"

"Again, no."

I was certain Gregor's children had every fence in town "bugged." If he didn't know of anyone trying to sell the Dawnstone, then no one had.

"Do you know who killed Varma?"

"My child happened late upon the scene, but arrived in time to see three members of the Red Tide departing."

The Red Tide. And three of them. When it came to believing in coincidences, I was an atheist. "Are you aware we had a run-in with some Red Tiders?"

"I am."

"Were the three who left the alley the same three who attacked us?"

"As I said, my child only saw them leave the alley, but I believe it was them, yes."

It was beginning to look like our encounter with the gang members in Gothtown hadn't been just random bad luck after all.

"Do you know where they went?"

"Alas, no. My children lost them in the confusion of the festival."

"What do you know about veinburn?"

"It's a relatively new drug, very powerful, created by a fusion of magic and science. It's effective on all of Nekropolis's species, with the exception of the completely dead, such as zombies and ghosts." He paused. "Since you're the city's only self-willed zombie, I have no idea whether it would affect you or not. It would be interesting to find out, wouldn't it?"

"After what happened to Varma, I think I'll just say no, if you don't mind. Who's making the stuff?"

"The Dominari is distributing veinburn. But the drug itself is made by the Arcane."

Arcane? That meant: "Talaith."

Gregor's head bobbled, his version of a nod, I suspect. "And the plants which are used to make veinburn are cultivated in Glamere."

"That's surprising," Devona said. "I wouldn't expect Talaith to use technology, not after what Matt told me about how she demands her people practice pure, natural magic – and especially with what happened with the Overmind."

"Times change," I said. "And the Darklords will do anything to gain an advantage over each other – including abandoning their principles. Assuming they ever had any in the first place." I suddenly recalled who Devona's father was. "Sorry."

"Don't be, you're right; even Father might be persuaded to set aside his hatred of technology if he thought it was to his advantage." She thought a moment. "Could the Hidden Light be mixed up in this somehow? After all, they manage to smuggle holy items into Nekropolis. Perhaps they also bring in technology."

I answered before Gregor could. "Doubtful. The members of the Hidden Light are capable of a lot of things, but working closely with Darkfolk isn't one of them. They have a deep aversion to associating with those of a supernatural persuasion."

"Then why do they deal with you?" she asked.

"Because I was killed while foiling one of Talaith's plots. They view me not as a monster so much as a victim of a Darklord's evil." I turned to Gregor. "What do you think? Could the Hidden Light be in on this?"

"I must concur with your assessment, Matthew," he said. "The Hidden Light has always worked alone in the past."

That settled, I returned to my original line of questioning. "Do you know where The Dominari have their lab set up?"

"Somewhere in the Sprawl, I believe, but the exact location is unknown to me." Gregor's mandibles clicked together once, twice, an action I think was intended to substitute for a smile. "The Dominari may not be Darklords, but their protective spells are still quite formidable."

"I don't suppose you know who Varma's veinburn connection was."

"Actually, I do, or at least, I have a suspicion. The only veinburn dealer I'm aware of is a demon named Morfran who works out of the Sprawl."

I frowned. "Only one dealer? That doesn't make any sense. It's not like the Dominari to work on so small a scale."

"I have the impression they've been field-testing veinburn," Gregor said, "trying to get the formula just right."

"I suppose." Still, it didn't sound like the Dominari's style. Like the criminal organizations back on Earth, they always went for the money, and they weren't exactly known for their patience. "Can you think of anyone in particular who would gain from stealing the Dawnstone?"

"You're asking me to theorize. You know how much I dislike doing so in the absence of facts. But if I were to hazard a guess, I would say someone who wished to harm Lord Galm – or perhaps even Father Dis. And in all likelihood, that would be another Darklord."

"Talaith," Devona said. "Relations between my father and Talaith might be cordial at the moment, but they haven't always been so. And if Talaith is behind the creation of veinburn–"

"She could have gotten Varma hooked on the stuff, and used his addiction as leverage to get him to steal the Dawnstone for her," I finished. "It certainly seems to fit. No wonder she was ready for us when we tried to cross her domain. Augury, my dead ass. One of her people probably saw us asking around about Varma in the Sprawl and alerted her that we were investigating the Dawnstone's theft and figured there was a good chance we'd consult Gregor."

"And the Red Tide?" Devona asked. "They came after us after we'd visited Waldemar – long before anyone could've been aware of what we were doing."

"Maybe Talaith's got an informant in the Cathedral, someone who saw us there."

"Why the Red Tide, then? They hardly seem like the type to work for Talaith."

"Darkgems are darkgems, no matter who pays them to you. And the Red Tide's tech can't come cheap, not when it has to be imported from Earth."

Around us, Gregor's children began getting restless. A sign, I knew, that Gregor himself was becoming bored and was eager to move on to another topic.

"Anything else?" he asked.

"Not that I can think of," I answered.

"Then on to the matter of payment." If there's such a thing as an insect version of a purr, Gregor's words were it.

Before I could respond, Devona stepped in front of me and said, "I'll pay."

"No you won't," I said.

She turned to me, her face set in a determined expression. "You paid Waldemar's price, Lord Edrigu's, and Silent Jack's. It's my turn."

"I could afford to pay them, Devona. I... Papa Chatha gave me some bad news. My body can no longer be preserved by magic. I'll be gone in a couple days, maybe less."

Gregor didn't react; he'd probably already known. But Devona came forward and took my hand.

"I thought your skin looked a little grayer than when we first met, but I told myself it was just my imagination. It wasn't, though, was it?"

I shook my head.

"And you're spending the time you have left helping me." She sounded bemused, as if she couldn't quite bring herself to believe it.

I felt a need to tell her the truth. "My motives aren't unselfish. I was hoping that if we recovered the Dawnstone, you would intercede with Lord Galm on my behalf and ask him to help me make Papa a liar."

"So you haven't given up."

I smiled. "It's not in my nature."

"Then the prices you paid – a page from your life, bearing Edrigu's mark, losing your finger – you paid them even though you still intend to continue living. Uh, existing."

"Yes."

She nodded, as if in understanding, but of what I had no idea. She released my hand and turned back to face Gregor. "I shall pay this time."

"Actually," Gregor said, his antennae quivering as if he could barely contain himself, "since the information I've provided may benefit both of you – Devona, by helping recover the Dawnstone, and Matthew, by providing a chance to avoid discorporation – you must both pay."

"What?" Devona nearly shouted, setting Gregor's children to rustling nervously. "That isn't fair!"

Gregor leaned forward, and although nothing else in his attitude changed, I sensed a hint of menace in the motion. "This is my home. Here, I decide what is and isn't fair."

From behind us came a soft whispering, like a distant wave breaking on the beach. I turned to see Gregor's children had left the ceiling and the walls and were massing behind us.

I put a hand on Devona's shoulder. "It's okay. Information is the only coin he deals in."

"Quite so," Gregor affirmed.

Devona sighed. "Very well, then."

I looked behind us; the mound of Gregor's children was growing smaller as they returned to their places.

"Ms. Kanti, you shall pay first." Gregor settled back once more. "As Matthew told you, all that interests me

is information. But as I mentioned earlier, there are
some places in Nekropolis – only a few, mind you –
where my children have a difficult time venturing.
Among these places, as I indicated, is the Cathedral. I
want you to escort one of my children into Lord Galm's
stronghold and then, after a period of precisely one
month, escort it out again. You need do nothing else to
pay your debt to me."

Devona considered briefly, and then said, "Agreed."

"Excellent." Gregor did or said nothing more, but one
of his insects detached itself from the others and scurried up Devona's leg, over her waist and chest, along
her neck, across her jawline, and then darted into her
ear.

She screamed in pain and clapped her hand to the
side of her head. Blood trickled out from between her
fingers. She swayed and then fell to her knees.

I went to her and gently pulled her hand away from
her ear. I saw no sign of the insect and, thanks to her
half-vampire physiology, the wound of its passage was
already healing.

"I apologize. I should have made clear what I meant
by escort." Gregor chittered softly.

"If you've hurt her–"

"No need for dramatics, Matthew. My child must be
hidden inside Ms. Kanti in order to be able to penetrate
Lord Galm's wardspells. Despite the initial… unpleas-
antness of the process, she will not be harmed by
hosting my child, and when a month is over, it shall depart and Ms. Kanti's body will heal the minor damage

caused by its leavetaking." He rubbed four of his legs together, maybe in anticipation of soon gaining access to a place so long denied him.

"I'm all right, Matt," Devona said, sounding a bit shaky but otherwise unhurt. I helped her to stand. "It feels... odd," she said. "But that's all."

"All right, Gregor," I said. "My turn. Let me guess: you want me to carry one of your little spies too, so in case I do rot away to dust, I can ferry it over to the afterlife with me."

More chittering. "Hardly. You have only to answer one simple question for me, Matthew: how do you feel about being a zombie?"

FIFTEEN

"I don't know what you mean."

"Come now, Matthew, it's a simple enough question. How do you feel about being a zombie?"

"Why do you want to know?"

Gregor chittered loudly. "Why do I want to know anything? Because it is there to be known, because I do not already know. Because by knowing, I can perhaps come to understand."

"Understand what?"

"Everything, of course. But to answer your initial question more specifically, I wish to know because you are one of a kind, the only self-willed zombie in Nekropolis, perhaps the only one that has ever existed. And unlike normal zombies, you are aware and can provide valuable insight into your state of existence."

"I'd like to help you, Gregor, but I don't experience emotions the way I did when I was alive. I'm not sure I have any feelings about being a zombie."

Gregor's mandibles clacked together slowly – *tik-tik-tik-tik* – a gesture and sound which I'd come to know as a sign that the big bug was losing patience.

"Come now, Matthew. You forget to whom you are speaking. My children have watched you many times since your arrival in Nekropolis. You pretend to help people solely for monetary compensation in order that you might purchase preservative spells. But the lengths you go to in order to help them, the risks you take, indicate a man who is interested in far more than just collecting a paycheck."

"When I take on a job, I do it to the best of my abilities. That's how I am."

"And is that why you chose to help Lyra? She was a spirit, Matthew, and unable to pay you."

"Not true; I got to keep Honani's soul."

"Which you did not know would happen when you decided to aid Lyra. You helped her because you felt sorry for her and because her death filled you with righteous anger and you wanted to make her killer pay. You cannot deny it."

Gregor was right, I couldn't. "So?"

"So that proves you still feel, Matthew. Now answer my question and discharge your debt to me."

I looked at Devona and thought of what she had said to me in the alley where we'd discovered Varma's body. *If you don't feel anything, perhaps it doesn't have anything to do with your being a zombie. Perhaps that's who Matthew Richter really is – a man who was dead inside long before he died on the outside.*

Had she been right? Was that really who and what I was?

I heard the soft whisper of Gregor's children gathering behind.

"Matt–" Devona said warningly.

"How do I feel, Gregor? Even in Nekropolis I'm an oddity – a freak in a city of freaks – the only walking dead man with a mind of his own. And that mind is trapped in a body that's little more than a numb piece of meat. I can't feel warm or cold, can't feel the wind on my face. Can't smell, can't taste. I'm cut off from the world around me, on the outside of life, looking in and trying to remember what it was like to be a man, to be Matthew Richter, instead of just a pale memory of him.

"And now my undead body's preparing to betray me, getting ready to fall apart like so much overcooked chicken slipping off the bone. And despite my hope that Lord Galm might have the power to restore me and that he might deign to do so if I can help Devona recover the Dawnstone before I rot away completely, I'm still scared that none of it's going to matter, my body will cease to be and my spirit–" I showed the E on my palm to Gregor. "I suppose Lord Edrigu will get that."

I lowered my hand. "You want to know how it feels to be me, Gregor? Right now, it well and truly sucks. Satisfied?"

Gregor slumped against the wall, legs curled across his abdomen and stroking it slowly with a faint rustling sound as of a mass of dry twigs being rubbed together.

His attitude was that of a someone who has just had a very large and very good meal. Or great sex.

"Extremely. Thank you, Matthew. And good luck on your dual quests to locate the Dawnstone and discover a way to avoid your impending dissolution. I truly hope you succeed. Nekropolis is a far more interesting place with you inhabiting it."

I felt humiliated at having been forced to bare my soul for Gregor's amusement, and that Devona had been a witness. "I hope your next visitor is a very big can of sentient bug spray."

I turned to go, and Devona followed. Together, we walked up the temporarily insect-free stairs, Gregor's chittering laughter following us all the way.

We walked through the dilapidated streets of the Boneyard in silence for a time after that. The wraith images of the domain's inhabitants seemed to be sharper now, maybe because we'd moved further into the Boneyard, or maybe we were just getting used to them. A few tried to talk with us, but they made no sound, at least none we could hear, and after several moments of attempting to communicate by gesture, they gave up and drifted away.

When Devona finally spoke, she said, "What do we do now?" No mention of my embarrassing little scene back in Gregor's basement, for which I was quite grateful.

"We have several possible avenues of investigation at this point. We could try to find Morfran, the demon veinburn dealer; we could try to locate the drug lab the Arcane and the Dominari have set up in the Sprawl; or we could try to learn who hired the Red Tide vampires that killed Varma and tried to kill us."

As if on cue, a crimson mist rolled forth from a nearby sewer grate.

"No need to bust your rotting ass looking for us, zombie," Narda's voice drifted forth from the vermilion cloud. "We're right here."

The fog dissipated to reveal Narda, Enan, and the Giggler.

Enan raised his right hand. The fingers blurred and shifted, becoming five large hypodermic needles, the points glistening with liquid veinburn. He grinned. "Time to plug and play, Deadboy."

The vampiric trio looked the worse for wear since last I'd seen them, but not as much as I'd expected. There were still traces of burns on their faces and hands, but the worst injuries had been covered by patches of what appeared to be blue rubber that seemed to have bonded to their skin. Narda's missing eye hadn't regenerated; rather, in its place was a camera lens which protruded several inches from the socket. Their tech bodysuits, which had been short-circuiting as they fled from us in Gothtown, had been repaired, but sloppily – exposed wires, mismatched parts, metallic glops from hurried soldering. The suits sparked here and there, and the power hum was overloud and sounded a bit strained. I imagined the air contained the faint hot metal and plastic smell of machinery working too hard.

"The Boneyard isn't exactly your normal stomping grounds," I said. "How'd you find us?"

"We want to find someone, they're good as found," Narda said.

"You can't hide from the Tide," Enan added.

The Giggler giggled. Big surprise.

"What's with the blue gunk?" I asked. "New fashion statement?"

"Plaskin," Enan said. "Helps burns heal faster – even for Bloodborn – but they still hurt like a bitch." He gnashed his fangs, and his eyes blazed with anger. "But not as much as you're going to hurt before we finish you."

The Giggler lived up to his nickname once again, and I decided now was not the time to point out that my body was incapable of feeling any sensation, including pain. It would just make them more determined – and inventive.

"I'd have thought you'd be used to burns by now," I said. "After all, don't the crosses embedded in your foreheads burn your flesh?"

"Sure they do," Narda said. "They show the Red Tide's hardcore, and that we're not afraid of anything."

The Giggler let forth another peal of his high-pitched, girlish laughter. I was really getting tired of that sonofabitch. I bent down and picked up a broken brick from the worn and cracked street.

The Red Tide vampires laughed.

"What do you think you're gonna do with that?" Enan asked.

"This." Throwing isn't easy as slow as I am, but I've had plenty of practice. With a wind-up and then a half-throw, half-lurch, I hurled the makeshift missile as hard as I could at the Giggler's forehead. It struck the cross set into his flesh, driving it inward. The Giggler screamed and clawed at his forehead, but it was no good. The cross's corrosive effect on vampire flesh and bone, aided by the impact of my brick, had buried the holy object in his brain. Steam curled forth from the wound, and then rays of pure white light shot out of his eyes, ears, nostrils, and mouth. The light winked out and Giggler now had nothing but open ruins where his sensory organs had been. He stiffened and fell forward onto the broken pavement. I was confident he was dead, but I half expected him to start giggling again anyway.

"You worm-eaten motherfucker!" Narda shrieked.

For a moment, all Narda and Enan could do was stared in stunned amazement at the body of their fallen comrade – long enough to allow me to pull out my garlic and holy water squirt gun, which was mostly empty. But before I could start pumping the plastic trigger, Narda pointed and tendrils of wire shot forth to wrap themselves around Devona's arm.

"Put the gun down, Deadboy, or little Miss Leather here'll get a few million volts. Enough to fry her up good."

Vampires, for all their strengths, have a surprising number of weaknesses. Beyond the ones everyone knows about – sunlight, holy objects, wooden stakes –

are others such as silver and fire. Vampires aren't as flammable as zombies by any means, but fire can kill them.

I dropped the squirt gun to the ground with a plastic clatter.

"Kick it away."

I did.

Enan grinned. "Now we're going to have ourselves a little fun. Put your hands above your head, zombie, and step toward me slowly. Make any funny moves, and Narda turns your friend into charcoal. Got it?"

I nodded and did as he ordered.

"Stick out your arm," he commanded.

I did; I knew what was coming. "Veinburn won't work on me. I'm dead. All the way dead, not like you overgrown mosquitoes."

"Then you won't mind if I do this!" Enan plunged his needle fingers into the unfeeling flesh of my forearm. After a few moments, Enan yanked his hand away – tearing five ragged holes in my gray skin in the process – and the needles thickened into fingers once more.

"Well?" he asked. "How's it feel, deader?"

"I told you, I'm not–" I broke off, my body beginning to shake all over. I collapsed to the pavement not far from the Giggler's corpse, flipping and flopping like a fish tossed live into a frying pan.

"I'll be damned again!" Narda crowed. "This shit's even stronger than they said it is! Look at him go!"

"I bet that's the best he's felt in a loooooong time!" Enan laughed.

My exertions became so severe that I rolled over onto my stomach, and when I came around on my back again, I'd drawn my 9mm and leveled it at Narda's head. If I'd still been a cop, I'd have given her a warning. But I wasn't a cop anymore.

Two silver bullets apiece later, Narda and Enan had joined the Giggler on the ground. I stood, walked over to the bodies, reloaded, and pumped another couple rounds into their hearts, just to be sure.

Devona had untangled herself from Narda's wire. "I take it the veinburn didn't affect you. Nice acting job."

"What can I say? I was in drama club in high school." I examined the patches of plaskin on the forms of the dead vampires. I wondered if the substance might help fend off my decay, but I decided it probably wouldn't. The plaskin likely only worked on living tissue. No loss; I don't look good in blue anyway.

Devona gazed at the remains of the Red Tide members. "Makes it rather difficult to question them, doesn't it? Their being dead and all."

"You complaining?"

She smiled. "Not in the slightest. But it does narrow our options."

"The Red Tide has to get its technology somewhere, and the only Darklord enamored of technology is Varvara. But none of this strikes me as her style. Varvara's charming, fun, and she'd betray her best friend in a heartbeat if there was a laugh in it, but the Red Tide are too déclassé for her. My money's on the Dominari. They have the connections to import technology from

Earth and supply it to the Red Tide, and from what Gregor told us, the Dominari are involved in the manufacturing and testing of veinburn, which Enan possessed in abundance."

I put my gun away and shook my arm; it felt heavy and swollen. "Stupid vamps. Not only doesn't this stuff work on me, you'd think they'd have realized I'd need a functioning circulatory system to distribute it throughout my body."

"What will happen to the veinburn?"

"It'll just sit in my arm until I have it removed. Papa Chatha can do it for me. If I'm still around in a few days." As soon as I said the words, I regretted them. It was one thing to think those kind of morbid thoughts, another to voice them.

"Oh, Matt, I wish you had told me earlier."

"We only met a few hours ago, Devona. My situation has no bearing on your problem or on our efforts to resolve it." I paused. "Besides, I didn't want you worrying about me."

"That's sweet." And then she did something that surprised the hell out of me. She leaned forward and gave me a kiss on the cheek. I hadn't been kissed since I'd died, hadn't even really been touched – in a non-violent way, that is – by a woman.

I didn't know how to react, so I didn't. Just stood there and looked at her. Pretty smooth, huh?

"I want you to know something, Matt. No matter whether we find the Dawnstone or not, I intend to ask my father to help you."

Now I really didn't know what to say. But Devona didn't wait for a reply. "I assume we're off to the Sprawl again?"

I nodded. "To locate either Morfran or the drug lab." I smiled. "And I promise not to kill anyone else before we've had a chance to talk with them."

You know the old punchline? You can't get there from here. Nekropolis can be like that sometimes. To get back to the Sprawl, we had to either go through Glamere once more – definitely not an option – or pass through the Wyldwood, Dominion of Lord Amon, King of the Shapeshifters.

When I brought this up to Devona, she said, "Couldn't we take a shortcut across the grounds of the Nightspire?"

The Nightspire rests on a small island in the middle of the pentagram that is Nekropolis. This island is surrounded by the fiery waters of Phlegethon, the same waters which enclose the city and separate the five Dominions from each other. But in addition to the main bridges, there is a second set of smaller ones which connect each section of the city to the Nightspire. Devona's suggestion made sense on the surface. It would make our journey to the Sprawl far simpler and less deadly if we could walk from the Boneyard to the Nightspire, pass the bridge leading to the Wyldwood and take the one which led to the Sprawl.

"Unfortunately, it isn't that simple. During my time here, I've had occasion to travel a good bit of the city. I had the same idea as you a while back and tried to cross over one of the bridges to the Nightspire."

"What happened?"

"It didn't work. Powerful winds buffeted me, nearly knocking me into Phlegethon. When I retreated, the winds ceased. I later learned from Gregor that the wind, which he said was caused by the invisible Furies which guard the Nightspire, repels all who attempt to cross – not including the Darklords, of course – unless they are accompanied by one of Dis's representatives."

"So that's out then," Devona said. "And we can't risk another encounter with Lady Talaith."

"I'd rather not," I admitted.

"Which leaves only the Wyldwood."

"Talk about Scylla and Charybdis."

Her eyebrows rose. "I didn't realize you were so well read."

"Yeah, well, when you don't sleep, eat or go to the bathroom anymore, you have a lot of extra time for reading. Let's go. And on the way, maybe you can talk me out of it."

SIXTEEN

Before leaving the Boneyard, Devona and I discussed the best way to make it through the Wyldwood. Devona argued that the Accord which established unrestricted travel on the Obsidian Way would protect us in the Wyldwood, and so we should stay on it. I countered that might be true – *if* we were traveling in a vehicle, preferably a very fast one that could outpace a speeding lyke. But by walking completely unprotected out in the open, we would be marking ourselves as prey for every denizen in the Wyldwood. And Accord or no Accord, no lyke would pass up the opportunity to attack a pair of morons who wouldn't even bother trying to conceal their presence. As far as a lyke would be concerned, anyone that stupid deserved to have their flesh shredded into bloody gobbets.

"But the lykes will still be able to catch our scent, whether we're traveling on the Way or not," Devona said.

"Off the Way, we can move through the trees, and that will help mask our scent somewhat," I suggested. "Plus, my zombie… uh, *ambience* will seem more like rotting carrion in the woods, where there's less chance of lykes seeing me and realizing the smell is coming from a walking dead man. If they think I'm just the remnants of another lyke's kill, they'll leave us alone and go off in search of fresh prey."

In the end we compromised. We'd travel overland but stick as close to the Obsidian Way as possible, so we could return to it if necessary.

We crossed the Bridge of Silent Screams, left the Obsidian Way, and entered the dense tangle of forest that was the Wyldwood. We picked our way carefully through the underbrush, searching for a path and trying not to make too much noise lest we attract the attention of any lykes that might be nearby. Lykes were chaotic enough outside their Dominion, but here they were totally wild, killing on sight any who dared attempt to cross their land. Like I said, Devona and I made our way very carefully.

Despite the thickness of the forest, we could still see well enough. Some strange quality of Umbriel's shadowy light? Or maybe Lord Amon's magic was responsible. Whichever, I was grateful. Otherwise, I would have been totally dependent on Devona's vampire vision to lead me – and I don't like being dependent.

Still, being able to see didn't help us navigate. I'd been a city boy all my life and death, and Devona had spent most of her existence within the Cathedral and the surrounding environs of Gothtown. Neither of us was exactly a skilled outdoorsman. In order to make sure we didn't stray too far from the Obsidian Way, Devona had to climb trees a number of times to check the position of Umbriel and get a fix on our location. She went up with an easy grace and came down the same way, and watching her, admiring her strength and beauty, I felt a strange tightness in my chest. I told myself it was probably the result of the numerous injuries I'd sustained since taking on Devona's case, but I knew better.

After one such check, Devona climbed down from a large oak, a deep scowl on her face and said, "As near as I can tell, we've been going in circles – and I couldn't see any sign of the Way."

"Maybe there's some sort of enchantment on this Dominion that makes navigating difficult." I said this to make Devona feel better, but in truth I figured we two city kids had simply lost our way. I would've killed for a compass, but I'm not certain one would work in Nekropolis's dimension. I thought for a moment, trying to get my dead brain to cough up what little woodlore it knew. "Maybe we should start marking trees as we go, so at least we don't–"

Devona put a finger to her lips to shush me, and then she touched her ear. I listened, but I didn't hear anything. Devona's half-vampire hearing was far superior to mine, though, so I listened again, and this time I heard it: a soft rustling of leaves, not very far away and coming closer.

A lyke? I mouthed. The Wyldwood was home to many ordinary animals as well, all prey beasts for the lykes to hunt. Hopefully, what we heard was only a deer and not a savage shapeshifter come to gut us and feast on our entrails.

Devona shrugged then sniffed the air. At first she frowned, and then nodded, but she didn't seem all that certain. I wondered why, but knew now wasn't the time to ask. Something was coming, and whatever it was, I doubted it was the Welcome Wagon. I wished I'd given in to Devona earlier and stuck to the Obsidian Way like she'd wanted, but it was too late for regrets now. We headed off through the brush in the opposite direction of the rustling, trying to be as silent as we could, but being two city dwellers, I sure we failed miserably.

The rustling became a crashing as something loud bounded toward us. I pulled my 9mm out and rested my finger easily on the trigger. I only had five silver bullets left – not nearly enough to get us through the Wyldwood, but I couldn't worry about that now. Whatever it was came around our left and then approached from in front, slowing as it neared.

I aimed my weapon at the spot in the brush where I judged the lyke would appear and waited.

A few seconds later the leaves parted and I tightened my finger on the trigger. But then I paused as a six-foot white rabbit with yellow eyes stepped out of the underbrush.

"Don't tell me," I said. "You're late for a very important date."

The hare scowled. "Funny. But if she's Alice, then who the hell are you?" The voice was masculine, if a bit on the high side.

"I'm the guy who's got a gun full of silver bullets pointed at your chest. Please tell me you're not a carnivorous bunny."

The rabbit's large amber eyes fixed on my pistol, but his voice remained steady enough. "Who ever heard of such a thing?"

"This is Nekropolis, pal. A meat-eating rabbit would actually be rather mundane here."

"Good point. But no, I'm not a predator." He opened his mouth and displayed flat rabbit teeth. And then his form blurred and shifted until before us stood a thin, but still rabbity looking young man his mid-twenties, with an unruly shock of white hair and wearing nothing but a pair of overalls.

"Where did the pants come from?" I asked, curious. "I mean, you weren't wearing them before, and now here they are."

He shook his head as if I'd just asked the stupidest question imaginable. "Magic. A far better question is where did you two come from?"

I lowered my gun, but I didn't put it away. I wasn't ready to trust Bugs just yet. "The Boneyard."

He looked me over. "That I could've guessed." He wrinkled his nose. "And smelled."

"Sorry, but they don't make deodorant for zombies." I gave him an extremely truncated version of who Devona and I were and what we were doing here.

"You'd have been better off taking your chances with Lady Talaith. The Wyldwood is never a safe place for outsiders, but it's even more dangerous now."

"Why?" Devona asked.

The wererabbit opened his mouth to reply, but was cut off by the sound of horns echoing in the distance. Hunting horns.

"That's why. Today Lord Amon is conducting the Wild Hunt."

I sighed. "Of course he is." Why, I wondered to myself, are these things never easy?

The lyke, whose name turned out to be Arleigh ("It means 'from the hare's meadow,'" he said proudly), led us through the forest and to a vast stretch of pasture where cattle grazed contentedly beneath Umbriel's shadowlight.

"Here in the Wyldwood, we produce most of Nekropolis's meat and blood – real blood, not that synthetic glop Varvara's factories have started churning out." Arleigh said. "Well, animal blood, anyway. Cattle, sheep, goat... Non-preds like me tend the herds. The carnies are too impulsive for the work and usually end up killing and eating the animals themselves."

"You're a farmer?" Devona asked.

Arleigh nodded. "Most herbs like me are."

"So you lykes have a caste system?" I asked. "Doesn't seem fair."

Arleigh shrugged his lean, bony shoulders. "It suits

my nature, and I enjoy the work. What's wrong with that?"

I thought of my own work as a "doer of favors." In reality, I had to admit to myself, I was really still just a cop. *My* nature, I suppose. "Nothing wrong at all."

I noticed Devona was frowning, and I wondered if she was thinking about her own work as tender of Lord Galm's Collection.

"We're safe along the pastureland," Arleigh said. "The Hunt's conducted in the wilder part of the forest, using animals Lord Amon has specially bred at his Lodge." He lowered his voice. "I've heard it said that this year, he's using animals that have been... augmented."

"What, you mean through technology?"

He nodded.

"I guess it's everywhere," I said. I wondered how long it would be before Waldemar installed flesh computers in the Great Library and Gregor set up his own homepage on the Aethernet.

"Unfortunately," Arleigh said," the pastureland doesn't extend all the way to the Bridge of Forgotten Pleasures."

"Let me guess," I said. "The way we need to go is directly through the section of the Wyldwood where the Hunt's being conducted."

Arleigh nodded, and I sighed again. Never easy.

Arleigh offered to help us through the Wyldwood and I, distrusting soul that I am, wanted to know why. He puzzled over my question for a few moments before finally smiling apologetically. "The only reason I can give you is because it's the right thing to do."

I didn't buy it, but then twenty years as a cop and two as a zombie had made me a tad cynical. Maybe the lyke was just following his nature again. Whatever his reason for aiding us, we couldn't afford to turn him down.

Arleigh led us through the Wyldwood's pasturelands, but even though he assured us we were safe here, I kept my gun out. Just in case. Before long, however, we had to leave the pastureland and return to the forest. Arleigh thought he'd be able to lead us past the Hunt, but I could tell by the nervous way the lyke kept sniffing the air and looking around that he wasn't as confident as he would've liked us to believe.

We periodically heard the hunting horns, sometimes closer, sometimes farther. Arleigh told us not to worry overmuch about the horns, for sound traveled in deceptive ways in the forest.

Eventually, we reached a small clearing, and Arleigh said he needed to stop a moment and get his bearings. He crouched down, his nose shifted back to a rabbit's, whiskers and all, and he sniffed the ground.

A horn blasted, sounding close by. It was followed by the noise of something large and heavy crashing through the underbrush directly toward us. Arleigh stood, rabbit nose quivering in fear.

"We need to get out of here!" I told him. "Which way?"

But he only stood, transfixed, staring in the direction of whatever was approaching, and trembled. I grabbed his arm and shook him a couple times, but I couldn't break him out of his terror-induced trance. I figured to hell with him, then.

"C'mon, Devona, we have to–"

Before I could finish my sentence, an animal unlike any I had ever seen before bounded into the clearing. It looked something like a muscular ostrich, only with a thick neck and a large, cruelly hooked beak. No doubt one of the "augmented" animals the Hunt pursued. The bird skidded to a stop upon seeing us. It cocked its head and examined us, probably trying to determine if we were a threat or not.

Evidently, the answer was not, for it let forth an angry squawk and came charging at us, snapping its hook-beak.

I only had five silver bullets left, and I hated to waste them on the lyke's prey, but I couldn't let the giant bird attack us either. I aimed for the thing's throat, but before I could fire, a spear whizzed through the air and sunk into the creature's back with a meaty-moist *thuk!* The bird screeched in pain and pitched forward, where it lay writhing in the grass.

A huge wolfman stepped into the clearing, powerfully built, lupine head held high in a regal fashion. Lord Amon, I presumed. He was followed closely by a half dozen other lykes of various predator species, one of which – a humanoid bobcat – carried an antler horn slung over his shoulder by a leather strap. I was impressed by how silent the lykes had been – they hadn't made a sound.

I didn't need Arleigh to tell us we had stumbled across the Wild Hunt.

The bird, though bleeding profusely, was still very much alive, squawking and thrashing its powerful legs. The wolfman walked up to the animal and regarded it for a moment. I expected him to finish it off, but instead the wolf-headed humanoid padded over to us. I thought he might do any number of things, all of them involving his teeth and claws and our flesh, but he stopped in front of us and then did something I didn't anticipate and couldn't have imagined: he fell to one knee.

"I have downed the bird, my Lord. Would you do me the honor of dispatching it?"

At first, for some crazy reason, I thought the lyke was addressing me. But then Arleigh replied, "You have done well, Rolf. Rise and claim the honor for yourself." The wererabbit's voice was no longer high-pitched but low and resonant.

The wolfman stood and grinned. "Thank you, my Lord." Then he turned and loped toward the bird and, with a single savage bite and twist of his jaws, broke the animal's neck. He ripped off a hunk of meat, and walked away from the kill to devour it. The other lykes waited until Rolf was eating before rushing to the dead bird, snarling, yipping, and biting as they fought for the best of the remaining meat.

"My people have never been much for table manners," Arleigh said.

Devona and I turned toward him, but the rabbity man was gone; in his place stood a broad-shouldered, ruddy-faced man in full fox hunting regalia – little black hat, red jacket, white jodhpurs, shiny black boots, even a riding crop held in one black leather-gloved hand. But despite his transformation, the being still possessed the same yellow eyes as Arleigh.

"Allow me to introduce myself," he said with a touch of British accent. "I am Amon, Lord of the Wyldwood." He smiled, displaying a mouthful of sharp teeth. "So nice of you to drop by."

SEVENTEEN

"Forgive my little deception, but once I became aware of you, I thought it best to investigate. And the guise of Arleigh seemed a perfect way to do so."

"And what did you learn?" I asked. It appeared Amon wasn't limited to one wildform as were his subjects – which made sense seeing as how he was King of the Shapeshifters. Still, I was more than a little angry at myself for being fooled so easily. The yellow eyes should have been a tip-off. Who'd ever seen a rabbit with yellow eyes?

"What I needed to know: that you're not a threat sent by one of my fellow Lords. This time of year, we Darklords tend to be busy with certain preparations. So busy that we're more vulnerable than usual to each others' machinations." He smiled. "I myself have set in motion several plots against my peers over the centuries, most of them around the anniversary of the Descension. Unfortunately, none bore much fruit. We tend to be too evenly matched. Still, the fun is in the game, is it not?"

"I'm not a Darklord, so I wouldn't know," I said. Devona gave me a warning look, but I ignored her. The English gentleman act was getting on my nerves. "And speaking of preparations, shouldn't you be conserving your energy for the Renewal Ceremony? I'm surprised you're out hunting instead of meditating or something."

The English fox hunter guise melted away to be replaced by that of a khaki-clothed big-game hunter, complete with elephant gun. The English accent disappeared, too, to be replaced by gravely American. "We each prepare in our own way. Galm meditates, Talaith engages in rites with her people, Edrigu communes with the spirit world, and Varvara throws a lavish party. I have been marshaling my power for weeks now. Today I prepare my mind and soul by engaging in the activity which is at the very core of my being – the Hunt."

I nodded to the ravaged corpse of the huge bird. "It didn't look like you were doing much hunting to me."

Amon ignored the dig. "My sons and daughters always accompany me. This was Rolf's kill."

I looked at the lykes of varied species scattered about the clearing, all of whom were hunkered down, greedily devouring their shares of meat. "Nice family," I said dryly.

Frank Buck gave way to a yellow-eyed Daniel Boone, dressed in the requisite buckskin clothing and coonskin cap, complete with Kentucky accent. "What they lack in manners, they make up for in enthusiasm."

"You're a busy monster, so let's cut to the chase," I said. "What do you intend to do with us?"

"The story we told Arleigh – told you – is true," Devona added. "We're just trying to get back to the Sprawl. We're on an errand of great concern to my father, Lord Galm."

"I believe you," Amon said. "Though you provided few details, I could sense what you told me was indeed the truth."

I wondered how Amon could be so sure of that. Because of his heightened shapeshifter senses, which functioned as an organic lie detector? Or maybe through other abilities he possessed as a Darklord? Whichever, he did seem to believe us, which was the important thing.

Devona started to talk but Amon, who had become a tall, lean, spear-wielding African tribesman, silenced her with a gesture. "Details are unnecessary. Regardless of whether your errand is of major or minor importance, if your failure to complete it will inconvenience Galm, that's reason enough for me to keep you from continuing your journey."

I still held my 9mm at my side. I wondered if silver would prove effective against Amon, who was obviously much more than an ordinary lyke. The way things were going, it looked like I'd find out soon enough.

"But I have another reason to detain you. Two, actually. And their names are Honani and Thokk."

I groaned inwardly and was uncomfortably aware of the soul jar containing Honani's spirit – which now seemed suddenly very heavy – still resting in my jacket pocket.

"Mr. Richter, you are responsible for Honani's body being taken over by another, and for the grievous injuries inflicted on his sister when she tried to seek justice."

"Vengeance," I corrected.

Amon, now a Native American brave, shrugged. "A mere difference in terminology. Honani and Thokk turned to science to alter their natural abilities. As such, they are outcasts among my people."

I gestured toward the nearly picked clean carcass of Big Bird. "You don't seem completely adverse to science."

"It has its uses," Amon admitted. "Provided it isn't taken too far. Still, even though mixbloods possess corrupted genes, they are shapeshifers and thus still family. You have transgressed against two of my subjects. As Lord of the Wyldwood, I have a responsibility to my people to see that justice is done." He smiled. "Or, if you prefer, vengeance."

I preferred neither in this case, but I kept my mouth shut.

Rolf had finished eating and walked over to us. "These two aren't worthy of your attention, Father." He licked blood off his muzzle. "Especially the zombie. Allow me to slay them for you so that you might not dirty your hands."

Amon, now a shaggy caveman holding an animal's jawbone in one of his thick-knuckled hands, affectionately cuffed his child. "You've had your fun, Rolf. Now it is your father's turn."

Rolf bowed his head and stepped back.

I wondered what the odds were of my squeezing off a shot at Amon before one or more of his children fell upon me. Not good, I decided.

Then I had an idea. I raised my left hand and displayed the mark upon my palm. "My master, Lord Edrigu, will be displeased if anything should happen to us."

Amon looked at the mark for a moment and then burst out laughing. "That symbol merely means that Edrigu has laid a claim on your soul, zombie. I'm sure he'd be happy to collect it earlier than anticipated."

"Then what of my father?" Devona said in her best haughty-regal voice. "I am not just his daughter; I am also the keeper of his Collection. He would be furious if any harm were to come to me or my companion."

She sounded convincing enough, but I could tell by the uncertain look in her eyes that she wasn't sure that Lord Galm would be all that upset if his half-breed daughter died in the Wyldwood. I felt sorry for her then. What would it be like to have known a father for over seventy years, to have taken care of his Collection for nearly thirty, to have worked hard for him in hope of some simple recognition and still not know whether he cared if you lived or died?

Maybe Amon sensed her uncertainty as well, for after a moment's thought, he said, "You have aided in an assault on one of my subjects and trespassed on my Dominion. Galm cannot gainsay my right to justice."

Amon shimmered and was now a beer-gutted, flannel-shirted, John Deere-capped, shotgun-toting hunter, complete with chewing tobacco juice dribbling down his stubbled chin.

"But as it's the anniversary of the Descension and we are in the middle of the Wild Hunt, I shall make you a proposition." He turned his head and spit a brown stream into the grass. "Several miles from here is a small glen. You will be taken there and set free. All you need do is reach the other side, and I shall let you continue on your way to the Sprawl and will seek no further action against you for what happened to Honani and Thokk."

"And the catch is?" I asked.

Amon smiled, displaying tobacco-stained fangs. "I shall be hunting you."

"You have been given a great honor," Rolf said. He and his feral siblings escorted us through the forest, Rolf leading, the others enclosing us in a circle.

"Yeah, it's a dream come true," I replied.

He snarled and his clawed hands tensed. I'm sure he would've taken my head off if we hadn't been his father's prey. Before we'd set out, Rolf had taken my gun from me and now carried it in his left hand. Lykes are highly allergic to silver, but my bullets were safely encased within the gun, allowing him to hold it without harm. Still, I thought I could detect a slight swelling of his hand. I was surprised and puzzled that the lykes hadn't gotten rid of my gun as soon as they'd taken it from me. But when we reached the glen, I understood why.

"The hunt shall begin as soon as we depart," Rolf said solemnly. "My father, in deference to your weakness, shall give you a head start." His sharp-toothed smile reminded me of Amon. "How much of a head start, however, you shall not know." He pointed a clawed finger toward the other side of the glen. "The rules are simple. Reach the other side and your lives will be spared. Fail to do so, and you die."

He dropped my gun to the ground. "Once we are gone, you may pick up your weapon and begin." Before we could ask any questions, Rolf and the others bounded away into the forest, moving through the underbrush with silent, liquid grace.

I retrieved my gun and checked the clip. The five silver bullets were still there.

"It seems Lord Amon doesn't believe in hunting defenseless prey," Devona said.

"Or that he isn't as vulnerable to silver as an ordinary lyke. Let's get moving; the clock's ticking."

As soon as we stepped into the glen, it became night. I don't mean the perpetual dusk created by the diffuse shadowlight of Umbriel; I mean honest-to-God night, with stars and everything. Despite our situation, I was so surprised that I stopped and stared overhead. They were the first stars I had seen in two years, and they were beautiful.

For an instant I had the dizzying sensation that we had somehow stepped through an unseen door between Nekropolis and Earth – that I was home.

"Are those stars?" Devona asked, her voice soft with wonder. "I've heard about them, but I've never actually seen any before. They're lovely – and so far away. They make me feel small, and yet somehow big at the same time. Does that make any sense?"

"It makes perfect sense. But they can't be real stars. What we're looking at is most likely an illusion, a distraction designed to slow us down."

"You're right, of course. I'll lead the way; my night vision is better than yours." She took my hand and pulled me forward.

"And keep a nose out for Amon. We don't know what form he'll be wearing when he attacks, but it has to have a scent."

"Right."

We ran. The grass was slick with dew, and the sound of crickets chirping filled the air. I knew it was all just special effects supplied courtesy of Amon, but a wave of homesickness hit me hard, and I thought that if I had to die for good, I could pick far worse places in Nekropolis.

We continued forward, Devona's gaze fixed unwaveringly on the opposite treeline, her heightened senses alive and alert; I held my gun at the ready, my comparatively weak vision and hearing working overtime, cop instincts on full.

Moments that felt more like hours passed, without any sign of the master of the Wyldwood.

"Why is Amon even bothering to stalk us?" Devona said in frustration. "He's a Darklord, one of the six most powerful beings in the city, including Father Dis. How can we possibly provide him with a real challenge?"

"I don't know much about Amon, but I've heard it said he gets as much pleasure from swatting flies as he does from stalking big game. To him, the hunt is everything."

Devona started to reply, but then she suddenly squatted down, yanking me along with her so hard I felt something pull in my arm. I heard rather than felt something large pass through the air above us, approximately where our heads had been. A shrill cry of frustration sounded, followed by the flapping of wings as whatever it was began gaining altitude for another run.

"Looks like our head start's over," I muttered, scanning the night sky for Amon. I looked for a black patch against the stars, but whichever shape Amon was wearing, he was moving too fast for me to locate him. And then I heard something large whistling through the air and Devona screamed.

The starlight didn't provide much illumination, but it was enough for me to see that Devona was struggling with a large bird – an eagle or maybe a condor; it was difficult to tell in the dark. Whichever the particular avian, I knew it really was Amon. I raised my gun, but didn't dare fire for fear of hitting Devona.

"Throw him off you so I can get a shot!" I shouted.

Devona grabbed the bird by the wings and hurled him forward. It was dark, the bird was moving fast, and my reflexes are not nearly as good as they were when I was alive. But I didn't worry about any of that. I squinted my left eye, aimed, and squeezed off a shot.

The bird shrieked and hit the ground with a heavy thump. I held my gun on it, waiting for it to stir, but it didn't move. Without taking my eyes off it, I asked Devona if she was all right.

"A few cuts on my face, a couple fairly deep. Messy, but otherwise I'm unharmed. I should heal before too long."

The bird remained motionless, but I didn't lower my gun an inch; I knew better. "He was probably going for your eyes. Makes sense, since you're the only one of us who can see in the dark."

"Is he dead?" she asked.

"What do you think?"

"I think a Darklord doesn't die this easily."

"I think you're right." I moved toward the bird slowly, keeping my gun trained on it the entire time. It didn't so much as move a feather as I approached and stood over it.

"What kind is it?" I asked.

"An eagle, I think," Devona answered. "I've only seen them in books, though."

I carefully toed the eagle and its body collapsed into dust. I bent down, intending to get a closer look, but within seconds, the dust too was gone.

"Perhaps we got lucky," Devona suggested.

"I don't believe in luck." I stood. "We'd better–" My sentence was cut off as a snarling piece of darkness detached itself from the night and slammed into me, knocking me to the ground, spitting and clawing. Ivory fangs glinted in the starlight as the panther buried its teeth in the undead flesh of my neck.

But as sudden and hard as the impact had been, I still had hold of my gun. As the big cat worried my neck, I calmly raised my pistol to its head, pressed the muzzle against its black fur, and fired.

The panther let out a cry and fell limp.

"Devona, could you help haul this thing off me?" I asked. "It's pretty heavy. Oh, and be careful. Its teeth are still lodged in my neck."

Together we got the panther off without much additional damage to my already ravaged neck. Devona then helped me to my feet, and I noticed that my head was canted to the left. I tried to hold it upright, but it wouldn't stay. One more repair to add to the list for Papa Chatha – if I found a way to survive past the next couple days.

"Matt, your neck…" Devona sounded concerned and, although she was trying to hide it, mildly disgusted. She knew intellectually that I was a zombie, but I think this was the first time she'd really understood what that meant.

"It may look bad, but believe me, I'm okay. Now let's check out Sylvester here." I kicked the kitty corpse as I had the eagle's, with the same result: it collapsed into dust.

"Amon must be cheating," Devona said indignantly, "sending other shapeshifters in his place."

"I don't think so. Lykes don't disintegrate like this when they're killed. I think we have been fighting Amon, but he's a far different kind of shapeshifter than his subjects. When we shoot him, we kill the body he's wearing at the time – not him."

"You mean he discards his shape, leaves it behind?"

"Like a snake shedding his skin. He'll keep coming at us in different forms until I've used up my three remaining silver bullets. And then he'll have us."

"Not if we can get to the other side of the glen first," Devona said.

"I've been meaning to talk to you about that. We ran for a while before Amon attacked, right?"

"Yes, I'd estimate for perhaps five minutes."

"Me too. And in that time, we should've been able to cover a significant amount of ground, right?"

She nodded warily.

I pointed in the direction we had come, toward the line of trees where Rolf had left us – trees that were only a few feet away. "Then how come we haven't moved?"

EIGHTEEN

"No wonder Amon steered us to this glen," Devona said. "It's enchanted."

"I hate Darklords," I said. "I really do."

"I don't know if we've been running in place, running in circles, running in a straight line through warped space, or have been standing still and just think we've been running."

As an experiment, I stepped back to the treeline – keeping an eye out for Amon's next attack, of course. I didn't seem to have any trouble getting there. I even reached out and touched the trunk of an elm. I looked back and saw Devona standing several feet away.

"Start walking."

She did, and it was the oddest thing. On one hand, she appeared to be walking away from me, but on the other, she seemed to stay in place. It was as two different films were being played at once on the same screen.

"Keep walking, but look back over your shoulder," I called. "And tell me what you see."

"All right." A pause. "This is strange; I appear to be moving away from you, but at the same time you seem to be almost right next to me."

"Okay, stop walking."

My vision lurched, and I experienced a dizzying moment of vertigo that might very well have nauseated me if I still had a working stomach. The far-off image of Devona was gone, and only the close-up Devona remained.

I returned to her side. "Well, that didn't help any." I scanned the sky and ground for any sign of Amon, but there was none. Maybe he had to recover, build up his strength again from having been shot twice. Or maybe he was just enjoying our confusion over the nature of his glen.

"No, it helped a great deal," she said. "The effect we experienced is similar to that of certain wardspells which operate by making someone believe he is walking toward the object warded, when in reality he cannot approach it."

"So how do we break the spell?"

"I said this spell is similar; I didn't say it was the same. We're talking about a spell laid by a Darklord. Even if I had the mystical ability to circumvent the normal version of this spell – and remember, my father made certain I was trained only in the monitoring of wardspells, not the laying or breaking of them – I couldn't begin to touch the enchantment on this glen."

"Just because Amon cast this spell doesn't mean it can't be broken. The Darklords can't afford to waste much power on such trifles as this, can they? They have the Renewal Ceremony to think about, let alone trying to defend themselves from each other. Maybe you didn't receive any formal training in getting around wardspells, but that doesn't mean you can't extrapolate from what you did learn. And if a person knows how a lock works, he stands a good chance of picking it."

"But I'm not a magicworker," Devona protested. "I'm a curator, and I suppose really little more than a glorified security guard."

I sighed. "Look, I'd like to do this gently, but we don't have time. What you are, Devona, is a half-breed vampire who gets her entire sense of sense of self-worth from basically dusting another man's treasures. Because of the way you were brought up and the attitude of other vampires toward your mixed heritage, you feel that being the keeper of your father's Collection is all you can do, that there isn't any more to you.

"But in the short time I've known you, I've seen much more. I've seen a woman who when faced with danger doesn't run, doesn't back away – she fights. I've seen a woman who when faced with a problem doesn't give up – she keeps working at it until she finds a solution. I've seen a woman who's intelligent and caring... and," I said softly, "who sees the man inside me, the man I thought had died along with his body. I've seen a woman who, having ventured beyond her tightly circumscribed life, is starting to find out who she really is and what she's truly capable of. Well, it's time to find out some more, Devona. It's time to find us a way out of here."

I didn't know how she'd react: tell me to go to hell, start crying, or haul off and belt me. Maybe all three. But she just looked at me for a long moment, her expression blank, eyes unreadable in the dark. And then she nodded.

"Let's start walking again. I need to examine the spell while it's functioning." She headed off without waiting for my reply.

I smiled as I hurried after her. Wholly human or not, she was some woman.

While we walked and walked and got nowhere, Amon came at us again, this time in the more classic form of a large gray wolf. He managed to take a hunk out of my right leg before I dispatched him, or rather, his shape.

Two bullets left.

"I have an idea," Devona said not long after Amon's wolf facade had disintegrated. "I'm not sure it'll work, though."

"I'm rapidly running out of ammunition. Anything's worth a try at this point."

"I don't have the mystical training to break the spell, but I do think I understand how it's constructed. It's really very simple, a mere matter of aligning psychothaumaturgic energy structures in a constantly rotating–"

"In simple English, please, for the magically challenged among us."

She grinned. "Sorry. Basically, the spell works by constantly assaulting our minds with false sensory input. The trick to overcoming such a spell is to block out the false input so that our senses can detect reality once more."

"Sounds like quite a trick."

"It is. But I think I know how we might accomplish it. Remember I said that as half Bloodborn I possess a certain amount of psychic ability? While I haven't been trained in its use, I believe I may be able to sense in which direction the Sprawl lies by focusing on the combined mental energy of all the celebrants there. Ordinarily, I might not be able to accomplish such a feat, but this time of year there are so many people crowding the streets of the Sprawl and the emotional atmosphere is so charged, that even with my untutored powers I should be able to get a fix on it. And once I know where the Sprawl is–"

"You'll be able to shut out the glen's spell and lead us across," I finished. Earlier, I'd been wishing for a compass. Now it looked like Devona had found us a psychic equivalent.

"There's a problem, though," she said.

I smiled. "Only one?"

"You'll still be affected by the spell."

"Why is that a problem? You can guide me."

"And if Amon attacks and we become separated?"

"You can use your powers to locate me."

"I don't know if I can maintain my fix on the Sprawl and locate you at the same time. And even if I could, Amon might take the opportunity to finish one or both of us off while I'm looking for you." She shook her head. "No, it would be better if we both were able to home in on the Sprawl."

"That would be nice, but I'm afraid a set of psychic powers wasn't included in my zombie membership kit."

"You don't need powers of your own; we can link minds. That way you'll be able to sense what I sense."

"Link minds?" I tried to imagine what it would be like to have my mind joined with someone else's, but I couldn't. The closest I could come to was some sort of psychic equivalent to a phone connection, and somehow I doubted it would be like that.

Devona must have sensed my reluctance because she hurried to add, "I really believe it's the only way."

It wasn't like we had a lot of options to choose from. "Have you ever linked with anyone before?"

She looked down at the ground, and when she answered, she sounded embarrassed. "I've had a few Shadows of my own over the years. And I've linked with some of them."

She said *Shadows* but the word I heard was *lovers*. I don't know why it bothered me – we were both adults, and Devona was older than I, in her seventies chronologically. And for that matter, I was a zombie. I had no business being jealous – but I was.

"Will it work on me?" I asked. "However my brain functions, I'm sure it's not the same as a living man's."

"I don't know, Matt. We'll just have to try."

I didn't like the idea of anyone invading my mind, no matter who it was. But it didn't look like I had a choice. "Okay. But we'd better hurry before Amon attacks again."

Without another word, Devona reached out with both hands and placed her fingers lightly on the sides of my head. I wondered what her touch felt like.

Nothing happened at first, and I was afraid that my zombie mind wasn't capable of linking with a living one, when all of a sudden a warm, bright light flashed behind my eyes. And then I felt Devona inside me.

There are moments in every person's life when they feel close to someone else. It could be something as simple as a shared look, a moment when you exchange glances and know that each understands the other perfectly. Or it could be a joke that you share, one that always makes the two of you break up even though no one else around you ever seems to get it. Holding hands while walking at sunset; running your fingers slowly, gently along each other's skin after making love; hugging each other tight, bawling like babies as your hearts are breaking.

Being linked with Devona was all of these things and more.

It had been so long since I had felt this close to another person – no, I had never felt this close to another person: not any of my friends, not my ex-wife, not even my partner Dale. And I didn't know whether to feel joy at this sharing of souls with Devona, or sadness because I had never allowed myself to experience it before.

And then I looked to the far side of the glen, and although it didn't appear any different than before, somehow I could tell that it wasn't very far away at all. Only a few minutes' run at most.

Race you, Devona said in my mind.

Not with the hunk Amon took out of my leg, I responded. How about a fast walk?

You're on, she thought playfully, and we set off.

Together.

I expected Amon to attack just as we reached the other side, but he didn't. We stepped out of the glen, through the trees, and then the night sky and stars vanished, to be replaced once more by Umbriel and the featureless gray-black sky it hung in.

And there, not more than fifty feet away, lay the Obsidian Way and the Bridge of Forgotten Pleasures, the crossing point from the Wyldwood to the Sprawl. We'd done it.

Without thinking about it, Devona and I hugged each other. Linked as we were, the gesture was automatic and completely natural, a physicalizing, however imperfect, of the closeness that we shared.

And then the link dissolved and one became two again.

Devona stepped back. "I'm sorry. I was so excited to see the bridge, I lost concentration."

"That's okay. The link had served its purpose anyway." I had never felt more alone in my existence. I felt like half of my soul had been ripped away. And yet, an echo of Devona remained inside me, the merest trace, like a memory of shared laughter, or a kiss that lingers on the lips long after your lover has departed.

I reached out and took Devona's hand. "Let's get out of here before Amon comes after us." I led her toward the bridge.

"But he said we'd be free if we made it across the glen."

A guttural voice came from behind us. "I lied."

I whirled around to see a massive yellow-eyed grizzly bear standing on all fours at the edge of the glen. Amon roared and charged. I raised my gun to fire, but before I could pull the trigger, the bear was upon us.

With a powerful blow of his huge paw, Amon knocked the 9mm out of my hand. It flew through the air, struck the ground, and discharged. It would have been nice if the bullet had happened to strike Amon, but it went flying off into the trees, wasted.

One bullet left.

Devona leaped onto the bear's back and grabbed double handfuls of its coarse brown fur. She then bared her fangs and sank them into the beast's back, using them like knives, slashing and tearing at Amon's ursine flesh.

Amon bellowed in pain and reared up on his hind legs. He tried to shake Devona off, but she clung to his back as if she were the world's largest and most determined tick. Amon then tottered toward the bridge in the stumpy-legged gait bears have when walking erect.

I ran – well, given the state of my chewed-up right leg, I half-ran, half-hobbled – toward my gun. I retrieved it, and galumphed toward the Bridge of Forgotten Pleasures.

Amon had crossed onto the bridge, and technically Devona and he were no longer in his Dominion. But he didn't show any sign of stopping his attack, and I didn't expect him to.

Devona continued ripping away at Amon's flesh. Her face was covered with blood, and she looked as savage and wild as the bear she battled. It was hard to reconcile this Devona with the one I'd so recently been linked to. But I didn't have time to think about that. Amon had backed up against the iron railing and his form began to shimmer and change.

So far he had only come at us in one shape at a time, and although that had never been spelled out as part of the deal, I'd assumed it was. Looked like I was wrong.

His interim form resembled a blurry amoeba, and Devona was having a tough time holding on. In a flash, I understood what he was going to do: he intended Devona to lose her grip on his fluid transitional form and fall into Phlegethon. If the river's mystic green flame didn't kill her, the Lesk which swam within it surely would.

"Devona, jump!" I shouted as I raised my gun and fired.

The last silver bullet struck Amon in the chest – or rather where his chest would have been if he'd been solid – just as Devona launched herself up and over the Lord of the Wyldwood. Devona landed easily on the bridge as the amoebic Darklord pitched backward over the rail and plummeted soundlessly toward Phlegethon's fiery green embrace.

I tucked my empty gun into my shoulder holster and hurried over to Devona. She was covered with blood, but it was impossible to tell if any of it was hers.

"Are you okay?"

She wiped a smear of blood from her mouth and nodded. "Do you think it's over?"

"It's possible Amon is more vulnerable in his transitional state and the last silver bullet did him in."

"Do you believe that?"

"I believe Darklords are very hard to kill. Let's get out of here before–"

A gigantic reptilian head rose up before us, fiery green water trickling down its black-scaled hide.

"Too late, zombie." The voice of Amon's British hunter guise, the one that annoyed me so much, boomed out of the Lesk's serpentine mouth. I'd never seen one of the great beasts close up before, only the black lines of their backs as they plied the waters of Phlegethon. The creature was far larger than I had imagined, and looked something like a snake encased in black armor. Its brow was spiked, and it had a row of bony serrated triangles running down its back. And of course it possessed Amon's feral yellow eyes – eyes full of fury and hunger.

"Let us go, Amon!" I shouted. "We played by the rules of your challenge and beat you, fair and square!"

Amon laughed, a harsh, brittle sound, as of a thousand bones breaking.

"The Hunt has only a single rule, little man: victory belongs to the strongest and swiftest." He hissed and his jaws opened wide in preparation to devour us.

"What of Honani, Darklord?" I yelled.

Amon paused and narrowed his basketball-sized eyes.

I reached into my jacket and removed the soul jar. "This container is what I used to draw Honani's spirit from his body. Honani remains inside. All I have to do to release him is pry open the lid." I gripped the lid in my fingers. "If I do, his spirit will be set free to wander Nekropolis for eternity. Or maybe he'll end up in the Boneyard as one of Edrigu's servants."

Amon's head swayed slowly back and forth as he regarded me.

"You told us earlier that despite being a mixblood, Honani was still one of your subjects – one of the family, as you put it." I gave the jar a shake. "Well, here he is, Amon. Are you going to abandon him just because his body now belongs to another?"

Amon hissed softly. "How do I know you're telling the truth?"

"How did you know it when you pretended to be Arleigh?" I countered.

Amon considered. "Very well," he said at last. "Place the jar on the bridge and you may go."

"Nothing personal, but I'd rather keep it with us until we reach the other side, if it's all the same to you."

Amon laughed again, and I was surprised to hear no malice in it. "Go on, then!"

We backed toward the Sprawl side of the bridge, keeping our eyes on Amon the entire way. When we reached the far side, Amon touched his serpent's nose to the bridge and flowed into his English hunter body.

I set the jar on the bridge and Amon gave me a little salute. "Well played, Mr. Richter. Well played, indeed. I haven't enjoyed a Wild Hunt this much in decades."

"I'm glad you liked it," I said wryly. And Devona and I turned and hurried into the Sprawl before the lord of the shapeshifters could change his mind.

From now on Amon would have to add a corollary to his rule about the Hunt: sometimes victory doesn't go to the strongest or swiftest. Sometimes it goes to a desperate dead man with deep pockets.

NINETEEN

"So that's the infamous House of Dark Delights," De-vona said, sounding less than impressed.

The Sprawl's best-known brothel was located on the southeast end of Sybarite Street, and the Descension Day celebrating was a bit more subdued here, mostly because by this time a majority of partiers lay on the sidewalks, in the gutters, and in the alleys, unconscious or worse, robbed of whatever darkgems they'd had in their pockets, and more than likely missing several pints of bodily fluids and an organ or two. At least it was easier to get around in this neighborhood for those us who remained ambulatory – if you didn't mind stepping over all the bodies, that is.

The House sat between a casino called, ominously enough, Bet Your Life, and a soul-modification parlor (slogan: *When you've done everything to your body that you possibly can*) called Spiritus Mutatio. The House of Dark Delights was a pleasant-looking three-story building painted white, with green shutters and matching shingles. There, the dark is all on the inside.

The facial lacerations Amon had given Devona were almost completely healed by now, after snacking on a couple blood-ices she'd purchased from a street vendor along the way.

"It doesn't seem very well protected – especially for this part of town," she said. "No fence surrounding the place, no bars on the windows…"

"You're good with wardspells, right?" I said. "Try checking out its magical defenses."

Devona closed her eyes and concentrated. A few seconds later her eyes snapped open, and she looked at me with an expression of shock. "The spells protecting the building are almost as strong and complex as those warding my father's Collection!"

I smiled. "Bennie doesn't like to take any chances."

"Bennie?"

"The owner and operator," I said. "I just use Bennie. It's makes things easier."

Devona gave me a puzzled look, and I told her she'd understand soon enough. As Devona had pointed out, there's no fence around the House of Dark Delights, and we strolled up the front walk, onto the porch, and I knocked on the door. The first time I'd come here, no one had warned me to knock first. I made the mistake of reaching for the doorknob, and as soon as my undead flesh came in contact with the metal, I found myself blasted across the street and through the front window of Les Escargot, a gourmet restaurant run by giant snails. The food's supposed to be great, but you wouldn't believe how slow the service is.

The door opened, and an extremely large and muscular mixblood lyke was glaring down at us – one that I knew well. After all, I'd seen him, or at least his body, walking out of Skully's only several hours ago.

"Lyra?" I said hopefully. I was thinking of how I'd traded the soul jar containing Honani's spirit to Amon for our freedom. Had the Darklord used his powers to force out Lyra's essence and return Honani to his rightful body?

The mixblood glared at us for a moment longer before dissolving into a fit of giggling. "Darn it! I knew I wouldn't be able to keep a straight face!"

I started to sigh in relief, but Lyra scooped me up and gave me a vicious hug, squeezing the rest of the air out of my lungs. When she put me down, I half expected to collapse to the porch in a mass of dead flesh and shattered bone. But luckily my skeletal system had withstood Lyra's affectionate embrace, if only just.

"What are you doing here, Matt? And who's your friend? She's cute!" Lyra turned to Devona and started to smile, but she frowned instead. "Hey, didn't I see you at Skully's when I walked out? I was kind of muzzy-headed from the transfer into this body, so maybe I'm wrong, but I could've sworn–"

"I was there," Devona confirmed.

"After you left Skully's, Devona asked me to help her out with a problem, Lyra. We're here because I think Bennie might be able to help us."

"Sure – come on in!" Lyra stepped aside so we could enter. When we were inside, Lyra closed to the door and even I, without any mystical training whatsoever, could sense a battery of defensive spells activating.

"So you decided to return to your old, uh, stomping grounds?" I asked Lyra.

Lyra grinned with Honani's mixblood mouth, and though she displayed a truly intimidating array of teeth, she still somehow managed look cute.

"More than that, I've got a new job! Bennie made me a bouncer!" Lyra flexed her right arm, and her new mixblood muscles bulged impressively.

I couldn't help laughing. "Perfect!"

"I know! Bennie's the best, aren't they? They also offered to get me an appointment with Dr. Moreau at the House of Pain to see if he might be able to give my new body a sex change, but I think I'm going to keep it as is for now. I always wanted to see how the other half lives, and I now I've got my chance!"

Devona looked at me. "They?"

"It'll all make sense soon. Trust me."

Lyra led us through the foyer and into the lounge which, as usual, was filled with customers waiting for appointments to begin, restocking on fluids between assignations, or bragging about their performance to their companions afterward. The lounge was decorated like a tasteful upscale neighborhood tavern back on Earth: black lacquer tables and chairs, a small kitchen which served appetizers and snacks, and – instead of flat-screen TV's – giant Mind's Eye devices were mounted on the walls, the orbs broadcasting news coverage of Descension Day activities throughout the city. But the heart of the lounge was undeniably the large circular bar in the middle of the room. The bartenders on duty could mix any type of drink you wanted, but every one of them was Arcane and their true specialty was potion-making. They could create any manner of aphrodisiac or performance-enhancing substance imaginable, and many that were beyond imagination, even in Nekropolis.

Every table in the lounge was taken by men and women representing all the races the city has to offer – Bennie doesn't believe in discrimination when it comes to love, or the reasonable facsimile on the menu at the House of Dark Delights – and it looked like Devona and I were going to have to stand. But Lyra escorted us over to a table where two vampires I recognized were playing a holographic game of bloodshards.

The male looked up as we approached, his holo-eye implants switching over to normal vision, and he groaned when he got a good look at us, or more specifically, at me.

"Not you again! My sister and I just want to be left alone to play in peace!"

"And that's all you've been doing for the last four hours" Lyra said. "This lounge is reserved for paying customers, Reshem. I let you slide because of the trouble Matt and I caused you at Skully's earlier, but now I have to ask you to take your game elsewhere."

The female vampire switched her implants over to regular vision then too, and the holographic game pieces vanished. "But this is the only place we've able to find where a fight hasn't broken out within ten minutes of our arrival," she protested. "We figured it would be safe to play here because the customers aren't interested in fighting."

Her brother grinned. "Because they have other activities on their mind."

Lyra put her large clawed hands onto the table and went into her pissed-off mixblood routine, teeth bared, brow furrowed, growl rumbling deep in her throat.

The male vampire sighed. "All right, we're going. Come, Halina, let's try the restaurant across the street. We should be able to get in at least a dozen games before the server arrives to take our drink orders."

The vampire siblings left, and Lyra gestured to the now empty table. "If you'd like to take a seat, I'll go find Bennie and tell her you want to talk to her. I'll have someone come over and get you something to drink while you wait." Lyra gestured to one of the servers, gave us a last smile, and then turned to go.

We sat and watched Lyra make her way back to the foyer, everyone in her path stumbling over one another to get out of her way. Lyra acted as if she didn't notice, but I knew she loved every minute of it.

"I think that girl has a bright future ahead of her in the nuisance-deterrent business," Devona said.

I couldn't help but agree.

While waited for a server to come over, Devona glanced around the lounge, taking everything in. She frowned. "All these people... the place hardly seems large enough to accommodate them all. As big as the lounge is, I don't see how they have any space left over for rooms."

"That's because only part of the House of Dark Delights is aboveground," I said. "There are seven levels beneath us, each more, ah, intense than the last."

Devona raised an eyebrow and I hastened to add, "Or so I've been told. I've never actually had the opportunity – or the desire – to explore beyond the lounge."

Devona smiled, obviously enjoying my discomfort. "Sure, Matt. Whatever you say."

A white-furred werecat server wearing an almost nonexistent black leather bikini came over and asked if we'd like anything to drink – on the house. I politely declined, but Devona ordered a glass of aqua sanguis. The server winked at me as she left, swishing her tail a bit more strictly than necessary as she headed toward the bar. I noticed Devona scowling.

"Why Ms. Kanti, if I didn't know better, I might think you were actually jealous."

Devona laughed just a little too loudly. "*Right*. As if I would be jealous of a cheap little thing like. Doesn't she realize that six breasts is just overkill?"

"You're right: you don't sound a bit jealous."

She smiled. "All right, I admit it, I am."

"I don't think you have to worry about anyone snatching me away. I'm not exactly the best-looking guy in the place at the moment." Cuts on my face, burnt arm, missing ear and pinkie, chewed-up leg, tilted head, and skin getting grayer by the minute – not to mention the state of my suit. I'd never been a male model, but I'd definitely seen better days.

Devona reached over and took my hand. "It's not the outside I see when I look at you. Especially after what happened in the glen."

All I could feel of Devona's touch was the slight pressure of her fingers against my skin. But it was enough.

"So you felt it too?"

She nodded. "It was the most intense experience of any kind I've ever had."

"I thought you said you'd linked with men before."

"I have, but it was never like that. Those men were Shadows in more ways than one, Matt. Shallow, hollow men who just wanted me for my body, or because I was Bloodborn and exotic, or because they thought I could make them Bloodborn too. But you – you're special. I don't think you realize just how much."

"Devona…" I didn't know what to say. We'd met each other less than a day ago, but after what had happened in the glen, after joining souls as we'd done, it was like we'd known each other for years. No, forever. But I couldn't let this go on, no matter how much I wanted it to, and believe me, I did.

The werecat brought Devona's drink, and we were silent while she put it down on the table. She saw we were holding hands, so she kept her winks to herself this time when she departed.

When the girl was out of earshot, I continued. "What kind of relationship can you have with a zombie? I'm not exactly fully functional, if you know what I mean."

"I don't care about that, Matt. We don't need physical love, not when we can link."

"Even so, I think it would be best for now if we just tried to concentrate our attention on the job at hand."

Her eyes grew cold and hurt and she tried to pull away, but I held her hand tight.

"I'm not rejecting you, Devona. I want to make that clear. I probably should reject you, to be honest, but I can't. But we shouldn't go forward with this until I know for certain that I'm going to... I guess 'live' isn't the right word. Survive, I guess. Unless your father can help me, I'll be gone soon."

"Then we can have that time together, Matt."

I shook my head. "I won't do that to you. I can't. We know how we feel about each other – know it in a way that two people who haven't been linked never could. Right now that has to be enough. If I'm lucky, in a couple days, I'll still be here, and then we can continue this conversation where it left off. I promise."

A crimson tear pooled at the corner of her right eye. "And if you aren't lucky?"

I grinned. "Would you smack me if I said we'll always have the glen?"

She squeezed my hand and I squeezed right back.

"Well, look who we have here! If it isn't Matthew Richter, the man who helped supply me with the best bouncer I've ever had!"

We looked up to see a tall, striking woman in a tuxedo striding confidently toward us. She wore her bright orange hair in a buzz cut, and her cherry-red lipstick contrasted with her ice-blue eyes. She stopped when she reached our table. There were only two chairs, and we were currently occupying them. I offered mine, but Bennie declined.

"Thank you, Matt, but there's no need." In a louder voice, Bennie said, "The first person who offers their chair gets two minutes alone with me in the Correctionary."

A near-riot ensued as men, women, and creatures of indeterminate species and gender fought to be the first to get a chair to Bennie, but in the end, a man with iron spikes jutting forth from his flesh like he was some sort of industrial porcupine won. He held the chair as Bennie sat.

"Thank you, love," Bennie said then added, with a dark twinkle in her eye, "Let's make it two and a half minutes, shall we? Don't go far; I'll come for you later. Or vice versa."

Spike-man looked so overwhelmed, I thought he might pass out, but he managed to hold onto consciousness long enough to thank Bennie before heading straight for the bar, no doubt intending to get some heavy-duty pharmacological assistance to prepare for his 180 seconds in the Correctionary with Bennie. If even a tenth of what I've heard about her skills is true, I figured he'd need it. Everyone else in the lounge was glaring jealously at Spike-man, and he was lucky no one present possessed the evil eye, or he would've been dead before he got two steps away from our table.

"Thanks for the floor show, Bennie," I said. "Do you take requests?"

She let out a hearty laugh. "You wish!"

I turned to Devona. "Devona Kanti, may I present the owner of the House of Dark Delights, Madame Benedetta."

Bennie reached out to take Devona's hand in the way some women will, intending to clasp it gently from underneath and give it a gentle squeeze. But halfway across the table, Bennie's slender fingers swelled and the slight reddish hair on the back of her hand became more pronounced. Bennie took Devona's hand in a masculine grip and gave it a good shake.

"Pleased to meet you," Bennie said in a voice that had suddenly grown deeper. "You're far too lovely to be keeping company with such a rough customer as Matt. However did the two of you meet?"

Devona stared at Bennie. His shoulders were broader, neck thicker, the lipstick was gone, and he sported a mustache and goatee the same bright orange shade as his hair. Bennie was still just as striking as before, but he most definitely was –

"A man?" Devona said.

"Occasionally," Bennie said. "There are so many pleasures to be had from life. Why limit yourself to experiencing them from only one perspective?"

"And now, Devona, you've also met Master Benedict," I said.

"But you can call me Bennie," our host said. "It makes things so much simpler."

Devona gave me an amused glance. "So I've heard."

"An ancestor of mine was a chemist who once tried to use specialized drugs to distill the good in man's nature and separate it from the evil," Bennie said. "My goals are somewhat less lofty. I use his formulae – along with some of my own devising – to make a buck or two." He gestured toward his body. "And, as you've seen, to enjoy myself. I also helped developed most of the aphrodisiacs and performance-enhancers we serve at the bar, although I must admit, my Arcane employees have helped a great deal with those formulae which require magic. And speaking of formulae…"

Bennie sat back and lifted his hand, and the werecat was instantly there, with a glass of scotch to put in it. Or at least, it looked like scotch. I wondered if it wasn't the special libation that allowed him and/or her to switch back and forth between genders.

"Thank you, Lourdes. That will be all…" Bennie gave her a smoldering look. "For now."

"Promises, promises." The werecat purred as she slinked off to see to other customers.

Bennie took a sip of his drink. "Lyra told me you needed my help with something. After what you did for that sweet child, Matt – not to mention what you did to the bastard who killed her – I'm forever in your debt. Whatever you need, just name it."

I spent the next few minutes giving Bennie the rundown on why we were there.

After winning our freedom from the Wyldwood, Devona and I returned to the Broken Cross, hoping that Shrike might know something about the veinburn dealer Morfran. Shike told us that Morfran was demon kin of a particularly rare insectine subspecies who mated only during a three-week period every year. This was the middle of week two for Morfran. It seemed he'd come into quite a bit of money recently – I could guess how – and that lately he'd been spending a good portion of his funds at the House of Dark Delights. According to Shrike, Morfran had been visiting the House several hours every day.

"Father Dis, do I know him!" Bennie said when I was finished. As I'd talked, she'd switched genders again and was at the moment a woman. "If you look up the word *indefatigable* in the dictionary, you'll find only a drawing of that disgusting little bug. But his darkgems are as good as anyone else's, and he certainly has a lot of them to spend. I'm not sure if he's here now, though. Descension Day is our busiest time of the year, Matt, and the customers come and go so quickly." She grinned at her own pun, but quickly grew serious again. "So you think Morfran sold the drug which killed Devona's brother?"

"According to Gregor, there's a good chance he did. We need to talk to him, Bennie – and we need him to give us some answers."

"I see." Bennie's scotch glass was empty. She held it up, and Lourdes swooped by to snatch it out of her hand and replace it with a fresh one. Bennie sipped as she thought. Then an idea came to her and she slowly smiled.

'I think I know how can help you. You know my motto: *Better living through chemistry.*" And her smiled became a broad grin.

Devona glanced at the four-sided clock mounted on a metal pole in the middle of the bar. Nekropolis follows standard Earth time: twenty-four hour days, seven-day weeks, twelve-month years – not that it means very much when you live beneath Umbriel's perpetual dusk and, like me, you don't need to sleep. Bennie had left us some time ago, to see about one thing or another. A gender-switching brothel owner's work is never done.

"We've been waiting here almost an hour," she said. "Maybe Morfran's already left."

"We'd have seen him." All of the House's customers had to pass through the lounge in order to get to and leave the rooms. Bennie didn't make nearly as much money on booze and drugs as she did sex, but she wanted to squeeze as many darkgems out of her customers as she could before sending them back into the streets, so she made certain her clientele had two opportunities to sit down and have a couple drinks. And, after hoisting a few on their way out, if they decided they'd rested up enough and were ready for another go, why, they could just head right back on through the lounge, and hire themselves some more fun.

I'd heard it said that Bennie is as wealthy as any Darklord. I wouldn't doubt it.

"Perhaps he left through a rear exit," Devona said.

"There is no rear exit. Bennie had it bricked over years ago to stop deadbeat customers from sneaking out without paying." Rumor had it that several such customers had been present – and bound in chains – when the bricks were laid. "Just try to relax."

"Shrike was probably wrong, and Morfran's not even here."

"Bennie sent Lourdes to check for us, remember? He's downstairs all right – with three girls: one lyke, one Bloodborn, and one demon kin. I can't begin to imagine the geometric and metamorphic possibilities."

And before I could add anything more, Morfran finally walked into the lounge.

The demon swaggered like he was, you'll pardon the expression, cock of the walk. Or in his case, gigantic walking stick of the walk. He was a twig-thin insectine demon, with a carapace resembling fluorescent-red Formica. He had a triangular face something like a praying mantis, with huge eyes like those of a too-precious moppet in a black-velvet painting.

As he scuttled past our table, I said, "Morfran!"

The demon stopped and swiveled his head back to look at me. His expression – assuming his bug face was even capable of making one – was unreadable.

"It's me, Matt. You remember, I was one of your customers, back when I was alive."

A few seconds ticked by, then he said, "Oh, yes" in a voice which sounded like a hive full of buzzing bees.

His voice was almost as difficult to read as his face, but I thought he sounded a trifle unsure, as if he knew he didn't remember me, but thought maybe he should. Exactly the response I wanted.

"Why don't you sit down and have a drink with us, for old times' sake?"

His head tilted quickly to one side, then to the other, then back once more, as if he were an insect version of a metronome.

"I don't know. There is much I should be doing."

"I've heard you're quite the ladies' man," Devona virtually purred. "Three at one time, they say."

Given his physiognomy, it was impossible for Morfran to puff himself up with pride, but that's what it looked like.

"Nothing personal, Morfran," I said, good-naturedly but with plenty of skepticism, "but three at a time? Come on!"

"Yes, three at a time." He sounded aggrieved. "Not only that, but once a day for nearly two weeks now."

"Really!" Devona said, leaning toward him and flashing more than a hint of cleavage. "Quite impressive!"

Even without the necessary equipment for facial expression, Morfran still gave the impression of leering at Devona's chest.

"I don't know…" I said doubtfully.

Morfran skittered up to our table and, since his body structure wouldn't allow him to take a seat, at least not comfortably, he stood. "Are you doubting my word, Mark?"

"Matt," I corrected. I signaled Lourdes and pointed to Morfran. She nodded and padded over to the bar, her tail swishing slowly back and forth, to get him a drink. I noticed Devona frowning at me, and I quickly returned my gaze to Morfran. "I'm not doubting you; I'm just saying that guys exaggerate sometimes, that's all."

"I am not exaggerating. It is the nature of my subspecies to be sexually prolific during this time of the year. It is our mating season."

I tried to imagine just how something so... alien could manage to have sexual congress with one humanoid female, let alone three. But try as I might, I just couldn't picture it.

Lourdes brought over Morfran's drink, set it in front of the demon, and gave me another wink before departing with more tail swishing. I really wished she hadn't winked. I had a feeling I'd be hearing about that later on.

"You mean the rest of the year you don't... Well, that explains it, then." I lifted my glass, and Devona did likewise. "Here's to you, Morfran; you're a bona fide sex machine."

"Only for three weeks out of the year," he said, but he seemed pleased nonetheless. He leaned his head over his drink and a needle-thin organ extended out of his small mouth and dipped into the booze. He drank greedily, with great slurping sips. Within moments, his glass was empty.

"Whoa! You must really have worked up a thirst back there!"

Morfran's body shivered. His equivalent of a laugh, I think. "One does tend to expend a great deal of fluid during mating."

I was glad my stomach was as dead as the rest of me; if it wasn't, it would've turned right then.

Morfran's eyes narrowed. "I must admit that I don't remember you as clearly as I would like, Mark. You said you were a customer of mine when you were alive? I certainly hope my wares were not the cause of your demise."

"Actually, I have a confession to make: we've never met before."

His head titled back and forth again, right-left, right-left, very fast this time,.

"We've come here to ask you a few questions," I said. "About veinburn – and about a vampire named Varma."

Sometimes the direct approach works; sometimes it doesn't. This was one of the latter times. Morfran's carapace turned completely brown – the same color as the table and floor, I noticed – he whirled about, and his twig legs became a blur as he fled for the foyer.

"I told you he'd run," Devona said.

"You were right." Neither of us bothered to get up and give pursuit. There was no need.

A few moments later, Morfran was carried back to our table, squirming, legs flailing madly, carapace rapidly changing colors from red to yellow to brown.

"He almost got past me," Lyra said. "I guess I still haven't gotten the hang of this body yet."

"You did great," I told her. "Now if you could just hold him still for a moment while I explain a few things to him?"

Bennie's newest – and strongest – bouncer smiled sweetly, the effect somewhat spoiled by Honani's jagged mixblood teeth. I hadn't had a chance yet to tell her about what had happened at the edge of the Wyldwood with the soul that had previously occupied her current body, and I'm not sure I wanted to. The knowledge that Amon had Honani's spirit – and worrying what the Dark Lord might seek to do with it – would only plague her. But I made a mental note to talk with Bennie before I decomposed. With her wealth and devotion to her staff, I hoped she could arrange for some way to protect Lyra from Amon, should it come to that.

Lyra squeezed Morfran and the demon's carapace creaked alarmingly.

"Careful," I warned. "We don't want to reduce him to kindling now."

"Oops. Sorry." She eased up. Morfran struggled a bit more, until it became obvious he wasn't going anywhere, and then he finally gave up and just hung motionless in Lyra's massive arms.

"Okay, here's the situation, Morfran," I said. "Before the waitress brought your drink over, I spiked it with a potion specially prepared for you by Bennie herself. She serves a lot of potions, you know. Some work to induce a state of sexual readiness in someone whose spirit may be willing but whose flesh needs a little more help. Other potions work just the opposite: they suppress sexual functioning. These are used these for clients who refuse to pay their tabs or for those who mistreat the staff."

I wished Honani hadn't been too proud to accept the aid of one of Bennie's potions when he'd visited Lyra. If he had taken one, she'd probably still be alive and in her own body.

I went on. "To put it simply, Morfran, you can't get it up anymore – or whatever it is males of your species do. And you won't be able to until you receive the antidote. If you cooperate and answer a few questions, I'll make sure you get it. If not, you'll miss out on the final week of your mating season." I'd learned from Shrike that Morfran's subspecies of demon was mindlessly driven to copulate during this time, and the potion Bennie had created for Morfran was a cruel one: it removed sexual functioning, but actually increased desire, making it all the more effective when it came to convincing delinquent customers to make good on outstanding debts.

Morfran's carapace edged toward black now. "It doesn't matter. I have quite a bit of money; I can easily afford to purchase an antidote from a witch somewhere else."

"You could try. But Bennie's enchantments aren't easily removed. It's true you might find someone who'll hit on the right formula to remove the spell eventually, but it could take some time. Easily a week."

"Oh, much more than that, I think," Devona said. "He might still be looking this time next year."

Morfran's shell had gone completely black now. I wondered if it was a sign of anger, or maybe fear. Whichever, it was clear we were getting to him.

"You don't understand," he said quietly, with an edge of desperation. "The people I work for would be most displeased if I told you anything."

"By 'people' you mean the Dominari, right? I sympathize with you, Morfran old bug, but all I can tell you is to ask yourself which is worse: talking to us and maybe having the Dominari find out, or going the rest of this year's mating season desperately needing to have sex, but without any lead in your pencil."

Morfran regarded me for a moment, his head tilting back and forth slowly this time. Finally, he let out an edgy buzz of a sigh that already sounded tinged with the beginnings of sexual tension and frustration. "Very well. What do you wish to know?"

We asked the demon some questions, and he answered them clearly, quickly, and concisely. I was fairly certain that he had nothing directly to do with Varma's death – it was clear the Red Tide vampires had been responsible for that – and so when we were finished, I had Lourdes bring over the antidote. Morfran practically inhaled the potion, and then scuttled off back to the more carnal sections of Bennie's establishment, no doubt intending to make sure the antidote worked as advertised.

And so Devona and I said goodbye to Lyra, who I wished well in her new profession, and Devona alone (as she insisted) thanked Lourdes. Bennie gave us both kisses on the cheek – despite the nasty condition of mine, Dis bless her/him – and we left the House of Dark Delights to follow up on what we had learned from Morfran.

We headed for Skully's.

TWENTY

The bar was still busy as hell, and there were a few new suspicious-looking stains on the floor since the last time I'd been here, but the atmosphere seemed calm enough now. But considering why Devona and I had come back, I doubted it was going to stay that way for long.

The juke box was singing "Bewitched, Bothered, and Bewildered" when Devona and I walked in, but as soon as the trio of heads caught sight of me, they stopped. The middle one said, "Not you again!" and all three shut their mouths tight and closed their eyes, as if they were little children who thought they could make me vanish by pretending I didn't exist. I noticed none of the patrons complained about the performance being interrupted.

Devona and I walked over to the bar and took a pair of stools suddenly vacated by a couple lykes in human form who wrinkled their noses in disgust as they left.

"What did you expect, roses?" I muttered as they walked off.

Skully was busy at the other end of the bar filling a mug of beer for the pierced warlock I'd seen the last time I was in here. The Arcane man still seemed somewhat familiar to me, and while he waited for his beer, I studied his face, but I still couldn't place him. When Skully handed him his beer, the warlock noticed my scrutiny, but instead of looking upset, he merely gave me a nod and walked over to sit at the same table he'd been at when I'd fought Honani earlier. I wondered if he'd been sitting there alone drinking the entire time I'd been gone. Maybe he was just a solitary type who wanted a relatively quiet place to hide out from the Descension Day madness. Still, there was something about the man that bothered me…

My thoughts were interrupted as Skully came down to our end of the bar.

"Hey, Matt! I'm surprised to see you back so soon – and with your arm reattached, I see. Business?" He nodded to Devona, and from the tone in his voice he would have smiled if he'd possessed the lips and facial muscles to do so. "Or pleasure? Wait, let me guess. Has to be business, as bad as you look. You shouldn't be in here: you should be over at Papa Chatha's getting some more work done."

"This is my new friend Devona. Her father lost something – something very important – and I'm helping her look for it."

"Oh?"

"Her father's name is Galm, and the object is called the Dawnstone. Sound familiar?"

Skully shook his fleshless head. "No, should it?"

"Yes, because according to my source" – who was at that very moment most likely *expending a great deal of fluid*, as he'd put it – "you're responsible for its disappearance from the Cathedral. Or at least your bosses the Dominari are."

Then something happened which I'd never seen before. Tiny pinpricks of crimson light began to blaze deep in the cold darkness of Skully's eye sockets. "I think maybe you'd better leave, Matt, and take your new friend with you."

He started to turn away, but I grabbed his pudgy, hairy wrist and stopped him. "I know there's a Dominari-run lab upstairs, Skully. A lab that's been awfully busy lately cranking out veinburn."

Skully yanked his arm away. "Your mind has finally rotted through, Matt, you know that? All that's upstairs are my quarters and some extra storage space."

Skully and I looked over the bar at each other for a moment. I knew his silver broadaxe wasn't far from his reach.

"If that's true, then you won't have objection to my taking a look, now will you?" And before Skully could respond, I jumped off my stool and ran-limped as fast as I could toward the iron door located the right of the bar.

Head aside, Skully has a fully fleshed body. A little too fully fleshed, and I thought given my current state, we'd be evenly matched with it came to speed. But even with his bulk, Skully was able to grab his axe from behind the counter and leap over the bar and come after me before I made it halfway to the stairs.

He shouted my name, and I turned in time to see him raise his axe over his head, the silver glinting even in the bar's dim light. "Don't make me hurt you, Matt. Please."

Everyone in the bar watched us play out our little drama, not only to see what would happen next but also to help them decide if they should bother taking cover. But no one observed us more intensely than the pierced warlock.

Where the hell do I know that sonofabitch from? I thought.

"If you really don't want to hurt me, Skully I have a suggestion: put the axe down."

"I can't do that, Matt," he said sadly.

The irony inherent in the situation was so thick you could cut it with Skully's axe. It was like a replay of earlier in the day, only instead of a murdering lyke, I now faced a friend. A friend who was about to bring a very large, very sharp weapon down on my head, but a friend nonetheless.

"I can't let this one go," I said. "It's too important."

"And I can't let you reach those stairs."

Stalemate. I had little in the way of surprises left in my pockets, and nothing that would take care of Skully. Hell, I wasn't even exactly sure what sort of creature he was, and I didn't have the first clue as to what sort of weaknesses he might possess.

"So what do we do now, Matt?" he asked.

"I figure you can just stand there, and I'll watch as Devona cracks you over your bony noggin with a chair."

"Come off it, I'm not going to fall for–" The chair connected with his skull with a sharp crack! and a shower of splintered wood. Skully dropped his axe, which hit the concrete floor with a loud clang, and a second later, Skully himself crashed down beside it.

I quickly examined him. He had a tiny jagged fissure in his skull, and the lights in his socket had been extinguished.

Devona held only a pair of chair legs in her hands now, and she let them clatter to the floor. "Is he unconscious?"

"Who can tell? But he's not moving right now and that's good enough. Let's go." I continued toward the stairs, this time with Devona at my side.

Skully's patrons didn't know what to do at first. They merely sat and stared. Then one particular Einstein among them shouted, "Hey, free drinks!" and a stampede for the bar commenced. I hoped Skully wouldn't get stepped on too badly, even if he had been prepared to turn me into filet-o-zombie.

The iron door that led to the bar's upper level was locked and – as Devona had figured it would be – it was protected by some seriously powerful wardspells. But Shrike had managed to borrow some magical lockpicks for us from a thief he knew, and using the knowledge Devona had gained from years serving as guardian of Galm's Collection, she was able to bypass the wardspells and open the door in surprisingly short order.

"I'm impressed," I said. "If you decide to stop working for your father, you can always take up a career as a cat burglar – or maybe I should say bat burglar."

She grinned, and we hurried up the stairs as fast as my bum leg would allow and exited onto the second floor. The short hall had only three wooden doors, all closed. I turned to Devona and touched the side of my nose. She nodded and inhaled.

"That one." She pointed to door number two.

"That one it is, then." I took out my 9mm, which was now loaded with purely ordinary bullets, stepped to the door, and was about to try the knob when Devona stopped.

"Let me see if it's warded." She waved her hands over the door's surface, careful not to touch it. "It's clean. I guess the Dominari figured the wardspells on the door downstairs were enough protection. Idiots." She tried the knob, but it wouldn't budge. "At least they weren't too stupid to lock it."

"As a macho type, I'd ordinarily kick the door in myself," I said, "but seeing as how you're somewhat stronger than I am…"

She smiled, leaned back and executed a swift, powerful kick to the middle of the door, which exploded off its hinges and flew into the room.

Devona stepped back and I moved past her into the room, fighting the urge to shout, "Police!" Instead I said, "Nobody move!" Hardly as satisfying, but it was the best I could do under the circumstances. At least it fulfilled my quota of tough-guy talk for the day.

There was no one in the room. I kept my gun out, though, just in case. Inside sat a table filled with chemical apparatus: copper tubing, black rubber hoses, beakers, vials, the whole junior chemistry lab bit. Next to that lay a stone altar upon which rested various flowers and herbs, along with the sliced-up body of a dead lamb and the rune-engraved obsidian knife which had done it in. Science and magic, working together to create a better world, or at least a more profitable one – for the Dominari, that is.

"So Morfran was telling the truth," I said. Even with the motivation we'd provided him with, I still hadn't quite believed what he'd told us. You can never trust drug-pushing scum, regardless of species or home dimension.

"And I'll make damn sure the bug pays for it, too."

I recognized the voice coming from behind us, and though I was dead, it sent a chill through my room-temperature blood. We turned to see the voice belonged to the shaven-headed punk warlock from downstairs. His piercings – multiple rings in the outer curves of his ears, across his bottom lip, in both nostrils, along his eyebrows, down both sides of his forearms, and who knew where else beneath his ratty jeans and *A is for Anarchy* T-shirt – pulsed with a silvery energy that wreathed his body in a shimmering argent aura.

I might have been a zombie, but right then I felt a fury inside me as strong as any emotion I'd ever experienced as a living man. I fought to keep my voice calm as I said, "Hello, Yberio."

The warlock smiled, displaying metal-encased teeth. "Surprised to see me back from the dead, Richter?"

"Are you kidding? This is Nekropolis. Half the people you meet here are one kind of dead or another. You've changed a bit from when we last met." I looked him up and down. "The new look suits you. What does Talaith think about it?"

Devona's jaw dropped. "Wait, this warlock is the one who created the Overmind for Talaith, the one who–"

"Killed Richter's partner," Yberio finished. "Indeed."

At that moment, I was painfully aware that I still held my 9mm in my right hand. It was down at my side, and I calculated my chances of raising the weapon and getting a shot off before Yberio could do anything to stop me. My reflexes would've been slow even if my undead body had been in its peak condition, but as beat-up and decayed as I was right then, I wasn't in danger of being crowned fastest gun in the Sprawl anytime soon. Yberio must've guessed what I was thinking – or perhaps he literally read my mind – and he evidently thought more of my threat potential than I did, because he made a small gesture with his hand and tendrils of silver energy flowed forth from his aura, snatch the gun out of my hand, and tossed it into the corner of the room with contemptuous ease.

"Not that I couldn't stop a bullet if I wanted to," Yberio said, "but I'm more conservative in my use of power these days, seeing as how I don't wield quite so much as I used to. But then again, what's the point of possessing power if you don't enjoy it from time to time?"

The warlock stretched his hands toward us and before we could react, two gouts of silver energy blasted forth, slamming us backward into the table holding the chemical and mystical apparatus used for creating vein-burn. Vials and beakers shattered, noxious chemicals spilled, the dead goat went flying, and the table broke from the force of the impact. Since I couldn't feel pain, I wasn't stunned, and I immediately tried to sit up. But before I could manage to do so, Yberio gestured again, and two more tendrils extended from his aura, the tips shaping themselves into large silvery hands as they came at us. The energy hands smashed into our chests and pressed down like iron weights, pinning us where we lay.

Yberio laughed softly. He sounded pleased, but also a bit sad. "You know, there was a time when I could've destroyed both of you far more elegantly than this. I was a Demilord once... but that was before you came to town, Richter."

I managed to wriggle my right arm free enough to reach up and attempt to clutch the wrist of the silvery hand holding me down. It remained attached to Yberio by an umbilicus of energy, but while it felt solid enough on my chest, when I tried to grab hold of it, my hand merely passed through as if it wasn't there. I felt a distant tingling sensation, as if I'd come in contact with a strong electrical field.

"Don't you mean before you decided to start killing people in my jurisdiction back on Earth?" I countered.

"Details, details," Yberio said.

I turned my head to check on Devona. She appeared unharmed, and while she too struggled to free herself from the grasp of Yberio's argent energy, she met with no more success than I had.

"Matt checked your pulse after the Overmind was destroyed," she said. "You didn't have one."

"I did," Yberio said. "It was just hard for him to feel it – especially since he'd become a zombie and wasn't used to his newly deadened sense of touch. I wasn't dead, merely in a deep coma as it turned out, and I spent a number of months in that state as my mind and body worked desperately to heal themselves. Talaith helped as much as she could, but she'd suffered her own injuries from the Overmind's demise and needed the bulk of her magic to heal herself. And when I finally awoke, I found myself... diminished. I still had my knowledge of magic, but I was only capable of accessing and channeling a fraction of the mystic energy I once could. It seemed the psychic backlash caused by the destruction of the Overmind had burned out a portion of my own mind, and I was no longer a Demilord, but merely an ordinary warlock." He paused, and his tone grew bitter, "And not a particularly strong one at that."

I couldn't reach any of my pockets, and even if I could, I didn't have anything that I could use against Yberio. I looked around at the wreckage of the lab table that I was lying amidst, hoping to find something, anything, I could use as a weapon. My gaze fell upon a half-broken beaker that still contained several ounces of a yellow-green chemical. Not veinburn itself, but one of its ingredients. The beaker lay just outside of my reach, but if I could manage to stretch a bit…

"That's why you wear all those rings," Devona said. "They augment your natural magical abilities."

"Very good," Yberio gave Devona an appraising look. "You're half vampire, right? Perhaps you have a bit of Arcane blood in you on your human side. But you're correct. My rings help me absorb, store, and channel the mystic energy, all of which I can no longer do on my own. In human terms, it's the equivalent of replacing a lost limb with a prosthesis or using a wheelchair if one can no longer walk."

I saw Devona give me a quick glance. She understood what I was trying to do, and she looked back to Yberio and tried to keep him talking.

"I bet Talaith wasn't happy about that," she said," considering how she feels about technology."

"My rings aren't technology in the strictest sense, but you're right. Talaith considered them to be the same thing. At the very least, she thought them… unnatural." Yberio let out a dark, bitter laugh. "As if there could be anything more unnatural than the likes of us! But she was angry with me for talking her into creating the Overmind, and she blamed me for the injuries that resulted in her loss of power. Darklords aren't known for their forgiving nature, but one thing they can never forgive is anyone who causes them to lose strength or, even worse, face."

I stretched my fingers toward the broken beaker. I was almost there. Just another inch...

Yberio continued his one-man pity party. "Talaith felt that I had made her a laughing stock in the eyes of her fellow Lords." He sneered. "As if that mattered. Arrogant fools, every one of them. They think they're better than we Demilords, simply because Dis chose them to help create Nekropolis. But did you know that Dis spent an entire year traveling the length and breadth of Earth, searching for the most powerful Darkfolk to help him turn his dream of Nekropolis into reality? And once he found them, he tested them in combat to determine just how strong they were. I was one of the Arcane Dis tested during the Wanderyear, and I acquitted myself admirably. I might well have been chosen to be a Dark-lord instead of Talaith – and I should've been! Dis might fancy himself a god, but in the end he's just another damned monster like the rest of us. He's not perfect; he's fully capable of making errors of judgment."

A half-inch now...

"But Dis didn't choose you, he chose Talaith," Devona said. "And Talaith banished you for failing her and turning to artificial means of enhancing your power, didn't she?"

From the face Yberio made, you'd have thought he was having trouble swallowing a crap-covered turdball rolled in shit sprinkles. "Yes – and that's when I realized I'd been a fool standing by her side all those centuries, helping her fight for one meaningless cause or another, all so she could increase her own power. First in the Blood Wars, and then in her endless pissing contests with the other so-called Lords. When I left Woodhome, I decided that from then on, I was going to work to increase my power and no one else's!"

The tips of my fingers brushed the beaker's glass surface. I thought I felt something snap in my shoulder, as if a tendon had torn loose, but it didn't matter. All that mattered was getting my hand on that beaker.

"But power costs money," Devona said. "You needed a way to make darkgems, so you began freelancing for the Dominari, helping them make new drugs like veinburn."

Yberio gave her a smug little smile. "Well. I do still retain my knowledge of magic, you know."

At last, I managed to wrap my fingers around the beaker.

"Tell me something, Yberio," I said. "Do you still know how to catch?"

Before he could react, I hurled the beaker toward him. As I'd hoped, he wasn't prepared for the attack and the half-broken glass container sailed through his silver energy aura without resistance. I got lucky and the jagged edge of the beaker hit him in the face, and the greenish-yellow liquid inside sloshed into his eyes. Yberio screamed and staggered backward, and as his concentration shattered, the silver hands holding Devona and I down vanished, along with the energy aura surrounding him. Crimson blood mixed with yellow-green chemicals as Yberio desperately wiped at his eyes, trying to clear them.

I sat up, intending to rise to my feet and confront the warlock who had killed my partner, but before I could stand, Devona leapt to her feet and closed on Yberio with the savage speed and grace of a jungle cat. She grabbed hold his shoulder with one hand, grabbed the top of his bald scalp with the other, and yanked his head to the side. Then she bared her fangs with a snarl and plunged her teeth into the warlock's exposed neck. Yberio shrieked as Devona tore out a chuck of his flesh and blood gushed from the wound.

Devona stepped back, her mouth and chest covered with the warlock's blood. She spat out the hunk of meat she'd bitten off and it hit the floor with a wet plap. Now Yberio pressed his hand to his throat, trying to keep his lifeblood from spilling out.

"A few hours ago, I was joined to Matt soul-to-soul," Devona said. "I experienced his thoughts, his emotions... and his memories. I know what you did to his partner, and more, I know what that loss did to him. You should've died the day the Overmind was destroyed, you bastard. But you didn't, and so I'm glad to finish the job. For Matt." She paused. "For my love."

I was so overwhelmed by what Devona had done – and even more by what she'd just said – that for a moment all I could do was sit there gaping like an undead moron. Her fangs were distended, her eyes were wild, and her mouth was smeared with gore... and I'd never seen any woman more beautiful.

But then Yberio's free arm flared with silver energy and he backhanded Devona, sending her sailing through the air to collide with the far wall. She bounced off and fell onto her side, moaning.

Silver power flickered to life around the hand Yberio held pressed to his neck wound, and I knew he was attempting to heal it. I slowly rose to my feet and started toward him.

"You know, Richter, as long as you and your little bloodcunt didn't find out about this lab, I was going to leave you alone. Sure, your destruction of the Overmind ruined my life, but I like to think I've risen above such petty things as revenge. If you don't stand in the way of my acquisition of power, why should I bother with you? But things have gone way too far now, and I'm –"

By this time I'd reached Yberio. I calmly took his head in my heads and gave it a single vicious twist. There was a loud *crack*, Yberio's eyes went wide, and his silver aura winked out. When I released his head, his dead body slumped to the floor. "You shouldn't have called her that," I whispered. Then I turned and went over to see how Devona was.

She managed to rise to a kneeling position, and I took her hand and helped her to stand.

"You all right?"

She drew the back of her hand across her mouth to wipe away Yberio's blood. "I've been better, but I think I'll live."

I intended to take her into my arms and give her the hug of her life, when I saw Skully standing in the doorway, axe held at his side. I searched for pinpricks of anger in his sockets and found none. He looked down at Yberio's dead body, his boneface expressionless as always.

"I never did like that dick," he said.

"I've known you ever since I first came to Nekropolis, Skully. Hell, I was still *alive* when we met. I knew you worked for the Dominari, but I never figured you'd associate with a scumbag like *that*." I gestured toward Yberio's corpse.

"I had my orders." Skully said. "And given who my bosses are, it's a good idea to do what they want, regardless of what I might think about it."

"Yberio was Arcane – not to mention Talaith's former consort," I said. "Was she in on this operation?" I asked.

"Not to my knowledge. The bosses don't like messing around with Darklords. Far as I know, Yberio worked here only for the money."

Did that mean Gregor – as impossible as it sounded – had been wrong about Talaith's involvement? Or was Skully not telling me the truth?

"What do you know about the theft of the Dawnstone, Skully? And what do the Dominari plan to do with it?"

"The bosses had nothing to do with stealing the Dawnstone. They were working with someone else, someone whose identity I don't know. I wasn't particularly chummy with Yberio, but we talked a few times. From what I gathered, someone approached the bosses with the formula for veinburn, but needed some capital and the technical know-how to produce it. For providing both, and giving a relatively small quantity of the finished product to their silent partner, the Dominari got to keep the formula."

"So the Dominari are probably setting up other veinburn labs around the city even as we speak. Great. Tell me, Skully, didn't it bother you what they were doing up here?"

"Sure it did." He gazed down at Yberio's body. "I may have to take orders, but that doesn't mean I always like it."

It was impossible to gauge his emotional state from his face (or lack thereof), but he sounded sincere. "And you have no idea who your Dominari's mystery partner might be?"

"No, and I don't think Yberio knew, either."

"How does Morfran fit into this?"

"He's one of the bosses' regular dealers, a small timer who usually sells mind dust. The bosses wanted him to try veinburn out on the market, see how people took to it."

"Which they undoubtedly did, given how addictive it is." I thought for a moment. "You said Morfran's a small timer. Why would the Dominari choose him for such an important project?"

"I wondered about that myself, but like I said, it's best not to ask questions."

"Perhaps because the Dominari's new partner asked them to," Devona said. "Because one of his regular customers was Varma."

"Who, fun-loving guy that he was, was probably first in line to try Morfran's newest product," I said. "Which got him hooked–"

"And after that, he'd do anything for more," Devona finished for me. "Including risk Father's wrath by stealing the Dawnstone."

"This unknown 'partner' probably made his or her own arrangements with Varma. The theft of an object of power from a Darklord is far too difficult an undertaking to involve a sleazy little bug like Morfran. And then, once we started nosing around, Mr. or Ms. Unknown decided to have Varma killed, in case we found him and got him to talk."

"And if Varma wouldn't have told us what happened to the Dawnstone, I would've had no choice but to tell Father everything myself, and he most definitely would've gotten Varma to talk. So Varma had to die."

I didn't want to think about what sort of persuasive techniques Lord Galm might have used on his blood-son. Varma's death by veinburn, ugly as it had been, might well have been kinder than leaving him to Galm's less-than-tender mercies.

Devona frowned. "What I don't understand is why wait to kill Varma? Wouldn't it have made more sense to kill him as soon as he delivered the Dawnstone?"

"Murdering Varma then would've drawn too much attention too early. Mr. Unknown wasn't worried about Varma spontaneously confessing. Varma would've been too afraid of Galm – and the punishment he would deliver – to admit his crime. It wasn't until we got too close that Varma became a liability and needed to be dealt with."

Devona's already pale skin grew paler. "Then... we're responsible for his death. No, I am, because I was afraid to go to Father, afraid of his anger, his disappointment. If I had spoken to Father instead of hiring you... Varma might still be alive."

I took her hand. "The only ones responsible for killing Varma are the Red Tide vampires, and whoever was pulling their strings – or in their case, wires. Okay?"

Devona didn't look completely convinced, but she nodded anyway. I figured it was the best I was going to get just then. I turned to Skully, who had been standing silently by while Devona and I tried to piece this mess together. "Do the Dominari have any connection with the Red Tide?"

"No, those tech-psychos are too unstable."

"So they worked directly for Mr. Unknown. I thought as much." There was something important about that particular tidbit of information, but I couldn't quite put my rapidly decomposing finger on it. Not yet.

"So where does that leave us?" Devona asked.

"Not much farther along than we were before," I admitted. "It appears Talaith doesn't have the Dawnstone and neither do the Dominari. It looks like Skully's bosses are the only ones who know who does have it, but I doubt they'd agree to share that information, assuming we could even locate them." I sighed. "I think it's safe to say that our investigation has run into a very large and very dead end."

"Uh, Matt?" Skully said. "There's something else."

"What? You know something you haven't told us?" I said hopefully.

"Not exactly. Remember when I told you it was a good idea to follow the bosses' orders? Well, they gave me some instructions about what I should do if you discovered the lab."

He lifted his axe.

"You don't want to do this," I said.

"No, but I have my orders." He took a step forward.

"If you really wanted to kill us, it would have been much easier to lead us up here in the first place, get us off our guard, and then let Yberio catch us unaware. But you didn't do that. You tried to send us away, and then you tried to stop us from coming up here."

Skully's grip on his axe tightened and loosened, tightened and loosened, as if were trying to decide his next move.

"So?"

"So I think you were disobeying orders, not following them, when you asked us to leave. And I think it's because you didn't want to have to kill a friend."

Skully gave forth a hollow laugh. "The Dominari and their servants have no friends."

"Then prove me wrong. Go ahead, make like Lizzie Borden. I won't stop you."

I heard Devona draw in a nervous gasp of air, but otherwise she did nothing.

Skully stood silently for several moments before finally lowering his axe. "You're right, Matt; I don't want to kill you. You're the closest thing to a friend I have. But when the bosses find out I couldn't go through with it..." His shoulders slumped. "Maybe I should just go ahead and turn myself in to the Adjudicators. Spending the rest of eternity locked away in Tenebrus would be a far gentler fate than what the Dominari will do to me when they learn I've failed."

Tenebrus was Nekropolis's prison, located deep beneath the Nightspire. Run by the ancient Egyptian sorceress Keket and her jackal-headed Warders, even in a city built from terror and darkness, it was among the most feared of places.

"Don't worry," I said. "We can make it look like you tried to kill us. Yberio is dead, and the lab's already trashed from our fight with him. We'll clonk you on the head again, this time with your own axe. We'll take off and you can just lie here unconscious until someone comes looking for you – or your customers downstairs steal all your booze, whichever comes first. With any luck, when the Dominari investigate, they'll believe you when you say you tried, but how could be you expected to stop of pair of dangerous characters like us who killed a former Demilord? "

"Won't they punish Skully anyway?" Devona asked.

"I doubt it. Skully's place has been a fixture in the Sprawl for years, and I bet the Dominari get too much use out of it – and its owner – to get rid of either." I turned to Skully. "If your bosses ask why I didn't turn you in to the Adjudicators, tell them you bribed me to keep my mouth shut."

"You'd do all that for me?" Skully asked.

I smiled. "Hey, what are friends for?"

Just then a solemn, sonorous tone sounded off in the distance. Several seconds later another sounded, and then another. They kept coming every ten seconds, soft and low, reminding me a bit of the lonely, mournful sound a foghorn makes.

"What's that noise?" I asked.

"Father Dis!" Devona swore. "It's the Deathknell summoning the Darklords to the Nightspire – the Renewal Ceremony will start soon!"

It was my turn to swear. We were too late. I was certain whoever had the Dawnstone planned to use it during the ceremony to kill Lord Galm, or maybe even Dis himself, if such a thing were possible. And there was nothing we could do about it. Unless…

I grabbed Devona's hand and pulled her toward the door. "I'm afraid you'll have to hit yourself over the head, Skully. Devona and I have to go." I shoved past him, and Devona and I stepped over the late and very much unlamented Yberio. We hurried down the stairs, taking them as fast as my bum leg would allow.

"Where are you going?" Skully called after us.

I shouted over my shoulder. "To crash a party!"

TWENTY-ONE

From the outside, Lady Varvara's stronghold is a glass and steel building ten stories tall, which wouldn't be out of place in the business district of any midsize city on Earth. Inside, Demon's Roost is a paean to pleasure, a twenty-four-hour-a-day bacchanalia that makes Las Vegas look like a kindergarten playground. It's an adults-only amusement park which contains such a dazzling scope and variety of decadence and perversity that it might give Caligula himself pause.

Beside the mass of partiers, getting inside wasn't a problem. Varvara doesn't believe in locking doors or posting guards. Anyone can come in and play, from the lowliest street beggar to any of the Demon Queen's fellow Darklords – but once inside, you're on your own and good luck to you. Just remember: there are no guarantees you'll ever make it out again. Devona and I made out way into the Atrium by squeezing through a mass of beings drinking, drugging, gambling, screwing, eating, talking, laughing, yelling, fighting – often, it seemed, all at the same time.

Any number of Nekropolitan luminaries were in attendance. After all, Demon's Roost is *the* place to be on Descension Day. The Scream Queen and her band Kakophanie provided the musical entertainment – if you could call the banshees' dissonant wailing music – and I spotted Marley's Ghost rattling his chains in time to the beat. Fade, who had made her way over from the Broken Cross, had gotten herself cornered by the Else, who was obviously trying to convince her to do a feature story on him, while the Jade Enigma looked on in cynical amusement, Antwerp the Psychotic Clown was stabbing himself over and over with a butcher knife and laughing uproariously, much to the annoyance of those unfortunate enough to be in range of his blood spatter. The Suicide King stood nearly, watching Antwerp's gory display with a critical eye and shaking his head. As Devona and I passed by, I heard him mutter, "That's not how you do it."

I noticed a trio of Demilords standing off to the side and keeping to themselves. Baron Samedi seemed to be enjoying himself well enough, if his broad grin was any indication, but Slitheria the Serpent Goddess watched the revelry with a reptilian gaze of cold disapproval. Molog, Demon Lord of Insects, stood with his arms crossed over his chest, the millions of six-legged creatures that formed his body scuttling about restlessly, making it look as if he might fall apart any second.

I'd seen them – and other Demilords – around the city before, but after our recent encounter with Yberio I now viewed them in a different light. Maybe they weren't quite as powerful as the Darklords, but they weren't saddled with the responsibilities of the five Lords, either. The Demilords were incredibly powerful beings free to do as they pleased, and they had no need to conserve their strength to help renew Umbriel once a year. In that sense, they were more powerful than the Darklords, and I wondered if – like Yberio – they resented being passed over by Dis during his Wanderyear in favor of the five current Darklords, and what they might intend to do to even the score one day.

The party wasn't confined to the ground, though. The Atrium extended several stories upward, and numerous beings flew or levitated above our heads, some swooping and darting about, while others merely circled slowly – perhaps hoping to spot prey of one sort or another below. Ichorus was there, no doubt having accompanied Fade. I wondered if they were an item. If so, I bet that would be one tidbit of gossip that would never appear in Fade's tabloid column. A number of ghostly figures were ballroom dancing in the air, their graceful moves somehow perfectly complementing Kakaphonie's thunderously strident melodies.

Devona kept swiveling her head this way and that, trying to take it all in and failing dismally. It was like trying to hold the ocean in your arms. No matter how hard you work at it, it's just not going to happen.

"Varvara has a one-word philosophy," I shouted to be heard over the Scream Queen and her band. "More!"

"She certainly appears to live by it!" Devona said.

The Atrium of Demon's Roost looks as if it had been ground zero during the explosion of an atomic kitsch bomb. Gaudy pastel-colored carpeting, black velvet paintings in neon-tube frames, mirrored disco balls spinning above… We passed a wall collage formed from thousands of tiny cheap toys from fast-food kids' meals, and soon after that, my favorite piece, a thirty foot-tall pewter statue of Elvis gazing benevolently down on a flock of plastic pink flamingos.

"Oh, my," was all Devona could manage to say.

"Quite a change from the Cathedral, isn't it?"

We stood for a moment and regarded at each other. Neither of us looked our best right then. I was a broken, decaying mess, and Devona was covered with Yberio's drying blood. Neither of us had commented on what had taken place in the veinburn lab, partially because we didn't have time to talk about it, but also I suspect because neither of us was exactly sure what to say. I was touched that Devona had felt the need to avenge Dale's death for me, but I was also once more painfully aware that we might have only a couple days, maybe even only a few more hours, together if Lord Galm wouldn't or couldn't use his magic to preserve my body. We'd come to mean so much to each other in such a short time, and I didn't want to face the very real possibility that what was growing between us would die before it had a chance to be fully born. So we looked at each other and didn't speak, but Devona took my hand and gave it a squeeze and that was enough.

Even with all the tumult in Demon's Roost, the tolling of the Deathknell could be heard, the sound muted and distant, but unmistakable. None of Varvara's guests seemed to notice, or more likely they just didn't care. After all, the Renewal Ceremony had been taking place every year for over three centuries. It was nothing special to them. They were far more concerned with obtaining their next drink and/or lover. But then, none of them knew about the Dawnstone and the use to which it would soon be put – unless Devona and I could stop it.

We continued on pushing, shoving, elbowing, and in a few cases kneeing our way through the crowd until we came to a bank of elevators. There were five, all the same, except the last on the left. That one had a red button, while the others had white buttons. And standing in front of the red-button elevator was an eight-foot-tall muscular creature with blue skin, shaggy black hair and a wild, unkempt beard. Its red-tinged eyes were the size of saucers, and huge incisors jutted down from behind its upper lip and curved outward like tusks. The thing wore only two items of clothing: a loincloth made from tanned human hide, and a necklace of tiny human heads.

"What is he?" Devona asked.

"His name is Jambha – it means *jaws* in Hindi – and he's a rakshasa, a demon from Hindu mythology. That's

Varvara's private elevator he's guarding. If anyone tries to use it without permission, he eats them."

Devona looked at me. "You're joking, right?"

"Well, he doesn't eat them right away. Among other things, back on Earth rakshasa were known for devouring the dead on battlefields. They like their food to age somewhat, say a week or two." I put a hand up to block my mouth so Jambha couldn't read my lips. "Watch out for his breath. I don't have a working olfactory system, and even I can't stand the stink of it."

Without another word, I led Devona over to Jambha. As we drew closer, we could see that the heads on the necklace were replicas of ours, little Matt-heads alternating with little Devona-heads, one after the other, all the way around. The neck stumps were ragged, as if the heads had been torn off by force, and they were fresh. Tiny drops of blood fell in continuous patters from the torn necks and onto Jambha's blue chest.

"How–" Devona began.

"Rakshasa are masters of illusions," I told her. "So don't believe everything you see."

When we came within three feet of the demon, I stopped us. Any closer, and we'd be instant demon chow.

"Hey, Jambha," I greeted him. "It's been a while."

The rakshasa looked me over from head to toe, and I felt like a piece of rotting meat in a demonic butcher's display case. A line of drool rolled down from his left tusk.

"You smell absolutely *appalling*," Jamba said, and licked his lips with a forked tongue.

"If that's a compliment, I guess I should say thank you, but keep your distance: no free samples, remember?" Since rakshasa love dead, rotting meat, in my current state I was like a walking ten course meal to Jambha, dessert included.

Jambha looked disappointed, but he recovered quickly. "No sample, no elevator ride."

I had a detached rotting ear I could give him somewhere in one of my pockets, and I started to fish around for it, but then I caught a glimpse of Devona's watching me with disapproval. I remembered what she'd said about the price I'd paid Waldermar – a page out of my memory. What kind of man thinks so little of his own experiences that he's willing to sell them for a few darkgems? So while giving Jambha the ear would've been the easy thing to do, in the end I decided not to.

'Listen, Jambha, we need to see Varvara right now. It's vital we catch her before she heads to the Spire for the Renewal Ceremony. Let us through."

"And I told you: no sample, no ride." He looked at me, his saucer eyes filled with carrion-lust.

The Deathknell sounded again, reminding me we didn't have time for playing around.

"Don't make me do it, Jambha."

The rakshasa scowled. "Do what?" he said warily.

"I have a pair of true-sight glasses in my pocket. If you don't let my friend and I use Varavara's elevator right now, I'll hand them to her and tell her to take a good look at you."

Jambha's scowl eased into a worried frown. "You're bluffing."

I shrugged." Only one way to find out."

The rakshasa and I stared each other down for a moment, but in the end Jambha sighed, pressed the button for us, and then stepped aside.

"Go on," he said miserably.

The door slid open and Devona and I stepped onto the elevator, both of us trying to ignore the disconcerting way the tiny Matt and Devona heads on Jambha's necklace all grinned as we walked by. Inside, there was only one button and I pushed it. As the door slowly closed, Jambha hurriedly said, "If anything *does* fall off, and you don't happen to have need of it, I'd appreciate it if you'd save it for me."

"I'll see what I can do." Then thankfully the door shut and the elevator began a smooth ascent. We rode upward to the lilting strains of a Muzak version of Blue Oyster Cult's "Don't Fear the Reaper." Varvara's odd sense of humor seemed appropriate given what had brought us here.

"This will take us straight up to the penthouse," I told Devona, "which is probably where Varvara's at right now, getting ready for the ceremony."

"Do you really have true-sight glasses?" Devona asked.

"No. I don't know if such things exist. I just made them up to bluff Jambha."

"Why would a rakshasa care if I looked at him with true-sight glasses – assuming any existed – or not? He certainly didn't seem overly concerned about his appearance before."

"Remember when I told you rakshasa were masters of illusion? In Jambha's case, he uses his abilities to hide his true body from everyone's eyes: in reality he stands a little under three feet tall and has arms like pipe cleaners. Not exactly the best look for a Darklord's guard. If word get out about his true appearance, Jambha would not only be embarrassed as hell, he'd never be able to work security in this town again."

"I'm just glad he let us get on," Devona said, "and I'm impressed that Varvara lets you use her private elevator. How do you rate? No, let me guess: you did her a favor once."

"Not quite." I didn't want to go on, but Devona was looking at me expectantly. "She finds me… amusing."

"Oh. In a good way or a bad way?"

"Honestly, I'm not sure."

"Do you think she'll listen to us?"

"There's no telling with Varvara. She might hear us out, or she might have us executed for bothering her before the Renewal Ceremony."

Devona looked suddenly alarmed.

"Relax; I was joking about the last part." At least, I hoped I was joking. It all depended on what sort of mood Varvara was in.

The elevator glided to a stop and the door opened to reveal a boudoir of silks, satins, and a thousand over-stuffed pillows scattered everywhere. Every possible shade of red and pink was represented, and I later learned from Devona that the air was thick with the mingled scents of a dozen different cloying perfumes mingled with a truckload of potpourri. The whole place was like a romance writer's wet dream.

Half of the large room was taken up by a monstrous canopy bed upon which lay the still, naked body of an obscenely muscled man. At first I thought he was dead, but he stirred slightly, and I realized he was only nearly dead.

I stepped off the elevator, and Devona followed. On the far side of the room, a stunningly beautiful redhead with a body that made most centerfolds look like concentration camp survivors stood before a mirrored wall, checking her outfit – a skin-tight dress made entirely of emeralds.

"That doesn't look very comfortable," I said.

Varvara didn't take her eyes off her reflection. "Comfortability is not the point." She turned around and examined her rear.

"Then what is?"

"Maximum amount of soul-gnawing envy from all women in the vicinity and maximum number of painfully unendurable erections from all men." She nodded. "I believe this will do nicely."

Varvara turned away from the mirror. "Hello, Matthew." She quickly looked me up and down. "You are aware, I trust, of your achingly desperate need of a makeover? So, what brings you into my bedroom this fine Descension evening? And with such a cute little friend!" Her brow crinkled as she frowned at Devona.

"Though you could use a good hosing down, dearie. A bit of advice: next time you decide to snack on someone, wear a bib."

She turned to me and smiled. "Don't tell me you want to get a foursome going, Matthew. I'm afraid I don't have the time, and Magnus–" She nodded toward the insensate slab of beefcake sprawled on her bed – "does not have the energy, and most likely won't for some days to come." She gave her boy-toy an appraising look. "I do hope I didn't break him. Victor Baron made him especially for me, and this was the first time I've had the chance to put the dear thing through his paces. He acquitted himself well enough, but there were a few moments there where I thought he might stroke out. Ah well, I suppose I can always send him back to the Foundry for a tune-up if necessary."

Now that Varvara faced us, her single non-human feature – unless you count her exaggeratedly feminine body as non-human – was evident: her slightly over-large eyes. They contained multicolored flecks which rotated slowly around the pupils. All demons, regardless of type, had those flecks, and they remained no matter what form a demon might assume. Varvara's eyes were more striking than most demons', though. They possessed an intensity that reminded me of an apex predator: cold, calculating, and always in the process of trying to decide whether or not to attack. She flashed us a dazzling smile that almost, but not quite, wiped away the eerie sensation of those savage eyes constantly sizing you up.

"Sorry to disappoint you, Varvara, but I'm not exactly up for those sort of games, if you know what I mean."

She walked over to us, every step runway model perfect, even with the incredibly steep high heels she was wearing. She leaned forward, nearly spilling out of her emeralds in the process, and whispered in my ear, "You could always watch."

And then she stepped back and laughed.

"Matt told me you find him amusing," Devona said icily. "Is it because he puts up with you cruelly taunting him like that?"

I shot Devona a warning glance. Maybe it was jealousy, or concern for my feelings, or both, that had prompted her to speak out, but talking like that to Varvara is not exactly conducive to your health.

The Demon Queen regarded Devona impassively for some time, but Devona stood her ground and stared at Varvara with equal intensity. And even though I didn't need to breathe, I held my breath anyway.

Then Varvara smiled. "I like you," she said simply. Underneath her words was an unspoken message: *I think I'll let you live.*

I released my breath.

"I'd really love to stay and chat, but I must dash. Have to help Dis and the other Darklords keep Nekropolis going for another year." She sighed theatrically. "Dreadfully dull, but I suppose it has to be done."

She started toward the elevator, but before she could reach it, I called after her.

"I have a favor to ask of you, Varvara."

She stopped and turned around. "A favor?" She smiled slowly. "Why of course, Matt. We demons love to do favors – for a price."

I held up my hand and displayed Lord Edrigu's mark. "I'm afraid I don't have much in the way of trade right now."

She frowned upon seeing the mark, and her manner became serious. "What in the Nine Hells have you been up to?"

So I told her.

When I finished, Varvara said, "I wasn't even aware that Galm had the Dawnstone, and now he's lost it. Intriguing."

"You know about the Dawnstone?" Devona asked.

Varvara waved the question aside. "Honey, when you've lived as long as I have, there isn't a whole lot you don't know." She turned toward the mirror and looked thoughtfully at her reflection. "I wonder if there's a way I can use this to my advantage."

"This isn't the time for scheming," I said sternly.

Varvara turned away from the mirror. "While the Dawnstone is a potent token of power, I'm not sure it really poses much of a threat. Still, I suppose it wouldn't hurt to telepathically check with my fellow Lords, especially since the Renewal Ceremony is soon to begin." She nodded to herself as if making a decision. "You two wait here." She turned and headed for a closed door on the other side of the room.

"Where are you going?" I asked.

She stopped. "To a private chamber where I can concentrate more effectively. We Darklords have built up quite strong psychic defenses against each other over the millennia, and it's going to take some effort on my part to get even a simple message past their guard – if I can."

"What about contacting Father Dis?" I suggested.

She gave me a withering look. "Darling, you don't contact Dis; he contacts you." And with that she walked to the door, opened it, stepped inside, and closed it behind her.

"Private chamber?" Devona said. "That looked like her–"

"Bathroom, yeah. But you have to admit, 'private chamber' sounds a lot classier."

"So what do we do?"

"You heard her: we wait."

Devona went over to the mirror and examined her transparent reflection. "I wish now that I had gone to Father right away. What if we can't stop whoever it is from using the Dawnstone?"

I joined her in front of the mirror, though I didn't particularly appreciate the chewed-up zombie it showed me. "There's no point in worrying about might-have-beens, Devona. All we can do now is our best. In the end, that has to be enough."

She didn't look convinced, so I decided to try to take her mind off her recriminations while Varvara attempted to contact the other Lords. "This is more than just a mirror, you know. It's Varvara's dimensional portal."

Devona took a half step back, as if afraid the mirror might suck her in. "You and Dale came to Nekropolis through here?"

"This is Varvara's personal portal. She has a larger one down in the lower levels of the Roost, which is what Dale and I used." I smiled. "I don't think we would've lasted very long if we'd popped out into Varvara's bedroom – especially if she'd been busy entertaining company."

Devona stepped back to the mirror. "I've never seen Father's portal. I wonder how it works."

"The one downstairs is pretty simple. All you have to do–" I reached out and tapped the glass three times with my index finger. The mirror shimmered and our reflections were replaced by an image of a park just before sunset – trees, benches, neatly trimmed green grass, birds singing, people walking, holding hands, riding bikes, in-line skating… From the trees and the way people were dressed, it looked like late spring. And then I realized: sunset. Horrified, I tried to push Devona out the way. But she planted her feet solidly on the floor, and with her strength, I couldn't budge her.

"What are you doing?"

"The sunlight!" I said. "You have to get away from the portal before–"

She laughed. "Matt, I'm half-human, remember? Sunlight doesn't destroy my kind, it just temporarily nullifies our vampiric abilities."

I wasn't sure, but it looked like her skin was slowly turning pinker, more fully human. I thought it would be a different story if I tried to shove her away from the mirror now. Her strength would be no greater than an ordinary human's too.

"So that's the sun," she said in a hushed voice. "It's redder than I imagined, but still quite beautiful." She touched her cheek. "And so warm."

For a moment I thought she was joking, but then I remembered Galm had brought her to Nekropolis soon after she'd been born. She really never had seen the sun.

"What are we looking at?" she asked.

"A park. It's a place where people in the city go to get away, feel close to nature, and relax." I smiled. "Kind of like the Wyldwood, only without the murderous shapeshifters."

"Everyone looks as if they're enjoying themselves. I wonder what it would be like to be human, fully human, and live in an ordinary house, work at an ordinary job, and go to the park at sunset."

"As I recall, it was pretty damned good." It had been a while since I had seen Earth except in movies on Mind's Eye broadcasts. But this was a hundred times better, and more heartbreaking, than any movie could ever be. Because I knew that all I would have to do to go there was to step through the glass. I was tempted. If I were going to die for good in the next day or so, at least I could die in the world where I'd been born and lived most of my life.

But I didn't step forward. There was still a chance that I could save myself. And besides, I don't like to leave a job unfinished.

"Pretty isn't it? Especially for Cleveland." Varvara had come out of the bathroom – excuse me, her private chamber – and was standing behind us. "Still, we don't have time for sightseeing." She snapped her long red-nailed fingers and the park evaporated and the mirror was just a mirror again. Devona looked disappointed.

"Any luck?" I asked.

"No, the fools wouldn't even acknowledge my attempts. Can't say as I blame, them, though. I'd have done the same thing; centuries of distrust are hard to overcome. I'll just have to try to talk to them once I get to the Nightspire, I suppose."

"You mean, once we get to the Nightspire," I said. "Devona and I have been through too much not to see this to the end."

"I don't think so, Matt. While you're fun to have around, Dis doesn't appreciate tag-alongs."

"The Darklords always bring a retinue with them," Devona said. "My father does, though I've never had the distinction of being part of it."

"So why couldn't we tag along with your tag-alongs?" I asked.

"Our retinues are primarily made up of Demilords, relatives, high-level city functionaries, and important Earth contacts," Varvara said. "Still… I suppose it wouldn't hurt anything."

"And think how much it'll annoy Talaith to see me there," I pointed out.

The Demon Queen brightened. "There is that. All right, you may accompany me. But we should go now.

There isn't much time left before the ceremony starts." She looked at us and then wrinkled her nose. "But perhaps you two should freshen up a bit first."

After Devona and I spent a couple of minutes in Varvara's "private chamber," the three of us headed for the elevator.

As we walked by the bed, I nodded to the still comatose Magnus. "What about him?"

"Let him sleep," Varvara said with a wicked grin. "He'll need all the rest he can get for when I return."

The elevator arrived. We got on and began our descent.

Varvara turned to Devona. "Before, you asked – in quite a snippy tone, I might add – what I found so amusing about Matt."

"I was just–" Devona began.

"What I find so amusing about our friend here is that he is a champion of order in one of the most chaotic places in the Omniverse – an undead Don Quixote, tilting at Nekropolis's windmills on what may very well be an ultimately futile quest to make this a better place." She smiled. "Besides, he makes me laugh."

"I'm just a guy who does favors for people, Varvara, you know that." I hate it when she talks about me that way. Probably because I'm afraid she's right.

The elevator stopped, the door opened, and we were off to the biggest windmill Nekropolis has to offer – the Nightspire.

TWENTY-TWO

Of all the ways I might have imagined traveling to the Nightspire in pursuit of a thief and murderer, riding in the back of a hot pink limousine (with matching interior) wasn't one of them. Behind us was a line of far less striking vehicles bearing Varvara's retinue, primarily demons, but a few humans – mostly music industry and Hollywood types – who served her as well.

Varvara sipped a frozen daiquiri whipped up from the tiny wet bar by her personal bartender, a creature which resembled a levitating sea urchin, and waved through the open widow at the cheering crowds lining the street. Psychographers captured mental impressions for live Mind's Eye coverage of the Renewal Ceremony as we passed, while reporters from both the *Tome* and the *Daily Atrocity* shouted out questions to Varvara, all of which she cheerfully ignored.

"It's so nice to receive the adulation of the masses, don't you think?" Varvara said. She downed the rest of her daiquiri and told the urchin to mix her another.

Varvara is probably the most popular Darklord, considering she lets her subjects – and anyone who visits the Sprawl, for that matter – pretty much do as they please. I can't say near-anarchy is my idea of effective social policy, but then Varvara's never asked for my opinion. And I must admit, the Sprawl is the most interesting place in Nekropolis, which is why I suppose I make my home there.

The driver, who I would've taken for just another pretty muscle-boy if it hadn't been for the ram's horns jutting out of his head, spoke over the intercom.

"I have to slow down, Milady. Several Sentinels are coming up behind us."

Varvara pushed a button on her armrest. "No problem, love, but when they're past, speed up a tad. We're running a wee bit late."

I turned around, and through the rear window I saw three Sentinels walking in a row down the middle of the street. They weren't running – I wasn't sure if they could – but they were walking faster than I'd ever seen any of the golems move before.

"Don't tell me," I said. "They're going to arrest us for assault with an exceptionally tacky paint job."

"Remember what I said about you making me laugh?" Varvara asked. "I take it back."

The Sentinels tromped around us and continued down the street, accompanied by boos and hisses from the drunk and drugged-up crowd. Father Dis's police force wasn't exactly beloved by the denizens of the Sprawl.

"Where are they going in such a hurry?" I asked.

"They've been recalled to the Nightspire for the Renewal Ceremony," Devona explained.

Varvara frowned at me. "How long have you been in Nekropolis now, two years?"

"Just about."

"And you didn't know the Sentinels are part of the ceremony?"

I shrugged. "This is only my second Descension celebration, and I spent the first helping a pregnant witch escape her abusive warlock husband. At one point, he actually switched my personality with that of the fetus, and I – well, suffice it to say the situation took some straightening out, and I missed a good part of the celebration, including the Renewal Ceremony."

"You have to tell about that one some time, Matt," Varvara said. "So many mortals wish to return to the womb, but you're the only one I know who's managed to do it!" And she laughed the rest the way to the Nightspire.

As we approached the slender black needle that was the Nightspire, I noticed something strange.

"Umbriel seems larger than usual."

"That's because it's descending for the Ceremony," Varvara said impatiently. "Really, Matt, are you going to be this tiresome the whole time?"

"More, if I can manage it."

The crowd was thickest as we neared the bridge that led from the Sprawl to the Nightspire. Varvara continued playing the gracious queen parading before

her adoring subjects, when a grizzled old man in a
yellowed seersucker suit and carrying a sheaf of paper
broke out of the crowd and came running toward the
limo, and Varvara's open window.

"Oh, no," I moaned. "Not now, Carl."

Carl thrust one of his homemade papers through the
window and into Varvara's face.

"Beware the Watchers, Lady!" he shouted wildly,
"Beware–" But that's as far as he got before Varvara hit
a button and the window slid up. Carl barely retracted
his arm in time. He released his "paper," however, and
it fell onto Varvara's lap. With a grimace of distaste, she
brushed it onto the floor.

"Usually I find Carl's rants diverting, but I'm not in
the mood tonight."

"I'm surprised he was able to approach the car at all,"
Devona said. "I'd think a Darlord would have better security."

"If Carl had any ill intent toward us, the wardspells
on my car would've fried him as soon as he came within
three feet." Varvara smiled. "Secure enough for you?"

Devona didn't reply.

The ram's-horn hunk drove us onto the bridge. The
winds of the Furies didn't rise, but then we were expected. As soon as we reached the dull, gray, grassless
earth of the island on the other side, the sonorous
tolling of the Deathknell stopped.

I looked at Varvara, but she said, "That merely means
that all five Darklords have now reached the Nightspire.
I'm usually the last."

"Why am I not surprised?"

The driver pulled up to the Nightspire and parked behind a double row of coaches and wagons – the other Darklords' vehicles, I presumed. The chauffeur came around and opened Varvara's door, and she slid out, taking his proffered hand and allowing him to help her, though she was doubtless the far stronger of the two. Devona and I had to haul our butts out unassisted, of course.

The other cars in Varvara's entourage parked behind us, and their occupants disembarked, more than a few of them giving Devona and me dirty looks, obviously wondering who we were and how we rated riding in the front of the procession with their queen – especially when they didn't.

The green flames of Phlegethon which surrounded the small island flared higher than usual. Because of the coming ceremony? I wondered. The air seemed charged with barely contained energy, and I looked up. Directly over the tip of the Nightspire, Umbriel, looking bloated and heavy, continued its slow descent.

Varvara started toward the rectangular entrance of the Nightspire, and gestured for Devona and me to follow. I heard a few mutterings from Varvara's other guests. It appeared we'd usurped yet another honor. My heart would've bled for them – if I'd had any blood.

As we walked, I saw Silent Jack atop his Black Rig, a pale woman in a blood-stained dress sitting next him. Jack had brought his wife, Bloody Mary, along with him for this special occasion. The ghostly coachman touched his finger to the brim of his hat as we walked by, but Mary just looked at us with the crimson hollows where her eyes had once been. I thought of the E on my palm, and a chill ran down my back regardless of the fact I had no working nerves.

As we entered, I thought that if Gregor had wanted Devona to carry one of his children so that he might finally get a look-see inside a Darklord's stronghold, how much more excited he would be to actually learn about the interior of the Nightspire itself. Inside was the same as the outside: featureless black, as if the Nightspire had been shaped from solidified shadow. We walked down a long narrow corridor lit by torches of green fire. Varvara's outrageously high heels clacked hollowly as she walked, echoing up and down the hall. She looked like someone who was trying to appear as if she wasn't hurrying, when in fact she was. I had a feeling we were running more than a "wee bit late," as she'd earlier told our driver.

A mural was painted on the corridor's wall showing scenes depicting key events in the history of the Darkfolk leading up to the founding of Nekropolis. The first scene was of a primordial swamp, like the kind you'd see in any Earth museum showing primitive lifeforms leaving the water to take their first tentative steps on land. But instead of amphibians, the creatures emerging from this swamp were shapeless sinuous shadows. I learned later that this event was known as Darkrise and the creatures were called Shadowings.

The second scene was more sinister, showing creatures that were obviously forerunners of vampires and lykes preying on primitive humans. The Darkfolk in the next scene were more developed – looking much as they do today – and they sat on thrones made from human bones while mortal men and woman bowed down to them, worshipping them as dark gods. The fourth scene showed the tables turning, as humans with crude swords, spears, and axes attacked Darkfolk, driving them away from human settlements and into the shadowy wilderness. The next scene skipped a couple thousand years and picked up the visual narrative with the Inquisition, showing Darkfolk being tortured by humans – vampires staked, lykes skinned, witches and warlocks burned alive.

The Wanderyear came next, showing a robed figure I assumed to be Dis traveling the length and breadth of the world in search of other Darkfolk powerful enough to help him create Nekropolis. Good thing Yberio was dead; he'd certainly have felt slighted to learn he wasn't among those portrayed in this scene. The Darksome Council came after that, when Dis met with the five current Darklords atop a wind-blasted mountain peak where the barriers between dimensions were thinnest. Here Dis showed the Lords the Null Plains, the new home where the Darkfolk would build their great city. After that was the Bedarkening – the creation of Umbriel above the Null Plans – followed by the construction of Nekropolis, and then the Descension, when Earth's Darkfolk finally emigrated to their new home. The second-to-last scene showed the city in flames, blood running red in the streets while the Darklords' armies fought with no quarter given and none asked: the Blood Wars. The last image was of Nekropolis as it looks today: the five Dominions at relative peace, the Nightspire rising above all, as if to keep a close eye on things.

The corridor let us out into a vast circular chamber which sloped inward the farther up it rose, and I realized that the Nightspire was hollow. But while the inside walls of the Nightspire were the same unchanging black as the exterior, white marble columns ringed the chamber, and the floor was made of tiled mosaics. Dis had once been the Roman god of the dead, and it seemed his taste in interior decorating hadn't changed since the Empire's fall.

In the middle of the chamber was a large, raised marble dais in the shape of a pentagram. Sentinels surrounded the dais, face out, as if they were guarding it. At a quick estimate, I figured there were maybe thirty Sentinels altogether. I hadn't realized the city had that many. I thought I recognized one, a Sentinel with a faint scar running down its chest, as the one who had taken Varma's body off our hands. I wondered if the golem had delivered Varma to the Cathedral, and if so, what Galm's reaction had been. I supposed I'd find out soon.

The Sentinels were far from the chamber's only occupants, though. Vampires, lykes, Arcane, and half-visible spirits stood in small groups, talking and sampling hors d'oeuvres and imbibing drinks brought to them by bald, red-robed men and women. That is, the living ate and drank. The dead merely watched them do so. Between two columns on the far side of the chamber, a tuxedo-clad pianist with four arms played soft, unobtrusive background music.

"I can't believe it," I said. "After everything I've heard about it, the vaunted Renewal Ceremony turns out to be nothing more than a cocktail party?"

"These are merely the preliminaries to the ceremony," Varvara said quietly. "The ceremony itself will begin shortly."

"Who are the baldies in red?" I asked.

"The Cabal," Varvara said quietly. "Dis's personal attendants. And it would be a good idea to avoid calling them 'baldies.'"

"They look like waiters to me," I said.

"They are whatever Dis says they are," Varvara replied. "Don't bother trying to talk to them; they only respond to their master."

"We must find my father and tell him of the threat," Devona said, and without waiting for either of us to reply, she set off for a group of nearby vampires nibbling on what appeared to be small animal hearts. Varvara and I hurried after her.

She asked the vampires – who were dressed in overdone Bela Lugosi drag – where Lord Galm was. The vampires, who I took to be out-of-towners from Earth by the way they dressed, pointed to the base of the pentagram dais, where Galm was standing talking to Amon in his English hunter guise, Talaith, and a thin man with the gaunt face of a mortician. I assumed the latter was

Edrigu. Devona made a beeline, or in her case a batline, toward them. There was one dignitary in attendance I'd never seen but heard a great deal about. Wrapped in ancient cerements, a crimson cape draped over her slender shoulders, a mask of wrought gold concealing her face stood Keket, Overseer of Tenebrus, flanked by a pair of her jackal-headed Warders. Keket held such a powerful position in the city, she sometimes was referred to as the Sixth Lord, though she had no official standing as such. She stood off to the side, ignoring everyone else, and being ignored right back in turn. Prison wardens are never among the most popular of party guests, no matter what dimension you're in.

I half-expected to see Waldemar there too, but supposedly he never leaves the Great Library. Sometimes I think he is the library, body and soul.

Varvara caught up to Devona and grabbed her arm to slow her down. "I think it would be best if I led the way, dear." From her tone, and the way her eyes flashed, it was clear Varvara wasn't making a request.

Devona looked like she was going to argue, but then thought better of it and nodded. We continued with Varvara in the lead, and as we approached the other Lords, the Demon Queen opened her arms and said, "Darlings! So nice to see you all!"

"And for us to see so much of you," Talaith said cattily as she eyed Varvara's outfit. "Why didn't you just come naked this year?"

"Is that a criticism, or are you voicing a regret?" Varvara shot back.

Talaith reddened but didn't reply. She looked smaller than the avatar which had attacked us in Glamere, older and more tired too. Physically, she appeared to be in her late sixties, with short gray hair, baggy eyes, and sagging skin. She'd looked better before the destruction of the Overmind: one more reason for her to hate me. In diametric opposition to Varvara's skimpy outfit, Talaith wore a simple black and white dress reminiscent of Puritan garb. I wondered if anyone had ever attempted to burn her at the stake. If so, I was sorry they'd failed.

Talaith turned to Devona and me, and her upper lip curled in disgust. "I knew your standards were low, Varvara, but really."

"Watch your tongue, witch," Galm growled. "The woman is one of my birth daughters." Maybe Devona, as a half human, didn't rate as high in the vampire hierarchy as the fully Bloodborn, but it seemed she was high enough for Galm to object to anyone insulting her.

"I was referring to the zombie," Talaith covered smoothly. She looked to the thin-faced man. "Really, Edrigu, isn't there something you can do about this... thing? After all, as one of the undead, he falls under your purview."

The corners of Edrigu's thin lips raised a fraction in what I assumed was meant to be a smile. He appeared to be in his mid-fifties and was bald save for a fine layer of black hair along the sides and back of his head. He wore a tattered white shroud covered with grave mold, and through the ragged cloth glimpses of not flesh but bone were visible.

"What would you have me do, precisely, Talaith?" His voice was a hollow monotone, a lonely echo in a deserted mausoleum.

"Oh, I don't know. Wave your hand and make him collapse into dust, something along those lines."

Edrigu gave me a look and I felt the mark on my palm itch. He knew he didn't have to do anything to me; I was due to turn to dust soon enough as it was.

"Sour grapes, Talaith," Amon said. "You're still bitter Mr. Richter and his late partner disrupted one of your little schemes a while back."

"Not much of a scheme, as I recall," Varvara said. "Even if Matt hadn't happened along, I doubt it would've worked."

Talaith glared at them both, but otherwise did nothing. The bantering Darklords reminded me of wary jungle predators facing each other over a water hole. They hated each other and weren't afraid to show it, but this wasn't the time or place to do anything about it. But I could see in Talaith's eyes that she was keeping track of every insult and adding it to her list of grievances against her fellow Lords.

Edrigu stepped closer to me and reached out to shake my hand. When our flesh touched, the E on my palm burned like fire, and I took in a hissing breath. It was the first pain I'd felt since I died.

"Hello, Mr. Richter," Edrigu said in that eerie voice of his. "It's nice to finally make your acquaintance. You are, after all, a unique specimen among my charges." He smiled with cold amusement. "By the way, my driver says you taste absolutely delicious."

I withdrew my hand. Edrigu's comment had rattled me – not to mention the burning sensation – and I quickly tried to cover. "You're a Darklord, Edrigu. You'd think you'd be able to afford some skin to cover those ribs."

Edrigu just smiled, his eyes cold as a tomb in deep winter. I turned away, unable to meet that awful gaze. The burning in my hand was mostly gone, but a distant echo of its pain lingered.

Devona went up to Galm and hesitantly touched his bare ivory arm. "Father, we must talk. It's urgent!

Up to now, Galm had been brooding and not paying attention to the conversation. But when Devona spoke, he looked up, startled, as if he'd forgotten she were here. "Not now, child. We received bad news at the Cathedral while you were out. Varma died the final death earlier today."

"I know, father," Devona said softly. "Matt and I found his body."

The other Lords fell silent and awaited Galm's reaction. Keket seemed especially interested, which only made sense since she represented what passed for the law in Nekropolis. I half expected Galm to destroy Devona and me where we stood, but instead the ancient vampire spoke softly in a voice thick with restrained anger. "Tell me what you know."

Devona hesitated, and then launched into a concise summary of everything that had happened since she'd discovered the Dawnstone was missing.

After she was done, the ice on Lord Galm's glacially impassive face broke and his features contorted in fury. "Varma was a weak, immature man who existed only for pleasure. If the Dominari hadn't introduced him to veinburn, he would have tried it on his own eventually. But if had you come to me immediately, child, I might have been able to locate Varma and use my magics to burn the addiction out of him, quite possibly preventing his assassination." He shot Varvara a meaningful look, and I imagined the two of them were going to have a few conversations about the drug trade in Varvara's Dominion not long after the ceremony.

"But you let your pride as keeper of my Collection interfere with your duty to your cousin – who was fully Bloodborn, I might add."

Devona hung her head in shame. "Yes, my Lord."

I wanted to shout at Galm, to tell him he was being unnecessarily cruel – not to mention just plain wrongheaded – to talk to Devona like he had. But I knew that despite my watering hole analogy, the Darklords' truce didn't extend to me, and I had to watch what I said.

"My Lord," I said, nearly choking on the words, "what about the Dawnstone?" I hoped this would distract him from berating Devona and also turn his attention to the most important aspect of her story: that whoever stole the Dawnstone likely planned to attack with it during the Renewal Ceremony.

But I was surprised by his response.

"It is of no consequence."

"No consequence!" I said. "I thought it was an object of great power!"

"It is," Galm admitted, "but one which takes much mystic knowledge and skill to operate. Such attributes are possessed only by my fellow Lords."

"And we would never use such a device," Edrigu said. "Not during the Renewal Ceremony."

"Edrigu's right," Amon said. "It would be one thing to employ the Dawnstone against each other outside of the Nightspire, but to use it here and risk Dis's wrath? Never."

"Not to mention what the effect of using an object of power would have on the ceremony itself," Talaith said. "We need Dis, and all five of us, to maintain Nekropolis. If the ceremony were interrupted before completion, Umbriel would fail to be renewed."

"And Nekropolis, and all its denizens, would be no more," Edrigu finished. "There'd be nothing left to rule over."

"Besides," Talaith pointed out, "there's no way anyone could sneak such a powerful artifact into the Nightspire, not with the powerful wardspells Father Dis has placed on the entrances."

"It's far more likely the Dominari have different – but no less nasty – plans for it," Amon said. "But that need not concern us at the moment."

I looked to Varvara for confirmation. "They've got a good point," she told me. "Several, in fact."

It sounded as if the other Lords had managed to convince Varvara. And truth to tell, what they said did seem reasonable. But that didn't mean I bought it. My undead gut told me that despite all the Darklords' arguments to the contrary, whoever had the Dawnstone would use it here, soon. But if the Darklords didn't believe us, I didn't know what we'd be able to do about it.

Evidently, Devona felt the same, too, for she said, "Father, please, you must–"

"Forget the Dawnstone," Galm said, icy reserve in place once more. "It is no longer any of your concern, for you are no longer keeper of my Collection."

Devona stared at her father in stunned disbelief.

"You have failed me and failed Varma. From now on you are cast out from the Bloodborn; you are no longer my daughter. Do not return to the Cathedral. If you do, I shall kill you." And with that, Galm turned and strode away.

Devona's eyes filled with tears which she fought desperately. Her hands clamped into fists so tight, her nails punctured the flesh of her palms and blood dripped from her wounds. She was shaking in both sorrow and anger. She opened her mouth – to call after Galm, I presume – but no words came. No matter what she might have said, I knew it wouldn't have helped. Lord Galm had rendered his judgment, and I doubted even Father Dis could get him to reverse it.

I put what I hoped was a comforting hand on her shoulder. I wanted to say something to console her, but it was my turn to be unable to find the right words. Everything that had defined her existence and her very identity for her entire life – seventy-three years – had been stripped away from her in mere moments.

I suppose I should have also been concerned that I'd lost my chance to gain Lord Galm's aid in staving off my final decay. But you know something? The thought didn't even occur to me.

Edrigu, Amon, and Talaith wandered off, the latter looking quite pleased with the way things had turned out. Keket – who, I'd noticed, had stayed out of the debate over the Dawnstone – gave us a last look before trailing after the four Darklords, her dog-headed servants in tow. Varvara remained with us, though I wasn't sure why.

And that's when a gong sounded, though there was none in the room to be seen, and through a doorway on the other side of the room entered a handsome man dressed in a dark purple toga.

Father Dis.

TWENTY-THREE

Everything stopped – the music, the conversation – and everyone turned toward Dis and slowly went down on bended knees. I don't mind showing someone respect, provided they earn it. But the idea of paying homage to a person I'd never meant as if he were royalty – even if in Nekropolis he was – really grated. Still, I knelt along with the others, though I gritted my teeth while doing so.

Dis strode into the chamber with the easy confidence of someone who is lord of all he surveys and doesn't feel a need to make a big deal out of it. He paused for a moment, smiled, and then gestured for us to stand. Everyone complied, but they remained silent, watching Father Dis and waiting for their next cue.

Dis wasn't what I had expected. There was nothing monstrous about him at all. He stood over six feet, had short curly black hair, a large but distinguished-looking nose, and a relaxed, charming smile. This was the ultimate Lord of Nekropolis? He looked more like an Italian movie star.

He walked through the crowd, smiling and nodding to those he passed, stopping once or twice to shake someone's hand (or paw or claw). And then he continued walking – straight toward us.

When he reached us, he stopped and flashed that smile of his. "Varvara, how lovely to see you, as always." He took her hand and kissed the back of it. His voice was a mellow tenor, but with an odd accent I couldn't quite place.

"My Lord," Varvara said solemnly, all trace of the shallow, fashion-crazed party-girl persona she affected gone.

Dis released her hand and turned to Devona and me. "I see we have two new guests this evening. Charmed, Ms. Kanti." He kissed Devona's hand, and she just watched him, flustered. "Mr. Richter."

I held up my gray-skinned hand. "If you're going to kiss my hand too, I have to warn you, it's seen better days." I couldn't help it; I'm even more of a smart aleck than usual when I'm nervous.

Dis chuckled. "I've seen far worse in my time, Mr. Richter, believe me." And then the pupils in his warm brown eyes dilated, becoming windows to a darkness deeper and colder than anything I had ever imagined. His pupils returned to normal and he shook my hand. "So glad you two could make it tonight. I hope it shall turn out to be a memorable experience for you both."

And with that he left us and walked toward the pentagram-shaped dais. "The time is nigh!" he called out in a commanding voice, the charming host gone, replaced by the Lord of the City. "Let us begin!"

He mounted the dais steps and climbed to the top, and passed through the ring of Sentinels. He took a position in the center of the pentagram and waited. The five Darklords, including Varvara, then joined him, each standing on the point of the pentagram which corresponded to the location of their stronghold in the city, facing Father Dis.

I half expected dramatic music to swell as Dis and the Darklords raised their arms above their heads, but the chamber was silent, the air charged with anticipation. Everyone stood gathered around the dais, watching, waiting. Dis chanted no harsh, multisyllabic words of magic, made no complicated mystic gestures. All he did was simply look upward – and the Nightspire began to open.

As if it were an ebon flower curling back its night-dark petals, the tip of Nightspire blossomed open to reveal Umbriel. The shadowsun hovered huge and heavy in the eternal night of Nekropolis's sky, its hue no longer pure black but now shot through with patches of gray. It seemed to sag in the sky, as if weary and barely able to keep itself aloft.

The Darklords lowered their hands until they were pointing at Dis. And then gouts of darkness blasted forth from their palms to engulf him in a turbulent, writhing shroud of shadow. Dis inhaled, drawing the darkness into him as if it were air, and then, with the Lords continuing to feed him with their shadow, Dis lowered his arms, threw back his head, and opened his mouth wide.

A torrent of darkness surged upward from deep within the being that called itself Father Dis, spiraling up through the interior of the Nightspire, geysering forth from the opening, and streaking across the starless sky toward Umbriel. The stygian bolt struck the shadowsun, feeding, restoring, renewing it. As we watched, the patches of gray began to shrink, and Umbriel seemed to grow stronger and more vital. It was a wonder to behold. A dark wonder, yes, but a wonder just the same.

And then, out of the corner of my eye, I became aware of movement on the dais. One of the Sentinels – the one I'd recognized earlier, with the scar on its chest – was stirring. It moved its thick-fingered hands to the line of puckered flesh, plunged them into the skin, and pulled open its chest. It reached into the cavity and brought forth a crystal a bit larger than a man's fist.

The Dawnstone.

I understood in a flash how the artifact had been smuggled past the Nightspire's wardspells. Concealed within a Sentinel, one of Dis's own guards, it hadn't tripped any of the mystic protections.

Some of the others in the audience had noticed the Sentinel's actions, and were shouting and pointing. If the Darklords and Dis were aware of what was happening, they gave no sign. The Lords continued pumping Dis full of darkness, and he in turn continued feeding it upward into Umbriel.

The Sentinel cupped the Dawnstone in its hands, and a warm yellow glow began to suffuse the crystal.

"It's activating the stone!" Devona shouted. "But that's impossible! A Sentinel is a golem, a mystic automaton without a mind of its own! It can't work magic!"

The Dawnstone's glow was getting brighter.

"Well, this one can!" I said.

People were shouting to the Lords, trying to get their attention, but it was no use. Whether the Lords couldn't hear or couldn't afford to be distracted at this point in the ceremony, they didn't respond. Neither, for that matter, did the other Sentinels, who remained motionless on the dais. Maybe they too were somehow part of the ceremony, or perhaps they needed Dis to command them to action. Whichever the case, they stood by, useless.

Dis's red-robed attendants, the Cabal, dropped their serving trays and rushed toward the rogue Sentinel, their hands flaring with crimson energy. But the Sentinel merely pointed the Dawnstone at the oncoming attendants. A dazzling lance of white light blazed forth from the crystal and washed over the Cabal. They didn't even have time to scream. One second they were there, the next they were gone. Not even dust remained.

A number of the Darklords' guests – the vampires especially – fell to the floor, crying and moaning in pain, injured from merely witnessing the release of the Dawnstone's awesome power. Keket managed to remain on her cloth-wrapped feet, but she'd averted her eyes, unable to face the Dawnstone's luminance. Her Warders huddled behind her, whining like terrified dogs. Everyone else either stood in mute fear or was trying to escape the chamber. No one headed for the Sentinel, which was slowly starting to turn around to face Dis and the Darklords.

It looked like it was up to the dead man. I drew my 9mm, aimed at the Sentinel's head, and squeezed off three shots.

I wasn't the world's greatest marksman when alive, but death has given me a much steadier hand, and my shots hit their intended target. But I might as well not have bothered; the bullets merely scratched the Sentinel's doughy gray flesh.

I decided to try a different target and fired three more shots at the Dawnstone. Because of the way the crystal was glowing, it was hard to tell if I hit it, but I believed I did. But instead of being rewarded with the sound of shattering magic crystal, nothing happened.

"I should've known it wouldn't be that easy," I muttered as I pulled out the spent clip and replaced it with a fresh one.

The Sentinel completed its turn and aimed the Dawnstone at Father Dis and, along with the five bolts of darkness still blasting into him from the Darklords, a stream of white light struck him full on the chest. The shadow streaming forth from Dis's mouth cut off as the Lord of Nekropolis screamed.

Take all the pain in the universe, not just physical pain, but all the mental and emotional anguish you can imagine. Put them all together, double, triple, quadruple them, and you still wouldn't match the intensity of the agony in Father Dis's cry.

And then the ground began to shake, as if the Nightspire shared its master's anguish. I wondered if the disturbance was localized to Dis's island, or if the entire city experienced the tremors. I feared the latter.

I finished reloading and turned to Devona. "Time to get your crystal back," I said.

She nodded grimly, and we started toward the dais, but before she could get three steps, she stiffened, grimaced in pain, and fell to her side. In my concern for Devona, I momentarily forgot about the Sentinel, the Dawnstone, the Lords, and the quaking of the Nightspire. I knelt by her side.

"What's wrong?"

She touched the side of her head and between pain-gritted teeth forced out, "My head… feels like it's… on fire…"

I feared she was suffering from some delayed reaction to viewing the Dawnstone's brilliance. I wanted to help her, wanted to take away the pain, but I didn't know how.

"Forget about me, go… stop… Dawnstone…"

I didn't want to leave her lying there in agony, but I knew if someone didn't do something soon, we'd all be destroyed. I nodded, squeezed her hand, then stood and half-ran, half-limped toward the dais. I weaved between weeping and wailing guests, my mind racing to come up with some sort of plan of attack.

I couldn't hurt the Sentinel by shooting it, couldn't shatter the Dawnstone. I certainly couldn't physically battle the golem, nor did I have any mystic knowledge that would allow me to attack it magically. And I didn't have anything in my jacket of tricks that would help. If only the damned thing's hide wasn't so blasted tough! Then I could – and then I realized: its skin might be impenetrable, but what about its insides? There was a gaping hole in its chest now where the Dawnstone had been concealed. If I could just get a shot at that hole…

I circled the dais, looking for an angle. It wasn't easy, considering the other motionless Sentinels in the way, not to mention the Darklords and Father Dis. But I finally found a space between a Sentinel and Talaith that, while not perfect by any means, would have to do. I aimed, doing my best to ignore Dis's cries and the chamber's shaking. Steady, steady… I fired.

One, two, three shots right into the open gash in the Sentinel's chest. Success! The creature staggered and the Dawnstone's beam winked out. But the golem didn't go down. Instead, it leveled the Dawnstone at me and I was blinded by the crystal's blazing light. I raised an arm to protect my eyes, but I felt no heat and no pain.

The light extinguished, and I blinked furiously, trying to force my eyes to work again. Within seconds, I could see once more, although my vision was peppered with floating purple and orange afterimages. I took a quick inventory of my body, and as near as I could tell, the Dawnstone hadn't harmed me. I was grateful the crystal produced no heat; otherwise, I likely would have burst into flame.

The Sentinel seemed to regard me for a moment – it was difficult to tell for certain since it possessed no facial features – and then it turned and began descending the dais. I checked Dis. He knelt in the middle of the pentagram, obviously shaken. The Darklords were still emitting beams of darkness at him, though, and the Nightspire continued quaking furiously. Dis got to his feet and looked up at Umbriel once more. The shadow-sun was covered with gray patches, many more than before, and jagged fissures criss-crossed its surface. The Renewal Ceremony was failing.

Dis opened his mouth and released a shout of equal parts frustration and determination, and pure darkness fountained from deep within him and rushed upward toward Nekropolis's dying sun.

The Sentinel, meanwhile, had reached the chamber floor and was stomping toward me, the Dawnstone held at its side in one massive hand. Magic hadn't harmed me, so it looked like the big bruiser was going to get physical. No problem; this kind of fight I understood.

I aimed for the gash and squeezed off three more shots.

The Sentinel took a step back, swayed, and then dropped the Dawnstone, which fell to the floor with a loud *clack!* but was undamaged. The rent in the golem's chest widened, and out spilled a black flood of tiny hard-shelled insects.

I stared in surprise, and suddenly a whole lot of things began to make sense.

I didn't have time to reflect on my newfound realizations before the insects were upon me, covering me completely from head to toe. I slapped at them, tore at them, hit the ground and rolled in an attempt to crush them, but while I got a few that way, there were just too damned many, gnawing, chewing, ripping away at my undead flesh. It didn't hurt, of course; I felt a certain distance from what was occurring, as if it were happening to someone else.

And then I couldn't move my left arm anymore, nor my right. I fell to the floor, my legs useless. I couldn't see, for I no longer possessed eyes. And my thoughts became erratic and sluggish, and I realized the insects had penetrated my brain.

I experienced a moment of vertigo, followed by darkness. Then I could see once more, only now I was looking down upon a carpet of insects that were picking clean a rag-covered skeleton, and I understood what had taken place. The insects had destroyed my body and released my spirit. I was dead, for the second time.

I wasn't upset by this development, didn't feel anything about it one way or the other. It just was.

Although I had no body, at least none that I was aware of, I did appear to have a limited range of vision, as if I were still using eyes to see. I wanted to know what the Sentinel was doing and, as if having the desire was all that was necessary, my vision focused at the golem.

It stood motionless while the insects finished their work, and then like a movie in reverse, they flowed back into the Sentinel. When they were all inside once more, the golem gripped its chest wound and pinched it closed, in order to hold the insects in, I presumed, and then stomped back toward the dais where Father Dis and the Darklords still struggled to renew Umbriel.

I watched, unconcerned, as the Sentinel retrieved the Dawnstone and mounted the steps of the dais. The golem then raised the mystic crystal and once more unleashed a blast of light at Dis. The ruler and founder of Nekropolis screamed, and the dark power he channeled upward to Umbriel was cut off again. He fell to his knees as the tremors which shook the Nightspire grew even more violent. I wondered idly how long the structure could withstand such shaking, not that it mattered much. Nothing mattered. The concept no longer held any meaning for me. Everything just was.

And then I felt a pull, as if something were drawing me toward it. I "looked" in that direction and saw a light a thousand times brighter than any the Dawnstone could ever produce. I began drifting toward that light, slowly at first, and then faster, leaving the struggles of the flesh creatures behind me, already forgotten.

And as I neared the light, I heard a voice, a voice that I hadn't heard in almost two years.

It's not like you to leave a job unfinished, Matt.

With a jolt, I remembered the Sentinel and the Dawnstone, Dis and the Darklords, Umbriel and the Nightspire.

And Devona.

Dale was right; I still had work to do.

Thanks for the reminder, pal.

I turned away from the light and moved back toward the chamber and the struggle taking place on the dais. I had no idea what I could hope to do as a disembodied spirit – I just knew I had to do something. I wished Lyra were here to give me a few pointers. She'd spent enough time as a spirit and probably could… And then it hit me. Lyra and Honani, one soul exchanged for another.

I didn't have a spell designed by Papa Chatha to aid me, but I did have a hell of a lot of determination. I concentrated on drifting toward the Sentinel, who was still unmercifully blasting Father Dis with the Dawnstone.

More specifically, I aimed for the gash in the thing's chest.

I slipped into the Sentinel's body and was suddenly aware of another consciousness within it. A fragmented, alien consciousness that I experienced as a million tiny voices whispering back and forth to each other. And then I sensed the voices become aware of me and begin speaking as one, only they weren't whispering this time: they were shouting – shouting for me to get out.

But I wasn't about to go anywhere. I concentrated my entire will on merging with the Sentinel, on becoming one with it, being it. I could feel the alien presence's grip on the golem begin to weaken, and I took advantage of the opportunity to seize control of the Sentinel's arms.

The alien presence shrieked within my mind as I brought the crystal to the chest of the body we shared, pried open the gash, and aimed the stone within. I sensed that all I needed to do to activate the Dawnstone was will it.

I did.

Light flooded through our shared being, and I could hear the presence's agonized screams, feel its death throes. And then the presence was gone, and the Dawnstone's light grew dim and went out altogether, leaving me alone in the Sentinel's body.

I began to feel my thoughts slipping away then, to feel my very Self begin to dissolve into an approaching night that was warm, welcoming, and eternal.

I didn't care, though. All that mattered was Nekropolis – and more importantly, Devona – was safe. I only wished I'd had a chance to say goodbye.

TWENTY-FOUR

I walked down the steps into Gregor's basement, my flashlight on high this time. I half expected him not to be there, but he was, crouching against the wall in his usual position, masses of his children – more than normal, I thought – all around him, covering the walls, floor, and ceiling. The ones scuttling across the floor remained outside my flashlight beam, but only just.

"Hello, Matthew," Gregor said.

"You don't seem very surprised to see me alive, or at least my version of alive. But then you wouldn't be, would you? We never did find the child of yours which Devona carried in her head. She thought it had somehow been destroyed by her proximity to the light of the Dawnstone. But it really escaped while Devona was half unconscious with pain and came back here to report to you, didn't it?"

"Getting into the Nightspire is one thing," Gregor said. "Getting out another. Your surmise is correct."

"Why'd you implant it in her? As a sort of fail-safe device?"

"As a precaution, in case either of you came too close to interfering with the plan. We would have tried to manipulate you into hosting one of us, Matthew, but we knew you would never agree to it."

"You were right. Speaking of people being right, I'm still shocked that crazy Carl actually reported a legitimate story."

"Even a lunatic is occasionally correct," Gregor said.

"That's what you are, isn't it? One of the Watchers from Outside... meaning outside the city."

"Yes, but despite our pose as Gregor, it is incorrect to refer to use as separate individuals. We are One."

"That's what I saw back in the Cathedral, when I looked out the window over the Null Plains and viewed what I took to be shifting waves of darkness. It was really millions upon millions of bugs, wasn't it? Millions of bits and pieces of you."

Gregor, or at least the part of the Watchers' group mind that appeared to be Gregor, nodded.

I became aware of insects gathering quietly around us. I had no doubt that if I turned to look, I'd find the entrance to the stairs blocked. But I continued talking.

"You know, I always wondered just what species you were. You didn't seem like any other being in Nekropolis. Now I know why."

"This dimension is our home, and has been for more years than your birth planet has existed. When Dis and the Darklords first entered this dimension and created

Nekropolis, we had no idea what had happened, for as One we had no concept of otherness. No concept of invasion. But we learned. We entered the city, tunneling beneath the flaming barrier of Phlegethon, and we spread throughout Nekropolis. It took over fifty of your years before we began to understand what had taken place, understand that others had come to our home, had stolen part of it and claimed it as their own. We became determined to do what anyone from your world would do in similar circumstances: repel the invaders and reclaim what was ours.

"We merely observed for the next century, learning as much as we could about Nekropolis and its denizens, their strengths and weaknesses, desires and fears, wants and needs. And when we felt we had learned enough, we decided it was time to begin. We created the guise of Gregor and began trading information. Not because we needed it; we collected more than enough on our own. But because we wished to make contacts with others that would be able to serve us. This is why we aided you over the last two years, Matthew, in the hope that we might eventually find a way to use you. Unfortunately for us, you proved adept at resisting manipulation.

"As the years passed, we slowly, cautiously began to shape the course of events in Nekropolis. Through our agents, we helped foment dissent between the Darklords, founded the Dominari and the Hidden Light, established street gangs, encouraged the growth of crime on all levels. We worked especially hard to make sure the Darklords did not cut off all contact with Earth. We wanted not only to make certain the Others had a way to leave our dimension, but that the developing technology from their former homeworld would continue to flow into the city to provide us more tools to fight with. And for the next two centuries, we gathered information, made contacts, manipulated, plotted, and schemed. And finally we saw our opportunity."

"The Dawnstone," I said.

"Gregor" nodded. "We have worked hard the last dozen or so years aiding the development of various thaumaturgically enhanced drugs such as tangleglow and mind dust. But when one of our agents created veinburn, a drug so powerful it would prove addictive even to the strongest of supernatural beings, we realized its awesome potential. As Gregor, we made arrangements with the Dominari to begin producing veinburn in limited quantities–"

"And made sure Morfran, who was the supplier to a bloodson of a Darklord, distributed it."

"Yes. Varma, indolent pleasure-seeker that he was, eagerly sampled Morfran's new product. And from that moment on, he was ours. By threatening to cut off his supply of veinburn, we convinced Varma to cooperate with us. He told us anything we wanted to know, all the secrets of his father that he was privy to. Including the contents of his vaunted Collection. And we learned of the Dawnstone.

"We had acquired much mystical knowledge over the last few centuries, and were instantly aware of the potential a crystal that produced actual sunlight would have here in a city of darkness. The Renewal Ceremony was fast approaching, and we realized it would be the perfect time to strike, for if Dis and the Darklords could not revitalize Umbriel – the power source which actually maintains the existence of Nekropolis within this dimension – the city would be destroyed and we would finally have gotten rid of the hated Others."

"So you had Varma steal the Dawnstone. After using your magical know-how to make sure his aura matched his father's so that he could get past Galm's wardspells."

The insects were all around me now; I was surrounded by solid walls of them. Only the illumination of my flashlight protected me. Still, I did nothing.

Gregor went on. "Varma delivered the Dawnstone, and we resumed his supply of veinburn. We saw no need to slay him at that time; there was no chance he would report his crime to Lord Galm, and we did not wish to draw any undue attention to the theft of the Dawnstone. Eventually, of course, it became necessary to have him killed in order to keep him from talking to you. He was a pathetic, weak creature, and would have told you everything with little prompting on your part.

"We had previously managed to implant some pieces of ourself into one of Dis's Sentinels, and we realized we could use it to ferry the Dawnstone into the Nightspire and then, once inside, use it to attack Dis and disrupt the Renewal Ceremony."

"So you stuck the Dawnstone inside the Sentinel, and waited for it to be recalled for the Ceremony. Tell me, why did you leave a scar on the Sentinel, even a faint one?"

"Our mystic knowledge, gleaned as it has been in scattered fragments over the centuries, is less than complete. The spells Dis used to create the Sentinels were unfamiliar to us, and we could only partially heal the golem's flesh. We had no choice but to go forward with the plan and hope no one would notice."

"I should have known it was you all along, Gregor. One of your children was on the wall listening when I first spoke with Devona. You were the only being in the city besides the two of us who knew we were investigating the theft of the Dawnstone, the only one who could have sent the Red Tide vampires to kill us after we left the Great Library."

"We knew you, Matthew. You wouldn't let go of this until you saw it through to the end, one way or another. You had to be stopped. Ms. Kanti was of lesser importance. If she had been been killed, it would have been solely due to her association with you."

"How did you manipulate the Red Tide members?"

"They were pathetically simple-minded creatures. To secure their services, we had only to promise them unlimited access to whatever technology they wished. They were no different than Varma, in that regard. They cared only for seeing their lusts fulfilled. Vampires' need for blood tends to make them highly addictive personalities in other regards."

"Thanks for the psychology lesson." The insects were only inches away from me now, and edging closer all the time. "I suppose you were behind all the attempts on our lives?"

"Most of them. Through various agents, we made sure Thokk knew you were in the Broken Cross, and that Talaith was aware of your passage through her realm. And of course, we made certain the Red Tide vampires were waiting for you after you left here. We also had the Dominari order Yberio and Skully to kill you. Unfortunately, the warlock proved too weak for the task, and Skully prized your friendship more than he feared his masters."

"And the insect we saw in the alley?"

"An error. It was one which we had implanted in Varma in order to keep track of him. The sheer amount of veinburn the Red Tide vampires injected into Varma was enough to affect the child, and slow its escape long enough for you to see it."

The writhing, softly chittering wall of darkness that surrounded my back and sides was only an inch away now. I knew if I swept my flashlight beam around, they would scurry off. But I kept the light shining at my feet. I wanted to lure as many of them into the basement as possible.

"I understand why you misled us into thinking Talaith might be behind the Dawnstone's theft; you wanted to draw attention away from yourself. But why did you tell us the truth about Morfran being a veinburn supplier?"

"Because the best lies are those mixed with some truth. And if the Red Tide vampires failed to kill you, we hoped that Morfran would lead you to Skully, who would finish you off. A hope that was in vain, as it turned out. It is a shame our plan failed, but we are nothing if not patient. We came close this time, and we shall succeed the next, whether it be tomorrow or a hundred years from now."

"I'm glad to see you're maintaining an optimistic outlook."

"We would have succeeded if not for you, Matthew. You have a fine, incisive mind and excellent instincts. Join us; help us free our home from the scourge of Others which infests it."

"Help you?" I said incredulously. "After everything that's happened, everything you've done, how can you even ask such a thing?"

"Because I have something to offer you, Matthew. I can make you mortal again."

"You're lying."

"The child Ms. Kanti hosted remained hidden in the Nightspire long enough to witness the Renewal Ceremony completed and Dis reward you for saving his city by removing your spirit from the Sentinel and restoring your body to you. But he didn't return you fully to life, did he?"

"He said it was beyond his power, that I had been a zombie too long to make me human again."

"Perhaps it is beyond the capabilities of Dis, but it is not beyond ours. Remember what you said when I asked you how you felt about being a zombie? You said you were a freak, trapped in a body that was little more than a numb piece of meat. Cut off from the world around you, on the outside of life. A pale memory of the man who was once Matthew Richter. We can end your suffering, Matthew. Help us destroy the invaders and we shall make you live again."

I didn't respond.

"Surely you have no love for this city or its inhabitants. Your kind regard them as monsters: unnatural, unholy things. You would be doing creation a favor by helping us destroy them."

"After nearly two years as a walking dead man, it's hard to see others as monsters, Gregor."

"Then consider it justice. This is our home; the Others are trespassers. They have no right to live in this dimension, no right to befoul it with their obscene otherness. Help us be rid of them, and we shall make you a man once more and use one of the Darklords' portals to return you to Earth. Perhaps you will not be able to resume your life where you left off, but at least you may begin a new one."

"Sorry, Gregor, but I can't do that. Maybe Dis and the Darklords shouldn't have built Nekropolis here, but they did, and you didn't protest."

"We did not understand! We knew nothing of otherness then! We did not know there were Others to protest to!"

"Even so, the city and its people have been here for almost four centuries. Isn't it time you learned to co-exist with them?"

"Impossible! Otherness can not be tolerated!"

"Then there's nothing I can do for you, Gregor. I won't help you. In fact, I'll do everything I can to stop you."

"You'll do nothing. It's a pity you won't join us, but that is your decision. You were foolish to come here alone, Matthew. We destroyed your body once, and we shall do so again – and this time there is no one to restore you. And don't think your flashlight will protect you. While we are creatures of this dark dimension and light does hurt us, there are far too many of us for your feeble beam to kill."

"I don't intend to use my flashlight. And you're wrong, Gregor. I didn't come alone." I clicked off the light and was plunged into darkness.

No insects swarmed over me as in the Nightspire. Instead, there was a rushing, moaning sound that made me think of a cold winter wind blowing across a blood-soaked battlefield. And then I heard the screaming of thousands upon thousands of tiny voices, the same as when I had shone the Dawnstone into the Sentinel's chest cavity, only multiplied to the nth degree.

And then there was silence. I waited a few moments more, and then I turned the flashlight back on. Its beam revealed Father Dis, standing alone in the now empty basement.

"Are they all gone?" I asked. I was grateful my flashlight had been turned off. I had no idea how Dis had destroyed the insects, and from the horrible sounds they had made while dying, I was certain I wanted to remain ignorant.

"All that were present at this location. I fear many more remain within the city, however, and even if none do, there are uncountable millions more outside Phlegethon's boundaries. I seriously doubt we've heard the last of the Watchers." He sighed. "I was of course aware of them when I led my people to this dimension, but I thought them some sort of native animal life. I never realized they were intelligent. If I had… well, it's too late now, isn't it?"

"Can't you do something? Like wave your hand in a godly gesture of omnipotence and smite them?"

Dis smiled. "As I told you when I restored you, there are limits to even my powers. The vast majority of my strength is used to maintain Umbriel and Phlegethon. The Darklords help, of course, but far less than even they imagine. Still, there's no use in letting them know that; everyone likes to feel they're important, don't they?"

"So you were telling the truth when you said you couldn't make me alive again?"

Dis nodded. "Though I was able to see to it that you are in no danger of inevitably decomposing again, provided of course you keep up regular applications of preservative spells. Barring accidents, you might very well exist forever."

Forever. The word had no meaning to me now. I wondered if it ever would. I figured I'd find out.

I showed Dis the underside of my hand. "My little finger grew back when you restored me, but I still have Edrigu's mark."

"Edrigu had a previous claim on you which I can do nothing about. Be careful what deals you make in Nekropolis, Matthew. They are always binding."

"I figured you'd say something like that. One more thing: back at the Nightspire, that mural in the corridor..."

"Yes?"

"The first scene depicted shadow creatures emerging from a swamp. Those things were the beginning of the Darkfolk, weren't they?"

"The Shadowings," Dis said. "There were indeed the progenitors of all of my kind that would follow. That was our only form for millions of years until humans began to evolve. Their dreams changed us, molded us, until we became dark reflections of their worst fears. Creatures that drank blood, changed into animals, worked black magic, and survived beyond death – all because humans imagined it so." Dis smiled. "So you see, Matthew, the Darkfolk really are your people's nightmares." But his smile quickly faded. "But the humans outgrew us, came to hate us and desire our destruction. Perhaps because we reminded them of the darkest parts of themselves."

"Maybe," I said. "But eating them might've had something to do with it too."

A hint of Dis's smile returned. "Possibly."

"When you and I first met, you allowed me to glimpse the true darkness that lies behind Father Dis. That darkness is what you really are, isn't it? You're one of the first Darkfolk – a Shadowing. One that's never changed for all these millions of years, not deep down where it really matters."

Dis didn't respond right away, and I thought he wasn't going to answer. But then he said. "It's why the Darkfolk call me Father, you know. I didn't literally sire them, of course, but my kind gave rise to theirs."

"That's why you wanted to create Nekropolis, wasn't it?" I said. "Because it's a father's duty to look after his children, to make sure they have a safe place to live."

Dis smiled fully once more, showing his perfect movie star teeth, but I knew that what I was really looking at was only a mask, a disguise for something so old, so utterly inhuman, that there was no way I could ever hope to understand it.

"You know, Matthew, you're really quite good at figuring things out. Have you ever considered becoming a detective?"

He laughed, and with that Dis began to fade, like the Cheshire Cat in a purple toga, until he was gone, not even leaving behind so much as a smile.

I picked my way though the rubble above what had been Gregor's lair, and walked down the steps to the broken sidewalk. Dis had brought me here after restoring my undead body so we could take care of Gregor before he abandoned his hidey hole, but for whatever reasons, the Lord of Nekropolis hadn't seen fit to provide me with a lift home. Not that I was ungrateful: Dis had already done plenty for me. Still, it was rude to leave a guy stranded – especially when said guy had just saved the whole goddamned city.

I started walking. But I hadn't gotten more than a block away from Gregor's when I heard what sounded like a water buffalo moaning in extreme pain coming up behind me, followed by a *blat* like a strangling trumpeter swan.

I turned and saw a hideous conglomeration of metal barreling down the street toward me. The thing screeched to a stop, and Lazlo hung out the window.

"Sorry it took me so long, Matt, but I had a little trouble getting the old cab running. I ended up having to cobble together a new one from what I could scrounge up in the junkyard – with a technical assist from the folks at the Foundry. I think it turned out pretty good overall, don't you?"

I walked over to the bent and twisted thing that coughed and shuddered alongside the curb. Not only was it patched together from different pieces of metal, but from swatches of living flesh as well. The hood opened a crack, displaying rows of teeth – some of which were now made out of iron – and I had the impression that the cab was smiling at me.

"This… is a car?"

Lazlo guffawed. "You really kill me sometimes, Matt, you know that?" He shook his head. "'*This is… a car?*' That's rich! Come on, hop in!"

I climbed into the passenger seat – once I figured out how to get the door open – and Lazlo said, "Where to, pal?"

"Demon's Roost," I answered.

TWENTY-FIVE

I found Devona standing alone in front of Varvara's bedroom mirror, looking at the image of a park at nighttime. Fluorescent lights glowed, attracting small clouds of insects, and even with the competition from the lights of the buildings downtown, the stars remained visible in the dark-blue sky.

I looked around, but Varvara was nowhere to be seen, and neither was the unconscious playmate Victor Baron had made for her. Maybe the Demon Queen was being uncharacteristically considerate and decided that Devona and I needed some time alone together. Then again, maybe Varvara had taken Magnus back to the Foundry for some repair work. Whatever the case, I was glad for the chance to be alone with Devona.

"Those are real stars, aren't they?" Devona asked without taking her eyes off the scene in the mirror. "They look different from the illusion in the Wyldwood. Crisper, brighter."

"Yes, they do."

"You know, I've never really experienced night before. I thought I had, living in Nekropolis, but what we have here isn't true night, is it? More like a perpetual gray. Real night seems more peaceful… soothing. And, even though everything is still, it possesses an energy all its own."

"Maybe that's your vampire half talking. After all, the night – true night – is a vampire's natural environment. Still, I know what you mean."

"I wish there was sound to go with the image," she said wistfully. "Birds singing…" She turned to me. "Do birds sing at night?"

I smiled. "Sometimes."

Devona turned back to the mirror. "Good. Birds singing, leaves rustling in the wind…"

Horns honking, brakes squealing, people shouting… but I decided not to mention these things just then. Why spoil the moment for her?

Devona took my hand and we stood silently and drank in the night.

Once the Renewal Ceremony had been completed and Umbriel was recharged for another year, Dis resurrected me – for the second time – and took me to Gregor's. Varvara offered to take Devona back to Demon's Roost while Dis and I dealt with the giant insect. Exactly how Dis and I traveled, I couldn't tell you. One moment we were in the Nightspire, the next we were standing on a street in the Boneyard. I guess when you're a god you can go wherever you want, whenever you want. When Lazlo later dropped me off

at Demon's Roost, I figured I'd find Devona up in Varvara's penthouse. I'd hoped she wouldn't be standing
in front of Varvara's mirror when I walked in, but I
wasn't surprised to find her there.

After a time, Devona said, "At first it devastated me
when Father fired me and cast me out of the Bloodborn. But now I see that Father never cared for me. A
creature like him is incapable of feelings like love, ten-
derness, forgiveness… I failed in my duty, and I had to
be punished. It was as simple as that to him. Never
mind that I served him for well on thirty years. That's
only the blink of an eye to a being like him." She turned
back to face the mirror. "Thirty years…" She shook her
head as if to clear it before going on. "But I've decided
to view my excommunication as an opportunity. I've
spent all my life in Nekropolis, most of it cloistered
within the Cathedral, tending a collection of someone
else's half-forgotten memories. It's time I created some
memories of my own."

"I think that would be a very good thing." I paused
and tried to sound nonchalant when I asked, "Any
thoughts about how you might start?"

"I'm not sure. While I can't return to the Cathedral,
I'm not entirely banned from Gothtown – though I
doubt I'll ever be very welcome there." She smiled
sadly. "I suppose I could try to find work in one of the
museums on the Avenue of Dread Wonders. I have the
right experience, though I worry the work might be too
much like tending Father's Collection. I'd just be trading one dusty old cage for another."

With her free hand, Devona brushed her fingers against the mirror's glass. She continued to hold onto my hand with the other.

"I suppose I could explore the other half of my heritage… get to know my mother's world, the world I was born into. I… spoke with Varvara while you were gone. I told her I was thinking about visiting Earth for a while, and she gave me the names of some of her people there who could help me get settled. She even gave me some Earth money."

If my heart had been beating it would've seized up in my chest at Devona's words.

She turned to face me then. "What do you think, Matt? Do you have any suggestions about what I should do?"

I knew by the look in her eyes and the tone of her voice what she wanted me to say: *I love you. Please don't go.* I knew it was crazy – Devona and I had met only yesterday – but the psychic link we'd shared in the Wyldwood had connected us on such a profound level that it was like we'd known each other all our lives. Maybe it shouldn't have made sense, but this was Nekropolis: nonsensical things happen here every day and twice on Sundays. The truth was that I did love Devona, more deeply and completely than I'd ever loved anyone before.

"I think you should go to Earth," I said.

A look of shocked disappointment spread across her face. She let go of my hand and took a step away from me. I hurried on before she could speak again.

"Earth is as much your birthright as Nekropolis. Maybe the new life you're looking for isn't here – it's there." I gestured toward mirror. "There's only one way you're ever going to find out, and that's to step through and see for yourself what's waiting for you on the other side."

Devona looked at me for a long moment, searching my eyes, trying to gauge my emotions. But my eyes are as dead as the rest of me, and they won't reveal anything I don't want them to.

When she spoke again, her tone was slightly reserved, the way it had been when we first met. "Maybe you're right."

Devona leaned forward as if she wanted to kiss me, but I held back. I couldn't bear the thought of her soft living lips touching my dead ones right then. Besides, no mere physical contact could ever compare to the link we'd experienced in the Wyldwood. After a moment she pulled away.

"You take care of yourself, Matthew Richter." Crimson tears welled in the corners of her eyes, and she fought to hold them back. If I'd been physically capable of crying... but I wasn't.

"You too."

She gave me a last long look before turning and walking toward the mirror.

I almost said it then: *Don't go. Stay with me.* But I gritted my teeth and held the words back.

And then she stepped through the glass and was gone. I wanted to watch her walk through the park a while, wanted to see her initial reactions to physically being on Earth for the first time since she'd been a baby. But as soon as she was through, the portal became a simple mirror again, and I was left staring at my gray-tainted face. I'd expected my expression to be completely emotionless, but the man I saw gazing sadly back at me from the mirror looked as if his undead heart was breaking.

"I thought it best if the portal closed as soon as she passed through."

I turned to see Varvara sitting on the edge of her bed. The Demon Queen was dressed in a skimpy red silk gown with a Chinese dragon embroidered in gold encircling the waist, its tail – which served as the robe's belt – clutched in its mouth.

"I should have known you couldn't pass up spying on us," I said bitterly. "I hope you enjoyed the show."

"I just teleported in this very moment, Matthew. I placed a spell on the mirror to let me know when Devona had gone through. I assure you, I know nothing of what occurred between the two of you – but I can guess. Noble idiot that you are, you let her go, didn't you?"

"She was born on Earth, Varvara. She deserves a chance to get to know her homeworld."

"You could've gone with her."

"It wouldn't have worked. I'd still need preservative spells."

"You could always come back to get them."

"Magic doesn't function as reliably on Earth as it does in Nekropolis, you know that. There's no telling how long a preservative spell would last for me there. I might decompose after only a few hours."

"Or you might not. You might be just fine. But that's not the real reason you didn't go with her, Matt, is it?"

"You may have been away from Earth for a few centuries, Varvara, but I bet you haven't forgotten what it's like. It's so much more than Nekropolis... Devona will have more opportunities, more chances, more choices than she ever could have here – especially since Galm made her an outcast among the Bloodborn. How could I deny her that?"

Varvara rose from her bed, walked over, and gave me a kiss on the cheek. For an instant, I felt her lips on my flesh just as if I'd been a living man, but the sensation quickly faded.

"I still say you're an idiot, Matt, but alive or not, you're a good man." She smiled, and the embroidered dragon around her waist winked. Her manner grew serious. "Are you going to be all right?"

"Of course. I'm a zombie; I don't have any feelings, remember?"

"Right. I forgot."

I knew Varvara didn't believe it, and for the first time in a long time, neither did I.

Lazlo was waiting for me in his cab outside the main lobby of Demon's Roost. He offered to give me a ride back to my place, but I told him I'd rather walk. If he noticed my mood, he didn't say anything. I turned away from his cab and started heading in the general direction of my apartment building.

Now that Umbriel had been renewed for another year, the Descension festival was officially over. Most of the partiers had already gone home to recover from the damage they'd done to themselves, but a few stragglers – or perhaps I should say staggerers – remained out, probably because they didn't possess enough command of their higher brain functions to remember where they lived or how to get there. The streets and sidewalks were covered with trash, most of it fairly innocuous – discarded fast-food wrappers, cigarette butts, Styrofoam cups and the like – but some of the debris was a bit more disturbing in nature and didn't bear close inspection. Already thick glutinous pseudopods were extruding from the sewer grates and stretching toward the trash, engulfing it, swiftly breaking down its molecular structure, and absorbing its mass. The Azure Slime lives beneath the streets of the Sprawl and functions as the Dominion's waste removal service. While the Slime feeds well all year, when Descension Day is over and everyone else's good times have ended, that's when the Slime's feast of feasts begins. It's usually good about not absorbing anything – or anyone – it shouldn't, but occasionallt it gets so excited by the grand repast laid out before it that it forgets and devours a passed-out drunk or a barely conscious partier who's hung around on the streets just a bit too long. I was walking fast enough that I wasn't worried about being absorbed, and the one time a bluish psuedopod did slither too close to my feet, I kicked at it, and the tendril withdrew almost sulkily.

Crimson ambulances from the Fever House slowly patrolled the streets, searching for those who'd been wounded beyond their capacity to heal themselves. When the Bloodwagon medics found someone who needed to be taken to the hospital, they stopped the ambulance, got out, and rushed to put their patient in the back of the vehicle before the Azure Slime got there. Sometimes they succeeded, sometimes they didn't, and sometimes they had to pry what was left of a patient out of the Slime's fluidic clutches and hope enough remained for them to restore to some semblance of health. The Bloodwagon medics had competition, however. Midnight-black hearses from the Foundry also cruised the Sprawl, the Bonegetters looking for dead bodies, severed limbs, or misplaced organs to salvage and return to their master. Victor Baron was always in need of fresh supplies, and the raw material his assistants recovered could keep the Foundry going for another year.

I saw more than a few predators lurking in the shadows, but those who made a move toward me took one look at the expression on my face and decided it might not be a bad idea to go in search of easier prey. Wise choice.

Now that they were no longer needed for the Renewal Ceremony, Sentinels patrolled the streets again – the Azure Slime made damn sure to stay clear of them – and I found it more than a little eerie to see the impassive golems after what had happened at the Nightspire. For a few moments, I'd actually been one of the things, and I knew I'd never look at them the same way again. Still, there was no doubt they were needed. Those Darkfolk who were unconscious but not in need of medical attention would be left to lie where they'd fallen until they managed to sleep off whatever had put them down. In the meantime, they were prime targets for thieves of all sorts, those who wanted darkgems, of course, but also those desiring to steal a victim's memories, soul, and even his or her potential futures. The Sentinels were the police force of Nekropolis, and they had their beat to walk, and while the impassive creatures made me uncomfortable now, as a former cop myself, I had to respect that.

I don't know how long I wandered, but eventually I found myself in front of my building. I almost expected crazy Carl to come running up to me with his latest bizarre expose, but he was nowhere to be seen. He was probably exhausted and getting some rest, like everyone else in the city. Sometimes I really miss sleeping. When you sleep, you don't have to think. Or remember. Or regret.

I climbed the steps to the building, entered the lobby, and walked to my apartment door. As I reached for the knob, I saw the door was open and slightly ajar. My cop instincts kicked into high gear, and I silently drew my 9mm and listened. I heard nothing, so I slowly pushed open the door and stepped inside.

Devona was sitting on the couch. She put down the book she'd been reading and smiled at me. "It's about time you got home."

I had no idea what to say, but at least I had the presence of mind to holster my gun.

"By the time I came back through Varvara's mirror and got down to the street, you were already gone. Lazlo was still there, though, and he gave me a ride here." She made a face. "Did you see what he's done to that cab? And I thought it was hideous before! When I got here and discovered you weren't home, I used the mystical lock-picks Shrike found for us, and I let myself in."

I walked over to the couch and sat down next to her. "I know Cleveland isn't exactly the grandest city on Earth, but I have a hard time believing you got tired of it this fast."

"That's not why I came back. There I was, standing in the park, drinking in all these wonderful new sights, sounds, and smells, when I realized something: I'd forgotten to pay you for helping me find the Dawnstone. If I remember right, the price we settled on was three hundred darkgems."

I was surprised, and truthfully, a bit insulted. "You don't need to pay me. Dis restored my body, and I'm as good as new. Well, good as a new zombie, anyway. Besides, it's not like I really did anything to help you. We found the Dawnstone, sure, but you ended up losing your job and being cast out from your people."

"Be that as it may, we made a deal and I intend to honor my part of the bargain. And don't tell me you can't use the money. Dis may have repaired your body with his magic, but you're still a zombie, and you still need preservative spells, right?"

"Don't worry about that. I've decided to get out of the business of doing favors and start an official private investigation business. A real one, with an office and everything."

"Good for you! But from what I understand, there are a lot of expenses associated with starting a new business – which is all the more reason to let me pay you. You're going to need the money." She paused. "Of course, I don't have a job at the moment, and I can't go to Father and ask to borrow some darkgems… so it might be a while before I can scrape up what I owe you."

I couldn't help smiling. "Tell you what, let's put it on your tab, and you can get it to me whenever you can, okay?"

She smiled back. "Okay." She leaned close and laid her head on my shoulder, and I put my arm around her. It felt so natural, so right, and I would've been content to sit like that for hours. But after a few moments, Devona said, "There's something I've been thinking about trying ever since we left the Wyldwood, Matt."

"What?"

"It might be easier if I show you." She sat up, touched her fingertips to my temples, and then closed her eyes.

I experienced a dizzying lurch, and then I was tumbling through a seemingly endless void. But it did have an end, and when I reached it, the falling sensation ceased and I found myself sitting on the grass by the edge of a pond, with Devona by my side. The sky above was a gentle blue and a light spring breeze was blowing. It was daylight, and for the first time in two years I felt the sun on my face. I looked down at my hands. Instead of gray, the flesh was a healthy pink. I turned to Devona and saw that her skin was no longer pale. We were both dressed the same as we'd been in Nekropolis, except now our clothes were clean and in good repair.

"What's happening?" I asked. The breeze blew across my skin, and I trembled. "Where are we?"

Devona placed her fingers on my lips and gently stroked them. The sensation was so intense, I couldn't stop myself from moaning.

"Home," she said simply.

Then she leaned forward and pressed her lips against mine. And you know something?

She was right.

ABOUT THE AUTHOR

Tim Waggoner is an American novelist and college professor. His original novels include *Cross County*, *Darkness Wakes*, *Pandora Drive*, and *Like Death*. His tie-in novels include *The Lady Ruin* series and the *Blade of the Flame* trilogy, both for Wizards of the Coast. He's also written fiction based on *Stargate: SG-1*, *Doctor Who*, *A Nightmare on Elm Street*, the videogame *Defender*, *Xena the Warrior Princess*, and others. He's published over one hundred short stories, some of which are collected in *Broken Shadows* and *All Too Surreal*. His articles on writing have appeared in *Writer's Digest*, *Writers' Journal* and other publications.

He teaches composition and creative writing at Sinclair Community College in Dayton, Ohio, and is a faculty mentor in Seton Hill University's Master of Arts in Writing Popular Fiction program in Greensburg, Pennsylvania.

To learn more about Tim and his writing, you can visit him on the web at **www.timwaggoner.com**

THE LONG, STRANGE TRIP TO NEKROPOLIS

It's January 1995. I'm thirty-one years old and I'm living in Columbus, Ohio. My then-wife is pregnant with our first child, and I'm teaching composition part-time at various area colleges while writing fiction full time. I'm in a writers' group with a number of wonderful people, including the fantasy novelist Dennis McKiernan, best known for a series of novels taking place in the wondrous realm of Mithgar. Dennis has become both a good friend and mentor to me, and he's introduced me to his agent, Jonathan Matson, who's taken me on as a client. I've published about a dozen short stories by this point, and I've got my first novel deal cooking: Jonathan is negotiating contract terms with a publisher for a surreal horror novel called *The Harmony Society*.

Life, as the saying goes, is pretty damned good.

In addition to my writers' group, I'm also in a gamers' group with Dennis and another member of our writers' group, Peter Busch. What's cool about this group is that each person takes a turn being gamemaster and designs an original scenario for the others to play. We've just finished playing a wonderful game Dennis designed, in which we were aliens – truly inhuman, scientifically plausible aliens – sent to investigate a mysterious abandoned space station. Now it's my turn to develop and run a scenario for Dennis and Pete.

I have to admit, I'm intimidated. Both Dennis and Pete are experienced gamers, and while I've played *D&D* and such before, I've never gamemastered, let alone designed a scenario myself. But Dennis and Pete promise to help me with the game mechanics as we play, so I roll up my metaphorical sleeves and get to work. For a few years, I've been thinking about writing a novel set in an otherwordly city full of monsters. So I decide to finally get to work on bringing this dark city of mine – which I've named Necropolis – to life. Or unlife, whichever is more appropriate.

I design the city and its inhabitants, come up with a nefarious plot for Dennis and Pete to deal with, and create characters for them. They're a pair of Earth cops who were trapped in Necropolis on a previous case: one who no can no longer withstand sunlight (though he's still fully human) and the other who has become a zombie. The two work as private investigators on the very mean streets of this shadow-enshrouded city.

I'm pleased with what I've developed, and when the day comes to begin playing, Dennis and Pete love the world and have a lot of fun with the scenario (even though I've made a rookie mistake and designed their characters to be too strong and they're tearing through my world like it was made of tissue paper – but then, maybe that's part of why they're having so much fun). We get halfway through the game scenario in our first session. It'll be a few months before we finish, though. My daughter Devona decides to come into the world five weeks early, and I'm a bit busy for a while. Eventually, we get back to the game and finish it up. Dennis and Pete had a great time, they congratulate me on doing a good job on running the game, and an even better one on designing Necropolis.

Life is still pretty damned good, even if now I'm suffering from new parent sleep-deprivation most of the time.

Then I get a call from my agent. The publisher's made an offer on *The Harmony Society*. It's a small publisher, and the money's not great, but I'm thrilled. My first novel sale!

Then Jonathan calls me a few days later to tell me the deal's fallen through because the publisher "No longer feels comfortable with the book." Whatever the hell that means.

Naturally enough, I'm devastated, and like any other first-time novelist in my position, I want to give up, want to curl up in a corner and die, boo-hoo, sob-sob. Instead, I get good and pissed and decide to write another novel. I turn my attention to Necropolis. I've already got the world designed, and I have a plot, plus, I've lived the story along with Dennis and Pete. So I sit down and, with some changes (combining the two detectives into one character, for example), I plant my ass in the office chair in front of my computer and my fingers start flying across the keys. Twenty-one days later, *Necropolis* the novel is finished. It only runs about 67,000 words, relatively short for a novel, but around the right size for a mystery, and since *Necropolis* is as much a mystery as it is fantasy and horror (with a little science fiction, humor, and romance sprinkled in here and there), I'm satisfied. After some revision, the book goes off to Jonathan to start sending around, and I move on to the next project.

Nine years pass.

It's 2004. My daughter Devona is nine, and her sister Leigh is four. I'm now a tenure-track professor teaching composition and creative writing at Sinclair Community College in Dayton, Ohio. I've published close to fifty stories now and a few novels, most of them media tie-ins. *Necropolis*, however, still hasn't found a home. It's too weird, blends too many genres, and publishers aren't sure what to do with it.

I decide to submit it to editor John Helfers for Five Star Books, a publisher that specializes in producing library-edition hardbacks (meaning sturdy books sold directly to libraries instead of in bookstores). I've worked with John on numerous anthology projects. He's a great editor, a swell guy, and we work well together, so I figure he might like *Necropolis*. And indeed he does. The book comes out from Five Star late in 2004, and I'm a happy man. I've come to really love that world and my main character over the last nine years, and I'm glad other people will finally get a chance to read about them.

More years pass.

I continue to publish more novels and stories, some original, some tie-in work, and the Internet continues to grow at an astonishing pace. I have a website now, and through it, readers send me e-mail, usually telling me how much they enjoyed this story or that novel (with the exception of the anonymous three-word e-mail I received which said, in all lowercase letters: *"you write badly"*). The most common e-mails I get are those telling me how much the sender enjoyed *Necropolis* – which they found at their local library – and asking when there will be a sequel. When I do panels at conventions people ask me when there's going to be a *Necropolis* sequel. People I run into at the bookstore recognize my name and ask about a sequel. It's getting so bad, I'm starting to have dreams in which nameless, faceless apparitions demand I write a sequel to *Necropolis*.

Hmmmm, I think to myself. Maybe I should starting listening to these folks. At least that way maybe I can stop having those dreams...

It's around 2007 now, and a couple new genres have become extremely popular in publishing: urban fantasy and paranormal romance. For the last couple years, I've been wandering through bookstores, seeing these books and thinking, Man, I guess I was ahead of my time with *Necropolis*. (And truth to tell, thinking this with more than a bit of envy.) Still, pragmatism is the hallmark of the professional writer, and I hope that the current popularity of urban fantasy means a publisher might be interested in bringing out a mass-market edition of *Necropolis*, hopefully as part of a new series. So my agent and I rededicate ourselves to pitching the book to editors. We get some nibbles, but no one swallows the bait. In the meantime, I'm getting even more people begging me for a sequel to *Necropolis*, and I tell them that I'm working on it.

Early in 2008, author, editor, and more-wonderful-than-you-can-possibly-imagine   person Jean Rabe is kind enough to ask me to write a story for an anthology of urban fantasy tales called *City Fantastic*. I've toyed with writing some stories about my main character from Necropolis for years, but I've never gotten around to it. I decide to quit stalling and write "Disarmed and Dangerous," zombie detective Matthew Adrion's first new adventure in thirteen years.

Then, almost as if that story sends out cosmic vibes into the publishing universe, one day in late 2008 I get an e-mail from British publisher Marc Gascoigne. Marc's worked with the Black Library, publisher of the hugely popular *Warhammer* and *Warhammer 40,000* novels, and with science fiction/fantasy imprint Solaris. I wrote an original novel based on *The Nightmare on Elm Street* franchise for Black Flame, an imprint of Black Library, a few years back. Marc knows my work and we've chatted at several conventions, and I've always been impressed with his intelligence, energy, professionalism, and enthusiasm for writing and publishing. In his e-mail, Marc tells me he's going to head up a new imprint for HarperCollins called Angry Robot, and might I have any novel projects to pitch to him?

As a matter of fact...

Marc agrees to take a look at *Necropolis*, and he's very enthusiastic about it. He wants me to add about twenty thousand more words to expand the setting in more deliriously gruesome detail, and he suggests a couple minor changes: calling the city Nekropolis to give the word a more sinister spin, and he thinks my main character, Matthew Adrion (a spin on the Latin name Adrian, which means dark), could use a better last name. Since it's been close to fifteen years since I named the man, I have to admit his last name has worn a little thin on me too, so he becomes Matthew

Richter (which has an association with rictus which works well for a zombie PI, don't you think?). Marc would also like me to write two more Nekropolis books for him.

And, as you're probably expecting me to say by now, life is once again Very Good Indeed.

The AR team want to bring the new and expanded *Nekropolis* out with the first wave of books released by Angry Robot, which means I have only a month or so to do the revision: nine more days than it took me to write the original. No prob, says I. And it isn't. I've lived with Necropolis – now with a K instead of a C – for fifteen years. I have no problem returning to it because, in truth, I've never left.

So here we are, Matthew Richter and I, in 2009, with *Nekropolis* in your hands, and two more adventures to follow, starting with *Dead Streets*. And after that, who knows? I'm not worried about what might happen, though. I've learned from experience that you can't keep a good zombie down.

If you're one of the readers who enjoyed the original version of the story and asked for more, I hope you enjoy the expanded novel and the two sequels to follow. After all, they wouldn't have existed if you hadn't kept asking for them.

And if you're an aspiring writer, think on this: professional writers often quote the famous line from the *I Ching*, "Perseverance furthers," not because they believe in fortune telling (though maybe they might – who am I to speak for all authors?) but because it codifies in two simple words a very powerful mental and emotional survival skill writers need to continue in the face of rejection and setbacks. So now that you've read this, if you're still wondering if perseverance really does further, let me tell you something, my friends.

You bet your undead ass it does.

Tim Waggoner
Centerville, OH, USA

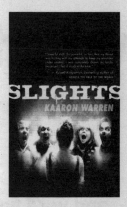